Ritual Blasphemy

A Shaman Detective Novel

Daylight Publishing
With Lulu Publishing

Roy. E. Day Jr.

Editing and Cover by Helen Manget

Dedication

Everything I write is for my family, friends, and this beautiful planet. This book is specifically dedicated to my spiritual teachers and those fellow travelers who were beside me on the spiritual or shamanic path, and to the people - the Northern Paiutes and to the Tule River people.

My spiritual teachers in order:

- Master Jack Johns – my first Karate teacher

- Ruth Stillman – theosophists – esoteric section, Co-Freemason – top 13 initiate

- Evelyn Monahan – taught parapsychology – GA State University

- Grandmother Evelyn Eaton – Metis Shaman – Co-Freemason – top 13 initiate

- Grandfather Raymond Stone – powerful Northern Paiute Shaman – who avoided fame, publicity

- Dr. Gayle Pierce – Healer, Buddhist, friend of Dali Lama

- Master Robert Quinn – my Karate Sifu

The fellow travelers were my friends Tom and Debbie, my girlfriend Peggy, my brothers Stephen, Winslow and his girlfriend Fay, sometimes friends from Theatrical Outfit, later Seven Stages. In California, my friends Laura and Chris were always there for me

I want to dedicate this work to the Northern Paiutes and to all on the Tule River Reservation.

Table Of Contents

Ritual Blasphemy

Tuhuki'ni said to the world, "Now this evildoer is dead. Hereafter the world shall be different. It shall be ruled correctly. All men shall be brothers."

Tuhuki'ni is black hawk, a Paiute mythic hero from

the Myths of the Owens Valley Paiute

Prologue

Leonard Wounded Face looked out at the peaceful California evening and knew somewhere there was a battle brewing. He'd fought battles his whole life, both inner and outer, and could feel them coming. *Numu*, the people*, nun' wa paya hup ca' a' otuu'mu* - the water ditch coyote children - the Owens Valley Paiutes – were not traditionally a warrior tribe, yet he had been a warrior most of his life, for the U.S. Army in Viet Nam, later for the American Indian Movement, and surviving prison during the years in between. The inner battles with anger, resentment, and alcohol were mostly won and laid to rest. Now an educator and historian, his days of physical conflict (he hoped) were also laid to rest, but as a shaman he was still an active spiritual warrior and his intuition told him a battle lay ahead.

He returned to the moment at hand and finished putting his Sacred Pipe into its soft deerskin pouch. He looked out again over *his* valley, from the north to the south. He certainly didn't own much of the Owens Valley in Anglo (from Anglo-American, meaning Caucasian) terms, and it didn't own him, but he *belonged* here. He was an Owens Valley Paiute, and they belonged here because they had always belonged here. It was where Mother Earth wanted them and placed them, and using a vast array of absolutely amazing survival skills, where they had always remained. Living in *harmony* with nature.

With a Ph.D. in history, a Masters in psychological counseling, and a Masters in anthropology, he was intellectually aware of the archaeological evidence supporting the various theories of migrations into the valley a thousand or two thousand years ago. So? As far as he was concerned, those migrations were absorbed by or merged with the original inhabitants, who were the Paiute or their direct ancestors. He knew in his heart and soul the Owens Valley Paiute had lived in the valley as long as human memory and experience had existed. His rational mind didn't believe Paiutes had really watched the Cascade Mountains rise up from the Earth as one of the Northern Paiute myths recorded, but was confident they had resided here continuously for at least thirteen thousand years through many climatic changes and geologic events. There was clear and overwhelming archaeological evidence that somebody had, and the Numu *knew* these first residents were their ancestors.

Sitting about halfway up Mount Whitney, the highest mountain in the Sierra Nevadas as well as the lower forty-eight states, facing east, he continued looking down at Lone Pine, the closet little town, then north to Independence, near the original Fort Independence, his home town, and then at the White/Inyo Mountains across the valley. He looked up as a murder of nine crows flew noisily overhead then glanced back down at the pouch holding his Sacred Pipe, and like his intuitive apprehension of the coming conflict; two other previously sublimated aggravations came back into his consciousness. He couldn't smoke the healing Pipe if his mind was out of balance so he had looked at the things bothering him before the healing ceremony, he had ddressed each rationally, calmed his mind and put them away. Now these thoughts wanted to be addressed more fully.

The first was his wife's mother's brother Vincent, over at Tule River for whom he had just smoked the healing Pipe. Vincent was in the hospital in Portersville for the third time for a mild heart attack or "cardiac event" as one of the doctors called it. Leonard had taken an oath to heal the sick and fight evil when he joined a secret spiritual warrior society, and he took that oath seriously. But his uncle wasn't doing his part. He took his blood pressure medicine, went to his doctor appointments, and went to the sweat lodge at Tule River regularly and sometimes made it over the mountains to the one at Big Pine - where he would confess he hadn't changed his diet or started exercising. It was time to open up a can of tough love on Uncle Vincent. If he wanted the shaman's blessing and healing, he needed to do his part, less greasy and fried foods, less starches, more fruits and vegetables, and some exercise. Tule River rez has many beautiful places to walk. Vincent needed to get off the sofa, push away the TV dinner tray, and get his fat butt outside for some fresh air and exercise.

Leonard knew his wife Sarah and her mother Sandy over at Tule River might not like it too much, but it was tough love time. Also, Vincent's wife needed to get with the program and change her menu some. Actually, a lot. *That* was going to go over great. He shook his head, drawing in a deep breath, these things needed to be said, Vincent needed to face the truth. So did his wife Ginny. Sometimes the repercussions of being a Pipe healer or shaman sucked, your clients are often friends or family with all the complications that ensues, but that was just part of the gig.

The Uncle Vincent aggravation had been low level and somewhat subconscious but the next aggravation brought him back, back to the deep anger that had been part of his life for so long he had once asked his mother as a teenager if he had been born angry from the very first day. Because he had lived angry for so many years. He didn't know at what age kids become consciously aware of discrimination or being looked down on, but they can feel it early enough. He didn't remember at any specific age learning the history of his people and the atrocities committed against them and their valley, more like he absorbed it. But growing up the anger was real enough, and never far below the surface. That anger had helped motivate him as a high school athlete to achieve, that anger had served him well in Nam with the 101st, the Rangers, and MAC SOG - who drafted him for a few special missions. There was no doubt the anger had served him well as an efficient jungle scout and killer for his country. That same anger served him poorly when he got back from his second tour.

Disillusioned with the politicians running things in D.C., unsure about the war in many ways, and convinced the army was one huge screwed up bureaucracy - at best most officers were inept and inefficient and at worst were just plain morons with way too much power - he walked away from that huge cluster fuck and back into civilian life; and the oppressively hot summertime of Columbus, Georgia. Where his still raging anger fueled by alcohol served him very poorly in a succession of bar fights; the violence and damage which he inflicted in the last of these incidents shocked even him when he came to consciousness the next morning in the hospital, handcuffed to his bed, with a very hostile policeman standing guard. If you cause thousands of dollars of damage and the hospitalization of five people, three of which are cops, two of which are hurt badly in the great state of Georgia, you *will* do time. He got five, did three years hard time.

It was ironic that he actually began to understand and control his anger for the first time in prison, although it served him well there a few times. He smiled and thought of Spooky, his young cell mate then, now his wana' (younger brother)/best friend/fellow shaman. Unconsciously his hand had gone to his tee shirt and was tracing a long scar from above the left nipple down to the top of the right pelvis. It was undoubtedly ironic that two men who later trained to become shaman together should meet in such environs. Reidsville was no cakewalk. He shook his head just thinking back, the noise, the violence, the hate, the smell of fear, a microcosm of the worst America had to offer.

This second aggravation reached way down inside him and definitely touched what remained of that deep anger again. He thought of his own feelings that first time he'd read the words in question as a young teenager - the shame, the anger, feeling his face flush, fighting back tears. He remembered as an adult, at one of his first public school jobs, being called in to a young Anglo teacher's literature class to help with a "situation." The bell had rung but a 9th grade Shoshone boy wouldn't lift his face, get up from his desk to go to the next class, or respond to anything she said. Her next class was filling up the room when Leonard walked in. Squatting next to the boy who had his face in his hands, elbows resting on either side of the book, Leonard had slowly reached in and lifted the book cover where he could read it. The anger boiled over in him then, because he remembered that same damned book and those same damned words.

He had quietly suggested to the young teacher that she take her class to the library, and added that the results of her thoughtlessness could *probably* be erased. He had gone back and slowly slid the book out from the front, as he bent and whispered to the boy that it was wrong and full of lies and to not believe a word in it. Keeping it open he'd handed it to her so she could read the tear stained pages as she took her class to the library.

Young and eager minds must be prepared by their teachers before they read certain books, they must receive some preparatory knowledge. In this case the knowledge that Mark

Twain, besides at times revealing a great understanding of human nature and possessing a gifted ability to reveal true slices of the Americana of the times, was also a product of his times. Literary geniuses are not always spiritually advanced people. Sometimes they say and do stupid things. Leonard recalled Twain's words, seared into his memory, as Twain referred to the Shoshone (and by likeness in life ways, to all Great Basin Indians) in his book *Roughing It* as, "the wretchedest type of mankind I have ever seen…inferior to all races of savages in our continent…their faces and hands bearing dirt…accumulating for...years…sneaking, treacherous looking race…indolent…prideless beggars…poor naked creatures…" The words came back so clearly and quickly; he knew they'd never gone away. He'd talked to the Shoshone kid for fifteen minutes, got him up and going, and again that afternoon for an hour. Nobody wants to hear one of America's greatest authors go on and on about how your race is the lowest of the low, the most despicable of the despicable. But when those same words came up today the counselor had handled the new Q (their nickname for quester) just fine.

They had just gotten through the July 4th holiday without incident, which hadn't always been the case. Indian and Anglos often look at national holidays with vastly different perspectives. Those that wanted to see the fireworks were shuttled into town in a couple of vans, and those not interested stayed at their remote camps. It wasn't easy, but things were going pretty smoothly, which hadn't always been the case in the seven years they'd run Personal Quest. The rich kids from over the mountains and the local Indian kids usually get along with each other and the counselors well enough but today this smart-ass Marin County kid finds out three year veteran counselor/psychology major David Johnson is full Shoshone and starts to dig. Smart-ass that he is, the kid was well educated and had a good memory because he almost quoted Twain verbatim. Then he congratulated David on his cleanliness and normal "American" appearance since his grandparents were dwellers in the Stone Age. The kid wouldn't let up, saying how David's grands were like Fred and Wilma Shoshone, making their flint arrowheads in a Shoshone Bedrock. When David had had enough, and he'd let the kid have his say, he responded.   "Two things you should know, new Q Jerry. My people lived here thousands of years in perfect ecological balance with the land, it took yours less than thirty years to destroy that balance and totally rape the landscape and then, then you let L.A. Water and Power come in and steal all the water rights in this valley, sending it all to L.A. Good job! And yeah, Mark Twain, in his own ignorance, he disrespected us Shoshone big time, but you know what? If someone had taken Mark Twain and that 'wretched, dirty' Shoshone thirty miles up in the the High Sierras, with nothing but the clothes on their backs, told them to survive and find their way back, only one would have made it back, and it wouldn't have been Twain. Unless of course, the poor wretched Shoshone helped him, then they'd both have gotten out."

With the Q put in his place, the day had continued without incident. Leonard shook his head back and forth unconsciously while smiling, thinking about all it had taken to get Personal Quest set up and running. Time, work, energy, love, faith, will, combining the various efforts of so many differt people and organizations. He shook his head again, thinking of the long way they had come, their learning curve and some of their mistakes. They no longer took court appointed kids, unless the judge talked to Leonard for a long time and personally convinced him to waive that rule, established for good reason. The questers had to be there on their own accord, if not completely voluntarily, at least in agreement with their parents that it was the next best step in their lives. If they weren't participating of their own free will, nothing much positive would be accomplished. Leonard had learned you can't help them all, but they had helped some problem kids dramatically and were helping to keep the old ways alive in the valley at the same time.

It had all started years ago, in the late 60's and 70's, the revitalization of Indian culture, and the powerful attraction of the Indian's traditional spiritual way to some Anglos as well as to Indians from all tribes who began returning to it. It was not organized, the revitalization spontaneously happened. Then A.I.M. warriors and Lakota and other traditionals started traveling to the various reservations, preaching pride and a return to the old ways. Many books were written and new sweat lodges started popping up on rez all over. Many of these sweat lodges were built in the Plains Indian traditional (often Lakota) style, and the Sacred Pipe made a comeback, also often presented in accordance with Plains Indian traditions. In fact, the sweat lodges in Owens Valley were built on the Lakota model instead of the much larger traditional Paiute sweat house, and the Sacred Pipes most Pipe healers and shaman smoked were hand carved from the catlinite of Minnesota pipestone. Each tribe had retained its own ways but there were some pan-tribal elements that seemed on their way to becoming universal, the Pipe and sweat lodge being two of them.

A Canadian writer who was a small part Indian, Eve Eaton had moved to the valley, come to the sweat lodges, and was healed of cancer by Paiute and Arapaho shaman. Grandfather Rayland, the valley's current shaman and Eve were trained by them to become shaman. The Owens Valley was no spiritual Mecca by any means, but the three books Eve Eaton wrote about her experiences during the 70's with the Paiute training to be a shaman did bring some spiritually minded people to the valley, some just to visit her and study, a few came to stay. During the 80's and 90's there were some Anglos running vision quest programs in the summer for troubled kids and there were Indians and some metis (mixed blood, part Indian) and a even few Anglos training to be Pipe healers under Grandfather Rayland. Under his supervision they went through the two night/one day fast, the three night/two day fast, and the four night/three day fast with the accompanying "putting in" and "taking out" sweat lodges for each fast that were the requirements set upby him to become a Pipe healer. There were museums and cultural centers in Big Pine and Bishop interested in keeping the Paiute survival skills and traditional lifestyle alive. Over the years after Grandmother Eve passed away, Grandfather Rayland talked to Leonard about putting all these separate efforts together.

Leonard finally talked to his wife Sarah who had the vision on how to bring everyone together. Then he talked to all the others - the vision questers, those training in the traditional shamanic way, and those interested in the traditional lifestyle from the culture centers and museums across the valley. It didn't always go smoothly, but now it was considered a model program and people from other tribes and government agencies came to observe it. Five years ago his wife applied and received a government grant which paid her a salary to run and coordinate it all and their older kids were counselors. Its smooth running took tons of pressure off his shoulders.

He blew out a long breath and returned to his premonition, his two aggravations fully dealt with - he returned to his intuitive warning that somewhere there was a battle brewing. It was no exaggeration that he could literally *feel* them coming. He *knew*. The intuition that had saved his squad in Nam countless times was something he had learned to listen to over the years. His intuition told him the battle coming was spiritual and would not be waged in Owens Valley. Things were peaceful in the valley, the battle would be fought elsewhere but would involve people he knew. He just didn't know who. Not yet.

The warm afternoon had turned to a cooler evening and he reached for his deerskin pouch and stood to go when the coyote rounded his truck. Years ago he might have walked further up the mountain to smoke his Pipe; he didn't have that luxury of time anymore. The coyote turned and stopped, they made eye contact and Leonard said, "Hello, Grandfather," quietly and politely, addressing the grandfather spirit of all coyotes and this, his representative. The coyote began walking away then trotted down to a bolder and turned back to look at him again. As they made eye contact a Great Horned Owl called, hooting loudly from the west behind him. The coyote broke eye contact, ran behind the bolder and out of sight. Leonard left his mind open for a few minutes, to see if his intuition had anything to add. Other than that the coming battle would involve fatalities, nada. Before he turned to his truck he said to no one in particular, to the mountain, to the valley, to the Mother Earth, "I guess I'll wait on the phone call."

As much as he hated cell phones and left his off and in the truck most of the time, with Personal Quest in full gear he kept it nearby and checked his messages often. In the High Sierra, sometimes they depended on walie-talkies or CB radios. When you are responsible for teenagers, comunication is extremely important. That's why he knew, whether at home or camping with the questers, he'd get the call. Leonard Wounded Face got in his truck, heading home to Sarah and their kids.

Chapter One – Early Saturday Morning

"It's the worst I've ever seen." His face was white, shining with a cold sweat, in the pink light of dawn. "Four tours in Nam, Project Phoenix and the CIA torture ranches, napalmed villages, burnt crisp babies, you fucking name it, I've seen it, but this - it's the worst thing I've ever seen." My brother John looked back inside the cabin, looked up at our brother Robert, looked back at me waiting on the ground by the steps, and shook his head. A double AKA (above the knee amputee) with huge arms, he popped a wheelie in his wheelchair, immediately attained his point of balance, and rolled down the porch's two steps maintaining the wheelie in perfect balance. Once on the ground, he brought the wheelchair down on all four wheels, shook his head again, and rolled off past me to his car.

Our oldest brother, who remained standing on the porch, checked his watch and looked back inside the abandoned cottage at the crime scene unit personel going about their business. He glanced back down at me as I switched the large metallic coffee mug into my other hand, pulled my badge out of my blue jeans' back pocket and clipped it on my belt. Even though it was just the gold badge of our private security firm attached to a round black leather base, it looks similar to a detective's shield, and I always feel strange wearing it out on my belt. Being an ex-con and all, it was only natural to feel a little weird. They say your self image is pretty much fully formed by the time you're twenty-one. By my twenty-first birthday I'd done four years hard time at Reidsville, killed three men with my hands up close, and still had one long year to go. Maturing in prison can play havoc with your self-image if you wind up wearing a badge.

I knew our oldest brother, APD Major Robert Mosby, had the watch command this shift, and had called our middle brother, John, who was now getting in his car, folding his wheelchair up, and pulling it in behind the front seats. When he first got home from Viet Nam, Robert and I tried to do stuff for him, just trying to help. He didn't want it, it just pissed him off. Now we know better than to even offer to help if it's something he can do himself. His wife Betty just calls him a macho asshole, but she plays it exactly like we do. I watched him pick up his cellular phone, and thought somewhat sarcastically, "Robert called his little brother John, so John called his little brother, me. Ain't family life great?" I knew John was calling our clients, the owners of this property. Being president of our private security firm, he was on his way over to personally consult with the Faulkners. They were, after all, very big clients for our fairly small company.

"You aboard on this?" the number one son asked, bringing me back to the task at hand.

"Yeah," I mumbled, nodded my head, drank some of the coffee, "that's what John-the-Boss said." I said it like it was some title, like Richard the Lionhearted. It's not like it was a private joke; when John answers the phone, that's how I address him. I use it to him and around him all the time, so do some of the other employees. If you knew John, you'd understand the "the-boss" part.

"Who's the DIC on this?" I asked.

My brother squinted his eyes at me, not much liking the acronym for detective-in-charge, "Danny Fagan's drawn this one." As if summoned on cue, Fagan walked out, stretched, and put on one of his trademark hats. He favored Panama hats, but not exclusively. Anything he looked good in, with a wide brim would do. He was street smart as well as educated, and he was cool, calm, coherent and well spoken in front of the news cameras, so he got many of the high profile homicide cases and was on the local news a lot. Danny's uncle was one of the correction officers I knew while I was in "the big house," so Danny knew me for what I was, and where I was coming from. At least to some extent. He smiled, walked down the steps and shook hands.

How ya doing, Spooky?" Even the cops called me by my jailhouse nickname. Pretty much everybody does, except my folks.

"Fine." I grunted in response. I wasn't a morning person, hadn't had enough coffee to get over the monosyllabic hump, and I didn't like to work this kind of case. I liked the more fun stuff like providing night clubs and titty clubs with off-duty cops, burglar-proofing jewelry stores, setting up back stage security at concerts, providing visiting VIP's with security, occasionally helping desperate victims get justice when the overworked system hadn't worked for them. But not this crap.

"So, ya'll provide security for this place." Danny said, while popping in a stick of gum. He looked wide awake, like he'd been up for hours. In some sick way Danny loved this shit. He got most alive when somebody else just got dead. All I could think of was that it was damned early on a Saturday morning, it was already hot, and I hadn't gotten enough sleep. Not near enough sleep.

"Yeah, we do their whole family, seven properties in the greater Atlanta area, and all their businesses. We've got alarm systems protecting the three houses, but on this part of the estate, other than no-trespassing signs and locks on the gates...." I trailed off, and gestured back with my hand. It was obvious that no one had lived in this abandoned caretaker's cottage, summer cabin, whatever the hell it had been, for generations. The occupied houses were through the woods, over a large hill a tenth of a mile away. The dirt road connecting this house to those was long overtaken by the quick growing pines. The driveway to the cottage began at the dead end of Thorn Road and was normally closed off by a locked steel gate. It looked like it hadn't been used much for years, until early this morning when the police found the bodies, due to an anonymous phone tip. Nothing around the abandoned cottage now but footpaths and horse trails.

"Yo, Danny, we're thuu, or wheel be, soon as the meet wagon shows. Where thu hails the M.E.?" a plump redhead in a CSU jumpsuit with a strong southside Atlanta accent yelled over to Danny, as she walked over to the crime scene unit van where her partner was loading up the tools of their grim trade. Danny went over and talked to them quietly. They finished loading up and as they drove away Danny yelled, "See you in half an hour."

By then Robert had also dismissed two of the squad cars, left a lone policeman/squad car to secure the area, and left. I was thinking that when the word got out about what kind of crime it was - its brutal, bizarre, and ritualistic nature, and on whose property it was perpetrated, the news hounds and scandal mongerors would be out in force. It was a little past dawn, the reports were just being filed, hopefully, it would be hours before the news buzzards began circling in numbers to feed off the carrion of modern life. However, if a reporter was listening to a police scanner, it could be much quicker. They would have to be held at bay, at the edge of the property. I knew our firm would have to provide some extra bodies in uniforms just to keep the over-enthusiastic journalists from trespassing. And APD would need more than one lone car to protect the integrity of the crime scene.

Danny walked back over, to find me riveted to the same spot. I knew not to invade a crime scene until invited by the DIC. "They're through for now," he said, referring to the CSU. "The M.E.'s been held up, they're going for coffee and will finish up when he shows." Danny waved me on in. "Don't worry about footprints, they used some kind of tarp. That's why I let John come in and take a quick look." I had wondered about that since arriving. I followed in his footsteps anyway; way too many crime scenes become unnecessarily polluted, something I didn't want to be guilty of. "I'm really glad you're here to help on this one, Spooky, this one's right up your alley."

Before he had even finished his sentence, I knew that his statement was not going to be accurate. It wasn't that this was my chosen, self-proclaimed, or advertised specialty, or that I enjoyed working such crimes. I had backed into my specialty by accident. You solve a few cases dealing with the occult, get a little notoriety and bam - you're an expert. It really boiled down to the fact that most cops were pretty much lost on any kind of crime with a major ritual or occult component, so to them, I *seemed* like a specialist. And with degrees in criminology and symbolic anthroplogy, and having been trained to become a shaman, I was their logical, as well as almost only option. Semantically speaking, most cops didn't know the difference between a psycho and a psychic, between a con man and a shaman, between a satanist and a wise one/witch. I would probably have been at this crime scene anyway, because we have the security contract with the Faulkners; but once I walked into that house with Danny, I was working as a subcontractor of special services to the Atlanta Police Department. Not that I charged them scale, and not that they'd pay it, but at least I got paid. Since that fee was in addition to my normal paycheck, and I definitely would have been called in on this case by John, for a non-lawyer, I was about as close to double billing as you can get.

But it's not like I enjoy this kind of work. It didn't come up much, thank God, but it was never enjoyable. Maybe challenging, or intellectually stimulating, but definitely not pleasant. Who wants to see, up close, that the dark side of humanity really does exist? Who wants to see the foul fruit of evil's labor? "Certainly not me," I thought to myself as I followed Danny into the dark and pungent house. "Certainly not me."

I couldn't help but think about crazy Larry, the first and last APD ghostbuster - a police term for a cop specializing in cult/occult crime. He had taken early retirement down on Florida's gulf coast after buying into a lot of conspiracy panic, and losing all credibility. When nobody with a rational mind could follow his logic, he began claiming all his detractors, like the mayor and the chief of police, were part of the same international satanic conspiracy that was undermining America domestically and Christianity internationally. They gave crazy Larry an easy choice, early retirement, or a loony bin. Hell, he's eating shrimp and crabmeat and going fishing every day. If he wasn't a right-wing fundamentalist Christian fanatic, I'd be tempted to think he'd planned it all out. After APD's crazy Larry experience they decided to go with a subcontracting provider of special services. Which translated, means me. If I weird out, they just cancel the contract, instead of paying out disability/retirement benefits until death. I took a deep breath and cleared my mind, I needed to concentrate on the matter at hand.

As I walked in, I immediately felt a tightness at the base of my skull, the small muscles over my medulla oblongata instinctively tightened. So did those of my lower abdomen below my navel. Feeling real uneasy I moved deeper inside the dilapidated house. Besides the normal musk of an old abandoned house there were two additional strong odors - one a heavy incense, the other the uniquely pungent odor of blood. I followed Danny to the back of the house and took a look around, and gasped. I was not mentally prepared for what my eyes saw. All the air rushed out of my lungs at once. I tried to be professional, to be calm, look around, be observant. But I was having trouble breathing deeply, among other things. I momentarily lost it, walked quickly out of the cottage, down the steps, and threw up my morning coffee. I tried to stop it and get control, but couldn't until my body had purged itself. Completly.

Too bad the mind couldn't do something similar. I wished I'd never seen the horror I'd just witnessed. And wished I didn't have to go back in. No choice. It was worse than the worst thing I had ever seen, it was worse than anything I could imagine. It was a nightmare from hell in physical form.

Danny waited at the doorway while I got it together outside in the sunlight. After I cleaned up with my red bandanna I took out my little pipe (as a quarter Cherokee/Paiute trained shaman I also have a large Sacred Pipe) and got out some kinik-kinik - an Indian smoking mixture of herbs, bark, and sweetgrass. I filled the pipe, said a prayer I learned from a Northern Paiute shaman, and moved the pipe up to the Sky and down to the Earth, and to the four directions. I held it for a second more, for the seventh power, the Star Child, and then pointed the stem up and drew a circle. Then as I lit the pipe and puffed, I blew the smoke into my cupped hand and took it in front, behind, on each side of my body as a purification. The lone uniformed cop had taken his squad car up to the gate where the public road dead end and the old driveway began, securing the only entrance, so I knew for a short time only Danny was around. I could feel him watching, but I didn't sense that it was disrespectful. Maybe curious. I repeated the six movements of the pipe slowly as I smoked and prayed. Prayed for a blessing, for help, for protection for me, for Danny, for the investigating team, and for the souls of the sacrificed.

After I finished and repeated the six movements, thanking the Great Spirit, the Earth Mother, the Powers of Air, Fire, Water, and Earth, and the power of the mystical Christ Light, I emptied the pipe and turned to go back inside. Danny's demeanor was that of someone calmly waiting. He was totally serious, no laughing, no scorn, no derision. But Danny and I had worked together before, which brought to mind another scene I'd have just as soon never witnessed. I felt an all too familiar ache in the pit of my stomach as another gruesome scene momentarily flashed before my inner vision, but I shook my head like a cat shakes off a stranger's touch, blew a long breath out of my lips, and got back to business. To dwell on a tragedy of the past would only hamper efficiency in the present.

In my imagination I had psychically armed and protected myself using techniques possibly dating as far back as 100,000 years and some not yet, but very close to 2,000 years old. Mean, sick, stupid violence is one thing, you see it every day on the streets. But cold, naked evil is another. Especially ruthless, dedicated, and determined evil. That is something entirely different. I joined Danny on the porch, and he looked at me and said, "I know Spooky, this is a bad one. A real bad one." He paused, glanced back to make sure I was following him, and said, "Let's do it." I followed him on in, now that I was *prepared* to tread through the valley of the shadow of Death.

About the time the M.E.'s meat wagon showed up, Danny and I had scanned the rooms quickly while he pointed out the relevant stuff. I went back out to my car, got my polaroid and my mini-cassette recorder. When I came back, Danny was showing the M.E. the crime scene. The Medical Examiner was said to be unshakable, but apparently not. He looked pale, at least paler than normal. He was trying to act like everything was business as usual but he was obviously shaken. "I've got to call for another vehicle." The M.E. cleared his throat and continued. "Nobody told me about the pets." He hesitated, "I shouldn't assume they were pets, it's just nobody told me about the three... animals, just the…." Atlanta's chief M.E. shook his head and walked out. So much for the ice in his veins, I thought. If it could shake up a man who's seen the quantity and quality of death, chaos, and carnage he has, I wasn't about to be embarrassed by my reaction.

The front rooms of the house looked like most abandoned houses look: dark, dusty, cobwebs in the corners. There were empty cigarette packs, beer cans, whiskey bottles, and obscene graffiti, all the normal refuse of young derelict behavior. The only obvious oddity was that the floors had been swept clean, with all the refuse swept into the corners. The only road in to the cottage was Thorn Road, basically a short straight dead end road with woods on either side. It was a local lover's lane that ended at the gate where the Faulkner's property began with the driveway to the abandoned cottage. Obviously, some kids got out of their cars and walked in to drink, smoke, or screw around. When we got the contract for the security work here and at the other Faulkner estates and businesses, the family informed us that the road in had been a local lover's lane for years, and since there had never been any problems, they didn't want to make waves. They must have understood that angry teenagers can be every bit as, if not more, vindictive than any other segment of our population and that the local teenagers might be angry if deprived of their hangout, and the resulting vandalism could be expensive. Since there had never been any problems, and no strangers had ever strayed near the inhabited houses, it wasn't a concern of theirs. Or ours, I thought. Until now.

The M.E. waited outside for the other meat wagon and the crime scene unit van while Danny and I went through the house again, this time methodically - me snapping polaroids and recording our conversation. Danny went over the physical details, while I commented on the occult aspects. Whenever I did this kind of thing, knowing that our secretary Dolores would transcribe and type it up later, I generally attempted to let my stream of consciousness go. However, it was difficult to open up and be intuitive in a place where scant hours before, such horrendous damage had been inflicted for someone's purpose, and probably pleasure, resulting in two such horrible fatalities. Or five, if you counted the animals. And one of the most obscene and blasphemous rituals known in the history of human behavior had been performed with purpose and precision.

After a long and arduous thirty-seven minutes Danny and I reemerged into the renewing sunlight. By then the other meat wagon had shown, the CSU van was back, and they were ready to bag 'em and tag 'em - take it all away to the labs and morgue. Danny and I waited outside. I smoked my pipe, he smoked his Marlboros, I poured coffee from my thermos, and we talked about the obvious oddities and inconsistencies of the crime scene.

He took me around to the window outside of the murder room and showed me the barely percievable smudged remnants of dusty footprints under the window where they got a few smudged fingerprints. The current deduction was that these were traces left by the kids that discovered the crime scene and called it in anonymously. We circled the house, looked at several paths between Thorn Road and the cottage, and then we drove around to the Faulkner's house, to join Danny's partner Schultz and John the Boss.

***

It didn't take the Faulkner clan long to circle the wagons. There in the library of the main house were three of the four Faulkner siblings, representing an impressive net worth, and not a small amount of social influence. They owned chains of furniture stores, were major stockholders in two computer software companies, owned a huge chunk of the leading building supply/nursery chain, owned forty-five liquor stores throughout the southeast, owned a timber corporation, two chemical plants, and two carpet mills. That's just part, there were other international investments, off shore accounts, etcetera. The Faulkners had close relationships with many of the top politicians and judges in the state. There was Emmet - the oldest; short, squat and bald. He was a bulldog of a man who ran the family businesses. Albert - the youngest, also bald, of medium height, lawyer for the family as well as senior partner of a successful corporate law firm. Phineas, Dr. Faulkner, was a psychiatrist for the rich neurotic housewives of north Atlanta, and their behaviorally dysfunctional children. Phineas was fairly tall, walked with a pronounced limp, and shared the same pattern of baldness as his brothers. They all had that Friar Tuck, Medieval monk naturally tonsured hair. They might have resembled monks, but there were no sheep in that library, it was a lion's den.

All that Schultz had told the family was that there had been a crime, a multiple murder, on their property at the abandoned cottage. John assured them that their security systems were functioning fine and that there had been no incursion on the inhabited part of the estate. Schultz had learned that there was no live-in staff. They had three full-time employees - a maid, and a man who served as a groundskeeper/stable master/gateman, and a chauffeur. All had been called and asked to come in immediately. The Faulkners were awaiting the appearance of their niece, the daughter of Alexi Faulkner-Davis. Samantha had been the last one awakened and was dressing. She attended a private school nearby and was staying with Dr. Faulkner while Alexi and her husband were in Europe for a prolonged visit.

Albert was asking questions one would expect of a lawyer. Was anyone associated with the Faulkners known to be involved, was there any threat to the family, was there any possible liability concerning the family, was there any chance the perpetrators were hiding nearby? The answers all seemed to be no.

Emmet's wife Gretta returned from being elsewhere in the house, a bleached blond with big hair, too much makeup, and whore-red lipstick. In the back of my mind I remembered having heard that she was a cheerleader at Ole Miss during her college days. I suspected she was not a card carrying member of N.O.W. She made a fuss that Emmet had to deal with, which gave Danny, Schultz, John, and me some time to huddle and talk. Danny told Schultz there was no physical evidence leading from the crime scene to these houses, and no reason, yet, to suspect anyone from these houses had anything to do with it, or had been targeted in any way.

Danny looked at John and me, and said, "I know that ya'll work for them, but right now, this is a *police* investigation, and you *will* be quiet regarding any details about the crime scene until we've asked all our questions and are through. Okay, boys?" We nodded, Danny was just being polite, and had been all along. It sure wasn't asking us too much to just shut the fuck up until they were through. Officially, I was working for Danny and APD as a contractor of special services and only John was representing our company. Of course, that's just legal bullshit, and I knew exactly what Danny was saying. I know I talk like a sailor, but you spend a few years "inside" and see how socially polite your language remains.

By the time Emmet had hushed Gretta, everybody with a badge was heading for their places. John rolled by and quietly told me to drop by later, and have some clams with Betty and him. I'm highly allergic to clams, that was John's private code way of saying something queer was afoot. I checked out the people whose large contract helped keep our company in the black: Emmet - the bald bulldog; Gretta - the bleached blond; Alpert - the corporate mouthpiece; and Dr. psycho-babble. What a set. More money than they knew what to do with, yet absolutely no reputation for philanthropy. But murder? The kind of brutality that produced the crime scene we had just examined was hard to imagine coming from the pampered rich, but who's to say? Evil is an equal opportunity employer.

The businessman looked worried, the lawyer looked tense, and the shrink began pushing around an old library book cart, shelving and removing numerous volumes from the shelves which covered all four walls. He didn't seem as stressed out as the rest, but he was a shrink. Coping was something he was supposed to be able to teach to his patients, so why shouldn't he be coping well with this? I didn't exactly like his looks or his body language, as those things go, but I readily admit to having a real problem with the God complex of far too many physicians, and I don't like the inherent arrogance of most shrinks. If they want to tinker with people's heads professionally, I want to see some hard evidence that shrinks as a whole have a good attitude about life and have their act together. Most of the shrinks I've known personally have gone through way too many divorces, and didn't impress me with their personal happiness in the least. In my opinion, most psychiatrists are really messed up people who major in their field at college trying to understand and heal themselves. Then they graduate and enter a profession attempting to fix up other people. By that point, some of them may be healed and understand themselves, becoming healed healers. But many (probably most) are not. I don't know the current stats, but at one time shrinks had the highest suicide rate of any profession, a fact by itself neither thrilling or reassuring to those in need of help.

I prefer a shaman's Sweat Lodge over some pompous stranger's couch, but that's just me. I spent years in the joint with a lot of really bent people, and I can't say that I ever witnessed much in the way of any psychological or psychiatric successes there. But, of course, I didn't witness much in the way of rehabilitation either.

Samantha finally made her way into the room demurely and sat down on the huge sofa with Alpert to her left and the blond beehive and bald bulldog to her right. She wore a black knee-length dress with black pumps. I felt something was wrong from the get-go. I'd never seen her before, had no reason to, this was John's gig. He didn't want to do the concerts or VIP stuff, his wife Betty didn't want him working the titty clubs, and I didn't want to wet-nurse some rich wimp who's scared some poor crack-head is going to rape his wife and kill him dead. And in this society, it might happen to him no matter what the hell we do. Anyway, I'd never laid eyes on her, but Schultz had told Danny, while he briefed him, that Samantha was fourteen, fifteen in a

25

couple of days. There was something about Samantha that was older than any fifteen. Much

older.

Unfortunately, because of a wayward youth, some bad luck, and my current profession, I

have spent way too much time inside holding cells, jail cells, barrooms, courtrooms, bus stations,

and pawn shops. The weigh-stations of the lost. I have seen three different kinds of "old for their

age." The first, the most common - is when a kid will get into things, go to work, generally just

mature years ahead of their chronological peers. The second is the "old soul" type - the kid who

takes care of his alcoholic/messed up parents and helps raise their siblings - those just born wise

and responsible beyond their years. The third type is something I have seen in a few unusual

cases of incest. In these few cases there seemed to be a genuine love between the individuals

before the adult gave in to whatever perversion, aberration, or demon drives someone to abuse

such a sacred trust. If kids can't trust the adults that raise them, it's very hard for them to ever

trust in anything. However irrational it may be, the children almost always feel guilty, thinking

they have somehow brought the situation upon themselves.

This betrayal of trust by an adult often leads the victim into developing a poor self-image,

a negative attitude towards life, and, in some cases, eventually into a life of crime. Just as

tragically, these young victims often grow into adults driven by unconscious compulsions to

repeat the aberrant behavior.

There's not much to do in jail, sometimes, but analyze the people society has lumped you

in with. Jails are full of people who weren't loved enough or treated well, and grew up bad. But

they say Ted Bundy and Jeffery Dalmer came from good homes, so who the hell knows? All the

criminals I've ever met had their excuses, their reasons, their stories. That's as dependable as

tomorrow's sunrise.

The "old before their age" syndrome I'm talking about is not found in the majority of incest cases - in which perversion and abuse are inflicted by the powerful upon the weak. I'm talking about those instances where what was once a genuine love somehow grew to be expressed in inappropriate, taboo, and illegal ways. In these instances the child, instead of being protected and nurtured, is seduced/coerced by the adult/relative/guardian into becoming a lover, forever losing their innocence as a child. In some extremely rare cases the child maintains and possibly expands her (or his) own personal power within that relationship and in their personal world. They know that what they are doing is wrong, and taboo, but they have developed a powerful secret - a forbidden love - an us against the world attitude.

I had been one of the investigators in a case in which a thirteen year old stepdaughter exhibited the attitude that she had victoriously taken her stepfather, as though away from her mother, and had virtually taken dominion over the household. In court she would not testify against her stepfather, and wouldn't speak to her distraught mother. It's hard to estimate the immediate or long range psychological damage done to the child and the family in such situations. In my personal experience at least 90% of men and women behind prison walls claim to have been somehow abused or mistreated as a child. Of course, that many also claim to be innocent.

I wish I had crystal clear intuition, or was extremely psychic when desired, or had the constant ability to discern a hunch - from real intuiton - from some neuron firing off because of some unconscious association in my subconscious mind. But I don't. However, I *felt* Samantha was old beyond her age, and I wondered if the good doctor was not so good. But for all I knew, she could be here to get away from some such previous harmful situation, and I was definitely jumping to wild speculations on a hunch, on a feeling, and nothing more. And even if such a wild hunch was accurate, odds were it probably had nothing at all to do with the sacrilege against life perpetrated at the abandoned cottage and would be a matter for DFACS and not Homicide.

Within a few minutes, Danny established that Dr. Phineas Faulkner and his niece lived in the other large house, Alpert lived here in the main house, and the small house was an infrequently used guest cottage. Emmet and Miss Beehive lived in Buckhead and were present just to lend support at a time of family crisis. The idea that Gretta was going to help support anybody in crisis was almost laughable, but since they do help to pay my salary, I kept a straight face. It seems Samantha's older brother was away at military school in South Carolina, Alpert was single and lived alone, and Phineas and his wife were divorced. She'd gotten the West Paces Ferry estate near the Governor's mansion. The three full time staffers worked Monday through Friday, and all three had worked all day Friday and left at their normal times. The cook, gardener/ stablemaster/gateman and the chauffeur were normally off on Saturday, unless needed for something special. Parties and special occasions were catered, so there had been strangers on the premises, but, of course, they used reputable companies. John the Boss spoke up, saying that part of our security contract included checking out their employees and that all three had clean sheets.

Schultz had already called them and asked them to come in, Danny informed everybody that the staff would be interviewed separately, as they arrived. He walked back and forth as he put forward his questions to the gathered family. I noticed he always managed to be facing them on the sofa at the moment he asked a question, searching for their facial responses. As the question and answer routine began, I listened on a subconscious level, getting the gist of the conversation, but not paying attention to the individual words. Alpert usually goes out Friday nights to various social functions, and had returned last night around one a.m. Phineas and

Samantha had been home last night. She was attending summer school, as were the rest of the students in the school's orchestra, because they had a prestigious invitational recital coming up soon in Washington D.C. at the Kennedy Center. Phineas, an accomplished musician, was augmenting the practice time she spent at school. They were home, but would have heard little - being in the music studio from ten to twelve. Samantha said she had been exhausted after hours of violin practice and gone straight to bed after a snack. Phineas said he was in bed by two, and dead to the world.

Nobody in either house had heard or seen anything unusual.

Mostly Danny asked, and mostly Alpert answered. I consciously relaxed my body, head to toe, and made my breathing even. I allowed my face to assume a relaxed appearance. I was acting like I was internally hanging on every word, while my eyes randomly roamed around the room, when actually I was trying to observe everyone in the room for their non-verbal signals and messages. I listened not so much to what the voices said, but to the stress they revealed, to the rhythm and cadence of their answers. I watched their body language, the position of their hands and head, and the movements of their eyes while they talked.

The questions had proceeded as expected, to establish where everybody was last night. Places? Times? Witnesses? Did anyone see or hear anything unusual? Could the police look over all the grounds? Certainly. It got interesting when Danny asked if he could look around inside the three houses as well. He slid it in like it was no big deal, but most of us knew he was asking for legal permission to search inside the houses. Alpert straightened up on the sofa, glanced back towards Phineas and began what sounded like a prepared statement. First, Alpert informed us that although there were no obvious boundaries, the old cottage and half of the estate's acreage was owned by a corporation. Everyone knew it was a family dominated corporation, but the legal point was made that the events didn't happen on the estate's private property, per se.

Alpert started talking about *the Bill of Rights*, this and that amendment to the constitution, how they had their own security, and how they had just been informed by Danny himself that there was no reason or evidence to think anyone from the crime scene came this way. Danny let Alpert run, just to see how far, and how energetically he would go with the ball. Alpert went the full hundred. Obviously the family didn't want law enforcement people ransacking their houses and turning up possible skeletons in the closets. I couldn't help but wonder what kind of skeletons, and how many, were in the Faulkner's closets. But they do employ our firm, so I spoke right out, forgetting I was supposed to keep quiet.

"Come on Danny, nobody wants the cops poking around their houses, turning everything upside down. The Faulkners told us they've had large catered affairs here. Suppose they let your boys come in, and they find a mirror shoved under some piece of furniture somewhere with some lines and half a gram of coke on it, left by a drunken guest or caterer. You're sworn by law to arrest the proprietor." Danny looked at me, mean. He didn't want me screwing around in his investigation, his eyes said I had been warned. But Alpert was already saying he just didn't think it was necessary, and offered to call a couple of judges for their opinions, despite, he grinned, the early hour. He said it would be no problem, after all, they were family friends.

"Of course," Alpert continued, "the family will cooperate with the investigation in every way, we just think giving you legal permission to search our houses is unnecessary and extreme. If the press found out you had searched our houses, every one of us would be subject to ridiculous and unjustified suspicion and intense media scrutiny. We are not suspects and don't think we should be treated as such. And as people who pay large sums in taxes each year, we think it would be a waste of our tax dollars and a poor utilization of your resources. You should be out there finding the real criminals, not going through our underwear drawers, or giving false impressions to the rumor mill press."

That settled, Schultz went out. The staff was beginning to arrive, and it's always prudent to separate employees from employers in any investigation, if you want any semblance of the truth. The good doctor had let his brother do all the legal arguing, but I noticed a couple of exasperated glances from Alpert towards Phineas. I had little doubt as to the source of the strenuous objections to allowing a search, or in whose closets the skeletons were most likely hidden.

I thought about my hunches. I believed that the niece was old beyond her years and she reminded me of a few incest victims I had been in the position to observe. I was also sure that the doctor didn't want his house searched. Neither of which, even if true, had any obvious or reasonable link to the crime at hand.

I continued studying the Faulkners. Everyone seemed to be acting naturally enough for such an unnatural situation. If anything, the girl and the doctor were too composed. It always pays to be suspicious, and God knows I've been burned bad before, for believing what I wanted to be the truth. "But no matter how badly you want something to be true," as I heard in my childhood, "that just don't make it so." Unfortunately, it can be very hard to discern whether someone is telling the truth or lying their heart out. A sociopath can beat a lie detector, so can someone using certain drugs. A Yogi or occultist can exhibit physiological control of the circulatory and respiratory systems. A practitioner of the black arts can create a psychic shield within his aura, and if a skilled hypnotist, can also work post hypnotic suggestions on their willing or unknowing accomplices - the manchurian candidate syndrome. People can lie skillfully, some can beat the best machines. Our military special opps and CIA spooks are trained to beat lie detector tests. Observations of body language are important indicators for discerning the truth, but certainly not infallible.

There are some people who can lie non-verbally just as well, if not better, than they do verbally. Just look at actors. Lying non-verbally and verbally *is* their art. They must make you believe in what they portray and temporarily get you to suspend your normal disbelief for them to be successful. In the performance aspect - actors, salesmen, con men, lawyers, and preachers all practice the same craft. They perform, we perceive. They sell, we buy. The motives behind their performances may differ greatly, but the performance art remains the same.

I waited until the doctor and his bookcart were in a position where I could observe him and Samantha simultaneously. "Samantha," I blurted out during a lull, a little louder than necessary, "what about your relationships?"

Samantha turned to stone. I couldn't observe any motion of breathing for what seemed like half a minute, she just froze. The doctor didn't, "What do you mean, this is uncalled for, this is outrageous!"

"Boyfriends doctor," I looked up at him, then at her, "or any friends from school, any acquaintances who might have had past trouble with the law? Any friends you might have taken to the abandoned cottage? Got any friends who are sadistic, Samantha?" She flung her hair black raven hair back, and her eyes glowed like smoldering coke in a steel furnace.

"No! Whoever you are, I don't like that many people at my school, *they're all so immature.* As to friends who have been over here, there have been a few, all girls, and none of them have police records, or have been to the abandoned cottage." She looked down, Phineas glared, while the other three Faulkners were quiet and oddly still.

"Excuse me, doctor," I said, making eye contact with him, remembering who contributed a large chunk to our yearly gross. "I just didn't want your niece to be in any danger. No disrespect was intended." Then I looked at Samantha, her burning eyes looked up at mine, and fourteen, almost fifteen or not, those eyes said "don't fuck with me" and they meant it. There was an icy depth to those eyes, as well as a raging anger, an intensity which belied her chronological age.

Danny had done most of the talking and I hadn't said much before so Samantha didn't know who I was. "And I'm Singleton Marcus Mosby, Miss Faulkner-Davis, the junior partner of Triple S Security. We provide security for your family," I said and nodded my head towards her in my best imitation of Old South gallantry. "At your service, ma'am." I smiled, but she looked down and away. She was obviously invulnerable to my lame attempt at charm. Danny loudly cleared his throat, so I quickly clarified my legal status. "Although at this point and time I'm working as a subcontracting technical expert for APD." Her response, "Whatever." Like she cared.

"Doctor," Danny continued along the same line, "do you have any patients, see any clients at all that might have sadistic tendencies, homicidal tendencies, or any cult or satanic ties?"

The doctor pivoted on his good leg, stood tall and looked squarely into Danny's eyes. "Detective, surely you know the sanctity of the doctor/patient or priest/confessor relationship. If you've done your homework you already know that I work regularly, at a very reduced rate I might add, with troubled youth and young adults from five jurisdictions - three county courts and two state superior courts. But I go to the penal facilities and probation offices, none of these court-directed patients have ever come here or to my office. This work for the state is part of a federally funded experiment, a pilot program which, if it continues to be successful, may soon become regional, possibly some day national." Danny was silent. He obviously didn't know about the doctor's penal work; from John's astonished look, neither did he, and certainly not *moi*. This wasn't my gig till this morning. John can keep wet-nursing the rich and I'll keep my concerts, nightclubs, and nudie clubs.

Danny asked for and wrote down the names of the judges and courts. I brought up my concern about the need for more security for the crime scene and the family - the onset of the hordes of reporters and the morbidly curious (the aptly named look-a-loos after the O.J. circus) was a matter of limited time. Danny said police reinforcements were already on the way. John gave the family our estimate of how many uniformed security personnel would be necessary for the family's privacy to be maintained and to secure the boundaries of their property. They concurred with his estimate and John rolled over and handed me his cellular, so I went out in the hall, called Dolores, and got things moving. While I was finishing the call, the meeting in the library adjourned. Samantha walked by as though I didn't exist, the doc glared once, but didn't say anything. Hell, he could have fired us on the spot, but wasn't so inclined. Danny told me to come see him downtown when I got through, as soon as possible. He didn't look too happy.

It was Saturday afternoon before Dolores got enough uniformed bodies out to really secure the estate. The TV crews showed up much quicker than I anticipated. Maybe they just pay the dispatchers at APD to keep them informed, or constantly monitor the police radio. I don't know, but boy, did they show up. The media circus began before APD or our guys were fully prepared. It was a real zoo. I was more than happy when, finally, I could leave. Who, I ask you, can possibly be more obnoxious than a pushy reporter? (Excluding, of course, salesmen, lawyers, and TV preachers.) We arrested one news crew, that just wouldn't take no, walked right past the no-trespassing signs and went bumbling through the woods, attempting to get a shot of the crime scene. We held them in handcuffs, despite their vociferous complaints until an APD squadcar came out and got them. Boy did they squawk, to us, to APD. I have no fucking sympathy. Two of my guards and I would lose an afternoon testifying in court, but I really didn't give a rabid rat's ass. I'm all for freedom of the press, but I'm also for the right of the individual in society to have some privacy. I think the pursuit of happiness, mentioned along with life and liberty in the *Declaration of Independence*, includes the right of privacy on your own property. I bet the founding fathers and most Americans today feel the same way.

I climbed in the company gas-guzzler and headed downtown for APD Homocide. When the company started growing, John bought the firm a shit-load of old DeKalb County police cars in one of those local government sell-off auctions. His idea was that old police cars look like police cars to the average Joe and thus were good for a security firm. That may be true, but that also means they aren't worth a damn for any kind of undercover work. Eventually, John had almost all the old cop cars repainted, some with our logo on the side, the others look like unmarked police cars, and our employees use one of our three nondescript vans, or get reimbursed for using private cars in undercover work. A friend of mine from "the inside" fixed our fleet up and keeps them in shape. He's an ex- (hopefully) car thief, and currently a dirt track racer/mechanic.

Driving towards APD I got pissed off, like I usually do, at all the new construction. I grew up here, and although I've been around most of this world and I try to be realistic in my desires, I was still hoping my little piece of this planet would retain the charm it held for me as a child. I loved the woods, the wildlife, the farms, and pastures of my childhood. I'll be straight, I think *overpopulation sucks*. There are already way too damn many people and I think we're reaching, very quickly, the carrying capacity of this small and beautiful planet. (If not pragmatically, then aesthetically, as in quality of life.) That is if we haven't already surpassed it. When I see any new construction I never think, "Oh! what wonderful progress!" I usually think, "another part of Mother Earth just got raped."

The people who don't love and deeply appreciate Nature should all go live in high-rises in the city, and not tear up the countryside. Suburbs are like a cancer consuming the surface of the earth. When I get on I-285, the perimeter highway surrounding Atlanta, I didn't think how convenient it is, instead I think, "I'm on the concrete circle of death." Circumference highways circling urban centers and the over-development within and outside of them isolate and destroy the breeding populations of so much wildlife it is a travesty against Nature. But besides environmentalists, ecologists, scientists, nature lovers, Indians, and metis shamans like myself, who gives a damn? The DOT builds roads wherever the politicians will let them, and you can bet your ass somebody somewhere is getting richer. Some of that money is then contirbuted to Pac's or candidates and the circle of greed continues. Now a second larger outer circumference highway is planned. And the beat of urban life goes on, as the elimination of urban/suburban green spaces and once rural farm land, woods, and wildlife goes on.

Downtown at APD Homicide Danny was semi-pissed off about my comments concerning his proposed search of the houses. I tried the honest approach as in, "use sincerity, sincerity always works." I could remember the line, but not the movie.

"Look, Danny, you were never going to get inside those houses without an obvious trail of blood to justify a warrant. What I did was to try to earn a little of the Faulkner's trust, just in case something wrong *is* going on there. Now I've got a better chance of finding out what."

"You'd be losing one of your biggest contracts if you nose around there contrary to family interests and get caught. If there's some conflict of interests, Spooky, we'll get another expert, or call the Feds."

It had already been a long, hot, tiring day. I hadn't gotten near enough sleep last night and I needed a good laugh and this was it. I started laughing because Danny hated working with the Feds. He thought they were a bunch of pompous white collar pricks who were over-educated in college and under-educated on the streets. He thought they were fine for chasing terrorists, that national security and the mob should be their main concerns. Let the real cops be cops, let the feebees (FBI) chase the wise guys and their goombahs, and the terrorists in the shadows.

"That's a call I'd like to hear you make." I kept laughing. Danny looked even more pissed.

"You know it's not like we couldn't catch hell for using you, if anybody checked *your sterling record*."

I got quiet quickly. He had a valid point. If the press got into my past and deciced to make a big deal…, so I tried making peace. "I'm sorry man, but that lawyer was not going to let you in, the good doctor would not allow it. And they are a very well connected family. But you know me, my loyalty to my clients only goes so far - on either side of that vastly huge grey zone in the middle, right is right and wrong is wrong. You saw that crime scene, Danny, do you really think I wouldn't want to bust whoever the hell is responsible for all that carnage, just so I wouldn't lose a contract?"

Danny smiled, "I didn't really think of them as suspects anyway, and didn't really expect them to let us in, but looking around might have helped rule them out. Any of them could have come and gone that night in a car with its lights off without being seen, they all have remote controls to come in and out of the gate electronically. But to answer your question, Spooky,"

Danny kind of groaned, "naw, youre not *that* greedy. You might have your vices, but greed's not one of them"

"Thanks for the vote of confidence." The chastisement over, we got down to work. We would spend hours going over every aspect of what we had. Soon, Danny would have to report upstairs with his plan of investigation and his estimates for how large a team he needed. Since this would be a high profile case with tons of media coverage, he'd have to be able to brief however big a team they gave him, assign tasks and manage the investigation efficiently. Danny knew he would be working under a microscope, but some perverse part of him loved it and thrived on it. A real sickee, I thought. I respected him, but still, a real sick boy. He loved this shit way, way too much, he absolutely thrived on it.

Chapter Two – Saturday Night

Walking into the candlelit room he felt like he owned the world. In his entire life he had never felt as powerful as he did now, and he was confident his power would continue growing. He had the world by the balls. Glancing down as he walked around the antique four-post bed he saw her black hair spread out on the silk sheets behind her head. She was lying perpendicularly across the middle of the bed, with her legs off the far side of the bed and her feet on the floor. Her pale wrists were tied with long red silk scarfs to the near head and foot bedposts. He slapped his hand loudly with his jet black riding crop as he rounded the footboard of the bed and then stood at its side, looking down on her as she lay naked before him, waiting.

Although slightly euphoric from the drug laced wine, she looked up at him with different feelings than those which had once so strongly consumed her. Her would-be savior thought he had become her master, but she was no slave. She had enjoyed the wide variety of their sexual games at first. Her detested older brother, whenever he could get away with it, had sadistically tormented her for as long as she could remember. When he began to go through puberty his activities had expanded to include sexual abuse as well. Her current situation, by her standards, was a definite improvement over life with brother.

These games gave her pleasure and this situation extended to her more control over her life than she had ever known before. But the love, commingled with the feeling of safety this man had once brought her, was long gone. His joy seemed to be in his mastery over her in the same way he manipulated so much in his life. Everything in his life. But he kept making two critical mistakes with her. He kept taking her for granted. And under estimating her. He would soon learn.

The man who had once been exciting and mysterious to her, now looked somewhat ridiculous. Standing there, bald head shining in the candlelight, shirtless, shoeless, wearing skin tight black leather pants. Around his waist was a wide black leather belt with a silver inverted pentagram side buckle. Hanging from the belt front and back were blacksmith aprons of black leather, thirteen inches square, each adorned with a bright red inverted pentagram. As she looked down at the five pointed star pointing to the floor, she knew the aprons concealed that the pants were crotchless in the front and had two large round holes in the back through which protruded his pasty white ass.

One day, when she had become master of this situation, she would tell him he was in lousy physical condition, his hands were corpse cold, and he looked totally absurd once the pentagram adorned aprons were removed. She bought into some of the philosophy of life he taught her, it suited her temperament and meshed with her experiences. She just wasn't sure the teacher could live up to the teachings. That remained to be seen. Sometimes she thought he was losing it, going further and further over the edge, especially recently, but other times he rose to the occasion. Either way, she was sure about what he represented to her now - a stepping stone to where she was headed, and the instrument and vehicle for her vengeance.

Many months ago, the sight of her naked body alone would have aroused him completely. Now, the sight of her with arms spread and tied, with the edge of her buttocks and her legs completely off the bed, waiting for him, was not enough for a strong and immediate physiological response.

She could see that once again there was no tell-tale bulge lifting the front apron. That meant the foreplay with the riding crop would be longer and harder than the levels she found pleasurable. But that would be okay, because when her turn came, she would give back tit for tat. Being her "master," he always went first. But unlike her brother, this man seemed to need to be punished and feel pain himself, as well as inflict it. Having been on the receiving end her whole life, she took much pleasure in the giving of pain, even if for now it was done as he instructed. He had gone to great pains to instruct her in his philosophy, that the strong take and the ruthless rule. That power is pleasure and pleasure is power. He might be the boss for now, but for how long she thought, how long till the student teaches the teacher.

He approached her, reached down and took her left leg by the calf, sliding his hand down to her heel, raising it high, lifting her leg towards the ceiling, and then pulling her leg over towards the foot of the bed, exposing the left half of her ass. He popped it lightly with the riding crop and she twisted her hips, exposing her bottom completely. Then he began with the riding crop using the pattern he always used: soft, hard, soft, repeatedly, interspersed with caressing, fondling, and digital manipulations. The harder he hit, the more aroused he got. She had a much higher tolerance of pain than he suspected, but she knew to make noises of pain so he got aroused quickly. Some day soon she was going to find out just how much punishment he could take. She doubted it was very much. The thought of that day aroused her, while her feigned but enthusiastic moans of pain drove him to drop the crop, twist her hips back to face him, spread her legs and pushed them up, rip off his aprons, and enter her. She pulled her legs up, then extended them straight out, and then drove her feet as hard as she could into his bare ass and began to grind against him. She squirmed to get him where she wanted him, and then began to pull on her restraints, working her pelvis furiously. She knew he was no marathon man, if she wanted hers she had to race. He leaned over her as he continued ramming into her, sliding his arms under her shoulders, reaching out with both hands and grabbing handfuls of her hair. Pulling. She fought to bring her face forward, found the spot on his shoulder over his left collar bone, opened wide and bit hard as she extended her legs again and kicked in, pushing him deep inside her. Their orgasms were simultaneous.

As he lay collapsed on her restrained body, almost unconscious from the intensity of orgasm, his weight driving her deep into the bed and making her breathing labored, she thought, "Get off soon fucker, your turn to hurt."

***

I was exhausted by the time I left Danny late in the evening, but would have been there even longer had I not repeatedly explained to Danny that I had to pick up someone at the airport. He reluctantly let me go, with the promise I'd meet with him again tomorrow morning before his briefing. He said he'd give me a call if he needed me before that. I gave him my most sarcastic, "Gee thanks," and hit the road. The word had come down that the power brokers upstairs were giving him a large team; the political pressure was already beginning to build to solve the case quickly. Rumors were already running rampant, fueled by media speculation. A brutal satanic ritual murder in the nice part of town gets attention, makes headlines, and troubles the rich and influential. It brings the city negative publicity on a national level, not good for a convention city. It is the kind of crime that the powerful elements of a community want to see solved immediately, not dragging out for weeks or months constantly in the papers, on the tube, and on talk radio.

I knew Danny's way. He'd push to accumulate leads, follow them thoroughly, and go over the crime scene and the related files

I knew Danny's way. He'd push to accumulate leads, follow them doggedly, go over the crime scene and the files repetitiously, until he had it figured. Out of the required questions: who, what, when, where, how, motive, and opportunity - we definitely knew where and had a general idea about when. Other than that, we didn't know squat. At least not yet.   On the way to the airport I glanced down to make sure I had the small posterboard sign I'd made with the name Laura Red Star in black magic marker. Leonard Wounded Face had called a couple of weeks ago, saying

On the way to the airport I glanced dwon to make sure I had the small posterboard sign I'd made with the name Laura Red Star in black magic marker. Leonard Wounded face had called a couple of weks ago saying his mother's younger brother's daughter would be coming to Atlanta for the Unity Convention. (Indians are often specific about relations because European kinship terms and theirs are not always equivalent.) I immediately offered to put her up, show her around, and let her use my truck or a company car because I could always use a company car or ride my scooter. I'd just gotten it out of the shop and been wanting to ride the Harley more during the summer weather anyway.

Leonard Wounded Face had been my cellmate when I went "down the road" into the state system. I got busted on my seventeenth birthday, a rather ironic birthday

Leonard Wonded Face had been my cellmate when I went "down the road" into the state system. I got busted on my seventeenth birthday, a rather ironic present from from Fate, and went into the adult penal system four months later. There wasn't a real long trial. Hell, I was guilty as sin according to their laws. I didn't remember me or anybody I know ever voting consent to those laws, but that's the way it goes.

Every prisoner in Georgia that goes into the state penal system for a felony must go through Jackson Diagnostic Center, where they have Georgia's death row. It's a real eye-opener

Every prisoner that goes into the state penal system for a felony must go through Jackson Diaganostic Center, wher they have Georgi'a death row. It's a real eye-opener at seventeen.

After they evaluate you, they give you your "EF number" and send you on to your new home in the state penal system. When I arrived at Reidsville I was given a bunk in Leonard's cell. He showed me the ropes of survival in "the big house" and we became best friends and brothers over the next three years. Growing up he didn't have a wana´ (younger brother) and had always wanted one. So over the years he became my pavi´ and I became his wana.´ I did a couple of years after he left, but by then I knew the score, had friends and allies, and had carved out my own place. In prison Leonard became, and today remains a big part of my life. Like I always heard church people say, the Lord works in mysterious ways.

Leonard was there when I got my nickname and like it or not, the name stuck. Leonard also helped lead me into my avocation, that of shamanism. My profession is

Leonard was there when I got my nickname and like it or not, the name stuck. Leonard also helped lead me into my avocation, that of shamanism. My profession is security facilitation and private investigation, but my avocation, my calling, is metis (may-tee, from the French Canadian meaning mixed blood) shamanism.

An Indian Vietnam Vet, who went down for hospitalizing three policemen, two very seriously, hospitalizing two other civilians, and destroying a bar might not seem to have a lot

An Indian Vietnam vet, who went down for hospitalizing three policemen, two seriously, hospitalizing two civilians, and singlehandedly destroying a bar might not seem to have much in common with a green kid down for growing herb, but we had enough. My brother John was Special Forces while Leonard was 101st Airborne and done Ranger training at Fort Benning. Both were warriors who had volunteered and done their jobs but afterwards had severe reservations about the politicians and policies which sent them to southeast Asia. Neither had much, if any, respect for the South Vietnamese government or for most of the South Vietnamese

Army they had been sent to support. When I told Leonard that the herb I had been growing with my cousins was from seeds brought home by vets, and that the main outlet for my herb was the patient population at two V.A. hospitals, he warmed up. When he found out about my grandmother and I found out about the medicine men and women in his family history, things got downright interesting.

My grandmother didn't die until she was 97. She was full Cherokee and quite a character. She was the local midwife and herb doctor in their rural moutain valley . She told us that as a small child she had been told her great grandfather had been a medicine man, and something of a prophet and visionary. Until the white soldiers killed him.

Some of my earliest and best memories are sitting around her with all my brothers and my sister and all our cousins, while she rocked in her rocking chair, smoked a corn cobb pipe, and told us about the Indian

Some of my earliest and best memories are of sitting sround her with all my brothers and my sister and cousins, while she rocked in her rocking chair, smoked a corn cobb pipe, and told us about the Indian ways, and stories of how the plants and animals came to be the way they are today. She told us that the Earth was our mother, and just like our human mothers bore us, the Earth Mother gives birth to all of humanity, all the animals and plants, and that one of the most important lessons in life is that we must love her and respect her the way we do our own mothers. You can call it corny, you can call it simplistic, but I believed her then, and I still do, with all my heart.

Leonard told me about his family, about the Numu, the people - the Northern Paiute, and his home - the Owens Valley. Leonard taught me a lot of stuff that U.S. historians never seem to put in the history books at school - about how the Indians had been treated, from the first

European contact down to the present. Things I later corroborated at college and in libraries, but they conveniently forgot to teach in public education. Certainly not in the elementary or high schools I know about. Nobody ever told me how within two hundred years of European contact, previously unknown diseases brought by the Europeans raced across the Americas killing off over half, high estimates range up to 96% of the indigenous peoples of North, Central, and South America. Nobody told me how, for decades the Indian children on reservations in the U.S. were taken away from their parents and forced to go to boarding schools where they were stripped of their cultural heritage and physically punished if they spoke their own language instead of English. Nobody had told me how the Bureau of Indians Affairs was looked upon by most Indians not as a friend but as an instrument of oppression. Nobody told me how in the land of religious freedom the Indians were not free to practice their own religion until Congress gave it to them in 1978. However, to this day there are restictions concerning the Sun Dance.

When Leonard told me that most Indians considered the European colonials and immigrants, in general, and the U.S. government specifically, to have

When Leonard told me that most Indians considered the European colonials and immigrants, in general, and the U.S. government specifically, to have been as hard on the Indians as Hitler was on the Jews, I had to pause and think. I had always known that the Indians got screwed every way to Sunday, but somehow the extent of the atrocities had not sunk in. I had no idea how widespread and effective the European/U.S. campaign of *genocide* against the Indians had been, but I had plenty of time to learn while inside, and learn I did.

Genocide and the United States are not words usually associated with each other, except by Indians. The original and true Americans are now an extremely small minority group in the United States. At the time I was in college, the number of Indian remains in museums and educational institutions throughout the United States outnumbered the population of living

Indians. That's fairly effective genocide.

The colonials, and the U.S. government which followed, dealt with the Indians first as a

resource to be taken advantage of, and then as a problem to be solved by forced migration,

military conquest, or genocide. Some soldiers and settlers really believed that the only good

Indian was a dead one. Blankets infected with smallpox were given to the Indians; women and

children were regularly and indiscriminantly massacred as though they were combatants. The

U.S. broke the terms of every treaty they ever made with the Indian nations during the first 200

years of our history. And these natioanl sins are not sins of some distant past with no

repercussions in the present. Just tour the reservations throughout the U.S. and take a good look

at the Third World quietly isolated inside the First World. Read the statistics concerning health,

education, employment. A few successful casinos have helped some tribes but the mistreatment

of the original Americans is not a thing of the distant past.

Most of the Indians killed in California between 1820 and 1920 were killed by drunken

settlers/vigilantes who killed men, women, and children in order to steal their land. There were

"social clubs" that existed for the sole purpose of killing Indians, often they took an ear, finger,

or scalp for counting purposes and as souvenirs. One governor of California in the 1840's, Peter

Barnett, publicly stated that it was obvious that the war between the White and Indian races

would continue until its inevitable conclusion, the extermination of the Indians. At the infamous

Wounded Knee massacre, where 300 men, women, and children who had peacefully gathered to

perform the Ghost Dance were savagely set upon and murdered by the 7th Cavalry, the soldiers

posed for pictures like brave heroes. Twenty-seven of these murderers of women and children

received the United State's highest honor, the Congressional Medal of Honor. Honor? Killing old men, women, and children? They don't teach that in the history books. Since Wovoka, the founder and prophet of the Ghost Dance movement was Northern Paiute, the Paiutes had it rough for years. And they still remember.

Our government no longer erects statues to commemorate the old massacres, but the Indians haven't forgotten. They, more than any minority in this great nation, are still waiting for their piece of the American Dream. Their original American Dream ended with European contact, and became their American Nightmare. Casinos have in no way solved the massive problems of 300 years of repression. Poverty and joblessness are still rampant on most reservations, the high school drop out rate is near half, and a high percentage of Indians will be victims of violent crime.

Leonard's father was an Owen's Valley Paiute and his mother from Tule River - over the Sierras on the western side. His great grandfather was the first Wounded Face, he was the "captain" of the braves who acquired horses and resisted the invaders. Although most Paiute took Anglo names after their subjugation, and today most Owens Valley Paiutes use their Anglo names almost exclusively; his grandfather and father had chosen and kept Wounded Face as their last name, to honor their ancestor with the long scar from the calvary officer's saber.

Most Paiutes had Anglo last names like Stewart, McBride, Collins, or Lewis, a few Anglicized their Paiute name, like his cousins the Red Stars. Leonard's father's cousin was a revered shaman, Grandfather Rayland Greyrock; and he wasn't the only one in Leonard's large extended family. Despite his occasional bouts of drinking and partying which often included fighting, Leonard had absorbed a vast amount of traditional knowledge and he taught me the Indian spiritual worldview. He found me an eager and patient student. Contrary to some of his behavior during the occasional drinking sprees that landed him in jail, Leonard was truly a

48

deeply spiritual man. He just had an inner wildness, and some anger and resentment he hadn't

outgrown or fully gotten a hold of at the time.

When you're doing time, time is what you've got. My attitude towards doing hard time

was to learn what I could, stay in the best physical shape possible, and to stay out of trouble - not

get raped, maimed, or killed. I'd been told going in, with good behavior and prison over-

crowding, I'd probably only do two years hard time and the rest would be on parole. Leonard had

a great wealth of knowledge and I had the questions. That's how we spent many hundreds, if not

thousands of hours, and that's how I got my nickname, discussing spiritual subjects.

One of the biggest black men in the house was James Cantrell. He was probably no angel

out on the streets but he was likeable on the inside. Cantrell wanted to get in better shape while

he was putting in his time so after watching a few of my workouts, he approached me and I

shared with him some of what I'd learned from my dad and brothers about strength and agility

training. We often worked out together. He was a powerful man in that environment, and a damn

good ally to have. To tell the truth, I liked him a lot, but I heard some wild and crazy stories

about him when he was out on the streets.

One day at lunch, Cantrell was sitting next to me while Leonard and I were deep, very

deep, in a discussion. Leonard was explaining that unlike the Judeo-Christian world view of

good versus evil and a world at spiritual war, the Indians see a much more harmonious whole.

They have nature spirits and spirits that are the equivalent of our angels and somewhat of our

demons, but they have no ultimate antithesis to God such as the Judeo-Christian Satan. They

definitely have trickster spirits, but they serve to teach, not torment. In some Indian nations, a

trickster spirit, Coyote, is considered to be the Creator. In Paiute creation myths Coyote is the

father of the Paiute, which is why the Paiute name for the Owens Valley Paiute is the water ditch (Owens Valley) coyote children—*nun´ wa paya hup ca´ a´ otuu´ mu.*

We were lost in our discussion when finally Cantrell stood up with his empty tray, laughed a little to himself, and said, "Damn Chief, you and Mosby talk all kinds of spooky shit all the time. All the time. Chief, you and Spooky here need to lighten up, lighten up! Talk about sports, or pussy, or somthun', but not all this demon and spirit shit all the time." He pointed at his temple and made the circling motion with his finger, the internationaly accepted symbol for insanity, smiled and walked away. He never called me anything but Spooky from there on out, and within a week, it was my name. That's life in the "big house."

After a couple of weeks of being called Spooky, I asked Leonard if he didn't mind being called Chief all the time instead of his name. He laughed, very exuberantly for him. He said he actually was a chief in a small warrior society, so although they used it as a nickname, they were actually doing him honor. I envied him his rationalization, for I had no such convenient coincidence to make my new name more tolerable. But just like going to jail in the first place, if you have no choice, you learn to live with it.

So I ended up being Spooky Mosby, and like it or not, will be, even if I live to be an old silver haired gentleman some day. It's not like I started out with John Smith or something ordinary. One of my father's ancestors was John Singleton Mosby, the Gray Ghost, one of the fathers of modern guerilla tactics. During the Civil War three counties in Virginia, not all that far from the nation's capitol, were known as Mosby's Confederacy. At the end of the war he dissolved his command, but he never surrendered. He had been the heartthrob of Virginia's belles, a southern hero, a thorn in the side of the Union, and he lived to be a gallant old man and write his memoirs. Dad's first son was named Robert, after his own father. The next two, John and I, got named after the Gray Ghost. Coming from a family big on military and law enforcement careers, it could be expected. I'm pretty sure my dad, the Colonel, is glad the one named John Mosby became a decorated and bonafide war hero. And that the black sheep of the family gets called Spooky. Sometimes life is just.

***

They always prepared and proceeded logically when acting out their sexual fantasies. Well, she thought, pretty much *his* fantasies so far. If bondage was involved, as it often was, the dominator would tie the submissive up, then leave the room, put on the appropriate outfit, return and play out the fantasy. Now it was *her* turn. She was down to only her black leather dog collar adorned with bright chrome spikes, her black lace-top thigh high stockings, her black six inch stiletto heels, and the riding crop. He was face up, spread-eagled on the bed, tied to all four posts with long black silk scarfs. She was facing the headboard which she grasped with one hand, while her other was busy with the riding crop. She was riding his tongue and nose like she was rounding the last turn in the Preakness with a four-length lead, going full speed for the finish line. Finally after one last quick whack, she dropped the crop, brought both hands down and grasped what he had left for hair on either side of his head, and got hers, again, and again. At times he blew out like a whale blowing out its spout and inhaled huge gasps of air. She didn't care if he had a little trouble breathing, this was her turn.

***

Leonard had told me on the phone that I wouldn't have any trouble recognizing her - how many beautiful American Indian women get off flights each night at Hartsfield/Jackson? I brought the sign anyway, but Leonard was right. As I watched the arriving throngs come out into the large waiting area outside of security, it would have been hard for me to miss Laura Red Star - primarily because I possess good vision, a functional male anatomy, am heterosexual, and breathing. I'm pretty sure everybody else meeting those requirements in seeing distance noticed her too. I had thought Leonard might have exaggerated, but if anything, beautiful was an understatement. She was thin and shapely, medium height, and had raven hair down to her waist. I knew I was maintaining my composure because I had not jumped up and down, high-fived strangers, or screamed thank-you Jesus. Not that I was taking anything for granted, and it's not that the romantic dry spell I found myself in was an extended drought. Not an extended-extended drought. And any sane single man would have welcomed the opportunity to show such an exquisitely beautiful woman his home town. She had those bright, aware eyes that always accompany a keen and perceptive mind. Down Simba, I told myself, down boy.

She scanned the crowd and immediately made her way towards me. My hair is the same as when I was living on the rez with Leonard - long, tied back in a pony tail with red leather thongs. It was a safe bet nobody else wore his hair warior style in the waiting crowd but me. I sheepishly raised the sign for about two seconds, she smiled, I rolled it up, folded it, and stuck it in my back pocket to dispose of properly. She was a smart traveler, all she had was a huge cloth purse - it looked like an Indian blanket with shoulder straps - on her shoulder and a carry-on she rolled. I offered and she let me take the luggage while she kept the monster pocketbook.

I had come straight from APD and it had been a hell of a day. It had been so full and I was running so late, I hadn't taken any time to consider my own appearance and wondered if I looked like the host from hell, or worse. I had on a white (no longer clean) tee shirt that said "security" front and back in large black letters and had a gold outline of a badge - front left. I had long since put my badge back in my back pocket. Knowing that airline food always sucks, if you even get any domestically, and being ravenous myself, I immediately suggested we eat dinner before she got settled in, and she quickly agreed.

Going through the new chrome and plastic airport monstrosity, I told her I wished she could have seen the old Atlanta airport. We went there pretty often as kids when we would sneak out, because you could be there late at night, not attract any attention, and have a ball. Besides a huge pinball arcade, the old airport had a restaurant on a mezzanine under which everybody flying in or out of Atlanta had to walk. The back wall of the mezzanine was clear plate glass through which you could watch the jets take off and land. It was world-class people watching. I spent many an hour there as an adult, enjoying a drink and the view, waiting to send off or meet someone. The new airport, like most of today's structures, is absolutely soul-less. All the bars have drink pouring machines, moreo soul-less effeciency.

As we approached my car and I pointed it out, she stopped, hesitated, turned to me and said, "Leonard said that you weren't a cop?" From the back it looked just like a police car.

"I'm not," I assured her. "It's the firm's car. We do security and private investigation work. It's supposed to look like a cop car, and it does, but believe me, it's not. And I'm not."

I couldn't help but think that for a journalist, she was awfully skittish about the police. Once we were loaded and on the way I her about it. "You don't seem too keen on cops or symbols of authority."

She responded pretty matter-of-factly. "It's a Pine Ridge thing. I married a Pine Ridge Lakota and lived there while the BIA, the FBI, and Dick Wilson's GOON's (Guards of the Oglala Nation) were conducting a covert war against members of the American Indian Movement, member's relatives, and supporters. Many people were killed, homes were destroyed, people were jailed on trumped up charges. All the symbols of government and power, all the authorities sided with the bad guys, or turned a blind eye."

I knew some things about this dark, recent-past abuse of power."Yeah, and twenty years later Leonard Peltier is still in jail for two killings which he didn't commit, in a firefight provoked by the Feds." I threw in. "It's one of the most blatant abuses of renegade federal power by the FBI in our history. They coerced witnesses, manipulated evidence, and really made a sham of the whole judicial process. The whole thing has been documented and presented to the American public on TV a couple of times, but still, no Congressional or judicial action. I thought maybe Clinton would rectify the injustice, right before he left office, right this one wrong, but no, he gave pardons to the big money white collar criminals. Nobody these days has the political courage to go on record stating that the FBI and BIA railroaded an innocent man, even though every prosecution witness at the Peltier trial later recanted their testimony, saying it was coerced by FBI or BIA threats.

"I remember hearing that during the covert war, the Pine Ridge Reservation had the highest unsolved murder rate in the United States. Years ago I thought Hawaiian Senator Daniel Inoye was getting some momentum going in Congress to free Peltier, but there was too much political risk and too little to gain for most of the professional politicians in Congress to take a stand and do the right thing. And nobody wants to look unpatriotic, right now, when the FBI is playing a major part in the war against Terror, so Peltier stays inside."

She didn't verbally respond. She looked down and shook her head back and forth in sadness, but I couldn't tell if it was conscious. She obviously didn't believe Peltier would ever find justice. We headed out on Atlanta's superfast highways. If you're not going fifteen over the speed limit, someone will run up your butt. She looked out at the trees flying by as we headed north on I-85.

"I don't know if Leonard told you," her voice grew softer, a little farther away, "I lost my husband on Pine Ridge."

I didn't know what to say, so I too kind of shook my head and said nothing.

"I married young," she continued, looking out the window, "at sixteen, to a much older Vietnam vet and A.I.M. warrior. They came into the Owens Valley to spread the word, I'd come over from Tule to hear, and I was swept off my feet by this Lakota warrior. We had a whirlwind romance, got married, and moved to Pine Ridge and lived on the rez. I saw him get blown in half by a shotgun blast on our own front porch. Although all I saw was a pickup truck speeding away in the dark, I had a very strong suspicion which GOON squad did it, and said so to the authorities. It remains an unsolved crime. And it probably always will. Lots of people died, lots of unsolved crimes."

I shook my head again and mumbled a lame I'm sorry and she said it was a long time ago. We took I-20 east and after twenty-five minutes got off on the surface streets headed home, via a restaurant on the way. As we rode on with the windows down the scent of honeysuckle filled the car, the breeze felt somewhere between cool and warm, and a one night past full moon was shining bright. With both windows down her hair was blowing back, sometimes caressing my arm as it danced on the air. It felt like cool silk. Laura Red Star was devastatingly beautiful in the moonlight.

"One thing I can say for your city," she broke the ice after a long pause, "it has more trees than any other city its size I've ever seen. Maybe any city I've ever seen."

"You should see it in the spring when the dogwoods and azaleas are blooming. It's gorgeous. But you should have seen it twenty years ago, it was a forest-city. There were large trees everywhere downtown, and there were small farms, pastures, and woods surrounding the city. It was uniquely beautiful as a forested city. It's getting over-developed so quickly these days, and there's no long range vision on how to keep it beautiful. We need to do what Colorado did, put a halt to unlimited growth, development, and desecration of nature. Have low-tax open area and green space laws. I'm scared that before the masses wake up, the beauty will be irrevocably gone."

"I certainly hope not. It is beautiful, for a city. From the air it looked very much like a large forest dotted with houses and lined by streets."

I liked this woman already.

***

Gary opened another beer. He'd been let go early again, third Saturday in a row. They only needed a second bouncer when the club was busy and the crowd rowdy. Lately it had been neither. But it really didn't matter shit to him, as he stared at the small brown paper sack stuffed full of money lying on top of a stack of his *Soldier of Fottune* magazines. It was filled with bundles of worn tens and twenties. It was thousands of dollars. More than he made in months, more than he'd made during his worst years.

He glanced over at the police uniform he had hung up neatly after its one use last night. It was so authentic. It had worked so successfully he knew he'd be using it again. Probably often. He couldn't believe it had everything: belt, holster, gun and ammo, flashlight, nightstick, shoes that fit, badge, police i.d. card with his name on it. Even a pamphlett with police codes and jargon. Everything was perfect. Whoever these people were, they were good, real good.

He got up and went to the fridge to get some red-hot sausages. He smiled and shook his head, thinking about the spell he'd done just weeks ago. It was a simple ritual. He'd done everything just like Kevin said, and it must have worked. Obviously, it worked. There was no other explanation. His whole life Gary had *dreamed* about being a hero, a soldier, a spy, a mafia hit-man, a tough guy. The kind of guy people write stories about and make movies about. He was a big, strong guy, with a natural inclination towards violence. He had always known he already had everything he needed, that he didn't need to do all that crap his teachers and coaches had shoved down his throat. He was big, mean, could take punishment, and enjoyed dishing it out. What more did he need? Certainly not all that fucking running and conditioning they tried to make him do in high school football before he quit. Certainly not all those damned repetitive movements the karate teachers had tried to make him do. And all that running so he could fight as a professional kick-boxer, what total bullshit. He had always known that he had what it took and all that discipline crap was just that, bullshit. And now, after doing one powerful spell without a single mistake, he had, at last, been found; been discovered.

He was being appreciated for his special talents, he was making money, he had been *recruited*. By somebody - the mafia, the CIA, some unauthorized covert agency - somebody. Somebody with resources. No more bouncing from job to job as a doorman/bouncer. No more scraping to get by. This was all his dreams coming true, definitely what he would have asked for, if he could have imagined it. Kevin had told him how to picture what it was he wanted, how to do the spell, and most importantly to tell no one, not even Kevin, until the request was granted. Gary had tried to be vague about what was going on, find out if Kevin was somehow asssociated with his new covert employer. He loved the sound of those words in his mind, so he said them outloud. "Covert employer." He laughed, spilled his beer, and cut a greasy sausage fart as he became a one man earthquake - a three hundred forty pound, six foot five inch earthquake, shaking on his ratty sofa. Between his long bouts of laughter, he would again say "covert employer," and go back into hysterics, spilling beer and expelling noxious fumes. He was one very happy, extremely twisted puppy.

***

Tonya came out of the bathroom wrapped in a towel and looked at the young slug. He wasn't much to look at, but he was enthusiastic, willing to take direction, and he could get another erection after orgasm quicker than any man or boy she'd ever seen. She thought it had to be his first time with a real woman, what else would explain the quick fuse and the short recovery period. But he had described some of his experiences and she could tell he had done something with somebody. He certainly knew how to use his hands to create pleasure or pain. That wasn't her problem. Her problem was the little prick kept shooting off like a Fourth of July fireworks show, and she was ready to take him to the next stage of his sexual development. The stage where he would last long enough for her to have fun. He was getting better, lasting a little longer each time, but the time for patience was over.

Tonya wasn't going to wait on him anymore and she wasn't taking any chances. She walked to the side of the bed and pulled from her purse on the nightstand a small plastic ziplock containing a surgical rubber cockring, and sat down on the bed next to him. His eyes were glued to her. She looked around at his uniform spread all over the room. It was obvious the military training wasn't taking on this teen. She had hooked enough soldiers, seen the ones who really took to the service, who were so well programmed they were neat, tidy, organized, efficient no matter the circumstances. Even with a hooker. This military school boy would never be one of those.

Tonya wondered just what the deal here was, why she had been paid so well, pharmaceutically so well supplied, why the john - a kid no less - had been researched so well, and why her instructions had been delivered so firmly. Threateningly. An old boyfriend/pimp pops up from nowhere, offers her a great job, and a plane ticket to Vegas for her and her daughter when it's over, set up with a new and better job working with a higher class clientele. Great pay and threats of serious bodily harm might be expected for doing a C.E.O. or politician in secret, maybe, but for Pugsley?

She stroked his penis with one hand and pulled the towel off herself with the other. His eyes were glued to her breasts. They were among the most beautiful things he had ever seen in his seventeen years and three weeks of life. Overweight and out of shape, immature in mind and body for his age, he had repeated two grades and still struggled. Stewart had few illusions as to his appearance, and his attractiveness to girls.

Stewart had no doubt that this weekend already qualified as the best weekend of his life. He had read the letters sent in to *Playboy* and *Penthouse*, but all the guys at school said it was all made up bullshit. This weekend was right off the pages of one those bragging letters, a fantasy fulfilled in flesh. And what flesh! God this woman should give lessons, he thought. He had no idea, no clue at all she was a pro. Even a deeply evil heart can find itself beating in a sheltered and naive chest.

Tonya was well aware the young slug had no idea what was going on, and he also had no idea just what he had in Tonya. His head came forward, his tongue already coming out, darting like a lizard's, hungry for her breasts. They were not big by any standards, but they were her pride and joy. She was petite, barely over five feet, just a misses size 6, 34 - 24 – 34. She was not the size woman found in titty magazines, and she was only an A cup, but she had beautiful breasts, breasts that were super sensitive, and she had killer nipples. Pugsley was busy kissing, sucking, and lightly biting them. As usual her nipples rose to the occasion, sticking out as long as the last joint of her little finger.

She continued stroking him as he played with her breasts. Her strong sexual response came into play as her throat and chest turned bright red and she grew moist. She had snorted four extremely long lines of coke in the bathroom and she was more than ready. She pulled away and brought her head down to his crotch. She blew on it. He was already fully erect. She reached up, grabbed his hand and brought it down to his shaft. He looked at her with a puzzled expression but he let her hands guide his.

"Look Pugsley, you just hold yourself straight up. Now this is going to feel a little tight." She pulled out on the fingerholds on each side of the rubber cockring and slid it down to the base of his shaft.

"Raquel, that's real tight," he protested. She had told him Friday afternoon when they met, that they must use pseudonyms. Explaining she was a respectable married woman whose husband was an important businessman, he shouldn't know who she really was. Likewise, he was probably underage, and she didn't want to know who he really was. He reminded her of the son in *the Adams Family* so she told him he would be Pugsley. He could call her Raquel, she told Pugsley, since he was about to find out who really had the greatest boobies in the world. Pugsley had no idea who Raquel Welch was and didn't care that she was the woman with the most respected chest when Tonya was little.

She had told him how everything must be discreet, done in just the right manner. God, she thought to herself, he was absolute putty in her hands. Hookers were used to being in control, it was a necessity in their profession. But this was different, like the kid was an awestruck apprentice and she was the master artist - and he was studying at her feet. No doubt, when it came to sexual games of pleasure and pain, the kid was a quick study. And no doubt he would

hurt her more than was pleasureable if she let him. She wondered if teaching really was the deal -

maybe this kid's father, uncle, older brother, guardian, whoever, wanted the kid broken in right,

and had the good sense to get a top professional in a discreet and controlled environment.

She slid the ring down to the very base of his penis and then worked her way back up with

her tongue. His hips were arching up and down uncontrollably, he was more than ready. "Okay,

Pugsley, here's the deal. You've been coming too quick and I haven't had enough fun. Last night,

my little S&M lover, was for you. Tonight is for me."

"Sure." He said. She could tell he didn't get it yet, so she explained the mechanics.

"Look, this tight little sugical rubber ring will keep all the blood where it is. Even when

you come, you'll stay hard so I'll have fun, too. Kid, the way you've been going, you might come

two or three times before I take this ring off." It turned out to be five, but who's counting.

***

He was standing in front of the mirror in his bathrobe, brushing the small clumps of wet

hair on either side and the back of his head. She came into the upstairs den in a silk kimono,

likewise still damp. Sexually satisfied, they chose to each shower in their own bathrooms. She

took her wet hair out of the towel wrapped like a turban and began to brush her's out as well. At

least she had something to brush. "He didn't call early, did he?"

He looked back at her through the mirror. "No, he'll call at the top of the hour, on the dot.

That's one of the reasons I selected him out of all the possible candidates, for someone of the

criminal underclass, he is reliable, dependable, and punctual."

"And ruthless," she had to add, "punctual, cold-hearted, and ruthless."

"Right you are." He smiled his charming smile. "Right you are." Then his smile crumpled, he violently threw his brush down on the table and as it bounced away he moved closer to the mirror. She could see his reflection, he wasn't smiling anymore. He looked pissed. He kept touching his nose, moving his head side to side. "Fuck!" He screamed louder than she had ever heard him. "Fuck!" He yelled again. "Look at what you did you little twit." She rose and came closer haltingly; she was scared he was going to lose it and hit her, but she wanted to know what the big deal was. Then the phone rang.

Chapter Three–Later Saturday Night

It was a nice little family owned Mexican restauraunt about fifteen minutes from our family compound. I still came sometimes with John the boss and Betty and the kids, but more often they'll come while I babysat for them and they bring me take out. I used to bring dates here, but I hadn't dated much lately. When something goes as bad as my last fiasco, well, let's just say I had been in no big hurry to get back up on the horse. Breaking up or getting jilted is one thing. You get thrown off the horse, you just get back on the horse. But suicide and mur... I can't believe I thought murder about myself. It was ruled a justifiable homicide as I attempted to stop an armed fugitive fleeing from justice. And her "suicide" was probably a murder in disguise. Anyway, it had been a while since I dated. Jose was smiling a little too much when he seated us on the outside deck, and he winked when he said it was nice to see me out again. It's bad when even your favorite waiter is a social critic.

She said she was hungry, I was ravenous, and we ordered a huge amount of food. There was one awkward moment when Jose asked, "I know you'll have a Tecate and lime, and a water, what will the lady have?"

She thought about it for a few seconds, "I'll take a Tecate, too." I sighed in relief. I try not to consume alcoholic beverages in front of medicine people and strictly traditional Indians as a sign of respect. In the long run, alcohol has probably been the single worst thing the Europeans afflicted upon Indian culture. (Diseases and warfare included.) Alcoholism is a terrible problem on most reservations, the saddest aspect of which is the high number of children born with fetal alcohol syndrome related birth defects and retardation. Because of alcohol's terrible impact, almost all the medicine men and women and the strict traditionals don't drink at all. (I use the term medicine here as it is used commonly, the academically correct term today generally is shaman or healer due to Christian influence. A traditional medicine person for many tribes was expected to know what we would call both white and black magic.)

A famous physical anthropologist, a professor at Georgia State, who until his death was Georigia's leading forensic anthropologist and had often helped out APD with skeletal remains, once explained the whole problem of Indians and alcohol. Dr. Blakely told me there were two factors at play with the Native Americans' trouble with alcohol. (Anthroplogists and PC people say Native Americans, but on the rez there are only Indians.) The first is known as "the culture of poverty syndrome."

Anthropologists have noted in many studies that when an outside, mechanically/ industrially/technologically superior culture comes into an area and conquers or dominates the indigenous, nature-dependent culture, and belittles that culture, its traditions and religion, such as happened in America, Australia, and parts of Africa and Asia, then the defeated and downtrodden culture often becomes a "culture of poverty."

The Europeans debasement of American Indian culture, the destruction of the Indian's resources and ways of sustenance, and the whole reservation system have led many anthropologists to consider the Indians in this light. Around the world, these outwardly dominated "cultures of poverty" almost always have lower average incomes and higher unemployment rates than the dominant culture which made them second-class citizens in their own homeland.

They also have higher incidences of alcohol and drug abuse, and domestic violence. There is no doubt that the European colonials made life miserable for the indigenous peoples; and today many Indians live in poverty and have few employment opportunities, but that is not the Indians' primary problem with alcohol. Indians may have a low mean income, but their culture is so rich, as an anthroplogy student I had difficulty with the phrase "culture of poverty."

It's no wonder many Indians look on anthropologists with disdain. The Indians problem with

alcohol is genetic.

Dr. Blakely told me those of Europeans descent have been exposed to mead and other

alcoholic beverages for a minimum of thirty thousand years. That's thirty thousand years Anglo

bodies and genetic material have been dealing with alcohol and building up a genetic tolerance.

Which is twenty-nine thousand six hundred years longer than the Indians. Minimum. Alcohol is

one of Nature's strongest drugs - a very serious depressant. It wreaks havoc with many, but

certainly not all Indians - its destructive power in Indian life too long misunderstood by most of

their critics.

Presumably Laura was not bothered by the genetically inherited alcohol susceptibility or

had otherwise learned to drink moderately. So we drank our Tecates, waited for our food, and

began what is always one of the most fun phases of any relationship, discovering somebody new.

***

The phone rang. He quit yelling, instantly regained his composure, and went to it quickly.

He let it ring the second and third time. At the end of the third ring he hit the button which put it

on the speaker phone.

"Hello." They both stared expectantly at the speaker.

"Good evening. This is George Greer, is Ginny there, please?"

"I'm, sorry. You must have the wrong number. But have an extremely good night."

"Sorry, and a very good evening to you." She jumped up and down. She seldom

did anything which betrayed her age, but the child in her came out. She jumped up and down and

shrieked. "We did it, we did it." She was facing him, with a hand on each of his arms and jumping. "He used five g's . We're going to get away with it."

He looked down at her, and mad as he was a minute before, even he couldn't help from smiling. "Of course we are. I've told you that all along, my little vixen, I've told you that all along." She was such a dichomtomy, sometimes an adolescent girl, sometimes a wise old woman, he never knew which she would be. Of course, he was concerned that he was trusting so much in one so young, but Fate or the dark prince had sent her at the right time/right place. He had not been around his sister or her children much before the current arrangement

For now, she believed him. But even if he didn't get away with it, *she* would. She had that angle figured out from the beginning. That's why she kept her secret, somewhat factual and detailed, but inventively fictional, diary. She was but a child being manipulated by influences beyond her ability to withstand. It was all there in her tortured words. That was her story, and she was sticking to it.

***

Stewart, alias Pugsley, thought Raquel spent an awful long time in the bathroom every time she went. And she went so often. He didn't have much experience with women for comparison, only his sister, his mother, and his nannies and servants. His mother had never really been around that much, she and his father preferred jet-setting around the world over the daily grind of raising children. That duty had always been left to the hired help. One of his older nannies had a weak bladder when he was five or six, but Raquel still spent more time in the john than that senile blue-hair.

Stewart was no angel, far from it, he had a violent and sadistic nature which he accepted and embraced, but he had led a relatively sheltered life. Money can provide a plethora of experiences, or it can isolate. He had no idea she was in the john filling her nose with almost pure Peruvian flake. A street ho would have beeen smoking crack, but she was no street ho.

Since Friday afternoon they had been having sex almost continuously. While he waited in the bed for her to come out and for their next session to start, he thought about just how lucky he had been to run into Raquel at the convenience store. Every afternoon after classes he would walk down the long driveway from the military academy to the street, cross it, and get his afternoon thrill. Stewart didn't have many pleasures in life. Anyone who looked at the pudgy kid knew he liked to eat. But eating was far from his only pleasure, and not at the top of the list. He had enjoyed the sadistic/sexual games he played with sis, but it was obvious that she never really did. Even when he brought her pleasure instead of pain, they both knew without his coercion she would never have played. But this, this was real sex, and this was great, great beyond his wildest expectations.

Stewart knew he wasn't academically the smartest kid at school, but he was clever and sneaky. He had swiped a set of keys, walked to the hardware store, copied the ones he wanted, and returned them without being caught. His best thrills at military school so far had been the times he snuck out at night with a .22 from the school armory and shot local dogs, or when he could befriend a cat or find other small animals to torture and slowly kill. Still, real sex was way better than even those highs.

Daily he would make his way to the convenience store, buy a Big Gulp slurpee, a hot dog, chips, and then some candy, and read some magazines. He would occasionally buy one to keep the Bangladeshi operator from yelling at him, but if they were found lying about in his room or on him it was serious demerit material. His folks had made it clear that if he got thrown out of one more prestigious prep school they would find the strictest, most spartan military school in the U.S. and dump him there without a car, without money, and without a ticket home on the holidays. Like now, but worse. If the state had run prisons where parents could unload their kids, he'd have been left a long time ago. Most kids his age from rich families already had awesome cars and credit cards, and a full social life, but not Stewart, no he'd been left with a small allowance, no car, few friends, and got nothing from his folks but threatening letters.

So there he was, Friday afternoon, Big Gulp half gone, candy and pie crumbs all over his uniform, with his afternoon hard-on, looking at the titty magazines. He was eyeing a picture of a large-breasted woman on all fours, looking back towards the camera, under which was a caption saying how she liked to be spanked, and asking the reader to spank her. He was lost in his own fantasy, not paying attention to his surroundings at all when a voice, the sexiest voice he had ever heard whispered into his right ear, "Wouldn't you rather do it than dream about it?"

Stewart began to blush, which was something of a miracle considering how much of his blood was below his waist. Nothing in his life had prepared him for such a moment and he didn't know how to respond. There was nothing negative, judgmental, or condescending in her voice. Unbelievaby he felt her hands on his shoulders and her face drew up besides his to look closer at the picture. So he just stood there, with a massive woody, not knowing what to do or say, as she peered at the picture over his shoulder. Then she whispered, "I like to be spanked when I make love, I like all those games. I bet you do too, don't you, little soldier?"

He nodded. He wasn't normally so honest, but this was no normal situation. She whispered with her lips almost touching his ears, "I've been looking for somebody special to play with, somebody like you. Would you like to be my playmate this weekend, little soldier?"

Stewart croaked out a yes at about three different octaves, his breaking voice sounding like a fingernail being dragged across a chalkboard. She seemed not to notice and didn't give him time to be embarrassed. "I'm going to buy a magazine, get in my car, and pull up to the pay hones beside the store. Meet me there in two minutes. But be discreet, I'm married, we can't let anyone see us together." With that, she picked up a Cosmo and walked away. Stewart watched her walk away, still not having seen her face, but the long honey-blond hair and the shapely legs below her tight miniskirt had even more blood headed below his belt. Feeling his zipper might break open at any moment, unable to contain his swelling organ any longer, he was thankul he always pulled his shirttail out, because he was really pitching a pup tent in front. He put the magazine down, still unable to see her face at the counter but he could hear the pleasantries of her commercial exchange. He waited at the magazine rack as she walked out the door and walked by in front of him on the other side of the glass on her way to the car.

She winked at him as she went by and he could see she was gorgeous, definitely as good looking as the women in the magazines. Opening the car door, she stared at him for a moment, winked once more and got in. She drove it around to the side of the building out of sight.

After counting to ten, he composed himself, put down the magazine and went after her. The passenger door was open, waiting for him. He hopped in and closed the door. They were in a white BMW with darkly tinted windows. She looked around once, saw there was no one in sight, and in a motion so quick it was a blur, reached down and undid his fly. His erection came flying out, like a bird escaping from a cage, and her hand went to it. Stewart wondered how much people on the outside could see through such dark windows. She must have wondered too, because she looked all the way around. Then in another motion so quick it was a blur, she moved her head down to his crotch. Stewart had known pleasureable sensations but he had never been with anybody that wanted to be with him, or that did things willingly and enthusiastically. He felt a thousand sensations at once, her hand, her mouth, her tongue, suction, pleasure, and before he knew it or could think about it, he reached down and grabbed handfuls of her hair as he exploded. Exploded like he never had before. Instead of pulling away she went hungrily deeper. He came so hard and so long he kind of lost consciousness momentarily. When she finally was done with him she pulled up and kissed him, hard. Stewart had played sex games, but this was his first french kiss. And an unusually sticky one, but he didn't know that. After the kiss, she pulled away. He looked dreamy, with his eyes still closed, so she slapped him. Not bruise hard, but not soft.

He opened his eyes then, but before he could speak, she said, "Your uniform says you're in school across the street, do you have a friend you can call at the school who can sign you out officially for the weekend?" He nodded. (One of the other unwanted loners stayed this weekend, and lived two dorm rooms over.) She continued, "Now I've got everything we need this weekend. You take this change, call your friend, make sure you're signed out and come back. And lover, not one word about me." In an almost threatening tone she said "Got it?" Stewart nodded again, took the coins and got out.

As the bathroom door opened Stewart came back from his memory to the moment, and Raquel walked out wrapped up in another towel. She sniffed a couple of times, went over and got her glass and fixed another vodka tonic. His eyes followed her wherever she went, he couldn't help it. Stewart was happier than he had ever been in his whole life, and she was the reason. As she sniffed loudly a couple more times, Stewart in his ignorance wondered if the air conditioner was up too high, or if she was coming down with a cold. He didn't know a hundred dollar sniffle when he heard one.

Smiling at him she sniffed and said, "That last time was a lot better lover, a lot better. She threw a CD in the blaster she'd brought, it sounded like Madonna singing something about hanky panky and spanky spanky. Raquel lifted the towel covering her hips and slapped her own butt, loudly, as she walked towards Pugsley. "Pugsley darlin, it's time you learned your next lessons about doggie style and hanky spanky."

***

Even though Laura Red Star was thin and shapely, she certainly had no reservations about being a hearty eater. I can put away some Mexican food and she was at least matching me. At least. The Unity Conference, she had explained to me was a convention of minority journalists. The Black, Latin, Asian, and Indian journalists met once a year, both individually and collectively. By all the minority journalists meeting together they became more sensitive to and aware of each other's situations as well as becoming a more powerful and influential voice speaking en masse.

"I would have come to the Unity conference anyway," she told me, "but I have other agendas." I must have had a quizzical expression, because I made her smile. "I'm between jobs, so I'm here job hunting. Networking, making contacts at the convention. After the convention I have some interviews around town."

"CNN?" I asked. After all, Ted and Jane, now minus Jane - she got Jesus and Ted couldn't take it - had run the biggest game in town. Then he sold it, but CNN didn't change.

"CNN and some others. It's not that I really want to quit being a print journalist. I always thought of news people on TV as being failed, frustrated actors or exhibitionistic personalities. I've found that sometimes that is true, but certainly not all the time. I did a little TV towards the end of my stay in the Bay area. I know my way around a studio, and the money's great. And if I'm in front of a camera, I occasionally might get to put the correct slant on pieces dealing with native rights, treaty disputes, that kind of thing."

She seemed to be defensive or sensitive about her changing medias. I wondered was she trying to convince me, or herself that it was all right to switch over to the tube. She explained it all herself momentarily.

"I just don't want people thinking I'm an airhead who got her job on looks."

That I could relate to; you see women on the news sometimes you know got the job more on looks than brains or competence. "Like the Eagles song, 'got the bubble headed bleached blond who comes on at five'..."

Laura finished it for me, "She can tell you 'bout the plane crash with a gleam in her eye. It's interesting when people die. Give us dirty laundry."

We smiled, but the song was all too true. However, I could tell she sincerely wanted to get where she got on merit, not just looks, and I respected the hell out of that. I also thought it was unfortunately all too rare in our culture.

"You don't have to convince me." I confessed, "Hell, I'm a CNN junkie. Whenever I get up, which can be morning, noon, or night depending on my work, if I have the chance, I spend a half hour drinking coffee and catching up on the world with Headline News, CNNI, or BBC; maybe MSNBC if there's anything political I care about.

Since Mike Myers had just relased a new sequel and she had spent part of her career in California I went into my Mike Myers/Austin Power's accent, "Oh Baby, it's not your fault you're shagadellic and the camera loves you." The result of which was she kicked my left shin under the table. It was the kind of thing my little sister would do, so I laughed and liked it. I felt amazingly at home with her, and could tell she was at ease around me. We were doing that smiling into each other's eyes stuff. Having not done that in a long time, it was feeling real good. Down Simba, I thought, down boy, remember, last time was a total disaster. I thought about

Svengali like control, hypnosis - leading to a tragic suicide. More probably a murder masked as suicide and my taking a life that needed to be taken, shook my head at the bloody memory and came back to the moment.

***

For one joyous moment it seemed just like it had been in the beginning. When there was affection just growing into romance. When there was the new thrill of breaking old taboos. When it was good for both of them. Before he turned out to be such a whacked-out power junkie ego-tripping control freak. He was bending down, she was straining up, they were holding each other tight and feeling good. But she was still curious about what had set him off before the coded call. She pulled back in his arms and looked at his face, searching. He was intoxicated with victory.

"He used five g's. Five, the absolute best conditions." He said with utter evil joy. He could see her searching his face, and then he remembered. "My nose, vixen, my nose."

She moved her head side to side and began to laugh. Wrong move. He slapped her with an open hand, quick and hard, but not hard enough to bruise. Her gymnastic gyrations during her pleasure ride earlier in bed must have bent his nose back a few times, it had a bright red strip running laterally across the middle. She calmed him. His face had become scary again, in a flash.

"It's not that noticeable." she assured him. "It was sunny today. It just looks like you got a little too much sun on the bridge of your nose. That's all. Remember, he used five g's. Your plan is working, the ritual was a success. Everything's going your way."

Inside she once more seethed. They actually had the old magic back for a fleeting instant, but it was gone in a flash, and he was back to himself. Instead of "the doctor is in," she often thought, "the monster is in." But let him be a monster, she told herself, as long as he doesn't know I can pull the strings. If I can manipulate the master manipulator, let him be a monster, my monster. The devil will have his due, and vengeance is mine, sayeth me. Vengeance is mine.

***

A man with three valid identities and as many jobs looked around once more, saw that he was of no interest to anyone, walked away from the dimly lit pay phone and got into his car. He left on his baseball hat and sunglasses, started the car and drove away. Normally someone of his age, background, and inclinations would have been drawn to own an American muscle car, something sporty with a big V8. Instead, he owned a nondescript, almost invisible sedan, much more likely to be owned by a school teacher, a salesman, or a retiree. But he was no normal denizen of the criminal underworld, his intelligence and self-discipline set him worlds above the average in the dark circles he inhabited.

***

Sitting out under the sky, we finally finished our mountain of food. The moon was still almost full, the sky was clear and the stars were bright. The ligtning bugs were lighting up and you could smell the swet scent of honeysuckle on the breeze. We both had about half of our second beer left, so we let them clear the food away but stayed. She had never been to Georgia and was amazed at the amount of lush greenery everywhere. Like so many people from outside the South, heavily influenced by the northeast media establishment and Hollywood's movies, she had never heard about the South's inherent beauty. Most people either expected antebellum mansions or crosses burning. Or both. The friendliness of the people and the beauty of the surroundings were quite a contrast to her expectations. The cicadas and tree frogs were doing their nightly serenade. Laura was fascinated by the lightning bugs doing their aierial mating dance, flahing their lights off and on, announing their presence, available to mate. It was a beautiful warm night and Laura appreciated the intensity of the natural life around her. Then she threw me a curve.

"You don't look like I expected." She said it out of nowhere and surprised me, I had been looking up at the moon and the beautiful star filled sky. I didn't know what she meant, so I kind of shrugged my shoulders and looked at her questioning with my body language. "Your grandmother is Cherokee?" She asked and I nodded. "I'm Scott-Irish-Cherokee."

She looked at me for a while, "You've got the almond eyes, epicanthic eyefold, the high cheekbones, the forehead, but not the nose. Most of your facial structure looks Indian, but your coloring, sure you've got a dark tan, but you're blond, dirty blond, with green eyes. Leonard never said you looked like an Anglo. Somehow, the way he talked, I don't know, I just thought you'd look more Indian."

"Well, being Leonard's cousin, I thought you'd be a lot homlier." She kicked me again. She really did act like my sister.

"I know you've come out and visited Leonard, trained under the Paiute medicine men, but also …Arapaho?" Leonard had obviously told her some things about me. "Well, Paiute mostly, but some Arapaho and Shoshone."

"Well, I think it's great the way you and Leonard didn't let prison ruin your lives. I once did a story on the high rate of residivism. It seems like that once some of those people go in, it's just a revolving door. You both did your time, but when it was over you got on with your lives, got educated, well Leonard got super educated, and you both made something of yourselves, and contribute to your communities. You were a grower? There's a lot of that on some of the rez."

I nodded, "I was a guerilla herb farmer, sold most of what I grew to the disabled Nam vets I met through visiting John and his friends at the VA hosptials. I just got unlucky, somebody got busted, gave me up to walk, happens all the time. I got popped the day I turned seventeen, in a big bust out in the fields."

"You went into the adult system? How many years?"

"Yeah, I went straight into the system, no juvy time or me."

"What was your sentence?"

"The original sentence was five years, I'd have gotten out in two and a half or three but there were complications. With good behavior, I did just two weeks under five years. My friends went to their high school senior year and then college. I did my 'undergraduate and graduate work' at Reidsville, by any standard an incredibly dangerous learning environment filled with violent, I mean studiply violent people. I learned a lot, about crime, about the dark side of human nature, about how fear and hate motivate.

"I don't think I would have made it through unraped without Leonard. He took me under his wing and protected me until I adjusted to the environment, learned the ropes and could handle myself. We had friends that were black, white, and Mexican. We tried to stay away from all that racial shit that goes down, but it's not always easy."

I looked up at the moon again, it truly was a beautiful night, the sensual kind where the night air feels good on your skin. I could feel her looking at me, as I looked back at her she started laughing. "Well, if you grew up as an outlaw in prison, what brought you to law enforcement?"

"I don't know if being a private eye really qualifies as law enforcement to your average cop, but Robert was an MP, and later in military intelligence, then MAC SOG in Vietnam. When he got out, he took some time off, then went and joined APD. John, with his Special Forces background wanted to do something active, but the cops weren't hiring double amputees. Robert pitched him the idea of a family run security and PI firm. John would be in charge, I'd work, and if I stayed out of trouble become a junior partner, and when Robert retires, he'll buy in and come aboard. John went for it. They figured, with all my prison contacts and the criminal knowledge I gained on the inside, I might really have something to contribute. And I suppose they didn't want me falling back into anything illegal.

"They know I hate theives, rapists, murderers, abusers, and the truly bad people. I just disagree with the state and federal laws concerning herb. I think alcohol is far worse and does more damage than herb. I don't know if I'd go as far as the Amsterdam model, but I'd give herb the same legal status and controls we have for for alcohol. Anyway, I went to college, as a double major in criminal justice and anthroplogy, and did some graduate work. I got all my rights back - to vote and everything, but it took ten years and lots of contacts and people pulling strings for me to get a weapons permit. But now I have the same priviledges and license as any Georgia private investigator. Depending on what's going on, sometimes my job is incredibly boring, and then other times, like now, when I'm working for APD, it can be all consuming.

She nodded. "I've had times where I was incredibly bored as a journalist, but there are time when it's a whirlwind and a huge rush. I'm deeply disappointed that I was in San Francisco and did't get to go cover the war. I want in with CNN, MSNBC, BBC, or a major network."

I nodded. "At least we don't have jobs that are boring all the time. I don't mean to change the subject, but how is Leonard? He was out here a little over a year ago…" I trailed off, I didn't want to go into why he had come to see me, the disastrous suicide and execut…, justifiable homicide. Leonard Wounded Face had gone on, after prison, to get a post graduate degree in history, then his PhD., and then a Masters degrees in counseling. Now he was an over-educated high school history teacher in Independence, taught part-time at a community college, and helped run a kind of survival/vision quest school for troubled teens each summer where they learn traditional Paiute survival skills, all in conjunction with those training under Grandfather Rayland. Among other things he regularly attended sweat lodges, knew all the sacred songs and myths, and assisted Grandfather Rayland. If Grandfather Rayland was travelling, Leonard ran the Sweat Lodge for him. There was always one concern about Leonard so I asked, "Is he staying away from the bottle?"

She kind of hesitated in her answer, which caused me a moment of concern that Leonard might have gone back to his old self-destructive pattern of binge drinking and bar fighting.

"I won't say that Leonard never takes a drink anymore, because I know that he occasionally does. But now, if he really wants to drink, he goes out into the desert alone, unarmed, sets up a camp, builds a fire, and sips beer all night. And that happens only once or twice a year, if at all. He never drinks in bars, or around other people. It's an urge he has gotten pretty much under control, but when he feels it real strongly, he goes camping by himself with a couple of six packs. It may not be an ideal solution, but it's one that keeps him out of trouble or from hurting anybody. He's a singer at the Sweat Lodge, he trains with medicine men, and he's on the tribal council. He's come a long way since you two shared a prison cell."

"How about his gambling?" I knew the Paiute love of games of chance existed long before the white man ever showed up, and Leonard definitely loves to gamble as much as any Indian I've ever met. The anthropologists who first studied the Paiutes thought gambling was their favorite activity.

"Did it ever become a problem? It wasn't any time I've ever been around him. God knows he's won almost every bet I ever made with him. Over the years he's taken me to the cleaners for close to a grand." She smiled at that. "No, Leonard loves to gamble, but it's never been an addiction, or even a problem. In fact, we have a wager concerning you."

Jose brought us two more beers, which we hadn't ordered. He said they were on the house. I was thankful he didn't just blurt out how long it had been since he had seen me here on a date. Although we thanked him warmly, I was relieved when he just smiled at us and walked away.

"What kind of bet?" Curious was a mild term, I couldn't imagine what kind of bet Leonard and Laura would have made concerning me.

"Well, I was hoping to get to know you a little better," she said, "before I tried to win Leonard's five hundred."

When she said five hundred I kind of spazzed-out with a mouthful of beer and did something between laughing, coughing, and choking, almost spewing beer out my nose. I grabbed a napkin before the mouthful made it onto the table, but it was a close call, and far from my most graceful moment. "Did you say five hundred, as in dollars?"

"Yes," she replied,"But whoever wins has to contribute at least three hundred of that to the fund for Indian colleges."

Leonard makes a decent living as a teacher, especially by reservation standards, but he has a wife and three kids now. Five hundred was a large sum for him to bet at one time. I figured he felt he was either sure to win or was going to contribute to the fund anyway. I don't exactly like being predictable either, no matter how close the friend.

"Okay, what's the deal?"

She looked at me for a second, hesitating, but now that the cat was out of the bag, what else could she do. "First off, Leonard makes a yearly contribution to the college fund, and this is one of the few bets he's made that he actually may be hoping to lose."

I was totally lost now, and had no idea what direction she was going in. "You know that Leonard has continued studying under a couple of shaman and training as a healer?"

I nodded. Leonard and I might not get to hang out with each other that much anymore, but we talk on the phone every month or two at the minimum. Sometimes once or twice a month.

"Well, Leonard thinks that you kind of repress some of your memories, and if that's true, then it puts you out of balance and in need of healing. He says you've got to face the darkest, most dangerous corners of your mind, accept yourself, forgive yourself, and get on with living a good life. He didn't exlain, but he said something that happened around a year ago made it worse."

Now there are a few things in everybody's life that are better not dwelled upon, but "repressed memories" was a phrase I didn't think could possibly could relate to me. "No offense, but that's bullshit. I appreciate his concern, but I don't think it applies to me. What exactly is the bet, and how can I help you win it? It would help even the score, even if I don't get the money, he's still losing. He's made enough off me over the years."

With that she pulled out a small micro-recorder very similar to the one I had used earlier that morning going over the crime scene. She said, "It's very simple, all you have to do is describe the events of one afternoon. Leonard says you can't do it."

I raised my shoulders and lifted my hands palms up as a nonverbal question. She pushed the record button down, and said, "Tell me, in your own words, as descriptively as possible, about the afternoon you saved Leonard's life. Explain the phrase I've heard Leonard use so many times, that you gave up three years of your life, to give him back his."

"What do you mean, phrase you've heard so many times? Why on earth would he be talking about that?"

"Oh, I've heard the story what seems like a hundred times. It's a favorite at large family gatherings, especially with the young boys sitting around a campfire. They love hearing how the brave young Cherokee breed (as in quarter breed, half breed) saved the strong Paiute warrior when he was surrounded by hostile cowboys. I could probably tell you the story. I'll even know if your account differs from his."

I shook my head slowly and looked down at her machine, I could barely hear its motor running. I couldn't believe that I had let my big, stupid mouth run on and put me in this position. If she hadn't been such an attractive woman....

"Explaining the phrase is simple, whether or not it's totally accurate. Leonard was about to be killed, I prevented that. It cost me two and a half, almost three more years in prison. Okay, that done, why don't you turn that thing off so we can head for the compound and get you settled in."

"That's only part of it, you have to describe the events. Leonard says it's part of your healing." She let it keep recording. "Describe what happened in as much detail as possible. If you can't do that I lose the bet." She hesitated for a second, then finished her thought, "And you're not as healthy as you think you are."

"All right, all right. No problem." I took a long swig of beer, and then another. But I knew Leonard was wrong, those memories weren't repressed, I could remember every fucking vivid detail. I simply chose not to dwell on it, or ever think about it, at all. But it wasn't repressed. I closed my eyes, opened up my memory, and it was all right there. Like yesterday.

"There were two floors on our block, each floor had forty-eight two-man cells, a TV and phone common area, and bathroom/showers. Four of the inmates were an armed robbery crew out of west Texas. Convicted in Georgia of four armed robberies and two vicious rapes they were considered likely suspects all across the south for a whole series of such incidents, from Texas to Georgia. They robbed banks, grocery stores, liquor stores, and raped their female victims whenever possible. Frank Hyatt was their leader, a tall thin mean son of a bitch. The rest of the crew was his brother James, and their cousin Lynell, and a little weasel called Lookout, who was just that, their driver/lookout."

With my eyes still closed I heard something sliding on the table. I looked up, she was pulling my empty bottle away and replacing it with her full one. I took another long sip and closed my eyes. It seemed the night had grown warmer, I was starting to sweat.

"Frank and James claimed they were from an old Texas pioneer family famous for Indian fighters. They would talk about this shit all the time, like it was some big deal. In their eyes they were cowboys, Leonard and I were considered by them to be Indians, and the only good one, to them, was a dead one. The animosity kept building. It was only a matter of time until their bullshit provoked Leonard. On the inside, there's only one way things like that get settled. I tried to ignore the bullshit, just do my time, but they were really getting to Leonard and words got exchanged that couldn't be taken back."

"We could shower any time we wanted from four in the afternoon until lockdown, and one afternoon working out Leonard pulled a muscle and quit early. I kept on and finished working out while he went on ahead to take his shower. When I got through and headed for my bed/locker I saw Junebug Carter, a black inmate we liked, come running up to me at full speed with nothing on but a towel. He told me that Leonard was alone in the shower when he left, but that the Hyatt gang passed him going in. At least three of them had shivs (knives made by inmates in jail). He didn't think Leonard was going to make it out alive."

In my mind's eye, I could still see Junebug's tense concerned face, could see the hall as I ran down it, could smell again that prison scent of men's sweat, stale smoke, and industrial cleaners. "I went running, I didn't have time to stop, think, or get a weapon. I just ran at full speed. When I turned into the bathroom area I saw Lookout at the entrance to the showers standing at the double door-sized opening with a mop in his hands and a bucket of water beside him on the floor. He was no trustee, that was not his job, and I instantly knew Junebug was right. I walked to the shower entrance and Lookout lowered the mop handle so it blocked the entrance. I could still see his smug, confident smirk. He started to say something like 'you don't want to go in there,' but I didn't let him finish. He got out a 'you.' My Dad, the hard ass Colonel, had taught me self defense and martial arts as far back as I can remember. Robert and John too, especially after they came back from Nam. I'd never had to use much of what they'd taught me before prison, but I certainly had practiced regularly and knew how. I also kept my thumb and first finger's fingernails long and sharp on both hands like Robert had suggested.

"I knew it was three on one and Leonard was unarmed so I heard "you" and my right hand shot out, palm toward his throat, thumb and fingers spread apart. At contact, I sank my fingers in and squeezed as hard as I could. I ripped Lookout's windpipe out. Not all the way out of his body, but my sharpened nails had sunk in deep and I crushed his windpipe and pulled it away from the rest of his throat. His right hand had been reaching to his back pocket to draw a shiv. With my right hand still in his throat I grabbed his right hand with my left hand. It was fairly easy for me to wrap my hand around his firmly, pull it out and down and then jerk his hand upward, ramming the shiv in between his sternum and the left side of his rib cage, directly up into his heart.

"I remember lowering him quietly and picking up the bucket of water. I was lucky. Killing Lookout had gone about as quickly and quietly as killing someone with your hands possibly can. As I listened I could hear some of the broken showers running as they always did, and the shower-echoes of a murmurred conversation, and figured they didn't know. I remember Lookout's blood dripping off my hand into the water in his bucket. It's strange how you notice the little things sometimes." In my mind I could see it so clearly, my blood drenched hand dripping his blood into the pail of water. I took another long swig of beer.

"I went into the showers carrying the pail of water. The shiv seemed stuck and didn't want to come out of Lookout so the pail of water was my weapon of choice.To my left at the far end I saw the backs of the three Hyatts standing next to each other, facing Leonard, whose back was against the wall, facing towards me. They had on clothes, Leonard of course, was naked with nothing but his towel. They all had one hand behind their backs clutching their shivs. The fight hadn't started yet, but the tension was building.

"I knew from hearing Frank Hyatt brag that he enjoyed seeing the fear on his victims' faces, it was part of the power rush. Leonard had turned his shower off. The Hyatts obviously hadn't heard anything because nobody looked back. I saw Leonard see me, but there was no expression on his face, no reaction, he looked away to not give me away. Frank was saying something, the rest of his gang laughed. Then I heard him say they were going to turn Leonard into a good Indian. Leonard just looked at them and began to wrap his towel around his left hand." I took another sip and wiped off my face with my napkin.

"I was scared I was going to slip on the wet floor. I walked quietly, quickly with the bucket of water in my right hand. I could tell the verbal part was about over and they would strike at any moment. Frank was directly facing Leonard, with James to his left and Lynell on the right. I walked towards Lynell. With the broken showers running they didn't hear my approach. I came up behind Lynell at the same moment they brought their shivs out in the open from behind their backs. They were looking for fear on Leonard's face, but the large Paiute didn't show any. Keeping my arm straight I slowly swung the bucket back so as to not spill the water and then with full strength and maximum velocity, hit Lynell in the neck and bottom of the head with it. It was still mostly full of water at impact and it snapped his neck and head and he went down as the water splashed. I could see Frank lunging and slashing at Leonard and Leonard fighting him off with the towel wrapped on his hand in my peripheral vision as I struck Lynell. James heard the whack as I hit Lynell and instead of rushing Leonard with Frank turned towards me. I brought the bucket back and swung it at his face as he charged me. I caught him on the left temple and cut him badly as he sliced my chest, but he stayed on his feet. I began swinging the mostly empty bucket in a figure eight, the way I'd been taught to use nun-chuks. As he slashed at me again I caught him in the same place on the temple and he went down on one knee. He slashed out again and I smashed it into his temple once more and he went down all the way. I pounced on him, took the shiv from his fingers and with all my strength drove it up under his sternum and left ribcage like I had Lookout, into his heart. I pulled it out and rose up as Frank lunged at Leonard again. I saw Leonard already had one long gash across his chest bleeeding profusely. The shiv went into Leonard's side, deep, but with both hands Leonard locked onto Frank's arm. I came at Frank from behind, grabbed a handful of hair, pulled his head back and I slit his fucking throat."

The beer was empty when I tried to take a drink. I shook my head, blew out, and opened my eyes. My face and eyes seemed wet. So did my shirt. She looked at me, with utter kindness and compassion. She said, "You're almost through, what happened next?"

I shook my head, "Isn't that enough?"

"No. Please, please finish the story. You're almost there. What did you do next? "I don't cry. Not ever. Not since the pen. I was a normal kid and all, but I kind of lost my emotional ability to cry out of self-preservation in the joint. But for the first time in the many years since I've been out, it seemed like tears were running down my face. I wasn't sobbing or boo-hooing or anything, but my face was wet. She reached out and grabbed my hand, and said, "Please, finish it."

So I closed my eyes again and went back to the shower. "Frank was writhing on the floor, blood spurting from his neck with each heartbeat. The air hissed and bubbled through the blood as his body fought to breathe. James was graveyard dead from the shiv in the heart, and Lynell was lying on the floor with his head and neck at a very unnatural angle. Leonard was bleeding bad all over his torso and was standing there, holding a towel over his wounds which was quickly becoming saturated with blood. He yelled my name, loud, to get my attention and to ground me. Then he yelled at me, "Spooky, finish it."

"I must have hesitated a second, 'cause he yelled the same thing again, telling me to finish it. You've got to understand that world, the way it works, paybacks and shit. Leonard was making me face the situation rationally. If any of them lived, they'd come back at us. It was total war - kill or be killed - once they made their move.

"I took the shiv and went to Frank while he writhed on the floor spurting blood. I knelt on the floor with my knees right behind his head and drove the shiv down then up under his rib cage back into his heart. I twisted it. He stopped writhing."

My eyes were still closed, my whole face seemed wet, I had to sniff so my nose wouldn't run. And then I heard her say, "You're almost there, what next?"

I blew out a long breath, shook my head a little and watched in my mind what happened next. I didn't want to describe it, and didn't see why it was necessary. Then I repeated myself, I wanted her to understand. "I did what I had to survive. In that world if I hadn't finished them all off, they would have come at Leonard and me later when we were vunerable. If was a life or death struggle to the very end and they had lost. They went in to take Leonard's life. They lost theirs." She waited silently for me to continue.   I waited, finally I said. "I did to Lynell what I did to Frank. The only way to make sure they all were dead was to stab each one in the heart. I knew if they didn't die, they would try to kill Leonard and me later. So I went from Frank to Lynell's unconscious body, stabbed him in the heart, too. I did it without hesitation. It was jailhouse justice, the law of survival in the big house. I'm not proud of what I did, but I'm not ashamed either. I finished off two attackers when they were totally helpless, but just seconds earlier, they had been trying to kill us. Leonard knew it was necessary, so did I."

I paused, hoping that was enough. Her silence made me continue. "I helped Leonard walk so we could get help. He was gushing blood, all over his torso, bleeding down all over him, my chest had two long cuts that were bleeding profusely, my right hand was cut, we certainly couldn't wait on guards to come help us. We'd have bled to death."

On the way out I saw my face in the bathroom mirror," I paused again, "but it wasn't my face anymore." I shook my head reflexively. "I saw the eyes of a cold blooded killer staring out from a face and body covered in blood. It wasn't pretty. I know that somewhere in the dark part of my soul, when suitably provoked, is a remorseless killer. Sometimes in my nightmares I go back to those showers, see Lookout's face with my hand in his throat…or my own walking out."

I had my elbow on the table, my eyes were closed, I was rubbing my forehead. "I was convicted on four counts of manslaughter, but due to the circumstances, our highly edited version of what happened, and what sorry-ass rat-fuckers those bastards really were, I was only sentenced to four additional five year terms to run concurrently, and only did two and a half, well almost three more years hard time and the rest on parole. That is how I lost three years of my life and gave Leonard the rest of his."

My face, my body was wet with sweat, my eyes were moist and my nose was running. I didn't know what the hell was going on with me. I was thankful there was no one sitting nearby. There I was in front of a beautiful woman, a total stranger, but who felt like family, a woman I might be able to care about if given half a chance, and I looked like a kindergarten kid who had bloodied his knee on the playground. I wiped my nose and face with my bandanna. She hadn't let go of my other hand. Hell, she was holding it so hard it almost hurt.

When I finally looked up at her I saw kind eyes and the traces of tears on her cheeks. She smiled at me warmly, and with her free hand turned off the recorder.

***

Gary was sleeping, lying down on his sofa, TV playing across from him. He was in a dream, working for his new employer, but the scenery kept shifting. One moment he was sure he was at Langely walking through the corridors of the CIA, the next moment he was in Don Corleone's mansion waiting to meet the Godfather. Agents or wise guys kept coming up and congratulating him on a job well done and welcoming him to the organization. Finally, when he got to go in to meet the Director/Godfather he walked into the office and waited before the desk. The man in the chair had his back turned and didn't speak. When the chair spun around it was neither Marlon Brando nor the Director of the CIA. The face was obscured by thick cigar smoke.

When the smoke settled, it seemed the face was changing - it looked like his father, then his old football coach who took so much pleasure in humiliating him, then it finally stopped changing. It was Jack Nicholson with devil's horns, he grinned demonically and screamed "Gotcha!"

Gary jerked, came halfway up, rolled off his sofa, hit his head on the cheap coffee table, fell on the floor, and managed to knock what was left of his last beer off the table and on top of him, as well as the bag of money. He was slow to get up, and could still hear "gotcha" ringing in his ears.

***

We didn't talk much on the way home. Maybe I was just embarrassed, maybe it was because I felt like something had just been ripped out of my insides. Other than in my dreams, I hadn't thought about that mirror vision of myself as a killer for years, as well as my feelings of revulsion towards myself and my actions on that day. I still believed I had done what was necessary at the moment, although they are horriffic memories - crushing throats, slicing throats, stabbing hearts, being cut and covered in your blood and the blood of your enemies. I guess some things had been repressed and my spiritual older brother Leonard was right. It certainly wasn't the first time and I damn sure knew it wouldn't be the last.

About the only conversation we had was when she asked me why I used the term family compound. I had to explain it wasn't like we were the Kennedys or anything. It was just that years ago, during his third year with APD Robert bought some land with money he'd saved from Nam. At the time, it was way out in the country, although the city and the suburbs have since taken most of what was rural and forested in the greater Atlanta area. Robert is a history buff and he would go on and on about the fall of Rome, the decline of Western civilization, and urban decay. When crack hit the city and all the kids started packing, Robert, with help from John, me, and some of our cousins, started building on his fifty-eight acres. Robert and I bought in. Now, John and I have houses around the pond, and further down the dirt road are Robert's original house and a little cabin on the five acre lake.

"Robert has one of those really large build it yourself log cabin kit homes, which is what I've got, except a smaller version, but John has a regular suburban style brick house. Where John and I live it's pasture land with a pond in front of the houses, and woods to the sides and back. There's a covered walkway between my house and John's. That's so he and I can get back and forth whatever the weather. Ironically, Robert got tired of the commute and now has a really nice house in the suburbs of northeast Atlanta and uses his log house for vacations and recreation.

Before we got there I explained to Laura how our company, Triple S Security, uses our compound as a real life display of some of the security equipment we sell and install. I didn't want her to freak out when she saw the razor wire on top of the chain link fence and the inner electric fence surrounding our property, the no trespassing/private property signs, the security camera at the dual electric gates, the flags on cables, and all the other stuff. I keyed in the code on my remote and the two gates opened electronically. As we drove the three tenths of a mile from the gate to the houses, Laura was surprised to see the deer among the sleeping cows peacefully grazing in the moonlight. Most of our visitors are. When she saw the barn down past my house she asked with some excitement if we had horses. When I told her yes, she said she loved to ride. I told her she could go riding any time she wanted and Laura seemed genuinely pleased. I should have guessed that, Paiute are renowned for their riding skill.

As soon as we drove past John's and before I could even get into my carport, John the boss came flying down the sidewalk between our houses at about twenty miles an hour. He had his badge clipped on his pocket, he was wearing his gun, he looked like he was ready to go to work. That and the speed he was travelling did not bode well for my immediate future. I stopped the car and he yelled, asking me if I'd talked to Danny, that we were running real late.

"Shit!" I muttered it, but it must have been loud enough for her to hear.

She looked at me,"What's wrong?"

"I have no idea, but this can't be good," I said as John came flying up and used his open-finger gloved hands to grab the wheelchair's tires and skidded to a halt right in front of my door.

"Have you talked to Danny?"

"Not since this evening, he said he'd call me if he needs me."

"Well, little brother, he's called, and we're already late. We've got to meet him at the crime scene for the luminol test. He said he didn't think he'd told you."

"I spent all afternoon with him, he didn't mention word one about luminol."

"So he forgot. He's got a million things on his mind. He's called, he wants you to be there for the test, now."

"John, say hello to Leonard's cousin, Laura Red Star." I said it with a tone to let him know he was forgetting his manners.

John, as comes so natural to him, began giving orders. "Spooky, go park your car and take her bags in to your house. Laura, hello, come with me, Betty wants to meet you and she will get you settled in, follow me." At that point John headed to his house. I just raised my shoulders, what can you do? So Laura got out and took off after the speeding wheelchair. John yelled back he'd pick me up in his car.

John burst through his screen door with Laura trotting behind him to keep up. "Betty, this is Laura, Leonard's cousin. Laura, Betty. Gotta go." Betty stood there holding one crying baby, another child was crying somewhere else in the back of the house.

"You woke up one of the twins with all your yelling," Betty said, as John was rolling out the door. Betty called after him,"You macho asshole."

But when Laura looked at Betty, the words didn't match her expression, she looked at her husband flying toward his car with genuine love and warmth in her eyes. Laura walked up to Betty, said hi and reached out and took the baby, freeing Betty to go get whichever twin was crying. Betty looked at Laura and said, "Why is it men have to make so much noise, make such a big show out of everything, when we women just know what to do, and do it?" Of course, it wasn't really a question. They both knew that.

***

Samantha lay there in her bed, trying to get to sleep. She had locked her diary in the box and locked the box inside the lower drawer of her nightstand. She had turned out the light, and was really tired, exhausted, but still, sleep was not coming. Despite her joy at success, her mind was filled with nightmarish images. Finally she reached over and punched the button on her cassette player to play the hypnosis sleep-inducing tape that Phineas had made for her. After twenty minutes, she was sleeping, deeply, and absorbing the subliminal messages Phineas had put on the tape. Messages she didn't know about, at least not consciously.

Chapter Four – Past Midnight/Early Sunday Morning

There was a squadcar guarding the gate, the uniform cop was sitting on the hood eating out of a Burger King bag, in front of it was a crime scene unit van with two tech leaning against it smoking. Danny was sitting in his car with the interior lights on drawing on his clipboard. John the boss, who had been driving like a maniac the whole way, running at a minimum of twenty-five to thirty miles an hour over the speed limit, skidded right up to Danny's car. Even though he's a double amputee, as long as he's strapped in, he's a hell of a driver. He claims he can use his hand controls quicker than an able-bodied person can use the foot pedals. Who knows, but after all that food and beer and as tired as I was, I was sure glad he was driving.

Danny got out and jumped into our backseat and told John to turn on the interior lights. He looked at me and said, "Where the fuck have you been? Out with some babe, getting some?"

"Fuck you, Danny. I told you I was picking up someone at the airport, and I got some food. You could have mentioned this downtown."

"I forgot, big deal. It's not like I don't have a thousand things on my mind."

"John says it's a million."Danny looked at John, smiled and said, "Okay, a million. I'm glad ya'll are here. Sorry I forgot.

We ought to be able to finish this fairly quick, so we can all go home and get some sleep before the 10 a.m. briefing."

"Ten a.m., how about an afternoon briefing?" I had to ask. But I knew the answer ahead of time. Danny was hot on the chase.

"I need you fifteen minutes earlier. You remember the first case you worked on with me when you gave me that background info, you know, the history of the devil and satanism, the magical mindset, the difference between witches, occultists, and satanists?"

"Yeah, sure." I hoped this wasn't going exactly where I knew it was.

"Well, I want you to give that same lecture tomorrow, and any insight you've got into the ritual nature of the crime. There will be Schultz, four other detectives, and two of the high-ranking uniforms in charge of the squad cars that patrol this zone. And some fucking feebee," he took on a sarcastic tone, "to observe, assist, and offer technical support." Feebee and feeb were among Danny's somewhat derogatory nicknames for the FBI. I use them too, but without the disdain. He hates working with feds, thinks they have no street sense, and steal the cases and the publicity from the people who do the real work. After 9/11 he told me he would gladly cooperate with the feebees on any kind of national security case, but if it wasn't national security or organized crime, they should stay the fuck out of the real cops way. In the back of my ex-con mind, a cop is a cop - local, state, federal, but Danny sure as hell doesn't see it that way. "The M.E. will have the preliminary autopsies done by tommorrow. Animals included. You got any input on who the four detectives should be, I get my choice. The rumors are going crazy, they want us to wrap this thing up quick."

"Input," I repeated, giving myself a moment to think. If this case was going to turn out the way it looked, we were dealing with people who believed in, and were committed to the antithesis of the Christian God - the devil. If we were dealing with a sorcerer on a reservation I'd want people who went to a Sweat Lodge regularly. When in Rome and all that. Since we were dealing with people who worship the Christian devil... I thought out loud in terms of theology. "Okay, nobody like crazy Larry, no right-wing fundamentalist Christians. They would get carried away and lose perspective. Since we're fighting the Christian devil," I stammered, realizing what I'd just said, "I mean people who believe in the Christian devil, just to be safe, make sure everybody's been baptized and has taken Holy Communion at least once. Theologically, in the

Christian faith, baptism and the eucharist ensure Christ's power over Satan, bought by the ransom of Christ's sacrifice. What would be ideal is people who grew up in some Christian faith, and still practice it but, you know, loosely. Seriously, no fundamentalist fanatics. Of course, I'll work with anybody, but that's what I'd prefer. And if we can get one or two of the women detectives, that would be great. We could use some intuition on our side, and a woman might be invaluable working the pregnant woman angle. The victim might have been recruited from a house for unwed mothers, a battered woman's shelter, something like that. They could work the clinics if necessary. Women often don't want to talk to men about things they don't think we really understand. At least one woman, please."

Danny paused for a second. He was not a chauvinist pig, not really, at least he didn't think so. Kind of like a lot of people don't think they're bigots, but they really are. Actually, Danny was not too thrilled when the number of female detectives started to grow past the token one or two. But as time passed he had seen some of them be successful and work with great diligence and they had won his respect. What he really didn't like was having to watch his jokes, his language, all the shit that was fine in a locker room but not in mixed company. "Okay, I can get two women, and I'll discreetly check to make sure about the religious stuff."

Danny handed me the clipboard. "You know the drill, we'll spray the luminol and look for blood traces, see what else we can find out. What I want out of you is to show me where to look, and to tell me what you can about the ritual. It looks like they swept and cleaned up ahead of time and then used tarps to cover their tracks, that's the only explanation for that much carnage but no bloody footprints. No bloody footprints in the house, on the steps, on the grass, in the dirt, anywhere. Not to mention no fucking fingerprints in the murder room. I wouldn't be surprised if they utilized the same plastic foot coverings our CSU folks wear; before, during, and with a new pair, after the ritual. But there's always a mistake. Nobody's fucking perfect."

I took the clipboard and saw that on the first page he had the outside layout - of the road, the old driveway, the paths and the house. On the second page he had the interior of the house. On the third page he had the murder room. I drew on that first. The room was square in proportion. I drew a circle inside the square and a triangle facing west inside the circle. I drew in the table/altar at the center and put crosses at the three points of the triangle. Then I turned to the house and drew where I thought the tarps had been laid, tarp upon tarp. They had to fold them in upon themselves, pulling them out after themselves. Down the steps and outside. I turned to the outside layout and drew two large tarps inside two larger tarps on the ground in front of the house. Then I looked at the road/gate/driveway layout. I had to figure out where they unloaded the materials before the ritual, and loaded the remains afterwards. I looked out at the gate, looked down, drew the most logical choice, and two alternatives, and handed Danny the clipboard. "Better tell the squad car and the CSU van to move up, they're on top of our best bet." I got out of the car. "Let's start outside, if it's okay with you Danny, inside will be easy."

***

The baby girl had gone back to sleep, the twin went back to sleep, his brother never woke up, used to sleeping through the noise. Betty and Laura were talking, while Laura was watching, really sampling, the news. Betty had given her the remote and said knock yourself out. It had been about a year since Leonard's last visit, and Betty was catching up on news of Leonard when a story caught her attention, "Leave it there, Laura, that's where our boys are."

Laura watched and listened. A multiple murder, under investigation, wealthy part of town, land owned by prominent local family, police wouldn't discuss the case except to say they were investigating, but rumors and unnamed sources said it was a ritualistic murder, involving the homicide of a pregnant woman and the death/torture of one to three animals. Details were sketchy, reports still unconfirmed....

Laura looked over at Betty and asked, "That's where Spooky and John are?"

"Sure, he didn't mention it at dinner?"

Laura just shook her head. Betty said, "They're not supposed to talk about it, but they're at the crime scene now, doing the luminol test."

"Luminol?" Laura had heard the word, but she generally had little interest in crime reports and crime reporting. She preferred political, social, and environmental issues.

"It's a chemical, John calls it a chemical reagent. When it's sprayed on blood stains in the dark, it makes the blood turn an eerie, luminous green. But you know the funny part, some folks claim bleach and taco sauce makes it urn green too, just like blood does."

Laura was thinking how things like this don't happen every day. Famous bizarre murders always have books written about them that sell, sometimes become best sellers. Here she was on the inside, at ground zero. She knew these were good people, like family to Leonard, and she couldn't take advantage of them. Still, she was a reporter, and the wheels in her mind were spinning like crazy.

***

There was a footpath to the right of the gate that led directly to the cottage. It was unfortunate it had been so unusually dry the last two weeks, or we might have had some decent foot impressions to work with. I tried to put myself in the perps place. If I was unloading and loading something covertly into and out of the cottage, directly adjacent to the farthest back path would be the place I'd choose. Shortest distance, least underbrush to deal with.

"Danny, if I was them, I'd have backed up the van, truck, RV, or car with a large trunk, whatever they had, to this point almost against the gate. It would be darkest, simplest, and quickest. Let's start here, work the path, then the open area in front of the cottage, and do the cottage last. You're the boss, so whatever you say goes, but that's my..." I started to say opinion, but changed my mind and used Danny's term, "input."

Danny gave the orders, the squadcar and CSU van pulled up, the techs got out the luminol and started spraying the pavement. We got lucky, I was only about a foot and a half off. The second spray hit the spot. We stood there and stared as little luminous green spots materialized before our eyes. I knew what was coming, some things are so predictable. It's like the old military joke when someone asks a question and the soldier responds, "That's top secret, I could tell you, but then I'd have to kill you." That stale line is twice my age at least. From the moment the green started showing up, I began counting. I got to seven when Danny said, "Hey Spooky, that green shit's really spooky looking, ain't it, Spooky." One of the techs started humming the refrain from the Classics IV's tune "*Spooky*. " The rest joined in.

I gave them my normal erudite reply in an Arnold Swartzeneger accent, "Fuck you assholes." Boy, I really had a way with words. They laughed. Cops love ribbing someone with long hair, even if he's on their side.

The luminol traces were not large or numerous. Sometimes the trick with luminol is to not spray luminol on everything, but spray enough to establish the pattern and get the unsprayed blood as samples because the luminol ruins the blood for other tests. In this case, we already knew inside there there was no shortage of blood stains and samples on the walls and ceiling. But here there were only six greenish spots about quarter-size, glowing eerily on the pavement. The area was marked in chalk.

As we began trying to trace our way back to the cabin we found no more spots on the ground, but a few traces on some bushes, at what would be about the right height for a medium tall man were he carrying a large bundle in his arms, occasionally brushing by or moving branches out of his way. Gloves I figured. The man carrying the tarps and whatever was folded up in them, presumably some of their blood stained ritual regalia, had blood on his gloves and when he pushed branches out of his way, the blood on his gloves rubbed off on the plants. That or blood from the tarps themselves.

There were a few minute drops closer to the cabin, on the ground as well as on the bushes. Outside the area where Danny had figured the tarps were laid out directly in front of the porch, we also found drops, outlining a large square area. But drops and spots were all we found outside the cabin, and nobody thought we were getting much surprising or of real value.

We checked the area outside the murder room window and found no evidence of blood, consistent with the theory that the smudged finger prints found there were left by the discoverers of the crime scene – our phone pals who called it in. Inside the house, there were small scattered spots outside of the killing room. Whoever the perps were, they were neat, methodical, and efficient. If this had been a normal homicide crime scene there would be luminous green chemical light shining everywhere and many trails of green footprints.

The only room where the luminol really picked up much was the murder room. There was blood on the floor along the wall, and blood spray patterns on the walls and the ceiling. The whole room had been awash in blood - was it really only twenty-four hours ago? It certainly seemed like much longer, but I was feeling more like a zombie than a human and I needed some serious rest. I couldn't help myself, "Damn Danny, it really is spooky looking in here." It really was an incredibly weird looking glowing green, on top of the evil and savagery done here, and the blood spray patterns showed just what kind of butchery was going on last night. I didn't have the severe reaction to the crime scene I experienced in the morning, but I still felt uneasy there and wanted to leave as soon as I went in. One of the techs was videoing everything so I didn't have to stay and study it. Anyway, in the murder room, all the blood was where I expected it to be. That was more than I could say for what we'd found outside. I didn't understand the six large spots where they loaded up, when they had been so efficient everywhere else.

John the boss had stayed at the gate with the uniformed officer in the squadcar. His chair could have picked up and tracked the luminol if he accidentally rolled through it, although that was unlikely with his skill. More importantly, he didn't want to show up on the video and get Danny in trouble. Danny had bent the rules this morning, he would be shattering them if he let John roll around the crime scene during a luminol test in the dark. I was there under official sanction, John wasn't.

After a few long looks around the murder scene, I asked Danny if he really needed me for anything else. "What's your hurry, Spooky?"

"Well Danny, I'm dead tired, I want some sleep, and I've got a house guest who I didn't even get to show around my house before John rushed me away. I want to go home. Now, do you need me for anything, or can I go?"

"Scat. I'll see you tomorrow at nine forty-five."

I looked at the blood splatter patterns in glowing green one last time and then split. Danny called after me, "Don't have beer on your breath tomorrow morning." I didn't turn around, I just kept walking, raised my hand, and flipped him off.

When John dropped me off in front of my house, the front door opened and Laura was framed in its light. The word statuesque came to mind. She was wearing what looked like a San

Francisco 49ers jersey and a loose fitting bathrobe. When I got closer I could see it was my bathrobe. She had just taken a shower, she still had her hair up in a towel turban. She stepped back and let me walk in and handed me a full beer which she had just opened. I said thanks and thought there could be worse ways of coming home than being greeted by a beautiful woman waiting with a cold beer.

She smiled a smile I couldn't interpret and said, "I've got a proposition for you." I couldn't think of an appropriate response, so I did my best Mae West imitation and said, "Like, why don't you come up and see me sometime?" For which she hit me playfully in the arm. I could tell she had grown up with lots of brothers; at times she acted, actually re-acted so much like my younger sister.

"Not that kind of proposition, Spooky, a business proposition. One that could make us both some serious money, and really accelerate my career. We sat down on the sofa, I attacked my beer. The TV was off and there was no music playing, except for the natural orchestra of crickets, treefrogs, bullfrogs, with the occasional call of a screech owl. The overhead fans were quietly running, the screen doors and open screened windows allowed the breeze to come in carrying the scent of honeysuckles. I don't use the air-conditioner unless it's real hot; I love fresh air. Out the living room window I could see the fireflies doing their mating dances while the moon's reflection shimmered in the pond. I looked out for a minute, closed my eyes, relaxed my body for another minute and came back. She patiently gave me those few minutes to relax, and I appreciated it. Finally I asked what proposition.

"I want to be your executive assistant, your personal secretary, your gopher, whatever, just let me work for you, I'll do it for free."

I was real tired, so I just asked, "Why?"

She really launched into it. She told me other reporters might lie and say she just wanted to see what a private investigator/security consultant did. But she was too honest for that. She explained that she didn't really like reporting crime, but books about infamous crimes sell well, many even become best sellers. Her excitement about the idea was obvious.

"We'll be partners - 50/50. You keep me informed, let me hang around and observe, I'll do all the writing, you get half the money and half the credit."

"No. First leak that comes out would be my ass in a sling, I'd get canned."

"I'm not talking about reporting it now, I'm talking about putting a book out after the crime is solved. I don't have a job right now, remember, I'd be working for me, for us. If it turns out to be a real sensational case and you catch the bad guys, books will get written anyway. You might as well tell the story right and cash in. I don't know about your profession, but in mine, a best selling non-fiction account of a notorious crime would guarantee me a great job. I could write my own ticket. This could be a really good thing for both of us."

She reached out and took my beerless hand, virtually forcing me to make eye contact. "How about if I work with you, be your secretary, assistant, whatever, we come home each night and compile the notes, work on the book, put it together, but you hold veto power on the wording of the final edition and the timing of when it could be released." I could tell how much she wanted it. I wondered how far my debt, duty, love, friendship – all I felt for Leonard was supposed to carry over to his relatives.

She kept up her assault. "You could make some serious money, be famous, be on Oprah, Leno, and Letterman. It'd be great for your business. Come on, I'll be quiet as a mouse when you work, you won't even know I'm there."

"I wouldn't mind the money if it worked out like you say, who wouldn't, but the last thing

I want to be is famous or on some stupid interview show. And a woman that looks like you and is as smart and ambitious as you - may try to be quiet as a mouse - but is always going to get noticed and be about impossible to forget."

She turned fully sideways to face me on the sofa, drawing her legs up under herself, and then she reached out and began holding my poor hand with both of hers. Her dark brown eyes were either pleading, or trying to will me to say yes, or both.

"Danny would get in deep shit if he knew about something like this and kept working with me. It could jeopardize the investigation and his, as well as my credibility as a prosecution witness." I shook my head. Even if I wanted to, and being around her definitely had an up side, there were just so many reasons why the logical answer should be no.

But Leonard had done so much for me inside, and then inviting me out to visit right after my release, introducing me to the Sweat Lodge and to lots of really good people, including the shaman who trained me. I owed him. I might not have made it through the joint without getting killed, maimed, or raped if I hadn't had him as a teacher/ally. And Laura was definitely right about one thing, if this case turned out to be a sensationally lurid affair and we caught the perps, books *would* be written. And money is money, and free publicity might help grow the family business….

"I can't really be part of writing a book until the case is over. It would hurt my credibility as a prosecution witness, which, if I'm called, is definitely part of my job." I looked at those pleading eyes and that alluring face and my resolve to say no, along with all my logical arguments that backed that resolve up, melted away. She had both hands on mine, her eyes, her whole body seemed so close, she had the scent of someone who's just showered…. I knew I wasn't thinking with the head that rests on my shoulders, but my resolve had been completely dissolved in her deep brown eyes and nearness.

"What I could do is let you work for me as a paid assistant, you could help me accomplish a few of my normal jobs while I'm working fulltime for the city. This case will take almost all of my time. When I don't need you, go to your convention or whatever. I can't be writing a book while I'm investigating, it would destroy my present and future credibility as a witness. But you could certainly work as my secretary each night as I go over the day's events and plan out tomorrow's. When this thing is all over, *then* maybe we could use my daily notes and write a book in retrospect. But no books and no book deals until it's all over. That's the only way I can remain a viable investigator and eventual witness. And you really would have to work to help me fulfill my routine work responsibilities, and our starting pay sucks. If you're interested in that arrangement, I would need you to video a lecture I've got to give to the investigating team tomorrow morning at ten. We're going to sell APD a copy. I'm tired of giving the same lecture every time a cult, occult, or ritualistic crime comes along. We can see how it goes tomorrow as a trial run and take it from there."

I had just practiced a game so often played by lawyers. Legal truth comes down to exactly what was said and what was done. I'd said and done the right things legally. I knew she could very well get exactly what she wanted in the long run, possibly to our mutual benefit and financial reward. But in a court of law we could both swear I'd refused to work on a book while investigating, and that I'd simply offered a part-time job to an out of work friend of the family.

She was every bit as aware as I was of what legal game we'd just played. She was so happy she rose up on the sofa, almost bouncing with excitement. She looked as happy and joyful as a child on Christmas. She leaned forward and kissed me lightly on the lips and said thank you. She hesitated close up, instead of moving back quickly, so I leaned forward a few inches, gave her a light kiss, and said you're welcome. Then she leaned back in and kissed me, deeply and fully. After about a minute she pulled away slightly, "I'm not usually this forward. I had a few glasses of your wine before and after I showered... it's been four months since my boyfriend and I broke up after three years together. It seems like a long time since I've been with anyone, or even wanted to be. Do you have... somebody?"

I shook my head, "There's no one, hasn't been for more than a year."

"A year? " She smiled, kissed me again, and repositioned herself on the sofa so we could hug and hold each other. She said, almost sighed, "And I thought four months was a long time. Spooky, my dear, we may be in for a memorable night."

And a memorable night it was indeed.

***

The man with three names walked into the small rented house and called to his brother, "Yo, Bobby, is everything ready? We need to get going. I'd like to get there while it's still dark."

Bobby came out of the back, "I got the bag you packed, my stuff, food 'n drinks, van's done been checked, all the fluids topped, 'n it's full of gas. Everythin' all right?" The big man talked in a slow way that didn't belie a quick intellect.

George looked at Bobby. He might not be a genius, or even as skilled a printer/forger as was expected in their family, but he could follow orders without fucking up. Which was invaluable. They had sent him to trade school to study locksmithing. Bobby had done fine work earlier tonight in the two break-ins and he had done excellent surveillance and reconnaissance in preparation for this weekend. He was calm and steady tonight, even when one of the marks came home early and they barely made it away without being detected. Bobby had what it takes to be a member of a good crew, he just didn't have the smarts to do anything by himself, or be a leader.

He answered his larger younger brother, "Everything's fine, Bobby, I called the doc, gave him the five G's, he gave me an 'extremely good.' So everything's cool. I even drove on the main road right by there. I didn't turn in or slow down, or anything, but I could see cop cars and a van at the dead end. I'm sure they're doing the night test, just like I told you. Let's book it. We've got to roadtrip."

Bobby followed his older brother out into the moonlit night with the bags his brother had doublechecked. George looked back and told him, "You can't be out on a job like this, be in the middle of things, and realize you forgot something. That's how people make the kind of mistakes that can cost a lifetime."

***

I woke up smiling for the first time in a long time and called Danny at home, but he was already at work. I think maybe his body overproduces adrenalin or some other chemical that keeps him wired twenty hours a day when he's on the chase. If I didn't know him better I'd think he was making midnight raids on the evidence room for pharmaceutical aid. But it wasn't from any outside chemical help, he was on the chase, big time. When I got him at work I told him I was going to bring an employee to tape my lecture so I could sell it cheaply to the city for posterity and I wouldn't have to keep repeating it. He said fine and asked me if I was ready to give an analysis of the ritual, and I said yes. I put the phone down and saw Laura was waking up beside me. As soon as she opened her eyes, she smiled. A big full natural smile. It was a good sign. I wasn't consciously hoping for it, but when I saw it, inside I went "Yeah!" I was feeling rather joyful myself. I wondered how long that could last once we went to work.

I called Leonard Wounded Face on his cell, he didn't respond, so I left him a message. It was way too early to call his house on a Saturday. Sometimes he camps out with the questers, but it was still real early in the morning out there, probably pre-dawn in California, so I wasn't surprised. He's like me about the cell phone phenomenon, your business or your life makes it necessary to have access to one, but generally I never carry it, I just leave it in whatever vehicle I'm using and check the messages.

I kept it short. "Pavi'(elder brother), Laura has arrived safely, she's settled in and set up fine for her convention. Pavi', I need you to send as much spiritual protection my way as possible. You wouldn't have believed the crime scene yesterday, we're up against the real thing - serious, organized, and disciplined satanic evil and we can use all the help and protection you can send Danny and me. Pray for us at the Sunday Sweat, I've got to go to work, but I'll call you later during a break."

***

The alarm clock woke Tonya up right on time. Pugsley was still out cold. He didn't have much exposure to alcohol and she figured he probably had no idea she had drugged his final drink both nights when she was ready to quit and get some rest herself. She popped pills knowingly, while covertly overdosing him so she'd wake up before he did. She guessed Pugsley whould be out cold for at least another two or three hours. George and Bobby Sanders would be by to pick her up in twenty minutes. Hopefully before first light. She knew she needed to eat something, she would make them get her food on the way. He was dead to the world, so she pulled the coke out of her purse and did a couple of small lines just to get going.

Showered, wide awake, and ready to go, she checked her overnight bag - Pugsley's shoes, socks, uniform and undies exactly as instructed. She looked out the window again as the white van pulled in next to her rental car. She put on her sunglasses and large floppy hat, took one more look at the passed out slug, and headed to the van.

***

Walking into APD Homicide I thought to myself that Laura looked just right. I had told her to dress down, and she imitated the dress of the news camera crews and technicians she was used to seeing as a reporter. The person you see on camera may be well dressed, but the rest of the news crew are always in blue jeans and tee shirts, which is what she had on. She carried the camera and the tri-pod very naturally, while I carried my briefcase filled with notes and some drawings I'd made after I woke up. I'd gone right to work, so other than a quick kiss hello and enjoying our coffee and breakfast, we'd been all business that morning. Had it not been for the horror of the crime, I'd have had difficulty not looking downright happy that morning, but a few reflections on the crime and it was no effort to be serious.

We made our way to Danny's desk. It was empty, but before I could even start to think about where to find him he came rushing in. He sat down, looked up at me, shook his head in disgusted wonderment. "You would not believe what the coroner just told me."

"I don't know, I'd believe about anything on this one."

"Naw, this is too weird. You won't believe what they found in the victim's stomach."

"Want to bet?" I was feeling lucky. I'd already won one bet for Laura in the last twenty-four hours, and I'd gotten lucky last night, in the romantic and carnal sense. And I'd thought deeply about the ritual, the precision of the perps, their mindset, and present day realities. Danny looked at me.

"Okay, you buy lunch today for me and Schultz if you lose, I'll buy lunch for you and your assistant if I lose."

I nodded, "Want to raise the stakes, and make it dinner at the Pleasant Pheasant?" Danny shook his head, I was being too confident. For the first time I realized I'd been real sketchy on details with Laura, all she knew was that it was a brutal ritual murder. Last night we'd been busy discovering each other, and this morning during the drive I was thinking, not talking. I hoped she had a strong stomach.

"No," said Danny," lunch at Merry Mac's is fine. I don't want to take advantage of you. Alright Mr. Know-it-all, what did the M.E. find in her stomach?"

Danny's confidence was returning. He thought I was stumped. But then he didn't know why the most infamous magician of the 20th century was booted out of Italy by Mussolini before World War II. "Blood." I responded. "Animal blood. In fact, the blood of all three animals were found in her stomach, probably mixed with some red wine. Undigested."

"Shit! I'm buying lunch," Danny exclaimed. I seldom get to impress a homicide detective as smart as Danny. I couldn't help smiling as I looked over at Laura. "You'll get a real taste of Southern cooking now."

Laura looked sick. Hunger was about the farthest thing from her mind at the moment. She didn't say anything, anything at all, but she didn't go toss her cookies, like I had yesterday morning.

After belated introductions we moved on to the briefing room. Schultz was moving around the room, playing with a screen, a slide projector, and a TV with a VCR, so Laura set up the tripod and video camera in the back while Danny and I conferred. Danny asked me in private if I could guarantee no leaks. He said he trusted me, but he didn't know about blindly extending that trust to my employees. I told him she was more than an employee and I guaranteed no leaks.

He looked at me questioningly, I just smiled and repeated, "No leaks. Guaranteed." He then made sure I knew that the city was only paying for me, not my hired help. All that cleared up, we talked while the team came in.

***

Tonya hastily ate her takeout breakfast, sitting uncomfortably in the flat back of the sparse old utility van as the sun rose. Bobby Sanders was driving to a spot he had found during the reconnaissance work he'd done for this job. George Sanders, his actual given name and the one Tonya knew him by, was interrogating her to see if she had followed the plan and script precisely. She had an uneasy feeling that if she came up with the wrong answers, or even if he just didn't *believe* her, she might not ever see Vegas, or even her daughter again. That bothered her for many reasons. She and George had a history. Growing up in the same neighborhood, dating him in high school, and five years ealier she'd been his girlfriend for over a year while he ran a small escort/call girl service as part of his multi-faceted criminal undertakings.

She knew George was ambitious, smart, coldhearted and was dedicated to crime not only by the family he was born into, but by choice. By philosophy. He was no dumbass, he'd simply come to the opinion at an early age that the rule followers were stupid and those who broke the rules intelligently were the really smart people.

George had done hard time for the sale of false documents when one of his former clients got seriously busted and turned stool pigeon on everybody he could think of. When George got out of jail a couple of years ago, he didn't go back in the flesh business, so he set her up with his cellmate, Kevin. Kevin was nowhere near as smart as George, although they were both equally mean sons of bitches. But Kevin had been a good protector, and he tried to behave like a legitimate business man, not some street pimp. All in all, in that world, he had been relatively good to her.

All she had told Kevin was that she was going down to Macon to her mother's to see her kid, just like she did every three or four weeks. George had approached her from out of nowhere, for what he called a once in a lifetime opportunity. Besides entertaining the john for one weekend under very specific circumstances and then going on to a new life in Vegas, part of that deal was leaving Kevin in the dark, and her mom, basically telling no one, for at least three months afterwards, maybe more. She had to do a one weekend job, and disappear. Now, riding in the sparse van she felt isolated and incredibly vulnerable. There was no doubt in her mind that the duffle bag beside her contained all the instruments necessary for her death and the disposal of her body. Probably Pugsley's too, not that she cared about the slug.

Years ago, maybe four or five times, she had seen George right before he had gone to do enforcement work, because of unpaid money or damaged girls. He'd looked scary then in a way she couldn't describe, but was way past anger or intimidation. She recognized that look and attitude, he looked that way now, real scary. If she'd known it was gonna be like this, she'd have never taken the job. After the third time of going through it all in detail, as they were on the dirt road that led to the unofficial rural trash dump, George's expression and attitude changed completely and he relaxed. Then she thought, maybe, she was going to make it out alive, and really would be flying on to Vegas with her daughter and hopefully, to a new and better life.

They piled out of the van, Tonya with her bag and Bobby with the duffle bag. Following George's orders she spread Pugsley's clothes out on the ground along with his socks and shoes. She didn't have a clue as to what was going on, and at this point really didn't want one, feeling the less she knew the better her possibilities of a long life. George had frightened her more the last thirty minutes than he had all the years they'd known each other. She told George she didn't want to watch or even know what was going on. George said that was an excellent idea, that she should just go back to the van and wait, which she gladly did.

George got a small cooler out of the duffle bag and withdrew from it four clear hospital plastic specimen jars half filled with a dark red liquid and a small plastic bottle with a trigger pump, the kind used to moisten plant leaves. It was about a third filled with a red liquid. He opened one of the specimen bottles, took a straw and sucked the red liquid half way up the straw, and began to blow it out on the bottom of the shoe's soles and between the rubber soles and the leather uppers.

***

Schultz and Laura were in the back of the room with the equipment. Unknown to me, but with the natural instincts of a reporter, she intended to tape the whole thing - not just my part. She put the camera on the tripod, turned it on, locked it in on the podium, saw no one was looking, placed a small square of black tape over the red "on light," left it running, and sat down beside it. The fan on the slide projector made a small a hum; no one could tell if the video camera was running or not. She stayed in the back, quiet and out of the way.

Eventually the whole team was there. Four detectives: a portly middle-aged white man, Dick Williams, an overweight middle-aged black man, Lester Wallace, a tall thin handsome black woman named Annie Wilson, and a solid, mannish looking white woman everybody called only by her last name, Potts. There were two high-ranking uniforms there, too. The chief of police walked the Fed in. Her presence showed how important the case was, her walking in the Fed meant she wanted things to go smoothly.

They were an odd pair, the tough small black woman police chief and the large whitebread Fed who still looked like the college football lineman he had been years ago. The

Chief introduced special agent Billy Ray Walton to everyone and left. Walton sat down and Danny, showing no sign of annoyance, began what was to be an extended briefing.

Standing at a podium to the right of the screen, Danny talked while Schultz worked the slide projector's remote control. I couldn't help but wonder if Laura had the stomach for what she was about to see. She didn't like cops or uniforms, but here she was in the middle of cop world. She didn't like reporting crime, but here she was with the core team investigating a horrendously brutal crime.

Danny didn't waste any time. "Around sunrise Saturday morning the 911 operator got a call from what sounds like a scared but excited male teenager reporting a crime at the old cottage at the end of Thorn road. You can hear two other male voices suggesting what to say in the background. We know the call was made from a nearby Waffle House and a waitress there has given us a fairly good description of the three boys. At this time, we do not think they are in any way connected with the doers, but the folks who left the smudged fingerprints on the outside of the murder room window. In the call they claimed to have been run off from the hangout/lovers lane at the end of Thorn by a uniformed policeman in an unmarked car around midnight, or a little after. They claimed to have heard odd singing or chanting in the distance. When the supposed policeman was asked about the noise, he said surveillance work was going on and it was time the kids moved on or they would be arrested. Of course, the kids left. About four a.m. they went to the Waffle House and ate, and before dawn returned to Thorn Road, curious about the noises and the supposed surveillance. They took a flashlight and checked out the cabin from outside, got a good look, freaked, went back to the waffle house and called it in. When asked repeatedly by the dispatcher to identify themselves, they hung up. We've analysed the tape, in the background one voice distictly says, 'Dude, get off the phone, we've got to be at the school in a few hours.' So we've assumed they are high school students who had a Saturday activity of some kind, and are probably attending summer school sessions at one of the two private or one public high school in that affluent area."

Danny drank some water. All that had been showing on the screen was the outside of the cottage. "Here is what the boys found." Schultz flicked the next slide, and there were audible gasps in the room. "The worst crime sene I've ever seen. In the center, on what Spooky says is the altar, lies a young caucasian female, mid to late teens, eight and a half to nine months pregnant. The baby was surgically cut out of the heavily sedated woman while both mother and infant were still alive. The woman's heart was then removed by a long incision under the left rib cage. The M.E. says her heart was cut and ripped out of her chest, resulting in her immediate death.

"You will notice that above her, between the altar and the upside down star painted on the wall is the infant, hung by wire to an inverted cross, crucified upside down, stabbed three times in the heart. The cross is made of pine limbs. Notice the three animals, also stabbed repeatedly, are also hung upside down, wired to inverted crosses of pine. You can't see it in these pictures, but all the animals have incisions slicing an artery, which were inflicted before they were stabbed and killed. Their blood was collected. The crosses stand up in holes cut in the floor, the weight of the crosses rests on the ground a foot and a half under the structure, giving them the stability and strength to hold a dog, a lamb, a goat, and a baby." Schultz flicked to different angled close ups of the woman and her baby, and the dog, lamb, and goat hanging upside down on crosses. In the dark, groans and gasps were heard of both male and female origin.

"The M.E. says the cutting on the woman was skilled and exhibited a knowledge of anatomy, but not so skilled as to be the work of a practicing surgeon. He says the differing strokes and penetrations of the wounds on the animals and infant suggest that this is the work of three different individuals. One person is fairly strong and knowledgeable of anatomy, right handed, the person that removed the baby from the mother. There is another extremely strong person, left handed, without precise knowledge of anatomy, who stabs deeply. Another person, smaller, not very strong, left handed, put only one relatively shallow wound in each victim. The M.E. guesses, and I repeat guesses, two adult men, one very strong, the other skilled and knowledgeable, and a woman, a medium to small sized woman, not a possessor of great strength."

The black woman detective, Annie Wilson, just blurted out, "How could any woman do that to another woman? These people are sick, no, way past sick, these people are evil." After seeing the close ups, no one in that room was inclined to disagree.

"We have some idea as to the order in which this crime was committed. We believe the ritual began around midnight and was probably over by one, one-thirty. The heavily sedated animals were wired and hung upside down on the crosses before they were bled, and then later stabbed to death. We found blood from the three animals undigested in the woman's stomach." There was a disgusted vocal reaction from most of the cops.

"So the animals were bled and some of their blood collected, mixed with wine and poured down the mouth of the woman. Then the infant was surgically removed from her mother's womb. The woman's heart was then cut/ripped out of her while it was still beating and drained of blood. The baby's umbilical cord was cut after removal, the M.E. says at this point it was alive and breathing. It was laid on its dead mother's bloody abdomen, stabbed to death, and then wired to the crucifix and placed upside down behind the altar. The M.E. says the animals' and the mother's bloodwork shows they were deeply sedated, heavily anesthetized. They probably made little noise or offered any resistance, making it likely they did not wound or mark their tormentors."

Schultz was flipping through the pictures; it seemed each one was more gruesome than its predecessor. Close ups of the animals, the mother, the infant. Some of the pictures showed the satanic graffiti on the walls. Annie spoke up again, "What's all the 'satan rules' gibberish on the walls? Are the satanic cult rumors true?"

The white woman detective, Potts, with a strong southern accent chimed in, "It certainly don't look like no normal crime scene." Danny told them we would get to the satanic angle in a minute.

"There are some obvious places to start our investigation, we know that the supposed cop reported on the scene was not one of ours on duty. We have a good description from the Waffle House waitress of the three boys who got a good look, we presume, at the impostor policeman, so we need to find those boys. In that wealthy area of town there is the one public school and two private schools open for summer school. Since Thorn Road is often frequented by teenagers, more than our three callers were probably run off from there by the impostor cop. Williams and Wallace," he said looking at the two men, tomorrow you will visit those three schools, find our callers and anyone else run off that night."

"The woman does not match any filed missing persons report. Wilson, you and Potts will work the pregnant woman angle. First make calls, if that's unproductive take her picture around to the shelters, clinics, and homes for unwed mothers. Where-ever she resides, since it's still the weekend, they might not even know she's missing. If nothing turns up in a few days, we'll give her picture to the press. But for now, silence to the press. We don't need all the crazies confessing or any copycat crimes to complicate matters.

"All four of you can divvy up the phone work: contacting the GBI and police and sherriff departments for info on any similar crimes, and contacting the animal control agencies trying to find out if the animals were bought, obtained from an animal shelter, or stolen. At the same time you talk to the other police departments check for..." He looked at me, so I threw in, "Burglaries of churches, especially Catholic, Episcopal, Eastern Orthodox, or any denomination big on showy rituals. Especially where the Host or any communion paraphernalia was stolen. Also search for church and graveyard desecrations, and mutilated animals. Go back at least two years. This bloody ritual was probably the culmination of a series of rituals, certainly not the first one these people have done. This was probably the first one they wanted us to find."

Danny sat down and motioned for me to go ahead. I went up to the podium and Laura rose, fiddled with the camera, then leaned back against the wall behind her. I'd told her I might have to move around some and use the green chalkboard behind the podium. She'd told me not to worry, that she'd do a good job. Once I started talking to the cops, I almost did forget she was there. Which was something, considering last night.

It was important that the task force understood who they were looking for, and also the notoriety this case would attain in the American law enforcement community as a whole. Because of that, they would need to do everything right. I hadn't even told Danny yet that we were sitting on top of what was bound to be an infamous first in American criminology. There was what some considered a Mexican/American case that qualified as the first, but it didn't, and I was about to explain why.

Chapter Five - Sunday Morning/Afternoon

George walked over and opened the passenger door, reached over to the keys and turned the engine on. Tonya had been attempting to rest with her eyes closed. He had, of all things, a hairdryer in his hand. It was plugged into an extension cord with a chrome jack. He pulled the cigarette lighter out, dropped it on the floorboard, and slid the jack into the lighter receptacle. He switched the hair dryer on, tested it on high, turned it off, and told her, "We won't be but a few more minutes, Tonya, then one more stop and you're back at work." He left the door cracked for the cord and rejoined his brother.

***

"The first thing I've got to get you to understand is that this murder, if it turns out in actuality to be the way it appears, was not committed for any of your normal reasons. This murder, murders, these acts of brutality were committed for a purpose, and that purpose is intimately tied up with religion and magic. And when I say magic, I don't mean any David Copperfield crap.

"Religion, by definition is a set of beliefs concerning the cause, nature, and purpose of Life, Existence, and the Universe. This usually concerns a superhuman agency or agencies, and usually involves devotion, rituals, and a moral code for human behavior. By contrast magic is considered a way of producing a desired effect, of making something occur as willed, through the use of various techniques thought to assure human control over supernatural agencies and the forces of Nature. Magic is the art and practice of making something happen in conformity to human will.

"While we're doing definitions, let's clear up two more. The first is cult, a word you hear often enough, but is seldom understood by its users. A cult, in its religious sense, can be any particular system of religious worship, especially its rites and ceremonies. Usually the word cult is used meaning that the religion is unorthodox or considered false by the more orthodox. The word occult is one of the most misused words in the English language, almost constantly misused by the media. Occult means that which cannot be seen. It is used to refer to that which is beyond the normal range of knowledge, is mysterious, secret. It can be the knowledge known only to initiates - knowledge of magic and the occult arts. Occult does not mean devil worship and occult does not imply evil, but you would never know that from what you hear on TV or read in the papers.

"Orthodox Christianity is a religion with God in three persons or aspects as the Father, the Holy Spirit, and Christ, supervising the agencies of the Archangels and Angels. In Christianity the enemy of the forces of Good is Satan, and he commands the infernal legions of archdemons and demons. They supposedly fight a spiritual war, the battleground of which is planet Earth. Whether or not you or I personally believe in this is not important right now, but we do need to agree on basic terms and mindsets. Christianity is a religion, but when a person is baptized and expects by that act to obtain salvation, or takes communion and expects a spiritual union with Christ, or prays for a healing, or for a promotion at work, religion touches the realm of magic because a result is desired. Religion is devotional. When one undertakes that religion's activities to produce a certain result, that is magical. In the most basic terms, magic for a good or benevolent purpose is called white magic, magic which is designed to do harm or is selfish at the expense of others is termed black magic.

"Whether or not Satanism is a religion can be debated, but however it is considered, it exists in relation to Christianity. Most religions and cultures have white and black magic, but Satanism, although inverted, is dependent on Christianity to supply its symbols and cosmology, and it is thought of as something practiced by black magicians in rebellion against Christianity. Of course, I didn't come up with these terms, and black or white magic has nothing to do with human racial appearance, just human intentions. A Satanist is always a black magician, but a black magician need not be a Satanist. Matamoros, Mexico can provide a graphic example of this. But before I go into that example, let me say that I believe that we have a genuine satanic ritual murder on our hands, and if this is the circumstance, it will be the first such documented case in the United States.

"Because of its unusual status, this case will receive a lot of attention in the U.S. law enforcement community, not to mention the media, and I can only urge you to think and rethink everything you do, and to doublecheck all your procedures. If APD drops the ball on this one, it will be a smaller version of something like being the Dallas Police Department in 1963 after JFK and Oswald got whacked – you will become a national laughing stock.

Before going further, let me relate the definition that Kenneth Lanning, the specialist in cult/occult crimes for the FBI, provides for what constitutes a satanic murder." I couldn't help looking up at Special Agent Walton, but he stayed quiet and attentive. "It is a murder committed by two or more people, is rationally planned, and is carried out primarily to fulfill a prescribed ritual calling for such a murder. Until now, according to the FBI, there had never been a single victim of a genuine satanic murder in the U.S. This crime may very well provide the first and second victims meeting the FBI criteria. If this leaks out prior to our apprehending the perpetrators, the press will go crazy, making this investigation a hundred times more difficult. The last thing we need is the TV sleaze hounds and the tabloids looking over our shoulders every step of the way, second-guessing everything we do, stirring up publicity that could generate confusing copycat crimes and tons of false confessions by crazies.

"Before you dismiss all this as irrational superstitious nonsense, try to remember that the age of reason and the scientific revolution are relative newcomers in terms of human history. For most of human history, at any point and time, most of humanity has believed in the power of magic as a causal force in physical reality. This belief in the efficacy of magic has existed within and outside of the Christian church throughout its history and at least two popes are widely believed to have practiced magic.

"Although certainly not as widespread in modern times, this belief in the efficacy of magic has certainly continued in industrial societies, despite all the exhortations of scientists and proponents of rationalism to the contrary. As an example of a magical mindset, let us briefly look at one modern magician, probably both the most famous and infamous magician of the 20th century, a British magician whose books still sell well internationally fifty years after his death.

"Aleister Crowley lived from 1875 until 1947, and like most modern magicians, was very eclectic. He developed his own complex system of magic, which he spelled m-a-g-i-c-k, which was a combination of magical systems from both the East and West. He combined the Kabbalah from esoteric Judaism, Hermetic and ritual magic from the classical civilizations of ancient Egypt, Greece, and Rome, and the Eastern practices of Tantric Yoga, among other things.

"Although Crowely was not a Satanist, his work and legend exerts a great influence on contemporary satanic phenomenon. He even went so far as to refer to himself as the 'the Great Beast 666' from the Bible, and 'Baphomet,' the supposed sinister deity of the Knights Templar, which probably didn't exist outside the imagination of the church's torturers. While some claim Crowley didn't believe in a devil others claim he made statements to the effect that Satan's second coming was imminent. But Crowley was known to have a bizarrely perverse sense of humor, and may have done and said much that was tongue-in-cheek and not meant to be taken literally.

"From the Kabbalah, the esoteric mysticism and practices developed by Jewish rabbis from the 7th to 18th centuries, Crowely accepted the idea that man was a microcosm, an exact duplicate of the universe, the macrocosm. Because man and the universe are indissolubly linked, an act by man, under certain conditions, may affect the world at large, just as an occurrence in the outer world can affect man individually. He saw the interaction between similarities, between a part and the whole, between a symbol and that which it symbolizes, termed sympathetic magic, to underlie all magic. Sex was a sacred act, an earthly counterpart of God's creative forces, symbolic of the energy which created the universe. Coitus was seen capable of linking man with divinity; by partaking in a sacred act, man becomes sacred.

"Crowley saw sex as a means of harnessing great amounts of internal and external power. He believed that sex set up vibrations, which under stringent control, could be directed and used by the magician for whatever purpose was desired. Crowley was considered by many to have started off as a white magician who was seduced by power and became a black magician. In a more modern context, like Darth Vader in the movie *Star Wars*, Crowley was seduced by the dark side of the Force. In the movie in which Vader is finally unmasked, the actor seems to be a Crowley look alike, some wonder if this was intentional.

"Contemporary Crowleyism teaches that Christian morality is oppressive because it blocks the expression of the genuine human propensity to take unrestrained joy and pleasure in sex and power. Christianity's oppressive morality is like an artificial dam unnaturally stopping a stream. They believe the releasing of sexual inhibitions unleashes vast quantities of both physical and psychological energy.

"I should also mention that Crowley divided magic into two basic kinds of activities. His magic was split into evocation - which was a directing of power, a calling forth in the external world, and invocation - a calling in, an identification with the godhead within.

"Now that we have looked at the beliefs of a modern magician, let's look at a series of documented black magic ritual murders, set in Mexico in 1989. Matamoros provides us with physical evidence, participant testimony, and extensive photo and press coverage of this modern example of ritual murder. At the center of this story is Aldolfo de Jesus Constanzo, born in Miami in 1962. He was raised by his mother, a native Cuban who practiced Santeria.

"I should explain that Santeria, Obeah, and other forms of Voodoo are examples of a syncretic religion, combining indigenous African beliefs brought by the slaves, with the Roman Catholicism forced on most slaves in the Caribbean, South America, and Louisiana. The fictional portrayals of Voodoo, especially on TV and in the movies, have generally portrayed all Voodoo as black magic, but this is patently untrue. Voodoo has healing rituals and beautiful marriage ceremonies. However, it is true that chickens are often sacrificed in Voodoo rituals, which makes Voodoo appear like black magic to the uninformed.

"Sacrifices in religion and magic are quite commonplace throughout human history. The Bible informs us that the Jews sacrificed rams and other animals up until and after the time of Christ, while in Christianity, Jesus is considered the sacrificial lamb whose willing sacrifice buys humanity redemption. Human sacrifice is found frequently throughout history, although it was often a criminal or enemy warrior who was sacrificed in a society's public rites. The classical Greeks and Romans sacrificed animals, as did some ceremonial magicians in Europe during and after the Middle Ages. Physical ritual sacrifice of a living creature might not be common in most religions today, but the concept of sacrifice is deeply embedded in many religions.

"Constanzo was an ecumenist of the black arts who apprenticed himself to practitioners of various Afro-Cuban and Haitian Voodoo cults including cults that practice black magic such as Palo Mayombe and Abakua. It is common where Voodoo or other forms of white and black magic are practiced for the practitioner of the black arts to publicly admit to only practicing white magic. Constanzo would not admit to practicing Abakua, he claimed he was practicing a combination of Santeria and Palo Mayombe. In Abakua, the practitioners are said to engage in torture, human sacrifice, and mystical cannibalism.

"What we know from those who paid Constanzo to do magic for them, and from those who worked magic with him, is that at least some of his ritual chants were in the Bantu language of central Africa and some of his practices were called Regla de Congo. We also know Constanzo revived the Aztec rites of human sacrifice, including the ripping out of a beating heart.

"By the mid 1980's he was living in Mexico city and had attracted a small group of followers who believed that Constanzo could predict the future using Tarot cards. He began to earn money performing rituals he claimed were rites of cleansing known as limpias. Each limpia is said to have included a ritual human sacrifice. His clients were said to be narcotics traffickers, Mexican government officials, and the elite of the Mexican entertainment community.

"His victims would be found in 'red light' districts, cruising homosexuals or prostitutes who would be invited or kidnapped, and then stripped and placed on the ritual altar. At Constanzo's instructions, the victim's chest would be split, the heart removed, and all present would drink blood directly from the heart. The victim's brains and other body parts were then placed in a cauldron with other symbolic items connoting death. The mixture would then be consumed by all present.

"Before the ritual killing it was considered important to inflict pain upon the victim, terrorizing him. It was thought that by using torture on the victim, the victim's fear placed the victim's soul and its power totally in the black magicians hands to be redirected as desired. Constanzo claimed his limpia 'cleansing' rituals gave his paying customers mystical power for professional success.

"It was said he sometimes performed up to three or four limpias a week, charging thirty to forty thousand dollars per limpia. Three or four a week, however, is most probably an exaggeration. He reportedly told one woman who came for a limpia something to the effect of - welcome to the house of the devil. If you want to be cleansed, you will no longer have God, but you will have other powers to call upon for success and inner strength. Constanzo reportedly made a good living as a black magician. He owned several houses, he had many cars for which he paid cash, and was said to have lived an aristocratic lifestyle.

"If Constanzo had not gotten involved with Americans and those who did business in America, who knows how long he could have continued. But I think we can assume Constanzo got greedy. He initiated a student from Texas Southmost University at Brownsville, named Sara Aldrete. Sara was said to be deeply impressed by the movie *The Believers* and encouraged the other members of the Constanzo cult to watch the movie repeatedly.

"Constanzo used Sara as a honey trap, as sexual bait to attract as a paying client a wealthy drug trafficker, Elio Hernandez. The honey trap worked and Constanzo offered to initiate Hernandez into his cult and provide him with magical powers that would greatly increase his American sales and provide him with magical protection from, and magical power over, the border authorities. His price for this service would be one half of Elio's profits from his American drug sales. Elio went for the deal and was initiated at Constanzo's Santa Elena Ranch on the outskirts of Matamoros, just across from Brownsville. One report said it took Elio two sacrificial murders to get the ritual right, one of which involved some kind of mistake which cost Hernandez' own cousin his life.

"Constanzo told Elio that to gain power over the American borders and expand his American market, he would need to sacrifice an American. Unfortunately for Mark Kilroy, a premed student at the University of Texas, he chose to spend spring break at Matamoros. He ended up on March 14, 1989, at the Santa Elena Ranch, lying naked upon an altar on which was a Buddha-like statue, Santeria and Roman Catholic candles, and objects associated with voodoo, specifically the black magic forms of Palo Mayombe and Abukua. He was terrorized and tortured, his legs were cut off and his chest was opened and his heart ripped out. His brain and his blood were mixed with animal organs in a cauldron along with a horseshoe to provide invisibility from law enforcement.

"On April 11, 1989 the Mexican police raided Santa Elena and dug out thirteen bodies from nine graves. In the raid they captured many cult members but didn't get Constanzo. The members confessed, the press was allowed in, and the photographs and videos were news all over the world. Eventually the Mexican police called in a curandero, a healer, to exorcise the place. Then they burned all the structures to the ground.

"Constanzo had fled to Mexico City. On May 6, with Sara Aldrete and his two homosexual lovers - Alvaro and Martin. He tried to burn two suitcases of money so the cops he had been bribing wouldn't get their hands on it. He then embraced his lover Martin while Alvaro shot and killed both with an AK-47.

"Now, we must note that the Constanzo cult was not satanic, they practiced black magic aspects of voodoo. More than a few seemingly intelligent people were buying into Constanzo's magical worldview, and at a very heavy price. Some paid huge amounts of money for his services. Just because these ideas may seem crazy to you does not mean that the practitioners or their clients were mentally deficient. They might have been evil as hell, but that doesn't necessarily mean they were stupid.

"The Satanists we're after may be every bit as evil as the Constanzo cult, but they aren't dumb. Their crime was well planned and organized, they went to great effort to prepare the ritual space, they executed a detailed and precise ritual, they coldly and effeciently cleaned up, and they disguised the crime scene. They purposely left the results of their work where it was bound to be discovered as an integral part of their ritual. They are flaunting their work at us, or they desire to manifest something that will exist publicly, out in the open. These are not deeply disturbed people crying out to be caught. They may definitely be deeply disturbed, but their precision indicates they have no conscious or unconscious desire to be punished. These are people practicing black magic, who seemingly worship the Christian Devil, or at the very least utilize satanic symbology, and they are deviously intelligent, ruthless, brutal, and efficient."

***

Tonya waited in the van while Bobby ran into the Waffle House. Since they had all eaten breakfast on the way out, she didn't know what the deal was. After a few minutes, Bobby came back and George ordered her to take his seat while he got in the back and played around with the food and Pugsley's uniform. He told her, "You're bringing back breakfast for you and your playmate. You took his clothes because you didn't want him to be seen by anyone, you didn't want to take the risk of him leaving the room and blowing your gig as a rich wife. You put ketchup on both of your hashbrowns. Carrying them back, you spilled some ketchup on his uniform. Got it?"

Tonya said yes real quick, George was beginning to have that dangerous look on his face again. "No problem, baby, just the way you say. I've done everything perfect, everything. Whatever's going on, I've been perfect, and I have absolutely zero curiosity. All you gotta do is tell me what to do, and it's done. No problem." She smiled, he looked cool again, and in a few minutes she'd be back in the room, and back in control, where she belonged.

***

"We are going to look at the four faces of the current satanic phenomenon. But before we look at Satanism in the present, we're going to look at in the past. Let's look at the history of the devil.

"Numerically speaking, most of us raised in modern Western culture get our ideas about God and the Universe from our Judeo-Christian predecessors. With those ideas we also inherited the devil. Some say that Satan is an archetype in the human unconscious - a remnant of our psychological evolution - the child of fear, fear being innate in all of us. Some simply say Satan is a personification of evil. However true these statements may be, Satanism as a religion or magical practice is the child of Christian repression. **Satanism is the child of Christian repression.**

"Look at the seven deadly sins: greed, pride, envy, anger, gluttony, lust, and sloth - laziness. They may not the best aspect of human behavior but they are certainly human. As the Christian church evolved, the growing emphasis on self-denial widened the normal gap between what is conscious and unconscious in a human, between the conscious mind and the unconscious being - our instinctive nature, our animal self. When people are told that the devil is found in the seven deadly sins, and they are all so very human, then people think the devil tends to remind them of themselves. **By making sex and lust and anger and so much of what is natural sinful,**

Christianity created great problems for itself. Problems not found in cultures and religions more careful about their social definitions of evil. Satanism is the child of Christian repression.

"Satan or his equivalent appears in monotheisms as the negative balance for a positive, all-good God. If God is all good, then a devil becomes necessary to explain the harsh realities facing humanity.

"Satan, as we know him today, began to make his appearance in the sixth century B.C. In 586 B.C. Nebuchadnezzar conquered Jerusalem and deported the Hebrews to Babylon (Iraq) where they worked as slaves. Three years later Cyrus the Great of Persia (Iran) conquered Babylon and gave the Jews a privileged status in the new social order. The bold action of the Persians putting the Hebrews in postions of authority over their previous masters caused the Jews to become more open, receptive and positively inclined toward Persian ideas. It is at this point that the Satan of the Old Testament undergoes a revision.

"Up until this point in Judaism, Satan was not a clearly described or important figure. Before this intertestmental period - the period after the Old Testament was established but before the Christ event - there was no myth of Lucifer rebelling against God, and falling from grace to become Satan. Satan is originally best translated as accuser, adversary. In the Judaic beliefs of the time he was an entity whose job was to accuse men before God, describe their wrongdoing, and bring about their punishment under the auspices of God - he was God's District Attorney. Scholars speculate that at this time Satan may have been considered figurative, not thought of as a specific entity at all.

"We have already touched on the idea of man as a microcosm and the universe as the macrocosm. Early Judaism taught that in both, the duality of good and evil is reflected. The early Jews thought of the inclination toward good as Yetzer Tob and the inclination toward evil as

Yetzer ha-Rah and saw these principles in both man and the universe. In early Hebrew thought Satan may have been the symbolic externalization of Yetzer ha-Rah and not thought of as a concrete entity. All of this changed dramatically with the Persian contact of 583 B.C.

"Persia's influence was not limited to Judaism. From the 700's B.C. until the Moslem conquest of 652 A.D., the religion of Persia, Zoroastrianism, spread with the Persian Empire. Today's India still has a large and active Zoroastrian community. With Zoroastrianism spread a doctrine of ethical dualism. Their religion depicts an eternal battle between good and evil. Ahura Mazda, the Principle of Light fights Angra Mainyu, the Principle of Darkness and source of all evil. This eternal fight continues until the end of time and the final Judgement, when Light triumphs. The universe, earth, and humanity were made by Ahura Mazda to ensnare and defeat Angra Mainyu. So man and Nature were created as traps by the Light to capture and defeat the Darkness.

"In preparation for the ongoing battle between Light and Darkness, both spirits created subsidiary spirits to help in the fight. Both sets of spirits were organized into vast military organizations, with a chain of command as in any military hierarchy. This concept of one evil being commanding an army of evil spirits - a vast demonic military hierarchy - had a tremendous impact on Judaic, Christian, and Islamic cosmologies. After the intertestmental period's Persian contact Hebrew literature underwent fundamental changes. Sheol, once a place of eternal sleep and peace became Hell, a place of damnation and punishment of the wicked. Satan became identified with the devil, the originator of all evil and the author of death. The serpent that tempted Eve in the Garden was then seen to be the devil in disguise. All of this is in total contrast to the original picture of God as presented in Isaiah, where God declares himself responsible for good and for evil, for life and for death. That original vision had changed to a highly evolved and complex Judaic angelology/demonology which conceived of Satan as an archfiend who headed up a formalized hierarchy, a demonic army attempting to defeat and overthrow the heavenly forces.

"This new outlook produced images of these demons of Satan consorting with humans to produce nonhuman offspring. The blood sucking she-demon Lilith preyed on man, as did her consort Samael, the Angel of Death, who would cut men down and carry them off to hell. It was this Satan and these demons that modern Judeo-Christianity inherited, lastingly changed from the original by the Persian contact of the intertestamental period. The entire New Testament *presupposes* the myth of the rebellious fallen Lucifer - whose name means the bearer of light, after the fall also called Satan, leading his spiritual rebellion against God, seeking new souls for his anti-kingdom in his war against the kingdom of God.

"Through this historical process the original Satan, the angel of accusation and Lucifer the light-bearer, the shining one, became the devil of the New Testament: the one today's Christians recognize, the evil one, the ruler of this (physical) world, the destroyer, the enemy, the murderer from the beginning, a liar and the father of lies. But this was not to be his final transformation, as time moved on and Christianity gained power in Europe, Satan grew horns."

***

Kevin was at the pay phone wondering what the fuck was going on. He was sweating before noon. It was a warm summer day, but it wasn't that damned hot. He was mentally willing Gary to answer. "Come on fatboy, pick up the fucking phone." Finally, after it had rung for what seemed like several minutes, the less than genius sounding voice of Gary came on the phone.

"'Ello."

"Gary, what the fuck is a detective car doing in front of your place. Are the pigs in there now?"

"Nope, nobody's here. Juz' woke up. Whazup?"

"Whazup is I thought you were get'n busted. Maybe they're staking you out. Look out your window, see if there's a pig sitting in the car now, there wasn't when I drove by a few minutes ago." Kevin waited impatiently, he could hear fatboy shuffling slowly across the room.

"No, thuh only car out there's my new car, 'n nobody's sittin' 'n it."

"Your new car, when the hell did you get a new car, a fucking detective car, no less?" Kevin asked in complete amazement.

"Thuh othur day. I thought maybe you knew somethin' 'bout it."

"No fucking way, man, I'm on my way over."

***

"The concept of Satan didn't change much while Christianity was in its infancy and fighting for survival. Christianity went through a series of persecutions up until 383 A.D., when it became the official religion of the Roman Empire. Up until 800 A.D. the attention of the church was still on survival, dealing with the external threats of the Teutonic hordes and then the Moslems. During the fifth century Saint Augustine wrote *City of God*, which among other things, put forth his concept of Satan and evil. He described legions of demons and the powers they exerted over humanity. But Augustine saw evil not as a creation of the devil, but created by God to separate the elect from the damned. Once more Satan was cast as the instigator and prompter of sin. But this view was not to dominate church thinking for long.

"As the church gained power and its influence spread across Europe, it absorbed and incorporated some pagan elements that were actually in conflict with orthodox Christianity.

Although the pagan pantheons - Norse, Gualic, Celtic - had different names for their gods and goddesses, there were great similarities among the various pantheons, including their holidays and celebrations.

"The original pre-Christian religions of Europe had various gods of fertility and many horned dieities. In Greece there were the bloody rites of Dionysus, a goat god of vegetation, and there was Priapus, who had the horns of a goat, a huge phallus, a god of the fields, bees, and sheep, and there was Pan, the god of the forests. In Egypt there had been the cult of Osiris, a god of vegetation, regeneration, fertility, and trees, and in Celtic Wales and Scotland were the remains of Druidism, and the craft of the Wise, the Wiccans, who had a mother goddess with a horned consort. The northern Teutonic peoples had their war gods, Thor and Odin, and the evil Loki, all of whom wore horned helmets. In Scandinavia there was Freyja, the May queen, the northern counterpart of Diana, a goddess of spring, of renewal, who wore antlers.

"In the original religions and myths of Europe the woods and glades were thought to be populated by nymphs, goatlike satyrs, and nature spirits. Horned fertility deities were originally found in all parts of Europe, however these horned deities were destined to be transformed by the church into the Christian Satan, who in the New Testament is called the ruler of *this* world.

"As Christianity was spread militarily across Europe, the initial attempts at converting the people to Christianity were often superficial. Charlemagne, to speed up the mass conversions of those he conquered, would drive the Saxons through a river, blessed upstream by a bishop. Such forced mass conversions were obviously not that meaningful to the coerced, who quickly reverted back to their old gods. The pagans of Europe may have found Christianity too foreign, being a product of the distant Middle East, or too unattuned to Nature, or possibly too simplistic, ignoring or rendering non-existent so much in which they believed.

"When the initial attempts at conversion were not as successful as desired, the church began to absorb and incorporate elements of the older religions it was replacing. This made the transition from one to the other easier for the conquered. Christian holidays were set on the same dates as the pagan holidays, and absorbed much from their predecessors. Many pagan deities were transformed by the church into Christian saints. Elements of pagan rituals and ceremonies sometimes found their way into the Christian services and in church artwork. An example of this can be found as late as 1282, when a priest was discovered leading a fertility dance on Easter.

"From the 500's on, pagan Europe became Christian, either through military conquest or through the conversion of the pagan kings. Thus Christianity spread from the ruling class downward on the social spectrum, sometimes very slowly. Even where genuine conversions of the populace were thought to have occurred, the peasantry frequently reverted back to their pre-christian traditional religion. The church, having a problem understanding why its grip on their converts was so tenuous, came upon the devil as a logical solution. There is an old saying that the gods of a conquered people become the devils of the conquerors. No clearer example of this can be found than in Christianity's conquest of Europe.

"Between 800 and 1100 there were several cases of women being burned as witches, but that was insignificant compared to what was yet to come, 'the burning times.' At the start of the twelfth century, Rome began to take a much harder line against those practicing the old ways, due to two factors. The first was the general populaces' persistent resistance to Christian conversion, the second was that attitudes within the church itself underwent drastic changes.

"As the church evolved, the influence of the disciple Peter, the rock upon which Christ said he would build his church, was eclipsed by the influence of Saul/Paul, a man who never met Jesus while he was alive, a religious zealot and persecutor of Christians. He was supposedly blinded by a vision of Jesus on the road to Damascus. When the blindness was removed, he became Christianity's number one zealot. Historians and scholars have debated whether or not Paul was a latent homosexual, and argued over the reason for his despising, contemptuous, and hateful attitude toward women. Whether or not you agree with this image of Saint Paul as a homosexual woman-hater, his influence was undoubtedly to have a truly perverse influence on the church.

"During the 1100's the Pauline influence resulted in two lasting, some would say diastrous changes in the Catholic Church. The first was the church splintering off into various sects dedicated to the principles of asceticism. These ascetics thought concern for bodily comfort was a distraction from the true means of attaining spiritual salvation. This earthly life was considered to be nothing but a preparation for the next spiritual life. Some of these ascetics denied the flesh by tormenting it, which openroke wide open ed the flood gates of perversion. They would inflict lacerations on themselves, and then keep the cuts from healing. They practiced flagellation and other self abuses.

"The religious heroes of the time were people like Saint Simon Stylites who lived his life in a pigsty, outside of which he would only stand on one leg, and Saint Anthony, who took delight in tormenting himself with sexual fantasies. The pious conducted holier than thou contests to see who could inflict the most self-abuse, to see how much pain they could endure, or how many lice they could grow in their hair.

"These ascetics expounded what can only be percieved as an extremely negative and pessimistic view of life. They considered the world with all its natural beauty to be created and maintained as a living hell which sole purpose was to prepare man for his heavenly existence.

They hated Nature as a whole and the human body, its comforts and pleasures, specifically. This craze within the church caught on in a big way and monastical orders popped up all over Europe.

"Paul's misogynistic attitude toward women as a whole, and his belief in the hinderance of the male/female relationship to Christian spiritual development, caught on with the clergy and celibacy became a way of life in the Catholic priesthood, the second lasting legacy of Paul. The Christian faiths around the world that allow or encourage their clerics to marry don't have the child sexual abuse/pedophile problems so rampant in the Catholic Church.

"As the church adopted celibacy the attitudes of the priests themselves changed. All of Nature was perceived as vile and corrupt and the material world was seen as nothing but the devil's trap for ensnaring man. All material pleasures were suspected as evil traps, drawing those tempted away from preparing for the spiritual afterlife. Sex was supposed to be only for procreation by those who were married. One book from this period even warned against the joys of gardening.

"Not everyone in the church could, or even wanted to live up to these ideals of asceticism. The iniquities of church administrators and of many priests were well known, the hypocrisy and corruption was often apparent and flagrant. Priests were constantly seducing the females of their own laities and some of the convents were rumored to be hotbeds of vice.

"In the social and economic system of the time the peasants were the *property* of their feudal lords. They were taxed, and subject to military foraging raids, in which the soldiers took food and sometimes women. The feudal lords, if they wanted to, could take the first fruits of any serf's marriage, i.e., sleep with the bride first, unless the peasant could make a large payment instead, which was always beyond their means. The church was a de facto part of the aristocracy. The church maintained that this social order was ordained by God, and if God wanted it changed,

He would. When the religion forced upon the peasants embraced their oppressors, it's not surprising that the church was not as loved and respected as the clergy desired. When peasant rebellions occurred, the military, with the church's blessing, would ruthlessly crush them. It is only natural that the peasants would turn away in their hearts from the corrupt nobility and the often corrupt clergy, both of whom could be seen as enemies of the common man.

"Not all the nobles were thrilled with the system either. New ideas were being brought back to Europe by the crusaders. The Knights Templars, the warrior priests of God, embraced chastity and poverty in a clear reaction to the corruption rampant in the church. The church began to have outside competition for the people's beliefs as the crusades were coming to an end. What they considered heresies were taking hold, the Gnostics, the Manichaeans, the Albigenses, and the Cathari were reactions to the corruption so rampant in the church. By the end of the 1200's as the crusades were ending, Christianity was rotting away from the inside due to its own corruption.

"The church, seeking to destroy its perceived enemies, responded with Papal Bulls decrying the heresies. The pope created the Holy Office of the Inquisition, and the church moved militarily against the heretics. In 1312, the Knights Templar were declared heretics and proclaimed an illegal order. Many Templars were tortured until they confessed as instructed. The seeds of modern Satanism were planted by these church sanctioned sadists, whose perverse imaginations invented sins against the church to which the 'heretics' would then confess, the only way they could stop the torture. With the application of endless torture, confessions of the most bizare nature were obtained. The church's and king's coffers were filled with possessions seized from these heretics. Wars were thus paid for.

"In 1275, In Toulouse, France a woman was burned, not for heresy, but for witchcraft. By the early 1300's most of the heresies had been wiped out, the heretics killed off, their property confiscated. The church fathers, intoxicated by blood, power, and money, looked for new victims. This left the peasants with their pantheons of nature deities open to attack.

"Most people don't realize that Adolf Hitler carried out the second holocaust during World War II, the Catholic church carried out the first. Pope Innocent VIII put out a Papal Bull in 1484 for witch prosecutions. In 1485, two Dominican Inquisitors put out a manual, *Malleus Maleficarium*, for inquisitors and witch hunters, which was widely used for two hundred years. The Bloodbath was on. Anyone who was different, any woman who was powerful, anyone who had something to be envied could easily and legally be burned as a witch. Europe's first holocaust was church sanctioned carnage without precedent.

"This church-sponsored insanity may be hard for us to grasp, but the numbers speak for themselves. From 1120 until 1741, *90 domestic animals* were tried for murder and witchcraft. That's right, 90 animals tried for witchcraft. The high end estimates for human casualties run between 7 to 9 million victims. Witch burnings were entertainment for the masses. The church got richer, women were kept down, and in the minds of the clergy, all the old religions were now satanic religions. Satan had shed his snakeskin and grown the horns of a goat."

***

"What the fuck do you mean you can't tell me?" Kevin was in Gary's face, screaming his head off in Gary's living room. "I'm your friend and your high priest. You better fuckin' tell me right now, what tha hell is goin' on?"

Gary was aware of the fact he was was no rocket scientist, no brain surgeon, no rocket surgeon, he wasn't even very bright for a nightclub bouncer, but he knew whoever his covert employers were, they had resources, and he had accepted their conditions for employment, one of which was absolute secrecy. He was also aware he wasn't even hired yet, one of the notes said his employment was conditional on how well he did during his probationary period. Besides that, it was Kevin himself who had taught him the four corners of the witches' pyramid: to know, to dare, to will, to be silent - to not talk about a spell until what was asked for was manifested on the material physical plane.

And if it was the CIA or the Mafia, or somebody like that, his house could be easily be bugged. He hadn't thought about that before, he hadn't needed to. But somebody could be listening to every word being said. He put his forefinger to his lips for silence. That just pissed off Kevin even more.

***

"Most of our ideas about Satanism come from the pervertred imagination of the Inquisition's sadistic torturers, combined with what little they knew, or their misconceptions about the old fertility religions of Europe. In fact, if Satanism can be considered as a real religion, which I personally doubt, it would be one of the first religions to come to us almost purely from fiction. Some experts even refer to Satanism as a literary creation. The initial fiction came from the imaginations of the perverted, torture-loving, sadistic Inquisitors who told their victims exactly what to confess. These fabricated confessions were promulgated by church propagandists, and over time absorbed into folklore, and were later embellished upon by fiction writers. Five hundred years after the creation of Satanism in France, it publicly reappeared in the U.S., with the publication of a single book in 1980. But we'll get back to that later.

"There was one small sect that was somewhat a predecessor of Satanism. It was one of the heresies during the 1200's called the Luciferans, who said that Lucifer, the bringer of Light, was the true God, and that the Christian god was an evil god who had tricked the world into believing in him. This heresy was wiped out, and was not really Satanism, because the

Luciferans looked at the corrupt church, thought it truly was evil incarnate, and searched for an alternative god, a good God. Supposedly, Satanists do not believe that Satan is a god of love and goodness. However, the church sponsored rumors, and the folklore they engendered about the Luciferans may have contributed to the supposed Satanism that surfaced in France in the 1600's, that associated with the infamous Black Mass."

***

Stewart, alias Pugsley, had woken up during a deep sleep with a tremendous pee buzz, he barely made it to the bathroom in time to relieve his bladder. It was only after he relieved himself and went back to bed that he noticed Raquel was not there. Since Friday afternoon he had not left the room, just as she had instructed. She'd get takeout for food. He wondered if she was gone for good, without even saying goodbye, but when he looked around he saw her boom box, her CD's, her suitcase, and her clothes lying around. It was at that point that he noticed none of his clothes were present. This he could not figure out.

He had seen enough movies and had heard enough stories to know that sometimes guys got rolled, they'd wake up and their money's gone. But he didn't have much money in his wallet, and what she had left in the room was worth more than his cash. She was married to a rich guy, so that wouldn't make sense, anyway. He sat down at the chair by the window, stark naked, looked out and saw her car in the same place. He was groggy, couldn't seem to wake up, but he knew things didn't make much sense.

So he sat there, looking out between the curtains, waiting for Raquel and his clothes to return. Things were weird enough for him to adjust the curtains, so there was just a big enough crack for him to look out, without much chance of anybody seeing him. There he waited, what other choice did he have?

Chapter Six – Sunday Morning/Afternoon

"With the Black Mass we have reached what some experts call classical Satanism. This is a perversion of the Catholic Mass, or more technically, an inversion of the Catholic Mass. The Black Mass of literature, which may have occurred in actuality, is a form of black magic and ritual rebellion. The Black Mass of literature and what is termed classical Satanism is thought to contain some or most of the following:

- The Catholic missal is read backwards, or more commonly, the words Satan and evil are substituted for the words God and good.

- The altar is the body of a naked woman.

- The ritual chamber is black, all religious paraphernalia is black, and the practitioners wear black robes with cowls.

- The wine is stolen from a church, or may, suppossedly be replaced with human blood, or urine. The host may be stolen from a church, or suppossedly, substituted for with feces, or the skin of a sacrificed victim. However, the use of urine, feces, or skin may only be a creation of literature, promulgated in urban legend.

- "The Lord's Prayer may be said backwards.

- The participants (all but sacrificial victims) must come of their own free will.

- They may make a disavowal of the Christian faith, they may be rebaptized in the name of Satan.

- The priest who officiates may be a defrocked or apostate priest.

"Some say the Black Mass just described *is nothing* but a literary creation with no basis in reality, combining the dubious confessions of the tortured victims of the Inquisition, the resulting church propaganda, and the imagination of the writers of novels like the perverted de Sade's *Justine* released in 1791, or the 1800's novel *La`Bas*. Whatever the origin, one form of the Black

Mass became a fatal reality. However, the Black Mass documented in French history is **not** the classical satanic service described by literature, but is more a black magic usurption of the Christian Mass.

"We have already looked at two modern magicians who tread of the path of black magic, Aleister Crowley and Aldolfo Constanzo; now we will look at the magical tradition within and outside of the Catholic Church to find the history of the Black Mass and the trail that leads to modern satanic phenomenon. The Catholic Church has a long history of which magic is an undeniable part.

First, it is important to understand that the efficacy of magic was widely believed among the clergy until modern times. Pope Gregory IX forbid sorcery by priests. Many high officials within the church were thought to be practitioners of the black arts. Pope Sylvester II was said to be a sorcerer and was accused of obtaining the papacy by magic. Pope Honorius III was rumored to be a black magician and a famous magical text was named in his honor or falsely attributed to him to make it more successful. In 681 A.D., the Council of Toledo forbade priests from saying the Mass of the Dead. The Mass of the Dead was a Mass said for someone who was living as though they were dead, for the purpose of magically ending their life. The church continually denounced this ritual for hundreds of years, but it was still being practiced one thousand years later.

"What we must understand is that to the people of the Dark and Middle Ages **the Mass was considered to be the ultimate magical ritual.** The power invoked by an ordained priest in the Mass was thought to be *automatic*, and could be manipulated, used or abused like any other natural force. This outpouring of energy was considered blind - not dependent on the morality or intention of the priest - thus it could be redirected magically to work for *any* chosen purpose, as the priest directed.

"By the 1500's, sorcery was so widespread in the church it became necessary to separate heretical from nonheretical sorcery. A long list of canons forbade the use of the sacraments or holy objects in magical rituals. Divination using holy water or blessed candles was forbidden. However, the church ruled that sorcery done by priests who used only profane objects did not come under the jurisdiction of the Inquisition.

"During the Renaissance, along with the breakdown of the feudal system and the growth of the mercantile class, it became accepted that personal and family Masses could be performed *for fees*. The lower ranking priests had become envious of their richer superiors and welcomed this outside source of income. 'Mass priests' filled this new need, with priests serving an individual's or family's needs for an annual tribute. Some of these Mass priests had questionable ethics and were a little too wild or unorthodox for the church and were excommunicated. It was from this body of Mass priests, especially those who were excommunicated, that the historical Black Mass emerged.

"One of the best and most thoroughly documented cases of a Black Mass comes from France during the reign of Louis XIV, arising from the famous '*Affaire des Poisons*.' This was not initially an investigation dealing with religion or magic, but murder. The witch hunt hysteria of 'the burning times' had ended in France by the 1670's, but profound belief in the occult sciences and magic was widespread.

"The court at Versailles was magnificent, the nobility and aristocrats wealthy. The needs and vices of this spoiled collection of opulence were met by swarms of hanger-ons who thus found employment. Among those who served the pampered rich, were apothecaries who made more than medicine: cosmetics, love potions, and poisons. There were also the sybils: the fortune tellers, card readers, palmists, astrologers, and clairvoyants. And there were the midwives, some of whom, for an extra fee, also performed abortions or infanticides. These were known as 'makers of angels.' This slang term came from an assumption of the times that if a baby was baptized and killed immediately, it would be sinless and go directly to be with God in Heaven. It was a corrupt and credulous time.

"In 1678, a lawyer reported to the Paris police a confession of crime he had overheard at a party, where a sybil was bragging about her clients in the nobility, and how after three more poisonings she could retire. The wife of a policeman was sent undercover to the sybil with instructions to complain vociferously about her husband. On her second visit she was sold a vial of poison. Arrests followed, but the investigation revealed they had only scratched the surface of a massive illegal undertaking - one which reaped illicit profits gained by providing paying customers with:

- abortions or infanticides by the midwives,

- poisons from the sybils,

- and in the extreme cases, ritual magic ceremonies performed by renegade priests.

"Police lieutenant Nicolas de La Reynie launched an investigation which resulted in a scandal reaching all the way to the throne of France. Reynie initially arrested only small fry, but he soon found out who was at the top of this huge pyramid of crime, a woman known as La Voisin. She was Catherine Monvoisin, a sybil who served the elite of Paris, who was considered an adept at reading the future from cards, palms, or astrology. She was so well known that in 1664 she had been issued an invitation and debated the case for astrology at the Sorbonne. She

had one husband, many servants, many lovers, and was running a 'murder incorporated' -
overseeing a widespread trade in poisons, abortions, and infanticides of unwanted infants.

Reynie's investigation led the King and his ministers to establish a royal commission, the Chambre Ardente, to investigate. La Voisin was arrested, her house searched, where they found an abortion chamber, and an adjoining furnace to dispose of bodies. On the grounds they found skeletal remains buried all over. She confessed, without being tortured, to many crimes: she had performed multitudes of abortions, often sold poisons, and estimated she had committed around 2,500 cases of infanticide. She was tried and executed in 1680.

"Besides all the buried skeletal remains on the grounds, the police also discovered what turned out to be a Black Mass pavilion. The walls were hung with black, behind the altar was a black curtain with a white cross, the altar cloth was black and concealed a mattress under it. On the altar was a tabernacle surmounted by a cross. All the candles were black. However, there were no symbols of Satan, it was a chapel designed for utilizing the Christian Mass for the purposes of black magic.

"After her mother's execution, Marguerite Monvoisin talked freely with the investigators about her mother's activities. She confirmed the disturbing stories others had told Reynie, and he dutifully went to the king, who upon hearing the evidence, temporarily suspended the Chambre Ardente by royal decree. The king's one time mistress, a woman who was his lover for twelve years, with whom he had fathered seven children, was said to have requested the performance of several Black Masses for the obtaining and preserving of his royal favors.

"The story told by the daughter and corroborated by others was that thirteen years earlier the Marquise de Montespan was envious of the king's mistress, and wanted to replace the queen. In 1667 she reached out to La Voisin for help in obtaining her goals through the use of sorcery.

La Voisin introduced her to a man, Lesage, and a priest, Abbe' Mariette, who would perform ritual magic for a fee.

"They performed a magical ritual for her three times, but it was not a Black Mass. Mariette in his vestments would perform before an altar, Lesage would assist, while the Marquise would kneel before the altar. Lesage chanted the "Veni Creator," then the priest read "L'evangile" over her, and then she recited a conjuration of what she wanted.

"She desired the queen to be barren, she wanted the king's mistress to lose favor, and she wanted to replace the mistress, and have her and her family in the king's good graces, and to eventually replace the queen. For the third ritual, in early 1668, she brought the two magicians to the Royal Court and had them do the ceremony in her sister's room.

"She didn't get everything she asked for, but she did replace the king's mistress. Her husband objected to no avail, and was ridiculed on the streets and at the theater. He was exiled to Spain. The Marquise was given a chateau and moved into the palace, and was given twice as many rooms as the queen. She ascended to such a position of power and influence she was referred to as the 'Queen of the Left Hand.'

"In 1669 she gave birth to the first of her seven children fathered by the king. Her position of power was stable for three years, but then the king roved in his affections and made her jealous. Her social empire was threatened. For fifteen days she would not see anyone, then she sent for La Voisin. Lesage and Mariette had been jailed for sacrilege and were gone, but La Voisin said she had somebody darker in magic, who did more powerful ceremonies.

"The Marquise met Abbe' Guibourg, who was a sixty-seven year old priest who held many benefices in and around Paris which provided him with a good yearly income. He had a reputation in the occult underworld as a black magician and was the father of several children with his mistress, some of whom, according to rumor, he had ritually sacrificed.

"In one of the most famous historical magical texts, 'The Key of Solomon' there are instructions for magicians that when working with demons, in certain instances, animals should be sacrificed. It suggests animals which are virgins, white animals for demons providing good things, and black animals for demons bringing harm.

"The priest Guibourg, however, preferred to sacrifice baptized infants. He claimed he was doing the baby a service, sending it sinless to be with God, and at the same time providing demons with the sacrificial blood they demanded, giving them the power to manifest change in the physical world. Guiborg called it a Black Mass. He performed the Christian Mass before the sacrifice, to give him the power to control the demons. He then prayed, sacrificed the baptized baby, supposedly sent its soul to Heaven, then he invoked the demons, offered them the sacrifice, and commanded what he desired. This is the actual and historical Black Mass, the use of the Christian Mass in the performance of black magic.

"For her ceremony in the Black Mass ritual pavilion on La Voisins's grounds, de Montespan lay naked on the altar. Her head was on a pillow, she lay directly in front of the priest, at the center of the altar. A cross was laid between her breasts, her arms were extended straight out, and in her hands she held black candles. The chalice was set between her thighs, and Guibourg stood between her knees.

"He said the Mass, then he prayed for the baby, saying how Christ had suffered the little children to come unto Him, and Guibourg willed that the sacrificial child should also come to Christ. He stated that he was a priest of Christ and by his hand, which the baby should bless, the baby was to incorporate with God. Then he slit the baby's throat over the Marquise. Having sent the infant's soul to God, he then invoked the demons Astaroth and Asmodeus and conjured them to accept the sacrifice which he presented to them, asking them to fulfill the Marquise's demand of receiving the king's affection, and the honor of the court, and that the king would look on her so favorably he would deny her nothing. As it worked out, she did return to the king's good graces for another three years.

"In 1675 the king had a bout of piety and threw her out. She had her allies slip the king love potions blessed by renegade priests. The king once more took her back. But the king not only wanted her back, he was back to his womanizing. She got so jealous, she had Guiborg perform three more Black Masses. The first, she performed with Guibourg at La Voisin's pavilion. The next two were performed for her by Guibourg and La Voisin. The next few years she was at her height of power, but in 1679 the king was taken by a young girl of eighteen.

"The Marquise was outraged and offered a fortune to La Voisin to poison the king and his young lover. La Voisin was arrested while undertaking the task, so the Marquise tried one of her associates. She too was arrested. Her story was heard by the detective Reynie, who went to the king. The king, upon hearing his tale, suspended the Chambre Ardente in October, 1680.

"The king tried to hush the affair up. The Marquise de Montespan never went to prison. She had already lost the king's favor to the eighteen year old before the arrests began, but she was mother to seven of his children. The king put everybody who could testify against the Marquise in jail for life. The results of the royal investigation were that 367 people were arrested, many of whom were priests. Out of the 367 arrested, 74 were sentenced, some of whom died in jail or were burned at the stake. Guibourg died in jail. Between 1673 and 1680 over fifty priests were executed in France for sacrilege. In 1691 the Marquise retired to a convent, where she became repentant in her old age and died in 1707."

I paused and drank some water. "This story just goes to show, once more, that hell knoweth no fury like a woman scorned." I noticed everybody laughed, but the women more than the men. They know, respect, maybe even enjoy the power of their wrath.

***

Stewart didn't have to wait all that long for Raquel. The sun had risen, as he sat drinking a warm coke left over from the night before. He saw a white van stop behind Raquel's car. She got out of the back. He stayed low with the curtains almost shut so he wouldn't be seen. She said something to the two men in the van, and walked towards the door quickly. He dove into the bed as she got the key card out and unlocked the door, and was under the covers by the time she walked in. He looked up like she had woken him up coming in. She smiled and said, "I got us some breakfast Pugsley, time to wake up and eat. You'll need your strength before our last session."

He was hungry from the previous night's exertions, so he sat up and dove into the food, not sure about what he had just seen, and not sure how to ask her about it.

***

"Another well documented case, one with some of the elements of the classical Satanism of literature, comes from England in the eighteenth century. However, many say it was only pseudo-Satanism, or really just orgies with satanic trappings. This may have begun as early as the 1730's, carried out by the infamous Hellfire Clubs. The Hellfire Clubs carried out parodies of Christian religious rites, but they may have just been the excuse for, or provided the atmosphere, for sexual debauchery. What is noteworthy is that the participants came from the upper strata of English society. From 1745 until 1768, the members of the Hellfire Clubs were a significant force in English politics. Among their members were famous poets, politicians, Earls, and the First Lord of the Admiralty.

149

"The Black Mass appeared again in France between 1848 and 1859, associated with two names—Abbe' Boulan and Eugene Vintras, and in the fictional work *La`Bas*. In Rome, an all black seemingly black mass chapel was discovered in 1895, at the Palazzo Borghese. In the 1920's William Seabrook revived the Hellfire Clubs in England. Again sexual debauchery was involved, but the ritual aspect may have been more serious. The requirements for their rituals were said to be an apostate priest, a consecrated host, a prostitute, and a virgin. There are rumors that similar activities are continuing in England today, but the same rumors say that they are really performances for paying tourists.

"Finally, we come to Satanism in America. Everybody is familiar with the Salem witch trials, but there is absolutely no evidence of any satanic activity there. It was more a case of hysteria than anything else. A newer theory is that some involved may have come into contact with a hallucinagenic fungus. There were accusations of Satanism leveled against Freemasons in the U.S. during the late 1800's, but they were unfounded.

"I have mentioned how Aleister Crowely was not a Satanist but how his work influenced them, and how his detractors said he predicted Satan's second coming. Other experts point to his writings which indicate he didn't even believe in Satan. They say that he believed the apocalypse of the Bible was the ending of one astrological age, the Piscean, and the beginning of the next, the Aquarian Age, and that he saw himself as the symbolic Great Beast. Whatever, we must come back to the Crowley saga for the birth of the American satanic phenomenon.

"In 1898, when he was twenty-three, Crowley became a member of the Golden Dawn, an extremely serious magical order in England, which included many famous personalities of English literature and many notable luminaries of occultism who later authored influential books. Among them were W.B. Yeats, MacGregor Mathews, Israel Regardie, and A.E.Waite. In 1904,

Crowley supposedly came into contact with his Holy Guardian Angel, Aiwass, who dictated to him *The Book of the Law*. Its' two leading precepts are: Do what thy will shall be the whole of the Law, Love is the Law, Love under Will, and that every man and every woman is a star. The star here is used to symbolize that every person has their proper course, their path, their natural orbit, just as Nature provides an orbit or path for every star in the heavens. This is a person's True Will, as provided by Nature. Every human conflict indicates that someone is not following the natural course of their orbit, that they are not following their True Will. Crowley thought that the way to discern one's True Will was to come into contact with one's own Holy Guardian Angel. Of course, for this purpose he recommended his own system of Magick.

"In 1912 Crowley joined the Ordo Templi Orientis, a magical order started by German occultist Karl Kellner. With his ritual ability and vast occult knowledge, Crowley became the head O.T.O. member in the English chapter. In 1920 he gathered some of his followers and went to Sicily and started the Abbey of Thelema (will), where they experimented with sexual magic, drugs, animal sacrifice, the rites of Dionysus, and even ritual bestiality. They were expelled by Mussolini when a cult member unknowingly sacrificed and consumed the blood of a distempered cat, and resultingly died. Crowley went through a decline, and in 1947, he died an impoverished drug addict. His books are still in print and sold all over the world.

"Among the several O.T.O. chapters that survived Crowley's decline was a U.S. chapter. Jack Parsons of Pasadena, California, a rocket propulsion engineer, was a member. In 1946, Parsons and L. Ron Hubbard, author of *Dianetics* and the father of Scientology, undertook a three day ritual attempting to bring down the 'Whore of Babalon' (their spelling) from the astral plane into incarnation. Parsons and his girlfriend had ritual sex repeatedly for three days, while Hubbard acted as a scribe. The woman, however, did not get pregnant. L. Ron Hubbard took off with ten thousand dollars of Parsons' money and his girlfriend. Parsons later caught up with Hubbard and recovered some of the money. In 1952, Parsons blew himself up experimenting at home. Parsons' mother killed herself two hours later. Satanists make much of the fact that the counter-culture and the Church of Satan were coming into existence thirteen years later.

"From 1963 to 1966, Mary Anne and Robert De Grimston were founding the Process Church of the Final Judgement, as they broke off from Scientology. The Process Church linked Christ and Satan together, and supposedly reversed the fifth commandment to "thou shalt kill." Charles Manson is said to have been influenced by the Process Church, and according to one author, so was the 'Son of Sam' killer, David Berkowitz.

"In 1966, Anton Szandor LaVey founded the Church of Satan in San Francisco. LaVey acted as a technical consultant for the movie *Rosemary's Baby*. The director of that movie was Roman Polanski, whose pregnant wife, Sharon Tate, was singled out for murder by Charles Manson. As to how or if all that ties in together, who knows.

"LaVey's Church of Satan claimed protection under the first amendment. They also claim they do not engage in any illegal activities. LaVey is the author of *The Satanic Bible* which came out in 1969. LaVey claimed that the more objectionable parts of his bible were meant to be taken as metaphors and he was not responsible for the actions of those who took them literally.

"LaVey grew up working in a side show/carnival atmosphere. He was repulsed by the hypocrisy evident in the many Christians he would see lusting after women on Saturday night and then being repentant on Sunday morning. Claiming to be a student of magic and a practitioner of the black arts throughout his life, he proudly treaded the left hand path of black magic. However, he did not embrace the classical Satanism of literature or that presented by religious propagandists.

"To him, Satanists are flesh-worshipers practicing a blatantly selfish religion. It is based on the belief that man is an inherently selfish and violent creature who is involved in the Darwinian struggle of survival of the fittest. LaVey put forth nine satanic statements which explained what (to him) Satan represents: indulgence instead of abstinence, vital existence instead of spiritual fantasy, wisdom instead of hypocrisy, kindness only to the deserving, vengeance instead of forgiveness, responsibility to the responsible, and that man is Nature's most vicious animal. Satan represents all the sins that lead to physical, mental, or emotional gratification, and according to LaVey is the Christian church's best friend, having kept it in business.

"LaVey's rituals in the *Satanic Bible* are not inversions of Christian rituals. To him such parodies are useful only as psychodramas. However, he did mock Christianity, saying that right and wrong and good and evil have been inverted by false prophets. He refered to Christ as impotent and mad, the true prince of evil - the king of the slaves. He claimed that no redeemer liveth, that there is no heavenly glory or hell filled with sinners, and that the here and now *is* our day of torment or our day of joy. God, by whatever name, was seen by LaVey as the balancing factor in Nature, a powerful force which permeates and balances the universe, but is impersonal and unconcerned with individual human existence. The causations of man and the actions and reactions of the universe are responsible for everything that occurs concerning humanity.

"LaVey's Satanism is as much, if not more, a practice of satanic ritual magic than a religion. He claimed that Satanism is not a religion of White-Light, instead it is a religion of the flesh, of the mundane, the carnal. A religion, he claimed, based on the universal traits of man. Satan is the personification of the left hand path, the use of power to serve the self, the aggrandizement of the human ego.

"LaVey taught Satan is not inherently evil, he has just been cast in that role for representing the carnal aspects of life, representing the same carnal side of human nature as did Pan and Dionysus. In LaVey's magical practices, they do not invoke demons, but invoke the devil, the various devils of human history, the gods and goddesses of hell, using their many infernal names found throughout the history of the planet. There is no selling of the soul, no pact with the devil, which he considered to be another invention of the church. He stated that most Satanists *do not believe* in an anthropomorphic being called Satan, but that Satan represents the forces of nature, the powers of darkness, and those aspects of human nature which have been left in the darkness by the White-Light religions.

"LaVey had interesting thoughts concerning ritual sacrifice. Traditionally the supposed purpose of a magical ritual sacrifice is to release the energy provided by the blood into the atmosphere of the magical working, providing more power and thus a greater chance of success. Contrary to that theory, LaVey claimed the energy in such sacrifices comes not from the blood but is a discharge of bioelectrical energy produced by the death throes of any living creature. Such a discharge of energy is the same bioelectrical phenomenon as that produced during any heightening of human emotions such as sexual orgasm, intense anger, terror, or grief. No Satanist would sacrifice an animal or child, he said, because they are pure forms of carnal existence and held as sacred. He said that Satanists will perform a human sacrifice, but that it is symbolic. Symbolically, ritually, the victim is destroyed by a hex which in turn is supposed to cause the physical, mental, or emotional destruction of the sacrifice/victim in ways not directly or legally attributable to the magician.

"The Satanism LeVey espoused does not express belief in reincarnation or the traditional Heaven and Hell, but talks vaguely about a strong ego being able to last past physical death and peek through the curtain of darkness to remain earthbound. Suicide, except as euthanasia, is frowned upon. Their holidays, as well as much of their ritual paraphernalia, seem to be borrowed from the pre-Christian European pagan traditions.

"The Black Mass is not one of LaVey's rituals. He considered it a creation of the Inquisition and fiction writers. LaVey espoused the theory and practice of satanic magic and presented one ritual form with three types of rituals. Ironically, he said that the ritual area, and the form and trappings of the ritual are a form of contrived ignorance; as they are in all religions. The difference for LaVey is that the Satanist knows he is practicing a form of contrived ignorance in order to expand and concentrate the power of his will.

"His satanic ritual chamber will have an altar, behind it a picture of Baphomet, the supposed satanic god of the Knights Templars. (Baphomet and the Goat of Mendes may be used by Satanists as symbolic of Satan, but actually both symbolize the universal life force, the great magical agent, the astral light.) They will also use an inverted pentagram with the head of a goat inside. They will use all black candles except for the altar on which there is a black candle to the left and a white candle to the right. A naked woman lies on the altar. Their magical tools and weapons consists of a bell, a chalice filled with a stimulating beverage, a sword, a phallus or phallic symbol as a wand, a gong, and parchment.

"Satanic magic as practiced by LaVey is an astral or emotional magic. There are three ceremonies: Lust, Compassion, and Destruction. The first to gain love or sex, the second to help or heal, the third to destroy one's enemies. The form of all three rituals is the same. The participants dress for ritual, men in all black, generally in robes with cowls, the older women also wear black and the younger women dress suggestively in black. All wear amulets with an inverted pentagram. Bells are rung to purify the air, Satan is invoked and the list of the infernal names of the devils are read aloud. They drink from the chalice, then turning counter-clockwise call the four biblical princes of Hell: Satan, Lucifer, Belial, and Leviathan. A benediction is performed with the phallus and then the priest reads the appropriate invocation for lust, compassion, or destruction. Then the emotions are heightened, mental imagery, symbolism, and sympathetic magic are employed to spell out what is desired and then psychically sent forward, they hope, to come into manifestation. For a lust ritual, this might include masturbation, for a compassion ritual this might require crying, or for a destruction ritual this might include sticking pins in an effigy of the victim. Requests written on parchment are then read and burned amid flurries of "hail Satan." The appropriate Enochian Key is read, the bell is wrung and the priest says 'so it is done.'

"LaVey didn't consider the Christian rituals of today as being powerful or important enough to be worthy of ritual inversion. Instead, he chose the work of the court astrologer and seer famous in England during the 1500's, John Dee, to provide his magical base. Dee is an excellent historical example of how one of the smartest people of his time could be a serious student of the occult, as well as a leading mind in the fields of mathematics and navigation. He was an adviser to two monarchs and his intellect helped guide England's maritime expansion. He was also the author, or as you might say today, the channel, for forty-eight 'keys' of invocation in a unique magical language.

"These keys or calls are in what Dee called the Enochian language and have been used by magicians like Aleister Crowley since first published in 1659. Dee claimed it was the language spoken by the angels before the biblical flood. LaVey reinstitued the inversion procedure with the Enochian keys, substituting the name Satan for God throughout the Enochian calls. One of LaVey's early disciples, Michael Aquino, broke off and formed the Temple of Set, in order to distance himself from the repudiation of Christ and to establish ties with the Egyptian god Set. However, they would probably still seem fairly satanic to the average American.

"The Church of Satan and LaVey's *Satanic Bible* constitute one of the four aspects of the satanic phenomenon in America today, public Satanism. LaVey is dead now, but his daughter has carried on her father's work and now leads what they call the CoS. The other three aspects are classical Satanism, the lone teenage dabbler in Satanism, and the self-styled Satanist. These four aspects are not separated by hard lines, there is some overlapping. We've gone over what classical Satanism was like in the past, we'll come back later to what it might look like now.

"American cultural interest in the satanic phenomenon peaked during the time of the McMartin and other nursery school witch hunt hysterias, well over a decade ago. These investigations and trials cost several states fortunes for almost (with the exception of one very questionable guilty verdict in Minnesota) universal not guilty verdicts; at least on appeal. It also cost the McMartins and some other victims jail time and the loss of their family businesses. "Taken in the light that the height of cultural interest in the satanic phenomenon has come and gone, and you know longer hear satanic cult survivor tales on Ophrah or outrageous stories of satanic nursery schools in the news, you might think that in 21st century America, Satanism is back to being mostly urban myth. I think that may have very well have been the case, except for the internet. Just like the internet caused an explosion in the number of Nazi/racist hate groups and in child pornograhpy, the internet has been a boon for Satanists. We'll come back to the net as a tool for Satanists later.

"The lone teenage dabbler constitutes the aspect of Satanism we hear about most often. A mental health worker's profile of these people would supposedly go something like this: the individual will be a loner, or have a very small number of friends, who feel powerless and want to have power, they are alienated. They may be into role playing games like *Dungeons and Dragons*, they may listen to the heavy metal music of Ozzy Osbourne, Black Sabbath, Motely Crue, Kiss, or more recent groups following in their black metal footsteps. They will: begin to investigate the dark side of the occult, buy LaVey's *Satanic Bible* and take it literally, possibly order satanic paraphernalia by mail, may experiment with black magic - often involving sexual activity or drug use, and are often prone to suicide and may take part in anti-social activity dressed up as Satanism, such as church or graveyard desecrations.

"It is important for police personnel to remember that historically a small amount of anti-social activity always takes place. Church or graveyard desecration may be anti-social activity, but is not necessarily satanic. And even if it seems accompanied by satanic symbols, it may not truly be satanic.

"In rare cases the lone teenage dabbler may also be a sociopath or a psychopath. If such a lone teenage dabbler in Satanism becomes a self-styled Satanist he may end up like Richard Ramirez, California's infamous 'Night Stalker.'

"The self-styled Satanist, like the Night Stalker, and according to some, the Son of Sam, borrows satanic themes as rationale for his deeply disturbed anti-social activity. The self-styled Satanist general profile would be an indiviual who: comes from a broken home, was abandoned or abused as a child, showed an early propensity for violence, is an outcast shunned by peers, is tormented by his own failures or others successes, and finds in Satanism a rationale for his outlook and actions.

"Having very briefly looked at the four aspects of the satanic phenomenon - classical, public, lone teenage dabbler, and self-styled Satanist, let us look at two perceptions of this phenomenon. Sociologist David Bromley says that if the Satanists represent a subversion

158

ideology, there are a group of people who represent a countersubversion ideology. These are 'the anti-satanists,' who hold a very dark perception of the satanic phenomenon, seeing it as a widespread danger. The people with the alternative perception of the satanic phenomenon are called the 'anti-anti-satanists.' The anti-satanists are the authors of a movement which perceives Satanism as a huge problem. The anti-anti-satanists think the huge problem is in the anti-satanists' own heads. The anti-satanists, at the peak of the phonomenon in the 1980's were made up of three groups of people: therapists, law enforcement personnel, and fundamentalist/ evangelical preachers.

"Hundreds of therapists who worked with patients suffering from MPD, Multiple Personality Disorder, what the layman calls split personalities, had heard similar stories from their patients about being victims of ritual satanic abuse. These therapists claimed these people told their stories with obvious emotional pain, that they told the same stories under hypnosis, that the stories were internally consistent, and that different patients from various locations told similar stories.

"The second group of anti-satanists were law enforcement personnel who had specialized in cult/occult crimes. These came from law enforcement agencies and departments, large and small, from all over the nation. People like crazy Larry, whose function I now fill. Several of these guys made a living for a time on the lecture circuit.

"The third group was and still is the preachers who are convinced Satan is lierally right behind so much of what they see as wrong in our society. To these three groups was added concerned parent groups wherever a satanic panic broke out, as in the McMartin case. These days you no longer see therapists or law enforcement personell in the media validating satanic phenomenon. But there is a hardcore of fundamentalists and fanatics who never let go. On both sides.

"The few remaining anti-satanists, generally speaking, are true believers who are convinced that there is a massive, organized, satanic underground which: practices ritual worship of Satan, sponsors molestation of children at preschools, kidnaps or breeds children for ritual sacrifice and the production of child pornography, is involved in the drug business, tortures animals, and sacrifices humans in a version of the Black Mass, practices mystical cannibalism, and is continually recruiting the young through games like Dungeons and Dragons, and through heavy metal music by groups like Black Sabbath.

"The anti-anti-satanists are comprised of social scientists who are more than skeptical about the anti-satanists' claims and law enforcement personnel who have become disenchanted by their anti-satanist colleagues. And of course, some of those practicing Satanism aren't too thrilled with the anti-satanists.

"It is logical to ask how the anti-satanists came to hold their beliefs in a satanic conspiracy. It all began with what are called 'satanic cult survivor' accounts as they were told to their therapists, predominantly by MPD patients, usually with the aid of hypnosis. This current chapter in the history of Satanism began in 1980 with one book, *Michele Remembers* by Michele Smith and Lawrence Pazder. Prior to this book there were ***absolutely no*** such satanic cult survivor accounts. The book is based on what Michele told her psychiatrist during the course of her psychotherapy, about her experiences growing up in a satanic cult on Vancouver Island during the 1950's. Many of the current images of Satanism held by the American public came from this and similar copycat books which followed. Remember when you hear the term satanic cult survivor to always think alleged, because there is zero proof.

"Also in 1980, Sandi Gallant, a San Francisco policewoman investigating ritual sexual abuse, noticed what she took to be satanic symbols were frequently found at crime scenes. Gallant typed up a brief police manual with six pages of what she considered satanic symbols. This pamphlet made its way across the entire nation, being photocopied and passed on. How many of you have seen this little manual?" Everybody raised their hands.

"Well, it was well-intentioned, but is absolutely full of misinformation, and should be thrown away, and Sandi Gallant would probably be the first person to tell you that. But once it got out, there was no getting it back. I'll go over its' mistakes later. Anyway, between *Michele Remembers* and its copycats, and the Gallant manual, and the sensationalist hype of the media, the American satanic phenomenon was off and running. How many of you have heard the term 'breeder' in relation to satanic crimes?" Again, everybody raised their hands.

"The concept of the breeder, someone who has children to be sacrificed or otherwise used by Satanists, was introduced by Lauren Stafford in her book about her 'experiences' in a satanic cult: *Satan's underground: the Extraordinary Story of One Woman's Escape.* She claimed to have been tortured and said she had the scars to prove it. Even worse, she said she had been a breeder, and had given birth to three children, one of which was ritually sacrificed. She claimed the other two were killed in kiddie porn snuff movies. She must have believed it, because she allowed herself to be medically examined. The results were she had never even been pregnant and the scars were self-inflicted. After the results were made public, the book was withdrawn by its publisher. Yet everyone here knows what a breeder supposedly is, but probably none of you knew the idea came from what would seem to be an obviously ill and self-deluded woman. The book was selling well until the publisher responsibly pulled the plug.

"In 1984, the First International Conference on Multiple Personality/Dissociative States was held. Many therapists at the time were convinced their patients were giving factual portrayals of a sinister phenomenon. By 1985 many Christian bookstores were filled with books and tapes advising how to fight the holy war against Satanism. By then Gallant's manual was omnipresent, and law enforcement, therapists, and ministers were fueling each other's fires. An uneducated media, geared toward sensationalistic stories that pleased the prurient masses, got on board and the train was rolling. Workshops and seminars were held to educate law enforcement personnel. Cult survivors were on shows like *Oprah* and *Geraldo*, and the train kept rolling. The public began to wonder how all these stories could be told if there wasn't something to it. A culture myth, an urban legend was taking hold, representing itself as true. The respectability of the therapists and the law enforcement personnel leant credibility to the uncorroborated cult survivors' books and personal appearances.

"But after a while, the social scientists, some of the law enforcement community, and other people with common sense began to have severe reservations about many of these claims of widespread satanic activity, and rightly so.

"In 1983, the McMartin preschool story broke. The parents went ballistic. They called in the authors of *Michele Remembers* and child psychologists to interrogate the children. The longer the children were interviewed, the wilder the stories got. Eventually they told stories of child abuse, kiddie porn, and of Satanists with black robes performing rituals in secret caves under the school. Within a decade there were 100 similar stories involving preschools across the nation. The satanic panic had hit big time. But it was time for a serious reality check.

"The McMartin preschool trial was the most expensive legal case in U.S. history at the time. Children were interrogated for hundreds of hours. Both sides incurred enormous legal costs. They even brought in earth movers and bull dozers looking for the caves described by the kids in which the rituals were held. But there was a scarcity of evidence, *any* evidence. There were no caves, there were no robes, no kiddie porn, no satanic paraphernalia, there was nothing. After all that money and all that time, there were ultimately no convictions that held up under appeal in the McMartin case. Although the jail time for the older women and the damage to their family and the community can never be taken back.

"In a similar case in Jordan, Minnesota there were 24 arrests, but they at least had one conviction. There are questions as to whether that one conviction was to save local face and embarrassment. But again, despite mass hyteria, there were no satanic trappings. Similar events happened all over this country. Many lives, careers, and reputations were destroyed needlessly. Thank God we have a slow judicial system, and we no longer burn the victims of our witch hunts.

"But in the beginning the anti-anti-satanists were not selling books, sparking prurient interest, getting any media hype, or raising anyone's Nielsen ratings so it took them a while to get their message out and be heard. But they did have some explanations and some facts on their side. They also weren't ruining peoples lives right and left with totally unfounded and outrageous charges. The anti-anti-satanists viewed the anti-satanists as either a curious phenomenon or else as a truly dangerous element in our society. Let's look at their side of the story.

"The first explanation of the anti-anti-satanists was that Satanism had become an culture myth/urban legend. An urban myth/legend is defined as a popular story that spreads swiftly by word of mouth and is accepted as true. Between the satanic cult survivor accounts, the convinced therapists, the talk shows, and the fundamentalist preachers, the word had definitely spread. Let's look at the phenomenon of satanic cult survivor accounts.

"The satanic cult survivors stories were almost always revealed during the process of therapy, usually including hypnosis. Three-fourths of the alleged satanic cult survivors are Multple Personality Disorder patients. The numbers these 'survivors' gave of the Satanists and the people sacrificed by them just did not seem plausible. The anti-anti-satanists theorized that the MPD patients could not discriminate between fact and fantasy and that the personalities, the 'alters' of the MPD, represented a type of self hypnosis. One contention is that the MPD patients are chameleon-like, manipulative personalities that feed the therapist what they think the therapist wants to hear.

"Anthropologist Sherill Mulhern theorized that the therapists constituted a professional subculture that had been inserting the idea of a satanic cult conspiracy into their diagnoses since 1984. She thinks that the patients were not all saying the same thing as much as they were all being heard the same way.

"Police officer and author Robert Hicks states that absolutely *no* police investigation has ever supported any satanic cult survivor allegations. That's thousands, if not millions, of books sold, and appearances seen by millions upon millions on TV, and not one police investigation verifying any of it - not one single arrest. A phenonomenon that was 100% hype and BS. As mentioned earlier, the FBI's Kenneth Lanning says that there have been no true casualties of satanic murder. He also wisely warns that the anti-satanists often make indiscriminate use of the words satanic, cult, occult, and ritualistic.

"In 1992 the False Memory Syndrome Foundation of Philadelphia was established. They collected 3000 accounts of families where an adult child, generally a female between twenty and forty, would supposedly recover a sublimated memory and then make some kind of accusation concerning incest occurring during their childhood. Some of theses 'recovered memories' included ritual satanic abuse. Four hundred and fifty of these cases went to court. The

Foundation's view of hypnosis, which had often been used with these MPD patients to 'recover' their satanic cult memories, was that hypnosis is a suggestive tool that intrinsically has the potential to create false images. They didn't deny that in the 3,000 accounts there were some cases of actual incest and abuse, some of which may have genuinely been sublimated in memories until therapy, but they stated strongly that every such accusation was not true. They implied most.

"Let's look at what the anti-anti-satanists do believe. They, as well as Sandi Gallant, author of the ubiquitous manual, do not believe in a widespread satanic conspiracy. There is no doubt in their minds that besides the public Satanists, isolated and ephemeral cults do sometimes come into existence, some are lead by psychopaths and sociopaths, some of which may profess Satanism. They dismiss most instances of seeming satanic activity as copycat manifestations of what the anti-satanists have made public and described in the media. They accuse the anti-satanists of actually being the authors of most seemingly satanic phenomenon, just as the torturers of the Inquisition gave us the original satanic legends and myths.

"Excluding LeVey's, and a few other examples of public Satanism in England, New Zealand, Canada, and western Europe, most of which don't agree with each other, where is any manifest international widespread satanic cult? In law enforcement we deal with evidence. There is **no evidence** of a single coherent organized satanic entity. There is no one set of accepted satanic belief systems, no organizational apparatus, no single accepted written source that traces the history of Satanism, nor spells out its philosophy, nor delineates its rituals and ceremonies. There simply is no continual satanic body or tradition to be found today or in history. To the anti-satanists who stubbornly claim the contrary, the anti-anti-satanists ask for evidence of such a conspiracy. Where are this widespread international Satanists organization's correspondences, their membership lists, their telephone logs, their travel records, their bank accounts, their meeting places, their crematoriums, their equipment used in the production of their pornography, where do they hold their conventions, where is any such evidence at all of this sinister widespread conspiracy? If it was there investigators would have found it. Occult and ritual groups are historically very prone to schism, defections, and internecine conflicts. Whenever ego and power are involved, such things are common, yet we have no evidence of such things occurring in the anti-satanist's widespread international satanic conspiracy.

"The anti-anti-satanists don't believe that the fundamentalist and evangelical ministers started the satanic culture myth, but they believe the ministers definitely helped continue it. Dollars were flowing at the Christian bookstores, many books and tapes were produced and sold. Some even postulated that the preachers thought if they could convince people of the reality of Satan, it would also convince people of the reality of God.

"The anti-anti-satanists think that the ministers are 'crying wolf,' when they attack everything they disagree with by labeling it as Satanism. Satanism is Satanism. It is not feminism, gay liberation, abortion, the erosion and destruction of the family unit, or New Age philosophy. If the ministers want to attack those things they disagree with, they should do so honestly and openly, not calling them all Satanists, which by definition they are not.

"New Age philosophy is about pursuing higher levels of consciousness and spiritual awareness, while Satanism is a selfish materialistic philosophy pursuing fulfillment through physical pleasure. Often, listening to fundamentalists on the tube, you would think New Age is Satanism. Satanism did borrow much from the European pagans who were persecuted by the church, but there is a big difference between Satanists, and the Wiccan or witches, the Neo-Pagans, and Neo-Goddess worshippers. This was where Sandi Gallant went wrong."

I moved back to the chalkboard. I could sense Laura moving from the wall to follow me with the camera. I picked up the chalk and drew as I talked. "There are some well-known symbols that Satanists practicing black magic might use, but there are not that many symbols which are purely satanic. Anyone who is an occultist or practices ritual magic may use a six or five pointed star. The Hexagram, the interlocking of two triangles in the six-pointed star, the Star of David of the Hebrews, has many occult symbolic meanings, the union of God and Goddess, of male and female, and in working magic, it means as above, so below. Above and below refers to the levels, planes, or dimensions of being. The magician does his ritual on the physical level, but using his will, he directs his emotional, mental, and spiritual energy to effect changes in those non-physical, spiritual dimensions which he believes will have causal effects on the physical world. The interlocking triangles represent the union of the microcosm, man, with the macrocosm, the universe   .

"Man, the microcosm, is also symbolized by the five pointed star, the pentagram. Everyone has seen DaVinci's drawings of man inside the five-pointed star. It has one point rising from the four, symbolizing the soul rising from the bondage of the animal nature or the union of the four elements in man, guided by his divine spirit. The four elements or dimensions of being represented in the pentagram are earth - the physical; water - the emotional; air - the mental; and fire - will, Life Force, spiritual fire. They are in harmony in humanity when guided by the divine spark/spirit, the Higher Self, the god within.

"Seeing a five or six pointed star, or the old pagan horned gods and goddesses does not imply anything sinister. The five pointed star with the point down may symbolize Satan, but it does have a few legitimate occult uses in Wicca and the Order of the Eastern Star, the women freemasons. But if you see a five pointed star, with the point down, and there is a goat's head in it, that is a legitimate satanic symbol. It represents the perversion or misuse of spiritual power to fulfill material desires. The numbers 666 and the phrase 'the Beast' both refer to the Anti-Christ of the book Revelations, and can generally be assumed to be satanic."

I paused for more water. "If any of you are interested in doing any background reading or research, I've got to warn you there's a lot of garbage out on this subject. I got most of the satanic history in this lecture from Arthur Lyon's *Satan Wants You* and the stuff about the satanic phenomenon in America from Ted Peters' *Sin, Radical Evil in Soul and Society.* Author Robert Hicks also has a great lecture about law enforecement and Satanism you can find on the internet.

"In terms of public Satanism and the internet, if you do research on the net, you'll probably find a book made reference to, the *Necronomicon* - the book of things dead and gone, or the book of dead names. Supposedly written in Damascus in 730 A.D. by Addul Alhazred, it is a compilation of occult wisdom, creation myths, and magic from the Middle East. In the 1580's Dr. John Dee and assitant Edward Kelly obtained access to a manuscript and produced an English manuscript. It was said to have a profound effect on their occult work with the Enochian calls. In 1664 a Hebrew translation was produced which had an influence on certain Kabbalists and Jewish mystics. Centuries later, Aliester Crowley obtained access to a manuscript, which supposedly had a large influence on his occult development and his *The Book of the Law*.

"Crowely, as the story goes, was lovers in the early 1920's with Sonia Greene, who later married H.P. Lovecraft. Lovecraft uses a Necronomicon in his fiction, but his is just that. Supposedly all the real manuscripts have gone missing and no major institution claims ownership of one. There are books for sale titled *Necronomicon*, but their validity, like so much in the world of the occult, is a matter of contention.

"On the net, with a good search engine, there is no short supply of satanic sites. Most of these claim that satanic involvement is a statement of individuality against the repression of Christian/societal inhibitions. Like LaVey's, many of these are probably relatively harmless, at least from a legal standpoint. But there are satanic groups much less warm and fuzzy than LaVey's. In New Zealand, England, and mainland Europe there are satanic groups known by names such as the Order of the Left Hand Path, now Ordo Sinistra Vivendi, the Fraternity of Baelder, and the Order of the Nine Angles. Some of these are vastly different from those forms of Satanism claiming to use satanic symbols as an expression of individual freedom and the throwing off of the shackles of repressive religious social inhibitions. Some of these groups seem to be genuine classical Satanists.

"England's Order of the Nine Angles disturbingly claims to be traditional or classical Satanists. They supposedly scare some of their fellow Satanists, claim to be over one hundred years old, put forth the *Black Book of Satan I,II,III*, have a developed ideology, body of rituals, and nine stages of initiation. They do traditional ritual inversion of Christian rituals in their Black Mass, are blatantly anti-Christian, and promulgate satanic black magic. You'll probably find the related web sites shocking, maybe revolting. One of their articles is a guide to human sacrifice, which they refer to as a gift for their prince. They describe both voluntary and involuntary sacrifice. One would be a euthanasia, go out while you're still healthy and strong kind of ritual. An involuntary sacrifice would be like our present victim, she sure as hell didn't volunteer to be mutilated."

"The room was quiet, I knew what they were thinking. "Right, and you thought porn, pedophiles, and Nazis were the main problems with the internet. Although the beliefs of the Nine Angles make most people very uncomfortable, they've never been linked to any crimes in the

U.S. - as far as I know. They also teach getting rid of the bodies of their victims so people don't get caught. They even have guidelines for choosing the victims of their sacrifice - their victims must show weakness, or be against them. I'm not about to say these groups aren't dangerous, their ideologies certainaly are, and it's hard for me to believe it's even legal to preach ritual murder over the internet, in England or the U.S. However, there is no indication of any symbolic link between the bloody ritual in the cabin and any known form of public Satanism." I looked at them, they had questioning faces. "The use of symbols here is not consistent with, or tie in to any known group. My reading of the ritual area and the ritual is that this would be a group of self-styled Satanists - sadistic, intelligent, but unaligned."

I looked at Danny. It had been a long lecture, on an esoteric subject, which, even if one accepts as interesting, was still pretty far away from the norms of modern police work. "Danny, if that's enough background, how about a break, and then we can come back and go over the satanic aspects of our present crime?" Danny assented, and people got up at varying speeds, depending on whether their feet were asleep or their bladder full. Laura put the camera on pause and joined me on the break. I also wanted to check in with Leonard while we had a chance.

Chapter Seven – Sunday Afternoon

Kevin was turning red and getting real pissed, all his muscles were tightening up. Gary was a big guy, wasn't scared of much, and he and Kevin had been tight for a long time, but he had seen Kevin go off on people before, and it wasn't pretty. Kevin was one of those guys who could always seem to come up with something handy and use it to do extreme damage to his opponent in a short amount of time. He had seen him almost beat a boy to death with a folding chair in high school. If Kevin hadn't been pulled off.... Gary found a pen, picked up a *Soldier of Fortune* and wrote on it that the house might be bugged. When Kevin read it, he yelled, "Shit!" real loud, but he started to pace around and act calmer. Kevin wasn't dressed for business since it was Sunday, and early morning by his schedule, he had on jeans and a tee shirt, and had a folding buck knife in a leather case on his belt. He walked around and closed the curtains fully, then sat on the sofa. Gary was glad he was calming the fuck down. He didn't like the idea of fightin' with one of his few friends. Especially one who was teachin' him things that could really make shit happen. Kevin pulled out what looked like a half ounce of crank in a baggie and threw it on the coffee table. He reached back and pulled his buck knife out of its case and flipped it open with his thumb. Inserting the blade in the open baggie of meth-amphetimine, he drew some out and dumped it on the table, cut out two long lines on the table, and straightened them out with the blade. Gary sat down beside him on the sofa, greatly relieved. Quickly Kevin snatched the ballpoint pen Gary still had in his hands and broke it in half, sliding the unconnected plastic half away from the pen, and used it to snort a huge line. He handed it to Gary with a look that said "do it," so Gary snorted a long thick line of speed. He could feel it burning into his nasal passages. He figured Kevin didn't have any sensation left inside his.

Kevin wanted fatboy to talk, and he knew just what would grease those wheels. He cut two more long lines out for a quick repeat. Then Kevin looked at Gary, smiled, and said, "Let's grab a couple of cases of beer from my carport and head up to the lake."

****

Pugsley had eaten with great abandon, even though his head was still unexplainably fuzzy. Raquel said she had eaten some at the counter while waiting for the takeout and wasn't that hungry anymore, so he ate hers after he finished his, while she was back in the bathroom for another extended stay.

He wanted to say something, ask questions, try to make plans to meet her in the future, tell her this was the best thing that ever happened to him, tell her something, but he was wary now, trying to figure out what was really going on. He had way too many conflicting thoughts running around in his head.

Below his waist the guy in charge told him to be quiet and not ruin it for both of them. Who could tell when he'd ever have it this good again. Stewart's mind acquiesced to the unerring and relentless logic of his penis.

****

"Talk about weird. You're chasing people that sacrifice animals and people to the devil?" Laura was talking low while I was throwing back some coffee. "Too bizarre… where did you learn about all that...that" she lowered her voice even more, like she was a schoolgirl who didn't cuss but was going to say something bad anyway, "all that weird fucking shit? I know about you and Leonard - Sweat Lodges, healing, spirit powers, animal spirits, spirit songs, dancing, I grew up on the rez, I know about all that stuff, but why did you learn about all this other crap, why would you want to know about Satan and demons and black magic? Why in the world would you want to do this kind of work?"

She was looking at me with eyes vastly different from those that opened to greet mine so joyfully hours earlier. It was like she was looking at me for the first time all over again, this time trying to look inside me. Looking for hidden demons. I looked into her eyes, and I attempted to let her in psychicly. I let her look into me and through me, I let her search. Finally I spoke.

"You hear the word healer alot, and shaman, not so much the term medicine man anymore, not at least around the reservations I've been to. Although it's still used in its popular sense, the term shaman is more apt. I don't know what you were taught, but I always thought of a healer as somebody who ran a Sweat Lodge, prayed to the Great Spirit, worked with spirit powers/animal spirits, carried a Sacred Pipe. Who may or may not also consider themselves a Christian as well. But I thought a medicine man, when the term is used correctly as it was in the past, had to know both sides, not necessarily use them, but know them, that it was part of his job. This is the same thing. It's not like lots of tribes don't have some fairly strong sorcery traditions.

She didn't say anything, so I continued. "The term witch is different for Indians and Anglos, but I know some fairly funky black magic gets practiced on some back corners of a few of the rez. A good medicine man is supposed to know both sides of the track. Same thing for me, this is my job, my work, I'm on the side of the angels, I committed my soul to the Light in a secret ritual you may already know about. I know it's a warrior soceity of men and women, so if you know, you *know*. I can't say anything more. Not here. But I *have* to know about the other side. In any conflict, you must know your own strengths and your enemies' weaknesses."

***

Samantha woke up very late, after having had another of her burning dreams. It had only begun in the last couple of months, but now at least once or twice a week she had the same dream. She was tied to a stake, on top of a large pile of wood. A priest was condemning her, while the peasants watched with open eyes, hungry for firery entertainment. An executioner held a torch, waiting for the priest to finish. Then, while the priest was still yelling his condemnation, she began to curse them, curse them all, the priest and the bloodthirsty church he represented, the feudal lord for letting it happen, the peasants for their eagerness for her blood. She cursed them all, to damnation, as the executioner came with the torch. The flames spread quickly. As they rose, at the first moment of the searing pain, she would wake up, filled with fear and hate and rage.

She had awoken from such a deep dream state that she went back to sleep, although it was a light sleep and fitful, it was at least without the tormenting burning dream.

***

They headed up to Lake Lanier on I-85 in Kevin's souped up black Monte Carlo. It had custom wheels, a big V-8, multi-port fuel injection, dual exhausts, the works. But since he was carrying speed and drinking beer, Kevin held it down to go with the flow of traffic. His partner in the escort agency was an older woman, mid-fifties, who had done well in real estate. When the market went soft for a few years and she had tax problems, she looked around for another source of income. She knew Kevin's uncle, who set up a meet and Kevin pitched her his idea. He had a small stable at the time (and was dealing some coke and crank although he didn't mention it,) but with her class and connections, and his strong arm and management, he knew he could put together a lucrative, classy escort service/callgirl operation. And they had. A highly profitable escort service, from which they both derived a substantial reported and unreported income.

Blanche had a house on Lanier, she helped Kevin buy a used houseboat and let him keep it at her dock. Kevin knew it was the perfect place to unhinge Gary's jaw. There was zero paperwork linking him to his houseboat's location.

"Thuh first reason I cain't say nothin' is the witches' pyramid. Yore thuh one," Gary said emphatically, "that taught me to know what ya' want, to dare to have it, to will to have it, to be silent until ya' really do have it. I done the ritual jus' like you taught, and what I asked for is comin' true, but it ain't come all the way yet. You told me, silence until ya fully have what ya ritually worked fer. The second reason's I said I woodn't."

"Said to who?" Kevin asked, trying to be patient.

"But if'a told ya that, I'd be breakin' thuh first rule of the pyramid."

"Awright, awright," Kevin sighed in resignation. "Drink a beer and forget about it."

Kevin knew he'd find out, sooner or later.

***

"They didn't leave much in the way of evidence." I continued with the task force. "We don't have any clear fingerprints or footprints, no cartracks, but we still have much to work with. We know there were probably three people working the ritual, and one fake cop on Thorn Road. The fake cop may have been too far away from the ritual chamber to have been what the Masons call the tyler, what at the Sweat Lodge we call the doorman. Somebody not participating in the ritual should be right outside as a guard; to keep the outer world from infringing while the ritual is underway. That would be five people. We know of one fake police car, but there had to be a van, trailer, RV, something to bring the animals in. How the animals were acquired and where they were stored are questions in need of answers. They must have already been drugged before being transported here, 'cause there's no sign they walked in. The easiest way to transport drugged animals or people is to bind their limbs, run a pole under the bindings, and carry them like hunters do game. So we have a minimum of four but probably five perps and two vehicles - one a van or truck with a camper, a horse trailer, an RV, something big enough to bring in the sacrificial victims. If the animals were bought or stolen, they would need to be kept somewhere before the ritual. Some of the people involved might have a lot of land, a barn, some privacy anyway. The animals may be a trail; the drugs used to sedate them may provide a trail; any vandalized or burglarized churches might provide a trail; in addition to working the schools for our phone pals who called it in, and the clinics and homes for the victim. What I'm trying to say is that this was a large, complex undertaking, any single aspect of which may provide us with a trail back to the perpetrators.

"Let's talk about how they prepared the ritual area, how they performed the ritual, and how they disguised the place when they left. You saw the black spray paint on the walls, the upside down pentagrams, the 'Satan Rules' graffiti. It is not artistic, the words were intentionally made to look like the script of an uneducated adolescent, but it's not. All of that was done after the ritual was over, right before they rolled up the tarps and took their travelling horror show back out on the road." I went back to the chalkboard to draw diagrams of the ritual.

"There are four inverse pentagrams painted on the walls, the one on the west wall has a goat's head spray-painted inside the pentagram. The artwork of the goat's head and the Hebrew letters at each point of the star is very precise, most likely spray painting over stensils. The disguising graffiti looks like spray-paint free-handed, but underneath the lightly spray-painted pentagrams we found precise well painted black pentagrams, perfectly geometrically formed, perfectly lined up with each other on the opposing walls. On the floor, encircling the altar and the four crucifixes are three large concentric black circles, spray-painted skillfully. There is a triangle, within the inner circle. It's base is in the east, and its point toward the west, the points of the triangle touch the circumference of the inner circle. Inside each point of this triangle is an inverted crucifix with an animal wired to it. The infant hangs on an inverse cross between the altar and the goat hanging on an inverted cross at the west point of the triangle."

Annie raised her hand, "What's the deal with the inverted crucifix? You didn't go over that."

"Well, first off, classical Satanism is about ritual rebellion and inversion of everything Christian, and since the crucifix is a major Christian symbol, it's natural that they would invert it. It's one element that sometimes shows up in classical Satanism, but not always. Our perps certainly didn't invent the inverted crucifix. Tradition tells us the Roman Emperor Nero had both Peter the Rock and Saul, later called the Saint Paul Paul, killed. The traditional story is that Peter was crucified upside down. Being crucified is obviously bad, done upside down it's supposed to be even worse.

"Think of all the preparation involved in this ritual. They had to procure the animals and the pregnant woman ahead of time. They had to be drugged and transported. The Satanists had to clean the ols cottage, prepare crucifixes, and cut the holes in the floor with battery powered power tools. They had to paint the circles and the triangle on the floor, and paint precise pentagrams on the walls for it to be a satisfactory satanic ritual chamber.

"The pentagrams, the black circles on the floor, and the goat's head all took time. The altar was an old table left when the cottage was abandoned, but still it was cleaned off and dragged in there. To prepare the ritual chamber, to bring in the tarps, tape them down, to bring in the black candles and the ritual regalia, then to bring in the sacrificial victims, perform a ritual of forty-five minutes to an hour and a half, afterwards to do some camouflage spray paint graffitti, then to untape the tarps and fold them in upon themselves, then to haul it all out and dispose of it - all this took meticulous planning and efficient execution. Among our perpetrators will be at least one highly organized individual, and possibly several.

"They brought in their own ritual regalia. They might have disposed of the bloody black robes with the tarps, but they most probably kept their magical ritual weapons. These symbolic weapons used for mastery in the elemental worlds minimally include: a sword or athame - the ritual dagger symbolic of fire, a pentacle - the ceremonial disk symbolic of earth with a pentagram on one side and a hexagram on the other, a chalice - which is symbolic of water, and a wand - symbolic of air, possibly phallus shaped. They may have also brought a bell or gong, and they definitely brought incense. Even if they burned or buried the tarps and the robes, it is highly unlikely that they disposed of their magical weapons - those a magician, black or white, left hand or right hand path, takes great care of and keeps for life. If we find the perpetrators, find their personal ritual chambers with their magical weapons, we'll find blood stains on all the athames and in at least one chalice."

I paused, took a long drink of water, and asked, "Are there any questions at this point, anything I can clear up?"

One of the uniformed supervisors asked how they could have so much activity and no footprints or fingerprints, so little physical evidence.

"Meticulous planning and execution. From the very first time, they went in using gloves and booties, probably dressed much like our CSU techs. They cleaned up, they made holes, installed crucifixes, painted the floor and walls, they brought in the tarps and even a pathway tarp, probably unrolled and rolled it up like a grounds crew would at a stadium. They knew the detail in which the crime scene would be analyzed and tried to foresee what we would do, and leave us nothing. Nothing in the way of solid clues, of course, but what they left they did so intentionally, for the general public."

Annie, the black woman cop who obviously had a sharp and quick mind, asked, "Can you tell us what the people doing this butchery thought they were accomplishing, and can you piece together their ritual?"

"When I was a college student majoring in both symbolic anthropology and criminology, I had already begun my apprenticeship with an Indian shaman, a healer. In class, I would see movies of shamans from around the world working, and even though I didn't speak their language, and some films had no sound, I always knew what the shamans were doing. Ritual is the language of the unconscious, or, if you're a fan of Jung, the collective unconscious. All that is a long way of saying I've got an idea what they were doing, I understand the mechanics of the ritual they employed, but why, and what for, is a different ballgame. I believe that this was the final ritual of a series of rituals, I would bet that animals were sacrificed previously, but this was probably their first human sacrifice.

"Remember how the Marquise Montespan wanted something specific, she wanted magical help to get it, and she didn't mind others being sacrificed so that she could obtain what she wanted. Many magical texts say that when asking demons to perform certain tasks, the magician needs to sacrifice a living being and supply that demon with blood, enabling it to have the physical power to manifest the magician's desires in the material world. Now, whether these Satanists were invoking a specific demon for a specific task, as Asmodeus and Astaroth were invoked by Abbe´ Guibourg, or whether they invoked Satan himself, as does LaVey, I do not know.

"I think they had a goal in mind, and they thought a sacrifice, a public sacrifice, was necessary. As efficient as they were, they could have cleaned up everything, left nothing behind. They didn't. Maybe they think they are pleasing their infernal prince by leaving the remains and flouting authority. More likely, I think what they desire, what they sought this ritual to magically manifest for them, is something in the public domain. What, however, I don't have a clue.

"I can give you a good idea of the order of the ritual. They cleaned the area, used a battery powered drill and saw to cut the holes in the floor, painted, and prepared the ritual chamber in the afternoon through the early evening, swept again and laid out all the tarps. They probably always had a guard hidden to protect the space. Then the satanic high priest would consecrate the area, and then they brought in the victims, animals, then human. The high priest would begin, state the purpose of the ritual, and invoke Satan or the appropriate demon. They would work themselves up emotionally - drinking wine, possibly stolen from a church, by song, chant, repetitive invocation, dance, by some technique to bring themselves to the required state of intensity. Once they were whipped up they drained some of each animal's blood into a chalice and made the mother drink it. Then, moving counterclockwise if they were attempting to harm or destroy, clockwise if they were working to make something come into being, they would invoke the devil or demons by name as they moved circularly, stabbing, killing the animals. The high priest would offer the sacrifice of the animals and tell the devil/demon what they wanted done while some kind of chanting would probably keep the other two participants busy and worked up. The chanting would become even more intense, the high priest invoking powerfully, at which point he cut the baby out. Then he cut and ripped the mother's heart out, instantly killing her. The blood in the heart was poured into a chalice half filled with red wine. The three participants would then drink from the chalice, to take the power/life force of the three animals and the mother. Because the mother had drunk the blood of the three animals, in their belief she had taken their power. By killing her, they took her power, as well as that of the three animals, whose blood she had consumed. This is a tricky magical way of getting the animals' psychic power without coming into contact with the animal's physical blood and any diseases therein. That done they sacrificed the baby to the devil/demon, in their perverted world view one of the most powerful of all possible sacrifices. At that point the high priest would be directing and willing the devil/demon to accomplish the appointed goal, spelling out exactly what was wanted, repetitiously, and psychically willing it to happen.

"After all this preparation was concluded they:

- performed an invocation,

- and performed the sacrifices of the animals,

- mother made to consume blood of animals in wine

- more invocation and statement of the desire,

- the surgical removal of the baby,

- the brutal sacrifice of the mother by heart removal

- the harvesting and consuming of her power through her blood,

- the sacrificing of the baby at the height of emotion and energy,

- the commanding of the devil/demon and willing their desire to be made manifest in reality,

- after the climax of this activity had been reached the priest would possibly hit the gong, or stomp, or clap – producing a sound accompanied by saying something to the effect of 'so mote it be' or 'so be it done,' a ritually prescribed number of times (possibly three) to end the ritual.

- Once it was over, they broke it all down,

- hauled away what they were taking,

- camouflaged the area to make it seem like illiterate teenagers,

- and left the rest for us to find."

***

Even in the titty magazines, Pugsley had never seen an outfit like Raquel was wearing when she came out of the bathroom. There was so much of it, yet it covered nothing at all. Nothing of interest to Pugsley. She wore a black cape held on a silver chain, she wore a black bustier with fully exposed breasts, a black garter belt and black hose. She had what looked like a cat-of-nine-tails in her hand, walking on six inch spiked heels. Stewart went to wood at the sight of her. Any questions about her, her honesty, the van, anything, were long gone. All the blood that feeds cognitive thought was filling his near-bursting member. Raquel lifted her left hand and popped it with the whip. It made a good pop, but Stewart could tell it wouldn't hurt too much, it wasn't a real whip, more a stage prop.

Tonya looked at the little slug and thought that in three days straight, even if he was a little sore, the kid sure could keep it up. "Let the games begin."

***

Annie raised her hand again and asked, "Are there any other options, between the two extremes of believing it - hook, line, and sinker, God and Devil, white and black magic - or disbelieving it all and being a total skeptic - atheist/non-believer? You study this stuff, what do you really believe about this?"

In a couple of hours, it was easy to tell who had the kind of intellect that searched and challenged and was desirous of knowledge. I smiled at her. I was hoping nobody would get into my personal beliefs. "You asked some difficult questions. I can give you some middle ground, or at least a psychological framework you can utilize to provide explanations outside the realm of religion. In the works of Carl Jung, a Swiss psychiatrist of Asian heritage who was a contemporary of Freud, the concepts of archetypes and the collective unconscious are put forth. His archetypes are non-physical, spiritual prototypes - the idea of a good mother, good father, god and goddess, or a good god, evil god. The collective unconscious is the collective unconscious of humanity. Now, the devil is derived from the bad god archetype, but its details have been filled in by the unconscious of humanity over the eons. Jung is fairly deep and not easily explained, but you can get his books or books about his ideas at the library. Aldous Huxley also put these things in a more modern context as he wrote about what he called 'the perennial philosophy.' As to what I believe - I'm somewhere in there philosophically between Jung, Jesus, and the Indian shaman. But Jesus said two things which bear remembering:

- as a man believeth in his heart, so he is.

- Possibly meaning as a person thinks consciously in his mind, and subconsciously in his heart, that will be his reality.

- and Jesus also said the entire kingdom of Heaven,

- (and I suspect Hell too), is within you."

***

Kevin had laid out some more large lines in the boathouse and then they went up on top to the roof/sundeck. The lake was noisy, too many damn boats. They were laying out, sunning in cut-off bluejeans, drinking beer. They were talkative. Speed or coke will loosen a tongue and give it the endurance to run a marathon. Gary wanted to tell his friend, but he didn't want to jinx things for himself.

Finally, Kevin, tired of running up against the same wall, and concerned about whatever the fuck fatboy was into, came up with an idea. "Look Gary, I keep my tools downstairs, and a little altar in a cupboard. How about I go down, do a ritual that you will get what you've asked for, but that it's okay to tell me, your high priest, what's going on?"

Kevin had studied the occult in high school with a few friends. He had gotten into Satan too. He loved Black Sabbath and all that satanic symbolism. In prison, his cellmate had opened up some insights into Satanism, satanic witches, satanic covens, the whole gig. Kevin had his own little coven now, of which he was high priest. There were five people total in his "coven," but his lady Amanda and fatboy were the only constant ones. The other two were in a heavy metal band, went by the nicknames of Beavis and Butthead, and kinda came and went.

Between the beers, the speed, and the social pressure exerted by a friend, and, as Kevin kept saying, his high priest, Gary really wanted to talk. Kevin's idea seemed the best way out. There was just no way, whoever his covert employers were, that they could have followed him up from Atlanta without his noticing a tail, because he was checking all the time. There was no way they could have set up a sophisticated sound detection system that could pick Kevin and him up on this speedboat-infested lake ahead of time, because nobody knew they were coming here, the lake visit was spontaneous. He knew he could talk freely, he just didn't want to blow his chance for having his dreams come true. He asked Kevin what he had in mind. Finally Gary said, "Okay, whut ya wont me tuh do?"

Kevin looked at him, "No big deal big man, just give me ten minutes to get ready, I'll call you down, and when we start the ritual, you just say 'Hail Satan' every time there's a pause. Once the ritual's over we'll do more lines, drink more beer, and you can tell me the whole fucking story."

***

Danny left Schultz in charge at APD Homicide, and left the guys to make calls to set up the school visits and check with other agencies while the women started calling the clinics and shelters. Nobody had reported a pregnant woman missing in the Atlanta area yet, and she had to come from somewhere. I gave Laura my old, but customized, '52 Ford pickup truck, with directions and a company pager; she was heading to a downtown hotel to see some friends who were helping set up the Unity conference. Danny had simply told me to come with him.

Danny was driving, and it didn't take a genius to see we were either heading back to the crime scene or to do interviews at the mansion.

"What did you think of the good doctor yesterday?" Danny asked me with a grin.

"I didn't like him too much, but I don't like a lot of doctors, and have little to no respect for a whole lot of shrinks. But working both sides of the law enforcement business, and having a brother go through the V.A. system might do that to anybody. Why, did the 'knowledge of anatomy but not a practicing surgeon' bring the shrink to mind?"

"Well," Danny paused, non-committal, "let's just say that I find him interesting, and want to know a little more about him. And also about the clients he gets from the courts."

"I thought about him too," I said, "but would a guy that smart do something that blatant in his own backyard? I didn't like the shrink yesterday either, but he didn't seem like a moron. It's not smart to commit such a horrendous crime on your own property. Leaving bloody carcasses around is not very subtle. Unless you think everybody in law enforcement is stump-dumb, or you're trying...to do what...I don't know. But I do know a lot of people that did great academically, but don't have shit for common sense. But this guy's rich, from a wealthy family; why would he get involved with something like Satanism, ritual sacrifice? I didn't care for his personality, but just because he went to med school on his way to being a shrink doesn't mean he's our doer."

"I doubt he is too, but I didn't want to do the calls or the clinics, so I figured you and I could go interview the doc, maybe some of the hired help." Danny smiled. He was a good cop, but he hated computers and he hated phone work. "If nothing else we'll just look around. Somebody chose the location for a reason. They had to know about it to use it. That pretty much narrows it down to family members, friends and acquaintances of the family, past or present employees, or kids that went to Thorn Road to hang out or make out. Who the hell else would even know the place was there?" I nodded my head in agreement.

"Taking into account that it seems illogical the doc did it, but having to look into the possibility that he may have - if he is dirty, that would implicate the niece, since she and the doc give each other alibis." I didn't want to say anything specific, so I let it dangle, "What'd you think about the niece?"

Danny looked at me, "Why? You pick up on something?"

I didn't have anything to go on, so I was vague, "She just seemed old for her age, definitely older than fourteen or fifteen."

Danny just shook his head and grinned, "It's not like when we were kids, they really do grow up younger and younger. Fifteen to them is about like eighteen was to us. Blame it on the movies, the media, TV, poor parenting, changing times, growth hormones in our meat and milk, whatever, kids are growing up quicker. Just look at the teenage pregnancy rate. It's ridiculous."

"Yeah," I said, "but do those high numbers mean they're growing up faster, are dumber about birth control, or that teen pregnancy and babies out of wedlock are just more acceptable these days?"

***

Kevin had finished with "So be it now Fully Done!" He sent Gary back up on top of the boat with some fresh beers. He put the candles out with his fingertips, and closed up his cupboard altar. He sat at the table, cut out a long line, snorted it, and headed upstairs. He was more than curious to know what the hell was up with fatboy.

***

Stewart was composing a letter to *Penthouse* in his head while Raquel was in the bathroom again. His anatomy was sore all over, but not so sore that he'd have to quit. She'd told him she had one or two more outfits left, but they'd have to get going after that. At that moment Pugsley would have been willing to stay in that room, doing just what they'd been doing, for the rest of his life.

Raquel came out with a maid outfit on, the kind you see on Halloween for the sexy French maid: white apron, black mini-skirt, cream thigh-highs, heels, and an unbuttoned top. She carried a tiny tray high like a servant in one hand, and a black teflon spatula in the other. The tray had Tonya's coke mirror with four lines of coke on it. Tonya wanted to see how the little slug would do on go juice. He had excellent hands, his tonguework was getting better, and he had proved himself as eager to give as to receive. She sat the tray down on the bed, lifted her skirt's back, revealing nothing but her shapely buttocks underneath, and gave herself a loud whack with the spatula. "All right darlin', the lessons continue...."

***

I knew we had four Triple S Security guards on the job at the Faulkner estate. One on the main gate, one at the Thorn Road gate, one in a car patrolling the roads around the estate, and one man on foot walking the perimeter. I knew Danny had a car at Thorn Road, too. My guys

had bagged another tabloid magazine news crew for trespassing. I promised them a bonus. As we

neared the estate I casually suggested something to Danny, "Don't drink the water."

"Good God, Spooky, we're not going to Mexico. What the hell you mean don't drink the

water? You think somebody that's not even a suspect would try to poison a cop. That's highly

unlikely."

"It's not a health thing, at least not physically, it's a psychic thing."

He looked at me like I was starting to remind him of crazy Larry. I tried to clear it up a

little.

"Don't worry about it at the main house. But if we go to the doc's house, and he offers

you something to eat or drink, especially water, just don't accept anything."

Danny didn't take to me telling him what to do. Some cop's egos are just as little girlishly

hyper-sensitive as actors and athletes. "Are you giving me orders? Don't forget I'm the guy in

charge. I could have your ass fired in five minutes. Hell, you work for me, I could fire your ass

right now!"

"Okay, Mr. Sensitivity," I said, "Call it an odd old superstition, but indulge me. I'm

asking, I'm suggesting, that you not take liquid at the doc's house if you have any suspicion at all

that he might be involved."

We pulled up to the main gate. I saw my man outside the gates and the gardener/

stablemaster/gateman in the gatehouse. The drive was closed by wrought iron gates that were

electrically operated remotely from cars or the gatehouse. When the gatekeeper saw us, he

pushed a button and opened the gates. Johnstone, one of our senior and more trustworthy

security officers walked over and talked to us through Danny's window.

Danny asked him if the reporters had been a nuisance. Johnstone said they were yesterday, but today only one news van had come by the front, and three at Thorn Road, besides the group bungling through the woods they had caught earlier that morning. Johnstone looked at Danny, "They know they'll probably get more info from sources at APD, or the M.E.'s office, or the city morgue."

I asked Johnstone had he seen much of the family.

"Naw, Spooky, since I got here today, and my whole shift yesterday, I haven't hardly seen a Faulkner step foot outside, go anywhere, or do anything. It appears they plan to ride the storm out at home. Probably a good idea." Danny and I both nodded. Johnstone went back, we drove onto the estate, and the gate closed quietly behind us.

***

"So they just sent you a typed, unsigned letter, in the mail, no return address, postmarked in town, said they'd become aware of you, were interested in you, and if you were interested in covert work, burn the letter and the envelope on your front porch at three o'clock in the afternoon, and you did that?" Kevin couldn't believe what he was hearing.

Gary nodded. They both paused while a speedboat pulled a woman skier in a skimpy thong bathing suit through their cove.

"So then they sent you another letter explaining a little bit more, you burned that as instructed, and this went on how many times?"

Gary thought about it for a minute. Kevin wondered if the chaise lounge Gary was in was going to break or not. Gary was so heavy his butt was almost down to the roof of the boathouse. Kevin figured if it broke, Gary wouldn't be falling too far, and he didn't want to insult fatboy, now that he was finally spilling his guts, so he didn't say anything. "Four times total," Gary replied. "Before last Friday when the car, uniform, and letter on the sofa were there when I got home from breakfast."

"So?" Kevin was impatient, trying really hard to be patient. He didn't know whether to be incredulous or envious. There had long been rumors that offshoots of official intelligence agencies, running off the book covert operations, hired criminals, drug dealers, burglars, whatever they needed from the criminal underworld to work for them; but at the same time, kept them far enough away from anything official to retain plausible deniability. He didn't doubt that things like that occasionally happened, but to fucking fatboy? That just didn't make any sense.

"So Friday, I read the note, burned it like I was instructed - on my porch at three o'clock, everything but the directions...and they took those back when I got there."

***

Danny only went twenty feet past the gate and pulled the car over. He looked over and said, "I'll be back in a second," and went back to the gatehouse. He talked to the man for a few minutes, then came back. When he got in I just looked at him. Finally I said, "Well?"

"Liam O'Thomas got the job from his father, he inherited it. He says they pay great, but they work him hard. Liam said any background questions, ask his dad, and so we will, when we get through here."

"So what now, boss, Alpert or the headshrinker?" I made the boss part as sarcastic as possible. Danny might get pissed at me, but he sure as hell wasn't going to fire me in the middle of the case. His only other option for assistance would mean the Feds, which was the same as no option to him. He had done amazingly well tolerating the Fed at the lecture, but I knew he wanted them as uninvolved as possible.

"The gateman's already buzzed him on the intercom. Dr. Phineas Faulkner should be expecting us." I wondered if Danny didn't like shrinks much either. There are always exceptions, but some professions…who likes lawyers? But I love good doctors and consider them a treasure and I really like my dentist and how often do you hear that? And when I thought about it - who likes cops and PI's?

It was past noon, but the doctor still had on a bathrobe, slippers, and pajamas underneath. Either it had been a long night, or he wasn't expecting to go anywhere. Maybe he just wanted us to feel like we were intruding on his Sunday, which we were. He had what looked like a bloody mary with a large celery stalk in his glass. I'd be lying to say it didn't look damn good. He offered us marys, coffee, or water. We declined.

He went back to the kitchen, we followed. It seems he wanted to freshen up his drink. He motioned to the table while he went about his business, so we sat down. From somewhere in the house we heard a female voice, shouting something like "Uuuuvalll, Uuuuvall, where are you?"

We heard feet going down steps rapidly and running our way. Instead of coming to the kitchen the way we had, from the main hall, through the dining room, and into the kitchen, the footsteps came down the steps and went off into a back hall and came into the kitchen through its other door. Samantha rushed in, a flurry of red. The doctor turned toward the noise. She ran to him, moaning, "Oh Uvall, I woke up, went back to sleep, then I had that fucking dream again." She ran to the doctor and buried herself in him.

Everybody knows that there are different ways of hugging people. You hug your relatives differently that you hug your lover. Well, Samantha hugged the doctor with a full body press. The hips are the dead giveaway in a body hug, you might hug your mom, your sister, your aunts with the top of your body, with back patting always optional. But you don't hug your relatives with the bottom half of your body. Samantha's pelvis was pressed against his. It was all the validation I needed of my earlier suspicions. Phineas grabbed her by both arms and pushed her out to arm's length at the same time he shouted her name. "Samantha! We have guests, snap out of it, you can tell me about your dreams later."

She looked around and saw us. As she turned toward us, Phineas let go of her arms. She could see us, and we could see her. Completely. She was wearing a tiny slip of a negligee, so thin you could see through it. Bright red, way past sheer. It stopped well above her knees, was slit on both sides to her waist, and had a neckline that plunged toward her naval. A skimpy nightgown of the same material hung open from her shoulders. When she saw us, she just stared, obviously shocked to find us in the kitchen. She looked at Danny, and then at me. She met my eyes, I looked at her, and then I looked her over and back into her eyes. She did not run or turn in modesty. This was no normal child, and this was no normal or natural relationship she had with the not-so-good doc. Finally she looked at Phineas, closed the nightgown for what little good that did, and said she'd go get dressed. She left, leaving a large silence. We could hear every footstep down the hall and up the stairs, and she was barefooted.

I had brought home from Europe a similar negligee for a girlfriend years ago. She'd put it on for our romantic evenings, but she never slept in it. Not without ulterior motives.

The bright sun was streaming in the windows, it was then that I looked at Phineas and noticed his nose, and its suspicious red streak. My guard said they hadn't gone outside yesterday or today. I didn't think it was sun anyway. I'd had a good friend with a rather enthusiastic and gymnastic girlfriend. I'd asked him one time how he'd sunburned his nose when it'd been raining for a week. He clued me in. Anyway, I felt that all my suspicions yesterday were probably grounded in reality. Of course, that still didn't mean the doc was our doer. Or that he and a fourteen - almost fifteen - year old, were brutal Satanists. But it didn't raise him in our public opinion poll either. And I kept thinking about her pet name for him, "Uvall." I knew that name, somewhere in the back of my mind.

***

"Okay. Okay, okay, okay, okay." Kevin was speeding bigtime on the crank and wierding out on the story. "Let me go over this again. You follow the directions, stop at the stop sign, and Bruce Lee jumps into your car."

"Not Bruce Lee, some guy dressed like uh ninja, all black - black hat, black sunglasses, black jacket wit' thu hood up, black pants, shoes, everthin'. Ev'n his fake beard was black. He looked like Z Z TOP meets thuh ninja homeboys. He directs me tuh a dark place, switches places, makes me wear a blindfold, and drives me tuh thuh job."

"Okay, okay, so at the job you park on this street well in front of a pickup with a camper, and you run off everybody who comes near - four or five carloads of kids and parkers. And they told you if a real cop showed up just say you were doing private security work. And after a while you heard muffled chanting and noises that sound similar to stuff we do in ritual. How long from the time you got there till the noises stopped?"

"Two hours, two and a half."

"Then what?"

"The Z Z ninja came out and told me to open the trunk and then wait in the passenger seat, which I did. After which he and some other guy put stuff in the trunk, it was dark, I couldn't see much. Then I was blindfolded, he drove for a while and put me out."

"Okay, okay, so he drove to this remote spot, you take the blindfold off and he tells you to get out, and that he'll be back for you soon, left, and after a while he came back and got you, in how long?" Kevin was still working for all the details.

Gary thought, "About fifteen or twenty minutes, not long."

"And then you got blindfolded again and he drives for twenty minutes. He takes your blindfold off at some remote spot where the camper from before is parked. He tells you to wait, so you waited for a few seconds, he came back from the pickup with the camper and gave you a bag full of money, told you how to get to 285, said they'd be in touch, and you drove away?"

"Yup."

"And you never seen this guy's face, he wears a fake beard, sunglasses, hat and hood up the whole time, at least when you're not blindfolded?"

"Yup."

Kevin just shook his head and watched a girl and a guy go by on jet-skis.

"Did you see anyone else at the pickup truck with the camper while you worked security?"

"Yup, there wuz one oth'r guy, who carried stuff tuh my trunk, but he had a hat and dark glasses, I couldn't see him no good, eethur."

"Have they been back in touch?"

"Nope, not yet."

Kevin thought for awhile. "Have you watched the news lately?"

"Nope, how 'bout you?"

"Naw." Kevin shook his head, "I hate listening to the fucking news."

"Me too."

***

The doctor just stood there, playing with the pitcher of bloody marys. Finally he came out with something lame like Samantha had many issues, was suffering from nightmares, and needed much reassurance. We just nodded like we understood, thinking the whole time that this was one

perverted, sick son of a bitch.

Danny asked him again about his patients referred by the courts, if anyone came to mind

with satanic leanings, sadistic tendencies, or who might have wanted to embarrass him. The doc

stayed with the same line as before, about doctor patient privilege, that he worked with a

significant number of disturbed kids, but none were out especially to get him. He was helping his

patients, not pissing them off.

I couldn't help but wonder how many juvenile girls the courts had sent his way for

counseling. Even if he wasn't our doer, I thought Danny's and my testimony, would be enough to

bring DFACS (Department of Family and Childrens Services) into this situation, and clean up

what looked like a nest of perversion. Maybe get this fucker, whatever the medical equivalent of

disbarred is, disbarred. Have the state revoke his license to practice medicine, put his picture in

the paper as a perv, do the perp walk, the whole nine yards.

***

Samantha sat in her room, shaking. She felt like those cops had seen right through her,

and *knew*. At the very least one of them had, the one with the dangerous eyes and the long hair

pulled back. Worse than that, and on a more immediate level, she feared what Phineas might do.

She was hoping he wouldn't be so stupid as to beat her or kill her in the midst of a murder

investigation. But was counting on his sanity and self-control a wise thing to do? It was too early

to throw herself at anyone's mercy. Phineas might be pissed, but he was bound to know it would

be his ass if anything happened to her. At least one decision had come out of this fiasco, when

and if she did play her last card, she now knew to whom she would run. She had seen birds of prey up close several times at the zoo, she would run to the one with the hawk's eyes.

***

After all his qestions had been answered two or thee times Kevin quit doing speed, just drank some more beers and laid out in the sun. Gary drank beer and floated out in the water without effort. Gary was hoping that telling Kevin wasn't going to jinx it all for him. Kevin had done an okay little spell, but he hadn't sacrificed anything. Gary had killed the cat he'd had for three years and kinda liked; now that was a sacrifice.

***

The old man lived in a beautiful and emaculate house, in a nice old part of Morningside. He had gorgeous grounds, a pool, and a plump and seemingly jovial wife. He was shirtless, cleaning the pool, and told us to follow him back to the pool. He offered us beers from a full cooler at the pool, to which I said yes immediately. It was Sunday afternoon in July and I was drained from the talk. Danny thought for a second, and said he'd love one. So Danny and I drank a cold one sitting at a poolside table, under the umbrella's shade while the old guy used the long handled net to scoop out the leaves in the pool.

He was an interesting, talkative guy. When I get that age I hope I'm in as good a shape as he was. Late sixties, early seventies, thin, tanned, muscular, he looked like someone who had worked physically hard his whole life. Danny started with general questions but once O'Thomas got going, he didn't need much prompting.

In minutes we knew he was born in Ireland, brought by his mudder and popper to the U.S. at age seven. At seventeen he joined the US Navy, and did twenty-five years. When he retired, he became a jack of all trades and ended up working for the Faulkners and did that for another twenty-three. He still occasionally helps his son out. He said the Faulkners were a private family, but he had been there a long time. He said they treated their employees fairly enough and paid well as long as you kept your distance and remembered your place.

"Just what was it you were wantin' to know?"

"You know we're investigating a double homicide that was committed at the abandoned cottage?" Danny queried.

Sean O'Thomas nodded and said, "Liam told me as much."

"Do you know of any enemies they might have that would want to srew them over or embarrass them?" Danny didn't want to steer him too much.

"Naah, it was the old man had the enemies, and he's long dead, he is, almost nineteen years. I don't think the boys are as hard or as mean as the old man, with the exception of Phineas, and he's a doctor, not a business man. The oldest boy just wanted to please his daddy; but he's a fair dealer from everything I understand, not the kind to make enemies. The younger lad didn't get pressured by the old man like Emmet and Phineas did, the daughter neither, I'd bet she hardly remembers the old man." Danny was going to let the old man talk, see if he wouldn't reveal some family secrets.

"Mary, Joseph, and Jesus, that old man was a tyrant, almost sadistic he was. Emmet never had enough spirit for him; passively went along with whatever the old man said. But Emmet had a good mind for business, the old man could see that early on, and that mitigated his otherwise dissappointments. He hoped Phineas would be a minister, and he almost was, was on his way to becoming one when the old man died. Then Phineas changed the path of his education. Went to med school, became a headshrinker."

This had gotten into my area of interest, so I pursued it. "Mr. O'Thomas, you say the old man was religious? We hadn't heard much about that."

"Call me Sean lad, call me Sean. You haven't heard anything about religion because the children are heathens, heathens they are, no religion at all now, from what I can see."

"So the old man drove Phineas toward the priesthood?" This definitely sparked my interest.

"Aye, now he might have made it all the way had the old man lived."

Danny, just curious, "What'd the old man die of?"

"A massive coronary, died instantly, he did. I was the third one on the scene, he was dead by the time I got there."

"Was there anything suspicious about it?" Danny was still curious. Death was his bussiness.

"Nah. Not a bit. His doctors had known it was coming. The man was too tense, had high blood pressure, kept everything bottled up except for when he'd lose his temper. A wild and dangerous temper he had. Phineas has it too."

"Ever see the old man beat the kids? Every see Phineas really lose his temper?"

"Aye, aye. Saw both. I saw the old man belt both Phineas and Emmet, many a time. The wife often had to stop him. Often. She fell apart when the old man died. Wasted away at the nut house, she did, just wasted away. Nannies raised the younger two, and now the worthless daughter has nannies raise her kids while she floats around Europe with her worthless husband and his Eurotrash friends." The old man shook his head. He obviously thought parenting was a hands on job for the parental units, not something to be assigned to an employee.

Sean opened another beer and took a long drink, then another. "And Phineas, Holy Mother, that boy was one of the meanest little shits I've ever laid my eyes on. Do you know about his accident, why he limps?" We shook our heads and Sean launched into it. "Well now, the old man, he thought stables, show horses, and equestrian competitions were one of the more acceptable things ymore than adequate but he was no competitive rider. Phineas showed real promise as a rider until the accident. T'was one o' the meanest things I've ever seen in my life. I wish I'd had a chance to stop it, but once he'd begun it was done quick."

He stopped scooping up leaves, he looked down with unseeing eyes; it was like he was watching something internally. We were lost, he'd jumped too far ahead in his story and then stopped.

Danny prompted, "The accident was mean?"

Sean looked up, looked a little surprised like he had momentarily forgotten we were there, lost in his mental pictures.

"Accident, mean? Naah, it was a normal enough accident, Phineas had raised a jump too high - the arrogance of youth - when he rode the horse at the jump, at the last moment the horse hit the brakes, and threw Phinnie forward. Compound fracture of his left femur, and his knee cap exploded. It was busted beyond what medical science at the time could repair. Traction for over a month in a hospital bed, then it was many weeks more before he could walk on crutches. On Phinnie's first day home from the hospital I was working with flowers in the front when I heard gunshots. I went running, with some caution, mind you, to see who was shooting. By the time I got anywhere near it was already too late. He had fired three times. The horse that had thrown Phinnie was laying there, making a huge ruckus, neighing and writhing in pain. Phinneie shot the horse with a twelve gauge shotgun, double aught buckshot, in each knee. At a distance I saw him shoot the last knee, the horse was laying sideways, helpless, two of its legs were blown clear off. Then he poured gasoline all over the horse, and threw a match on it. Jesus, Mary, and Joseph,

I've never seen such a horrid sight. Or heard any living thing make such an agonizing sound. I came up behind him, grabbed the gun from off the ground where he'd thrown it when he torched the mare. I shot her in the head, twice, to put her out of her agony. Phinnie hardly noticed what I'd done. He just stood there, leaning on his crutches, watching the mare burn. With a sick and evil grin on his face. The grin of a demon, it was, I tell you it was like watching Satan himself smiling at the gates of hell."

It was silent for a while. He was lost in memory. We wondered about the implications of such a revelation. I came back to a previous question I hadn't asked. "What religion was the old man, being he was so strict, beating the kids, forced one towards the priesthood?"

"That was the crazy part of it, he was a whiskey-palion." He started laughing. I guess Danny looked blank. Before I could explain, Sean beat me to it.

"An Episcopalian." Sean explained. "They're very liberal compared to most, the priests marry, they drink, they have fun. Most wiskeypalions are liberal, but not the old man, he should have been a Catholic, Primitive Baptist, or something strict. He was the meanest, strictest Episcopalian I've ever seen. God have mercy, he drove the oldest two something fierce. I thought my popper was mean but he couldn't hold a candle to ol' man Faulkner."

"So Phineas was studying to be an Episcopal minister when the elder Faulkner died. And he switched over to psychiatry. Did he and Emmet stay in the church?"

"Naah, I imagine their mother's funeral was the last time a Faulkner graced the inside of a church."

We asked about Samantha and Stewart. They hadn't grown up as children on the property, but he had seen them often enough. "They were both bed-wetters. After every visit, I had to Lysol and dry the mattresses, turn them over - what a pain. And they kept doing it way older than they shoulda."

"The little girl was all right, I guess, never seemed like a child though - always seemed like a little adult, somewhat withdrawn and brooding. The little boy was a mean little shit, always; he'd kill any bird he could with his BB gun. Would torture and burn frogs, caterpillars. anything he could catch. A right little shit he was, would kill the pretty robins and the throw their eggs and break them. Couldn't leave him unattended around kittens or puppies. You'd come back and one wouldn't be breathing. Happened too many times to be coincidence. His parents have tried shipping him off to different schools, lately of the stricter military variety. The parents never knew how to deal with him. If he'd been mine, I'd have taken a leather strap to him like my dad did me, in the days before all this political correctness bullshit. And I'd made him spend many an hour at church, on his knees, praying for the redemption of his evil soul."

We stayed a while longer, but nothing much more came of it. He hadn't been around much the last few years. But Sean had been invaluable on general background. We had plenty to think about.

****

After the investigators left, Phineas had another bloody mary, and then another. He finished the whole damn pitcher. He couldn't believe what the little fool had just done, all she had put in jepoardy. Those cops might not be as smart as he was, not even in his league, but they weren't blind. Maybe they would believe she was a scared kid seeking solace, but her outfit certainly didn't aid that impression. Cops, by law, had to report sexual abuse and incest. He could wind up with DFACS sniffing around or before a review board. He was seething, his temper had been building, his inhibitions draining away as he drained the pitcher of marys. He thought about what one of his penal clients told him about justice in jail. He stormed upstairs and got a pair of socks and he put one inside the other. Then he rushed to the bathroom and got a slightly used bar of soap which he put in the toe of the socks. Holding the top of the socks, he began to twirl the soap weighted sock. After twirling it around five times he crashed it into the palm of his hand. He couldn't believe the force of the blow, or the pain.

Since Phineas had not rushed up to punish her for her mistake, Samantha had erred, concluding he was dealing with it. She was upset with herself as it was; she had still been sleepy when she charged downstairs, and she wasn't sure how it looked to the cops, but the one that had pissed her off before seemed to have read her like a book. At least that's how it felt to her. She was sleeping in late and had heard the intercom buzz through her sleep, but she hadn't heard the doorbell, or heard people come in. Maybe she'd gone back to sleep after the buzz. She didn't know how she had made such a blatant mistake. In a week or two, such actions might have been on purpose, but this early, she may have ruined everything. Through her own mistake, her best chance at vengeance might slip away.

Phineas burst in. One look at his face revealed he was in a mad drunken rage. He had blood in his eyes. At that moment she doubted he had any sanity or control left. "You stupid, stupid little twit. Why don't you just ruin my life, as well as all our long thought out plans. Why don't you just ruin my fucking life completely, you stupid little slut." He began hitting her in the midsection with the weighted sock. Buttocks, breast, stomach, back, anywhere where bruises wouldn't show. While he swung at her, he remembered what he couldn't earlier. Four to six guys hold down the sheet, while the one trapped under it takes a relatively bruiseless beating in bed – called a sock party. He wailed on her while she flopped around, trying not to be hit. He was exhausted by the time she got by him and ran away. He had controlled his rage enough to limit his blows to body shots. She had been smart enough not to scream loudly, instead she tried to stay agile and take advantage of his intoxication. She knew he had no endurance. But she felt like twenty horses had kicked her by the time she ran outside and hid in the barn.

***

Stewart had never seen anything like it in person. Raquel came out in what looked to him like a catwoman suit. It was really just a crotchless black body stocking. She stood before him as he found out it had two removable patches over her breasts which she removed as he watched. He went to wood immediately, there was catwoman in a crotchless, exposed-breast body suit. She crawled catlike up on the bed, moved forward and grabbed the headboard. Raquel looked back at him and said, "Since I'm dressed like a cat, we have to do it like cats." She purred and moved her buttocks up and down. She had already taught him doggie style, so he crawled up right behind her.

***

She was crying quietly, but inside she raged. Samantha hadn't been that angry or that scared since the first time she told on Stewart and got him in trouble when she was six. She thought he had smothered her kitten and she told. He woke her up in the night with a fork one inch away from her eyes. Stewart calmly told her about the kitten. He hadn't killed her cat or her horse, yet, but he would if she ever squealed on him again. And he would do that before he stuck the fork in both her eyes and blinded her. So complete was her submission to him from that moment on, that the sexual abuse, once it began, was almost something she had been subconsciously expecting. Definitely not wanting, but expecting. Stewart was a sadist - manipulative and ruthless. She had been scared of Stewart for most of her life, and now she was scared of the doctor who was supposed to save her from Stewart. She quit crying and started to think about revenge, revenge on both her abusers. Revenge she could still walk away from.

***

Leonard Wounded Face arranged his eagle wings, still hot from the steam, between the canvas back of the sweat lodge and the willow branch frame which supported it and sat down in the darkness between the door and his primary patient. He was finished for today with his physical doctoring. It was toward the end of the third round, with the Old Man in the Mountain song still going strong.

As usually happens when Grandfather Rayland was away, Leonard was running the regular Sunday Sweat. The round dome shaped canvas and parachute material covered Sweat Lodge was filled with eighteen people, sitting, singing, praying, sweating close to each other in the darkness in a circle around the fire pit - filled with rocks which had been heated in the fire right outside the Sweat Lodge for hours. The rocks in the central fire pit didn't glow red hot, crackle, and shoot sparks like they had in the beginning, but they were still giving off scorching heat - despite the three rounds in which Leonard had poured dipperfull after dipperfull of water upon them from the bucket at his side - producing in excess the cleansing, purifying, and healing steam. Leonard had treated the young Indian man next to him, to fight an infection he picked up in the hospital when they used a rod to fix his broken femur. If his body didn't defeat the infection quickly, the surgeons wanted to operate again. The other patient was a woman with a chronic bronchial infection, the doctors hadn't cured her yet, so she'd come for spiritual help. These days most of the shaman's patients were going to the Sweat Lodge in conjunction with going to the doctor. Generally speaking, everyone was most comfotable that way, except maybe the doctor, often left out of the spiritual part, mistakenly thinking it is just him/her, instead of being part of the more effective patient/doctor/shaman triangle healing the body, mind, and spirit.

At the propper place to end the song Leonard shouted "Ho!" to which the other sweaters quit singing and responded in kind with a chorus of individual "Ho!'s"

Usually the Sweat Lodge ritual is comprised of four rounds, in between which the front and back door flaps may be opened or not, and water may be drunk or not, at the discretion of the shaman. The first round begins with prayers and invites the healing spirits in, the last and usually fourth round is the thank-you round and is completed by smoking the Sacred Pipe. In all rounds those present sing sacred songs to invoke and then to some extent carry and deliver the healing power. The middle, usually the second and third, are the working rounds in which those present in need are physically worked on by the shaman and those absent are prayed for and cured at a distance either by "sending" them healing energy or sending an animal spirit/spirit power to heal/aid them.

Leonard's physical treatments were performed in the darkness and in the punishing heat of the second and third working rounds. The people sit on Tule reeds, spread around the outer circumference of the Sweat Lodge, the inner ring next to the fire pit is bare earth. Because the shaman moves around inside the Sweat Lodge, using his eagle feathers, his hands, and certain techniques for sucking out the bad and casting it into the fire pit - he moves on that bare dirt inner circle, closer to the fire pit than the others - taking more of its punishing heat. Leonard was drenched in sweat as he spoke out in the darkness.

"Singer, I want you to lead the bear song then go into the wolf song. These will be our final songs this round. Pray for yourself, your own healing and the blessing and healing of those here and of your families and friends. Call on your spirit powers and any loved ones who've passed on who might want to help. I want everybody to keep in mind our friend Spooky all the way down there in Atlanta, and the people he's working with. I talked to him on the phone earlier and he wants our help and support. He told me about a terrible crime, some people killed a pregnant mother and her baby. The people that have done this have given their souls to the devil, to the evil side of darkness, and they must be stopped. There is a danger to the souls of those involved in fighting such battles, so he needs us to send our help to him in the days to come. Ho!" All the regular sweaters knew Spooky and responded with enthusiastic "Ho's!" The singer began the bear song, joined immediately by everyone else. Leonard also began to sing along, but in his consciousness, deep in trance he was already transforming into his spirit wolf. "Un a ki′ ta a ya′…"

Chapter Eight – Sunday Afternoon, Evening, and Night

The best time of Stewart's life was coming to a close and he wanted to do something to prevent its ending, or at least make sure that it would be repeated. He still wondered about her absence that morning, and the men in the van, but his overwhelming desire was not to lose the happiness, pleasure, and contentment he had discovered with Raquel - this exquisite and accepting fellow sado-masochistic sexual entity.

She came out of the bathroom fully dressed, and began gathering her stuff and preparing to leave. She bribed him to get his ass in gear, she promised to repeat the way she initially greeted him when they parted. The promise got him moving, however hesitantly.

"We had a great time," he tried reason, "why can't we meet and do it again?"

"Look, Pugsley, I told you how it had to be in the beginning. Just drop it, and let it end happy."

Knowing he was fighting a losing battle, as he had been for twenty minutes, he attempted to fill his other curiosity. "Who were those men who brought you back this morning?

She swung around and looked at him, with some of the CD's she had been putting up in her hands. Her face startled Stewart. She looked both questioning and angry at him. "What?'"

"I saw you get out of the white van, I saw two men sitting in it."

Thoughts were tumbling through her mind, but primarily she thought how dangerous George had looked hours earlier. She tried to stay in her role as a rich housewife out on a fling. "Oh, the guys in the van. I wanted to be outside and felt like walking, so I walked to go get us breakfast, but it was much longer distance than I thought. At the restaurant I saw some men on a construction crew who had done some renovation work on a few of our commercial properties. I asked them for a ride back, and their discretion."

Stewart digested her response and *changed* tact.

 "If you loved your husband a whole bunch, you wouldn't be doing this, so *why* can't we keep meeting?"

She was tired of arguing with the kid. He seemed to have bought her bullshit about the van. She just wanted this job to be over, and be with her girl safely in the skies on the way to Vegas.

"You're fucking a dead horse, Pugsley, let it go."

His mind was whirling, to have found such happiness and then to lose it. But if she didn't love her husband, which seemed likely, then she had probaby married for money. Stewart thought to himself, he had money, or at least would have when he came into the trust funds.

She had finished putting up her CD's, and was putting the blaster's cord up, when he fired his last shot.

"I'm very rich." It was a phrase he personally had never uttereded before. She turned around again, this time more slowly, but definitely interested. "I'm Stewart Faulkner-Davis, I come into my first trust fund, worth twenty-two million dollars, when I turn twenty-one. That's in less than four years. If you married once for money, maybe you could get divorced, and marry me."

Tonya stood there, speechless. This child's brainless words were probably the best offer of financial security she had ever been given. She wouldn't need to get divorced, but if she could get this little dork to California and marry him when he turned twenty-one, she would be worth eleven million by state law. She could even stay married to the little shit for a year or two for that kind of money.

"Let me get this straight, Pugsley. Your name is Stewart Faulkner-Davis, you're very rich, you get your first twenty-two mill when you turn twenty-one, and you want to marry me."

"Yeah," he stammered, "yeah."

"Well Stewart, sweetie, you just write your name, addresses and phone numbers down on a very, very small piece of paper, and I'll stay in touch. But I still want you to play everything like we agreed in the beginning. If anybody, I mean anybody asks you anything about this weekend, you stick to the original story. If that breaks down, you go to story two. If number two crashes and burns, I gave you the absolute last resort. Got it? Never vary from this plan. Now if you feel the same way in a few years about marriage and all, what the hell, we'll talk about it." In her heart Tonya knew she was looking at the best chance she ever would have of getting rich. She had lied to George about little things before and gotten away with it. She would just have to do it again. No bigee, she lied to herself.

"Will you give me your real name and number?" Stewart had noticed the distinct change in her attitude with his revelation of financial wealth. He thought he would press the advantage.

She thought about it for a few seconds. "Not now sweetie, but I'll call you in one or two months, and tell you how we can stay in touch."

He wanted more, but this was better than nothing. He still planned to memorize her license plate number, just in case.

***

Kevin would move in and out of the part sun induced/part beer induced daze, and try to make sense out of it all. Fatboy's incredible story and several other things that had bothered him lately weighed on his mind. Empty pauses on his answering machine, not that long, but several of them. There was the occasional feeling he was being watched, and a couple of times he felt like somebody had been in his house, but nothing was missing. What was up? Fatboy being recruited by government spooks seemed highly unlikely, but whoever was running fatboy, they sure seemed to have lots of resources. He tried to think about entrapment, but by who and for what? What law agency ran this kind of sting? None he had ever heard of. What if it was real, would he be jealous. Fatboy just didn't seem the James Bond type. Even if some offshoot CIA group or mafia family was recruiting fatboy, those who are deniable are vunerable and sacrificable. It just didn't make sense. But if somebody was watching fatboy real close, they sure as hell had seen him and might even know who he was, maybe what he did. Who the fuck are these people? Maybe they were watching him as well as fatboy. Anyone could have gotten the police uniform from Atlanta Costume, or gotten the car at an auction, bought the gun and holster, but the Police ID's looked genuine. Generally things are logical, reasonable, but this wasn't, this bothered the shit out of him.

***

Tonya let the slug off where she had found him after she brought him pleasure one last time as promised, then drove on to the rendezvous a block away from the rental place. She and George went in where they had rented her car early Friday morning. She almost couldn't keep a straight face again, just like when they rented it, because of George's beard. He had on a ball cap, sun glasses, and a huge mountain man beard. It didn't look that bad for a fake, you couldn't tell unless you looked hard up close, and she noticed in the pictures on his ID's he had a beard, she assumed the same one. The car was fine, the paperwork done quickly, and Bobby picked them up in the van. She was ready to get her baby girl and go, the sooner the better.

***

Stewart sat on the curb at the convience store and attacked two honey buns and a Big Gulp. Fucking was hard work, he'd had no idea. Were it not for the pain and soreness between his legs, and sore muscles all over his body, it could all have been a dream. Things like that just don't happen. Now he had to get back in, with ketchup stains smeared all over his uniform, meaning serious demerit trouble if he ran into the wrong asshole. He didn't want to get kicked out of this place now, who knows, she might change her mind and want to play with him again. Second honey bun finished, he dragged his tired and aching body up and walked slowly over to the phones. Big Gulp in hand, he was thinking "Dear Playboy, I've always read your letters and wondered if they weren't fiction. Until the other day when the strangest thing happened...."

***

Danny and I ate at the bar at Applebee's where Danny could sit in front of a phone, eat, and drink a cold one. It was Sunday, and he might not have to go back in today. Anyway, he'd already had one at the pool and was ready for another. Schultz filled him in. The men, Williams and Wallace, after hours on the phone, had gotten hold of all the right people, they would go from one school to the other Monday until they found their phone pals and brought them in for questioning. We all knew a description of the fake cop could be a godsend. The women, Annie Wilson and Potts, had called the womens shelters and unwed mothers homes in the greater Atlanta area and throughout north Georgia, and left stern instructions that if anybody out for the weekend didn't come in on time to call APD immediately. There weren't any missing persons reports in the southeast U.S. that matched her, and her prints revealed no criminal record, so she was still Jane Doe, mother of Baby Doe. No more reports were due in today from the M.E. or GBI, so Danny told them over the phone to draw straws, one person stays, the rest go home, and be in early tomorrow.

"What a fucked up family. More money than god and are they screwed up. A shrink boffing his niece, a kid that likes to kill and torture animals, parents Eurotrashing away...."

Danny was disgusted at the sorriness and perversion of this wealthy family.

"The sins of the parents will be passed down, even until the seventh generation." I couldn't help myself. Danny just stared at me, seeing if I was serious quoting the Bible.

"How about the psychological problems and complexes of parents are inherited/learned by their children, who repeat them, whose kids repeat them, until some kind of healing takes place and breaks the chain."

"Whatever." Danny wasn't as concerned with the transmission of mental disease as he was with solving this case. "What we've got to do is figure out what to do about this sadistic kid - Stewart. Where he goes to school in South Carolina is two, two and a half hours by car. The kid certainly knew about the cabin, who knows how serious his psychological problems are. He could be one of our doers." Danny paused for my opinion.

"In some ways he definitely fits the profile. But what about the shrink and the little witch?" As soon as I said the last word, I wondered why I had, and where it had come from. Danny looked at me funny and on reflex I said, "Shrink and the little rich girl. Do you call in DFACS, check it out, see if it ties in...?"

"DFACS can wait a day or two." Danny looked at me. "I've seen your library, and some of the stuff you've got and use. If this kid was involved, could you tell by the way his room looked, by what books and stuff he has?"

"Maybe at his house. But at a military school?" Danny called APD and got Annie. He gave her the name of Stewart's school and asked her to give them a call. Find out if he's there, and if he's been there all weekend. Then he asked me what I thought.

"He's the only person we know about, besides the doc, that fits anything of the profile. The doc because he almost went into the priesthood but rebelled, might cast him in the apostate priest satanic role. It still seems illogical and farfetched that anyone would do such a crime on their own land and leave it all to be found. Serial killers and people drawn to this kind of perverted black magic usually start off as kids torturing or killing insects, small animals, and then graduate to people. Which sounds like Stewart. We also know he was a bed-wetter. With a history of starting (horse) fires, he had all three of the major known indicators of serial killers - bed wetting, sadism, and pyromania. It's not much, but Sean seemed reliable. If Stewart wasn't on campus this weekend, we definitely need to know where he's been."

I'd left a message for Laura and she called in. Danny said he couldn't let me go until he found out about Stewart, that he and I might have to roadtrip. I suggested that if she didn't want to stay at the convention hotel, she go on home, hit the hot tub or go for a moonlight horseback ride with Betty. She said she'd do both and hoped I could join her. I hoped so, too. Of course, we had to roadtrip.

***

Stewart kept trying Jimmy's number. He didn't answer, which was bad for Stewart. He had to sneak in, go up to his room, change, sneak out and then sign in before seven o'clock. Without Jimmy opening up a side door, sneaking in would be difficult. He didn't know how Raquel could have been so sloppy, his uniform was a mess. The last thing he needed was more demerits, he was running out of schools to go to, and his parents were running out of what little, if any, patience they had left.

***

Bobby took the large bags into the house while George and Tonya transferred to George's sedan. Bobby drove the hour and a half down to Macon while George went over everything with Tonya. A few miles from Tonya's mama's trailer, he went over it again.

"Jasmine will meet you at baggage claim, you can't miss her, six feet tall, gorgeous, elegant, hair like a lion's mane. She'll be your new house mother. Now Tonya, this is your big chance, don't blow it. We're talking up to a thousand a trick, twenty-five hundred for the night, five grand for the weekend. You can save up and buy a house."

"You'll be doing etiquette classes and maybe even foreign language classes. Jasmine's got kids, your girl will be in pre-school with hers. This is big, baby, so don't fuck this up. Absolutely no contact with anyone in Georgia until I call and say it's okay. Got it?"

"Yeah, baby, I've got it and it all sounds great."

George handed her the tickets, and the rest of the money, and he genuinely smiled at her. "I always wanted good things for you, sweet tits, and this is it." As soon as they pulled down the dusty drive between the scrawny pine trees and stopped in front of the single wide trailer resting on the white concrete blocks, the door flew open and her little girl rushed out screaming, "Mama, Mama." Tonya started crying when she held Maria in her arms. She thought she knew George well enough to be certain of one thing. George might kill her if it was business, but he wouldn't kill a child. She really would make it to Vegas and a better life. It was unlike Tonya to cry, but her eyes poured. It was good she didn't know just how wrong she was about George.

***

Colonel Williams S. McIntyre, U.S. Army, inactive reserves, was a South Carolinian who felt fortunate he had been able to land such a good job in his native state. A first lieutenant in Nam, he'd made it to captain by the end of his third tour in country with the 101st Airborne. He was retired career army, now commander of this Cadillac of military academies, and the military expert for the best local TV station. After meals, and two or three other times a day, weather permitting, he walked the perimeter of the two large buildings - the school/dorm and the gym/swimming pool. Resting and leaning against one of the large oaks which ringed the edge of the school's large central building which housed both classrooms, dorms, and administrative offices, he often smoked his pipe or the occasional cigar while contemplating his domain. His inner office and living quarters were the only places on campus he could smoke, besides the great outdoors, and he enjoyed the alone time outside.

The Colonel was thinking about their policy of taking the discipline problems of other institutions. He had instituted a rule five years ago mandating the tuition for someone kicked out of two previous institutions was raised 50%. He was thinking it should be doubled or tripled. Speak of the devil, he thought, as he caught sight of one such multiple military school reject slinking, sneaking along the side of the school. He puffed his pipe and watched, saying quietly to himself, "This should be interesting."

Stewart had waited as long as he could, calling Jimmy. He couldn't wait any longer. He walked a third of the way up the school's drive and then headed for the trees which ringed the main building. The student running the front desk where they signed in would not be a friend of his and willing to risk any demerits for helping him out. Jimmy, his only friend, and a fellow outcast, was as unlikely as Stewart to ever be trusted with running the front desk. That only went to rule followers and ass kissers. Since there was no way to sneak in the front door, it had to be a side door, or the back door of the kitchen, which was sometimes left open by the kitchen and janitorial staff.

During the school week, the side doors were left open until after dinner, but on weekends and nights all student entry and exit was through the front doors. The side doors couldn't be opened from the outside. Stewart would have to be lucky enough to see someone walking in the halls, whose attention he could get by knocking, who liked him or disliked the rules enough to walk over, and push open the door for him; a clear demerit earning violation of the rules if caught. It wasn't highly likely, but it was worth a shot. He might be able to sneak in the back door, but someone on the staff would probably see him, and if so, was supposed to report him immediately. Like they cared.

He moved from the trees to the side door, and waited. After what felt like ten furtive minutes, seeing no one walking the halls, and feeling he was running out of time, he moved to the back door of the cafeteria. It was open. A flood of relief came over him. Then, right as he stepped inside the open door, a large hand clamped down on his shoulder from behind, and the very last voice he wanted to hear said, "Gotcha!"

I was dipping the last of my fries in the honey-mustard and knocking off my first cold one when Annie called Danny back. Three seconds into the conversation I could tell Danny was on fire.

"They need to put him under immediate supervision so he doesn't destroy evidence. We're going to need cooperation with South Carolina, we'll need a search warrant. No shower, nothing, total supervision immediately. He can pee, being watched, but he can't wash his hands."

As we ran to the car, Danny told me Annie had talked to the kid at the front desk of the military school, who put her through to the supervisor, who put her through to the commander, Colonel McIntyre. Stewart was in the process of getting read the riot act by the Colonel when Annie got him on the phone. Seems Stewart had tried to sneak back into the school and been caught by the Colonel himself. Annie talked to the Colonel, who spent three tours in Nam and said he knew bloodstains, and wondered why there were blood stains on Stewart's uniform. He also told her Stewart had signed out to spend the weekend at his Uncle Alpert's house. The Colonel said Stewart had a problematic record and that he'd be glad to stay on top of Stewart till we got there. It sounded too good to be true. An obvious lie and possibly blood stained clothing. Life, as well as the criminal element, is often not always rational or consistent, but still, it seemed too good to be true.

So I went roadtripping with Danny instead of going home. After my first night with a woman in a long time, instead of going home to Laura, I'd be spending the night playing cops and robbers (cops and bad guys, really) with Danny. At least I knew it would be a quick trip. A police car going 95 to 105 miles an hour can make a normal two hour trip in an hour and twenty minutes.

On the way Danny used his cell phone to coordinate with the South Carolina agencies and had them send a state trooper, ostensibly to tell Stewart about a murder committed on one of his relative's properties, but in reality to sit on top of the kid. They had a case for a search warrant, they had a lie, no alibi, possible blood stains, knowledge of the crime scene, and a personality matching the profile they were looking for. Before calling South Carolina, Danny got on the phone and explained to the Atlanta DA what he needed, adding that if "the powers that be" wanted a quick solution to the crime, he needed a quick search warrant and a lot of cooperation in South Carolina. The DA got on the phone, talking to city and state bigwigs. More calls got made. Danny wanted cooperation in South Carolina, and he got it.

***

Kevin and Gary broke into the second case of beer and took his bass boat to the marina for some bait, and found a likely spot. Refreshed after their afternoon naps, they had become surprisingly active. Kevin didn't get to come up and fish enough as it was, so he'd take the opportunity to do some dusk and night fishing, and being out on the water always cleared his head and helped him think. And he needed to think long and hard about this current situation. It was strange by any standards. He needed to figure out how what fatboy was into could come back on him. Kevin threw another line out while Gary fumbled with the bait. His fat fingers weren't very good at some tasks. Especially after that fourteenth or fifteenth brew.

***

Samantha had sneaked quietly back into the house after several hours and made it to the safety of her room and immediately locked her door. A long hot bath helped. Then she ventured out driven by hunger, only to hear the loud snoring of Phineas, who was passed out cold laying sideways on his bed. Back in her locked room after eating, she once more took her diary out, this time to record the truth, the details of her beating.

During the ride to South Carolina I repeatedly told Danny not to get too excited about the kid. People who plan and execute things as well as our perps were not likely to forget to change clothes or have a prepared alibi. Danny would agree, but he had seen so much outrageously stupid criminal behavior and there was so much pressure on him he couldn't help wanting a quick break and couldn't stop himself from wishful thinking. I hoped for his sake we got a quick solution to the crime, but I didn't expect it. Not this quick.

When we pulled in, there was a state trooper's car, a plain clothes car, and a S.C.B.I. mobile crime lab van. The detective was waiting outside with the search warrant, while the trooper was upstairs with the suspect in the Colonel's office, and the crime lab techs were waiting for us to hand them something to work on. We explained a little about the case to everybody and made our way in. Institutions, whatever they may be, have distinct odors. Hospitals, nursing homes, jails, boarding schools, all have their own unique institutional smells. This military school smelled like industrial cleaners, waxes, brass and wood polish, and money. There was no doubt it took some serious jack to send a kid to this place. The sound of our footsteps resonated loudly in the empty hall as we made our way to the front desk and the excited kid manning it. The presence of the police and the mystery of what gave rise to their presence had the kid agitated and tongue-tied. We finally got led to the Colonel's office.

The beast we'd heard about earlier was a frightened Pillsbury doughboy with mean, squinty eyes. And a stained uniform with stains that sure as hell looked like blood. After introductions we went into the Colonels office and Danny called Annie to check with the authorities near the school and ask the pertinent questions about desecrated churches and missing or murdered pets and livestock. She reported back surprisingly quickly that there were no church or graveyard descrations in the vicinity, but it seems some dogs were found shot, and a few cats mutilated. There was no guarantee it was Stewart's work, but it sure seemed possible. We didn't know who did what behind the scenes, but we were certainly impressed with all the cooperation and what was in place. The local detective was staying quiet and out of the way. With the mobile crime lab there to do the preliminary work on Stewart's stained uniform, if it wasn't ketchup like he claimed, but human blood, he'd either be taken into South Carolina custody or hopefully coming with us.

Danny started real slow, Stewart was obviously extremely nervous. The kid was surrounded by Georgia and South Carolina law enforcement personnel, was already in trouble with the Colonel, and he knew he had done things society frowns on, but he didn't know what the specific problem was. Ketchup stains aren't a state offense, neither is lieing about weekend plans. Danny looked at the sign in/out book. "So Stewart, you went home this weekend to stay with your Uncle Alpert?"

"Yes, sir."

"And how is your Uncle Alpert?"

"Fine, sir."

"Stewart?"

"Yes, sir?"

"Cut the bullshit. We've been at your Uncle Alpert's all weekend. You might have been there Friday night, but you sure as hell weren't there the rest of the time. So why don't you cut the crap and tell us about your weekend. You've just lied to a police officer in the investigation of a murder in front of multiple witnesses. That' prosecuteable crime. You can be arrested right now for obstruction."

Stewart gulped. It was so strange, Raquel had made him learn two extra cover stories, and now he had to use one.

"Camping sir, I was camping in the woods with a local boy named Arnold."

"What's Arnol's last name, whats he look like?"

Stewart launched into the story Raquel had told him. At the end of his recitation, Danny asked the Colonel if we could all talk in his inner office. We went back in the inner sanctum while the South Carolina State Trooper stayed with Stewart.

Danny and the Colonel talked about Stewart, his record at the school, his files, what the Colonel knew about his past. We showed him the search warrant handed us downstairs. The Colonel obviously had no great affection for Stewart, referring to him as "one of our problem transfers" - kids with behavior problems already booted out of other such institutions. With the Colonel's permission and cooperation, the S.C.B.I. mobile crime lab techs came up and took Stewart's uniform, shoes, and socks to test for blood. They combed his hair and scraped his fingernails. They took pictures of him with his undershirt off, lots of pictures of the scratches on his back. Raquel's little reminders. After all the activity, Stewart sat in the Colonel's outer office, under guard, wearing a robe brought to him from his room.

Stewart was experiencing something he never had before. He was shaking, shivering, while everybody else was comfortable. His knees were knocking against each other. He could feel the drops of sweat trickling from his underarms down his sides. Sweating while he was chilled, all he had on was his briefs, and the undershirt and robe they brought him after they had taken his clothes. The Colonel had told him to undress and hand over his clothes, and do whatever else he was asked, so he had. But he didn't understand any of this.

At first one of the uniformed cops told had told him some kind of murder had taken place on his family's land, but hadn't said which estate. Then some Atlanta cops came in and asked him where he'd been this weekend and he went with the sign out story, that he was at Albert's. They obviously knew that wasn't true and said so, so he had gone on to the next one. Nobody had said anything to him about sneaking the target practice .22's out and shooting the dogs, or asked about the mutilated cats, and nobody had asked him about his sister. He had broken some laws in his perverted but at the same time sheltered life, but Samantha had always been too scared of him to ever give him up. He didn't understand the sense of importance of what everybody around him was doing.

Without consciously understanding, Stewart piacked up they all had a hurried self-consciousness of people doing work that others would see or judge. Work that meant something. Stewart thought back over his weekend, there were several things he had questioned, but Raquel always had good answers.

Danny told the Colonel that Stewart could be arrested for making false statements to the police during the investigation of a murder; that was enough for him to be taken into custody. While we were waiting for the stain report, Danny said we'd like to execute the search warrant and go through Stewart's things. So all three of us proceeded to Stewart's room while the trooper stayed with Stewart.

On the way out, Danny stopped in front of Stewart, showed him the South Carolina search warrant, and informed him that we had already taken his clothes under its authority and were going to search his room. Stewart slumped in the armchair, with a defeated look. I wondered what we were about to find.

"Oh, shit," Stewart kept thinking, "oh, shit." A search warrant for his room. Things had gone from absolutely wonderful to totally crappy in a matter of hours. He thought about the weird things Raquel had done. Taking his clothes when she vanished, and then reappearing from the van. How she had cleaned the room before they left. Once she had put on her street clothes, she put on yellow rubber gloves and wiped off everything. Tub, sink absolutely everything. He had asked her about it and she said her husband was so rich and so jealous that he sometimes hired private detectives to watch her. She was sure she was safe this weekend, she'd said as she smiled and winked at him, 'But it's always wise to never leave a trace." She had wiped off the door handles as they left. She'd been very thorough.

Raquel had given him the first backup story if his sign out story failed, the one he was sticking to now, camping with a local boy named Arnold. If that fell apart, he'd go to story number two. Raquel had told him about a girl that worked for one of her husband's companies who had become a good friend of hers over the years. Raquel had found out the girl had a checkered past, and used that knowledge to persuade her to always provided Raquel with alibis when needed, and in exchange Raquel paid her well on the side. She said to use Amanda for the absolute last ditch alibi if need be, but to never mention her, she said she'd call Amanda and set it up as soon as possible.

All along Stewart had understood why a married woman needed an alibi, but never why she was so insistent that he have one, no, three. If he had to, he would vaguely describe his weekend but put Amanda in Raquel's place as instructed. All he knew was Amanda Stone from Atlanta, and he could describe her, at least repeat Raquel's description, which she'd made him repeat, and repeat, and repeat.

The Colonel led us to Stewart's room and watched from the door as we put on our latex examination gloves and conducted the search. The school might be expensive, but the room was the same small room found in most dorms. He had a desk, a bed, a set of drawers, and a closet. Not much to search, and it didn't take long. He had no books that interested me, no sign of any occult interests, no posters of bands or babes, not much in the way of decorations or anything revealing clues about his personality.

The last place we searched was the closet. Danny went through it as I took out the lone suitcase and used my locksmith's pick-it pack - a small leather case with the few tools needed to pick most common locks. When I opened it, both sides seemed filled with towels, but under the towels the real Stewart started to emerge. On one side there were several porno mags, as sleazy as one can get short of the big city specialty shops or black market operations. On the other side was an odd contraption and a cloth tool roll, the inexpensive kind used to hold a set of socket wrenches or similar tools. Inside it was a bizarre assortment of knives, exacto blades, razor blades, pliers, scalpels, tweezers, scissors, and a couple of small hacksaws.

Danny came out of the closet, the S.C. detective and the Colonel took a couple of steps forward once I said, "I think we've got a fucking jack-the-ripper here." Sure enough, it was all you'd need to kill, maim, and torture. It could be for small animals - squirrels, rabbits, cat; but some of the tools could also be used on people. We didn't know what we had yet, but there was nothing benign about what lay before us.

The contraption in the suitcase was nothing but a wood frame, but one like none of us had ever seen before. It was made of 2" by 1" oak and fastened firmly by multiple screws at the corners, as big as it possibly could be and still fit in the suitcase. All around the inside, every couple of inches were half-inch eyebolts, and in between them facing inside were strong bands of once white elastic cloth tipped with alligator clips, attached by screws to the frame. The elastic strips were heavily stained with what looked like blood.

It was crudely made, not skillfully assembled, but it was functional. We all just looked at it for a minute, this homemade dissection/torture kit laid out before us. If this boy wasn't a serial killer yet, he had all the makings.

Finally, Danny asked me what I made of the frame. "The only thing it remotely resembles is a frame used when tanning the skin of a deer, rabbit, coyote, whatever. I doubt this one was ever used for that. I think this one was used as a portable torture rack for whatever small animal was unfortunate enough to be in Stewart's path." In a paper bag were larger cloth straps tipped with larger alligator clips, probably to be tied to the eyebolts, with the alligator clips holding the victims in place.

Evil is disgusting and revolting. What Stewart did to small creatures was evil. I still didn't know if that made him one of our doers in Atlanta, but he did seem a more likely candidate once you examined his hobbies.

Laura had made her way back to the family compound, followed Spooky's instructions, and gotten herself in the gates. As soon as she got out of the truck, Betty stuck her head out and yelled for Laura to come eat dinner. John, Betty, and the kids made Laura feel right at home amidst the fried chicken, mashed potatoes, green beans, potato salad, biscuits, and sweet iced tea. It was good she had gone to the Unity planning meeting because it had put a buffer between her and the realities of the morning's work. The free lunch Spooky had won them had been postponed, thankfully. She hadn't had an appetite all day, until she walked into Betty's kitchen. Once she sat down, she ate like a horse.

After dinner over coffee and blackberry pie topped with vanilla ice cream, Betty told Laura Spooky had mentioned she liked horseback riding, and suggested they go for a moonlight ride while John put the kids down. In actuality, both women stayed and help put the kids down before their ride.

The moon was only two days past full, the lightning bugs were out in number, and the crickets and tree frogs were filling the night with natural music. It was not her native landscape, but it brought her a sense of peace and harmony. And she did feel very at home here, for only a few days.

After the ride, Betty and her made use of Spooky's hot tub while they sipped wine. They talked about Leonard and his wife and kids, about Spooky, about John and the kids, about her work. Laura wondered about Betty raising her family in the security/law enforcement world of John and Spooky, using the family compound as a model, security gates, cameras, and guns. It was very peaceful inside the compound, but there were a lot of guns. So Laura asked Betty about living with her self-described macho asshole and his brother in an armed camp.

Betty's reply surprised laura. "You see, I'm an army brat. My dad served as an MP and then made his way up through the ranks in military intelligence. I was raised inside army bases and learned to shoot about the same time I learned how to ride a bike. There are plenty of guns here, but they are properly secured or on person, the boys know I won't tolerate anything else."

"It's beautiful here, and peaceful, I'm just not used to being around badges and guns."

"Spooky told me about your loss. It must have been a terrible time for you."

Laura just nodded. "It was a long time ago."

Betty could only imagine the loss. But Betty would have shot back. "Who knows, if you'd been raised like I was, maybe you'd have gotten one or two of the thugs that killed your husband as they drove away. I know you say you don't like guns, but I could teach you how to shoot while you're here. Believe me, I'm a better shot than either of the boys. I was on the national team for years, and competed in the '92 and '96 Olympics. I was eighth in the world in '96."

"Wow, the Olympics. That's very impressive Betty. I appreciate the offer, I'll think it over." Laura thought she might need some knowledge of guns if her career shifted toward the area of crime reporting, after her book....

By the time Betty announced she had been away long enough and must return, Laura felt that sisterhood bond that happens between simpatico women, and they hugged warmly when she left.

Betty had told her not to expect Spooky back that night, so Laura skipped sleeping in her sexy nightgown, and wore her 49'ers jersey. Her suitcase was still in the guest bedroom she was yet to sleep in. She thought about things for a second, was she being presumptuous to assume she should sleep in his room. She laughed, shook her head, and climbed on in his bed. She knew men well enough, and she knew what had passed between them last night. They were well past the guest bedroom stage.

***

Besides his porno and torture chamber, Stewart didn't seem to have many possessions. He had a few fantasy/science fiction paperbacks, a slingshot, three marksmanship trophies, and a few postcards from his mom. There was not much left to do in Stewart's room when one of the S.C.B.I. techs stuck her head in the door and yelled, "Bingo! We have a winner. We have multiple spots which are definitely human blood." Danny showed the tech the stuff we needed bagged up and they talked about transferring the clothes and test results to Danny to take back to Atlanta. No problem.

The Colonel was legally responsible for Stewart in the absence of his parents, and the Colonel thought Stewart should head on back to Georgia with us, be under his uncles supervision, and face the music. He would either be placed under arrest in South Carolina or Georgia, and his uncle was a lawyer in Georgia, all his relatives were there. So going back to Georgia was the obvious choice. The level of cooperation was amazing to Danny, as well as to me. Whoever greased the wheels here had the juice to do the job right. And Stewart, obviously no legal scholar, did whatever the Colonel told him to.

We checked Stewart's locker in the gym locker room, but there was nothing there. On the way back, Danny asked if the Colonel had access to a few flashlights. The Colonel came back with three of the long, multi-battery variety and we went to go visit our suspect in waiting.

***

Stewart knew if they looked inside his suitcase he had some explaining to do. He would say he was interested in becoming a biologist, maybe a vet or a doctor, and he dissected the dead animals and roadkill he found in the woods or on the road. So far they were yet to mention anything he had actually done. Nobody had mentioned sneaking out rifles, dead dogs, cut up cats, or his sister. The wording of the search warrant confused him. He understood there was some kind of crime committed on Alpert's estate. He didn't know what that had to do with him. He ostensibly had a room at Alpert's, but his parents generally kept him at school year round. The crime on the estate sounded like murder, and for some reason, just because he lied about being there this weekend and had some ketsup stains on his uniform, he was a legitimate suspect, and they could take his clothes and search his room.

Danny came in strong, followed by the Colonel and me. Holding a big flashlight in his hand, he got up in Stewart's face, still sitting in the chair in his robe. "Stewart Faulkner-Davis we may soon place you under arrest for making false statements to a police officer during the course of a murder investigation - for obstruction of justice. Anything you say can, and will, be used against you in a court of law. You have a right to an attorney. If you cannot afford one, one will be provided for you. Do you understand your rights as I have represented them to you?"

Stewart was trying to swallow, but couldn't. He croaked out a hoarse "Yes."

"You will very likely be charged with murder. I'm giving you one last chance to tell me what you did this weekend, and to prove it."

Stewart managed a weak, "I was camping with Arnold." He was looking at the floor when he said it. In the long annals of human deception, this was one lame pathetic attempt.

"If you were camping with Arnold, then you can lead us to the campsite. We've got flashlights, you said it wasn't that far from the school. Let's go." He pulled Stewart up by the arm and pointed him to the door. "But one thing Stewart, you take us on some wild goose chase, and I'm going to charge you with *felony* obstruction of justice. And you will do time, whether or not you did the crime in Atlanta, I'll get you for obstruction and the felony charge will follow you forever. It will be very disappointing to your family. This is your last chance. If you want to come out of this thing okay, you better think, and think right."

Think is what Stewart did, he froze. He thought it out. He closed his eyes and thought it out. He could take the cops on one of the paths through the woods and meadows behind the convenience store. This area was part rural, part suburbs, there was always the chance he could find some kids's recent campsite. But if he failed to find one, this asshole seemed serious. Getting kicked out of another military school was one thing, getting arrested for a felony was another. His already pissy parents would go ballistic. Eventually he would get his trust fund and his freedom, and maybe even Raquel. She had told him she would set up the third alibi as soon as possible. Surely she'd had time by now.

***

Tonya gently brushed her daughters hair with her hand while she slept on the smooth flying plane. Right after take off and her daughter was already asleep. She thought about the money she'd been paid, her new life. Her mother wasn't thrilled that it would be months before she heard from Tonya and that where she was going and what she was doing was secret. Tonya said she'd be in touch when she could. It was hard, she didn't always like her mama, but she was great with Maria. And she didn't drink half as bad as she had when Tonya was a kid. But Tonya was more than willing to risk pissing off her Mama to have a better life and take good care of her daughter.

She tried not to think about the Pugesly gig, but it was hard not to. The instructions, the money, the coke, the warnings, the dialogue, she'd had to remember so much she felt like an actress when she finally got to deliver her lines to Pugsley. Pugsley with the mean squinty eyes, too close together, and an evil grin. Tonya had always been in control of their sex games, but she thought he might be genuinely dangerous when he became a man. Genuinely dangerous. She didn't feel bad about doing the job, she was a pro, and if she hadn't done it some other girl would have gotten the money and the fresh start. She owed it to Maria to take advantage of the opportunity. Who knows, she might eventually contact Pugsley, get him to California, marry him, and obtain her half of his trust fund. Live in L.A., become high society, rub shoulders with the stars, steal Brad Pitt away… She could do all that for her daughter, well Brad would be for herself. At that point she looked around the full flight, nobody was paying her attention, most around her were asleep. She took her shoe off and shook down from the toe a very small piece of paper. She took her phone book out and wrote down PGLY-SFD and his number. But the area code and first three digits she changed to one number higher, the last four digits one number lower. It was a simple code, but it had always worked for her before. She took the piece of paper, stuck it in her mouth and chewed it like gum.

The police were at least attentive and polite while he told his third story. Stewart, somewhat dazed and confused by it all, just kept hoping Raquel had talked to Amanda and set it all up like she said she would. He stuck to the third story, Amanda Stone had picked him up at the convience store, made love with him all weekend at the hotel, and dropped him off when it was over.

They told him to describe her. "Amanda Stone is like five foot six, 120 lbs, has light strawberry blond hair, and a Cyndi Crawfford mole over her left lip. She lives in Atlanta, and is in the phone book."

"How old is she?" Danny put to Stewart.

Stewart didn't have a clue, having had only one experience with a woman, and since he didn't know Raquel's age, he sure as hell didn't know Amanda's. "I don't have any idea. She was a woman, years older than me, but not like really old."

Danny then asked Stewart to stand up. "Stick out your hands." Stewart did as was told.

"Spooky, take a look. You see any signs of trauma, like this boy was in a fight?"

"Nah, he ain't been in a fight. Not unless he didn't land a blow. And he shows no signs of having been hit in a fight. Cat scratch fever on his back, maybe, but no fight. The stains aren't from any bloody nose or a fistfight."

"Stewart," Danny said, with his most serious voice, "you had blood stains all over you. Where'd all that blood come from, Stewart?"

Stewart didn't have a clue, ketchup does not blood stains make.

Being from a wealthy family, with an uncle who was a lawyer, and having seen enough movies and TV, he knew to say he didn't want to answer any more questions until he had seen his lawyer. So he said so.

***

The ride back was quicker than the ride there. Less traffic. Stewart was clueless we really hadn't arrested him yet. We'd told him we were *about* to arrest him, but by waiting until Atlanta to make it official and having him come with us under the Colonel's insrtuctions we skipped the whole extradition hassle. In absence of the parents, the Colonel was his legal guardian, and the Colonel told him to go with us, so go he did. We couldn't question Stewart any more because he had made the smart move and asked to lawyer up. And we couldn't talk about his case because he was right there in the back seat.

Danny asked me about my good looking assistant that I had assured him he could trust. Despite the fact he'd only met Leonard a couple of times, he knew my history with Leonard. Leonard's cousin in town for a convention, looking for a job, working for me part time, was honest and factual. I wouldn't lie to Danny, but I sure as hell wasn't going to mention a possible future book in the works. That would be stupid, and blow his credibility if I told him and he kept me on. Legally, the book was an idea that got turned down, and *might* be resurrected later.

When we got to APD Danny turned to Stewart and said, "I can't ask you any more questions without your attorney present but I'm going to say something and you can listen and think about it, and decide how you want to play things out. If you change your story, admit there's blood on your uniform, explain how it got there, and give us something we can verify quickly, we don't have to put you in the system. If you remain quiet, I'm gonna assume you are sticking by your statement that there's only ketchup on your uniform."

Stewart remained silent. Danny looked down and sighed, then lifted his face and made eye contact with Stewart. "Stewart Faulkner-Davis you are under arrest for giving false information to the police in a murder investigation - for the obstruction of justice. Because your've seventeen and this involves two murders to which you may be a material witness, you'll be booked and held as an adult. Once you're processed, you'll get to call your Uncle Albert or whoever you want. You'll get a phone call and you'll be arrainged and there'll be a bail hearing. You remember your rights as I already explained to you."

Stewart said, "Yes, sir."

"Okay, let's go inside." Danny opened Stewart's door and helped him out. The boy looked to be in a state of shock.

Stewart was booked inside and the collected evidence sent to the labs for complete analysis - both APD and GBI. Danny didn't know what he had yet, but it was promising. There was absolutely nothing for me to do for at least four or five hours, I hoped, so I demanded that Danny get my butt home for some much needed sleep. One of the uniformed squad cars had to take me home. The good thing was we were both in a hurry.

***

The Captain pointed out the Mississippi as they flew over it. Tonya was on her second Vodka and tonic, her baby girl was sound asleep, and she and was just beginning to enjoy the flight. Up until her period of reflection during this flight, she had maintained not knowing what was going on was her best strategy. Now that she had the money and a better life set up, she figured it might be to her definite advantage to keep current with what was up in South Carolina and Atlanta. She had her daughter to watch after now, ignorance was no longer bliss. Or safety.

I had to get out of the squad car and manually key in the numbers at the gate to get the squad car in. Thank God the electric eye took care of letting it back out. I got him to take me down to my house, told him the protocol to get out, and hit the door.

I went in, grabbed a cold one, and began to think about the night. I was tired, but still wired. There was so much stuff that just didn't make sense. I checked my machine; Leonard had called me back, left a message that Rayland was travelling, he'd run the regular Sunday Sweat Lodge and they had concentrated protection on me and those working with me, but I should call him back and give him more details. It was too late to call him back, I'd try him in the morning.

***

Chapter Nine – Early Monday Morning

Danny looked at Stewart in the holding cell at APD homicide. The kid looked scared, bewildered, confused. But with what Danny had seen in Stewart's room, knew from Sean O'Thomas and the fact he looked like such a mean little shit, not one iota of sympathy for him lay in Danny's heart. He just wondered if this sick fuck was one of the doers, and if so, who were the others? Obviously this little shit was not the ring leader or advanced black magician at the head of some satanic cult. But he certainly could have been one of the ones chanting and stabbing. Danny walked over to the bars of the holding cell and stood across from where Stewart sat.

"Stewart, you don't have to talk if you don't want to, and we will let you have your phone call once you've been processed but if you're not responsible for the murders, and you know something about them, or were coerced into participating, now would be the time to come clean. Better you get the deal than someone else. Because somebody will get the deal, and everybody else will do the time, or take the needle for the big sleep."

Stewart was once more confused. He'd been charged with lying, not murder. Why did they keep saying the ketchup stains were blood?

Stewart screamed out in frustration and desperation. "Why do you keep talking about murder? I haven't killed a single human being yet!"

Danny paused, had the kid meant to say what he'd said? It was scary, but it also sounded honest. What if he wasn't one of the killers. Maybe he was the watchman, and helped fold up and carry out the bloody tarps. Whatever, the kid refused to acknowledge he was splattered with human blood. Danny needed to run Amanda Stone through the computer ASAP and he hoped he'd have lab results soon to tag Stewart for the murders.

Half an hour later Danny came into the holding cell and told Stewart to put his hands out. Danny once more clamped the handcuffs down on Stewart's wrists. They were cold and too tight, but when Stewart said that, it was as though no one heard him. Danny had to take Stewart over to the jail to be processed. Generally speaking, for minor arrests, the bail is set routinely. But Danny and the Assistant DA on duty thought Stewart needed to go through the entire, very slow process of being put into the system, getting his phone call, and then going before the judge, where Danny and the ADA would push for no bail. Everybody, every step of the way, would be told the kid was a murder suspect with evidence being analyzed before charges could be made, and to move slowly.

The sun was rising as Stewart was walked into the city jail. The morning before he had been without his clothes, Raquel had taken them. Now he was without his clothes again, this time the police had taken them. He was still in his bathrobe and undies. The cop had told him they were going to take his underwear to test, keep his robe in lockup and return it to him when everything was over, and give him his new clothes and put him in the system. Stewart wasn't exactly sure what being put into the system meant, but he didn't like the sound of it at all. The white jumpsuit they gave him was clean and soft from a thousand washings.

I felt good hearing Leonard's message, knowing strong protection was sent our way. I decided to go out on my porch, sit in the hot tub, drink a cold one or two, smoke my pipe, and unwind. An intuitive flash or two would be nice, but so would relaxation for fifteen to a half, and then some much needed sleep.

Danny told the supervising deputy at the jail that Stewart was barely seventeen and from a prominent family, and although he was arrested and charged as an adult, he shouldn't be thrown in with any hardcore population. The deputy nodded in agreement, thought to himself,

"Yeah, whatever," and immediately forgot.

Stewart waited in the holding cell beside the desk, while Detective Fagan signed on a couple of clipboards. He got Stewart out and walked him to a phone. "Stewart, because you're seventeen and my responsibility, I'm making sure you get you phone call."

Stewart had thought this one out, Uncle Alpert was the logical choice. Stewart dialed Alpert's house and got the machine. Alpert had been called away to Augusta on business yesterday and hadn't returned yet, which left Stewart clueless. He left a message on the machine repeating what Danny told him, he'd been arrested for obstruction and was in the jail downtown. Danny told Stewart his number which Stewart repeated into the machine. Stewart pleaded for help to come quickly. Danny put Stewart back in the holding cell and left. Stewart didn't exactly like the detective, but at least he'd spent several hours with him and he was familiar. Now Stewart was in a holding cell with seven men, all who looked dangerous and like they could kick his butt at will. He was in a strange, dangerous new world where he knew no one, and nothing going on around him really made any sense. He might have done some bad things, but he wasn't being charged with anything he knew he'd done. But whatever was going on, it seemed to be getting more and more serious all the time and he wished his Uncle Alpert would come and get him the hell out.

The four black, one hispanic, one white, and one Asian man in with him all had on street clothes, but the man who came by and pushed through the plastic breakfast trays was wearing an orange version of what he had been given, a one white piece prison uniform jumpsuit with long pants, short sleeves, long zipper in front, looking like something a mechanic or janitor might wear. The other prisoners being escorted in handcuffs down the halls had on white prison uniforms like him. Stewart heard the guy in the orange uniform get called a trustee, but he didn't know what that meant, and was afraid to ask. When Stewart took the lid off the tray, he didn't find much underneath: a pint of milk, a small cup of lukewarm coffee, a small box of cereal, and a cold piece of white bread toast. Stewart thought he was glad he wasn't hungry, that wouldn't be much food for him.

Then he experienced his first act of jailhouse kindness. Something which happens more than those who've never been inside would ever know. An old black man with very bloodshot eyes and a strong smell of alcohol leaned toward him and told him quietly, "Et up boy. Once you in heaah, you nevah know how long it might be fo you et again. They move you, you go to court, you miss a meal, nobody give a fuck. You et evah time they serve you food, and you et evahthin." The old man smiled a gold-toothed smile and leaned back, and picked back up the conversation with the younger black man he'd been talking to. Stewart took the advice.

Ten minutes after he finished his less than delicious meal, one of the Fulton County Deputies came to the door and called out three names and Stewart's. He and another deputy handcuffed them as they walked out and they were escorted to the processing area where they were fingerprinted and photographed holding up a sign with their name, the date, and a number on it. Then they were taken to the shower area, everybody's clothes were taken, to be returned to them when released, except for Stewart whose clothes had already been taken for testing, with the exception of his underwear, which was now sent for testing. The orange uniformed trustees gave the new inmates flea and lice baths, and then the deputy gave them an all-cavity full-body check. Stewart, without articulating the thought, felt the whole process demeaning, dehumanizing, and belittling. When it was over he was given another clean white prison jumpsuit and a plastic toiletries kit with toothbrush, toothpaste, a bar of soap, a comb, and a pair of plastic shower sandals. Some with him had obviously been here before and knew the routine.

Stewart was getting bothered by the feelings of permanence and routine of everything they were doing, like he was going to be staying. He had been scared all along, but he was hitting far deeper, possibly more realistic levels of fear.

***

As I sat in the jacuzzi, steam wafting, I smoked my pipe and watched the sun rise over the trees and pastures, and it was beautiful - a pink, then red, then golden sunrise, with the morning birds enthusiastically greeting the new day. I had thought about the case, and it just didn't make sense - the evil precision of the crime scene, and a dork caught bumbling his way back sneaking in wearing a blood-stained uniform, with dubious alibis. The two didn't fit. The kid never acknowledged or explained the blood, kept insisting that it was ketchup. How the hell did it get there? So far we didn't know if it was our victim's blood or related to our case. But if he wasn't involved, where'd all that blood come from? Somebody's blood was on his uniform, I thought about Desi and Lucy, "Stewie, you got some 'splaining to do." Seriously, he had some explaining to do.

All of a sudden, there was a shadow blocking the rising sun. I looked up to see a truly beautiful sight, Laura Red Star in her 49'ers jersey.

"I'm sorry if I woke you up."

She had sleepy eyes. "I got up to use the bathroom, heard the jacuzzi running." There was a moment of easy silence as we smiled at each other, then she took off the jersey and stood there for a second. She was beautiful in the dawn light. Her long raven's hair was blowing gently in the wind, lifting off her exquisite bottom. I noticed the textured beauty of her brown aureoles and intimate skin in the morning glow. She didn't say anything, she just got in. She wasn't exactly smiling, it was more of a Mona Lisa half-grin. She was gorgeous, radiant, and had that knowing look that women have, saying that they are at harmony with Nature, that they understand it in ways no man ever can.

I had just grabbed a towel, my pipe, and two beers and come out, so I was naked. Now, so was she. I thought I was exhausted, but I was wrong. However, I truly was exhausted an hour later, when I finally got to sleep. But it was a wonderful way to greet a glorious morning.

Tonya had been nursing her third vodka tonic, drifting in and out of sleep, checking on Maria and then drifting back off to sleep. She was woken up by the approach announcement and the fasten your seat belt lights. The stewardess came by and took her drink, and Tonya began to wake Maria up for the landing. Looking out the window they saw the glistening adult disneyland in the desert. Tonya pointed out to Maria the large shiny pyramid next to the airport as they landed and watched her eyes grow big. It was a beautiful clear bright sunrise and Tonya felt it was a good sign - for a new and better life for her and Maria.

On the way to baggage claim Maria asked again and Tonya tried once more to explain about the cops and the security checks. When Tonya and Maria came to baggage claim, there was a beautiful, elegant woman with a luxuriant head of wavy golden brown hair, at least six feet tall, and wearing heels and an evening dress. The beautiful lady leaned down and said, "Come give your Aunt Jasmine a hug, Maria." The little girl had never seen a lady that elegantly dressed in real life before, was captivated, and ran into Jasmine's open arms. She was swept up in Jasmine's strong arms, hugged, and settled comfortably on her hips. Maria was amazed at how wonderful her new aunt smelled.

"Let's find your luggage and get ya'll settled in." Tonya wasn't sure where, but she heard the South, maybe Texas in Jasmine's voice. "And you, sugar bear, you precious thing, you're gonna be in nursery school with my youngest treasure, Chelsea." She put her finger lightly on

Maria's stomach and turned it like she was starting a car. Maria giggled. Jasmine turned and said to Tonya, "Carl's got to quit using these dawn flights, this is the second time in three days."

Tonya must have looked confused. "That's right, you call him George, when he comes here, he's always Carl Lewis." Jasmine laughed at the name. "You know, like Carl Lewis the runner." Tonya smiled, but she had no idea who the runner was, but she knew George, Carl, and Marty were all the same person. Jasmine continued, "What can I say Tonya, I'm a sucker for a handsome, intelligent, cruel and ruthless man that's good with the ladies."

Tonya could genuinely smile at that, "Well George - Carl is all of that, and sometimes even charming." And as in the last 18 hours, dangerous, possibly deadly.

***

Danny needed all the help he could get as fast as he could, but damn if he was going to call the "FBI liason" if he didn't absolutely have to. The feebees were publicity hounds and would gladly take credit for solving a case that wasn't theirs. Sure they had great facilities.… The local feebee/UGA jock was snooping around on the outside, offering assistance, but so far had been held at bay. From what Spooky said, if it was the first crime that fit the FBI's criteria as a satanic ritual murder, he thought they'd want to take it over, but they hadn't. He had all the resources of APD and GBI at work, now he'd call his frat brother. When they were SAE's at Florida. Danny thought Bernie the brother most likely to make the ten most wanted list, but damn if he didn't become DEA. That was Danny's way around, Bernie would run the names through the Fed's computers and see what came up.

It cost Danny two tickets to the Georgia/Florida game – also known as the world's largest cocktail party, but Bernie said he'd run Amanda Stone and Stewart Faulkner-Davis through the federal computers. As soon as he got off the phone, it rang. It was the Colonel, who felt he had an obligation to Stewart's family to inform them. He had agreed to wait until Danny told him he could contact them, but he hadn't heard anything back.

"Colonel, whom may I ask, will you inform? His parents? His uncle? Stewart tried his uncle already but only got the machine." The Colonel had no great love for Stewart, but he did have the reputation of his school to think of. He had also seen and understood Stewart's suitcase of horrors. The Colonel, hard man that he was, was an animal lover. He figured out Danny was looking for even more time. "I guess, under the circumstances, maybe I should attempt to reach the parents in Europe, before trying the uncle. But if I can't get hold of them in a couple of hours, the school must let some relative know he is no longer in our care, but in yours."

Danny thanked him. He thought the Colonel was an okay guy. The phone rang again, "We've got nothing on Stewart Faulkner-Davis, but we've got three hits on Amanda Stone, one plain hooking, two hooking and possession, all small time stuff, I'm going down to Records now to pull the files. It may take a little while, but I assume you want to look at everything?" Shaneeqa Lewis knew Danny and what he would want. She was by far the best in her department. A single black mother with three kids, a woman who made her house payments, made her kids do their homework, made it to church every Sunday, and took pride in her own professionalism. And managed to keep a good sense of humor about her almost all the time. Danny was damn lucky she'd taken his call.

"Shaneeqa, you're a sweetheart."

"Yeah, forget that, bring me a dozen Krispy Kremes and then tell me you love me."

"You got it." At this rate Danny would loose half this month's paycheck bribing his fellow law enforcement officers to do their jobs. Or his job. Whatever.

***

Stewart, feeling odd wearing his soft and obviously old and used bleached white jail uniform and carrying his new basic jailhouse hygene kit was led to the door of a large jail cell. It looked to Stewart like there were hundreds of beds, but it was really only a 50 bed cell. The deputy escorting them and the deputy at the cell couldn't decide something about Stewart and his companions. It had something to do with sheets and blankets and being assigned bunks. Finally their deputy escort came back over and asked them, "How many of you are likely to be bailed out today, how many will be with us a while?" Two seemed optimistic about bail, one didn't, and Stewart was clueless. The deputies took the easy way out. They'd be assigned beds and given linens after their court appearances. For the moment they could take any bunk that was bare. Stewart looked around. Near the deputy's desk there were five empty bunks with two inch green mattresses on the cold steel frames with one bare pillow, with no linens or signs of habitation. His companions spread out and each took one. Stewart did the same. It was hard, and not comfortable, and the AC was up too much and a little cool for no covers, but Stewart had been through many new experiences, good and bad, in a small amount of time. He crossed his arms over his body for warmth and settled in. The adrenalin well finally ran dry, shock and exhaustion finally kicked in and Stewart fell to sleep. Deep, coma sleep.

So a couple hours later when the roll for morning court was read, Stewart didn't hear his name. No one was aware of him or bothered to wake him, so he missed morning court.

***

The priest was holding a wooden cross out at her and praying, the crowd was yelling, the executioner in the black cowl was just feet away with the torch. She was spitting at the priest, cursing him, damning them all for their hypocracies. Bang! Bang! Bang! The door was booming, he was hitting it so hard the whole room was shaking. "Samantha, Samantha! Wake Up! Wake Up!"

To go from one terror to another in a half sleep state - she was confused. "What!"

"The door's locked. Let me in!"

"Why?"

"What do you mean why, let me in. Why is this door locked anyway?"

In her most sarcastic voice, "Gee, I don't know why. Maybe it's because somebody beat the fucking shit out of somebody yesterday, that might be why."

Phineas had forgotten. He had woken up/come to from being passed out dead drunk and it occurred to him that he hadn't done the final sweep yet, so the house could stand up under any search. He needed to get in her room, and he didn't want to waste time. His memory wasn't real clear. The cops were there, she had almost ruined everything, he had been drinking early, kept drinking, and then punished her. Hard. "I'm not mad at you anymore." He didn't want to say the next part, but time was of the essence. "I'm sorry. It will never happen again. I'm sorry."

Those were words she'd never heard him use before. She double checked to make sure the bedside drawer was locked. She let him in.

"What about school?"

"I'm not going. Under the circumstances...."

"Fine. Where're your tapes? The sleep tapes."

Samantha didn't get the big deal, but if the tapes were all he wanted. She handed him the three tapes.

"You didn't make any copies?"

"No. Why?"

Phineas didn't answer, he just took the tapes and headed for the door. At the door he stopped and turned around. "I'm glad you're staying home, after breakfast we're going to go over every square inch of this house. We can't afford any mistakes. Any *more* mistakes." He left. She looked down at the bedside drawer. If he took one look inside her "diary," he would, quite literally, kill her.

***

Danny's team came in early as requested. The two men went out to the three schools as soon as they'd been apprised of the situation. The two women continued to expand their search for the mother's identity, looking at new missing persons reports throughout the southeast, alerting shelters and homes, when a home for unwed mother's in Toccoa, Georgia called in. They had called their local police who had told them to call us immediately with the description. We called the Toccoa police, they dispatched a car to bring us the lady who ran the establishment, the lady running the desk when the misssing woman checked out, and their sign in/out book. Did a man come get her? Yes. Did they get his name? Kevin Eubanks.

Danny thanked them, asked everybody to hurry, and to bring with them any photos or belonging's of the woman that might be of help in identifying her. And please, please, hurry.

Shaneeqa called in, just the person he wanted to talk to. She had two of the three files, but was having trouble hunting down the first one. He told her to bring him what she had and then run the name Kevin Eubanks.

Shaneeqa started laughing. "You jokin,' right? Kevin Eubanks." She laughed again. Danny thought the name sounded familiar, but he thought maybe it was a criminal's name he just couldn't recall.

"So somebody told you I got a crush on him, right? And you jealous."

Danny paused. He hated not knowing what was going on, any time, any where, about any thing.

"You do know who Kevin Eubanks is, don't you Danny?"

Another long pause. Finally, "No."

"Ever watch Leno? He's the guitar player/band leader. You know."

"Right. Well actually, we have a real potential perp using that name, might be real, might be an alias, run it after you bring me the files. Please." It was good to use that word often if you wanted Shaneeqa to hurry.

***

The Colonel was very patient about trying to find Stewart's parents. He'd make a call, find out they'd been there and moved on, be given some more numbers, several of which were on yachts. He'd make a call, take a break, use the bathroom, and go walk and smoke his pipe. He worked steadily at finding Stewart's parents, averaging one call every fifteen to twenty-five minutes. It wasn't his fault they were hard to track down. Every time he started to think about hurrying the process, he saw in his mind's eye Stewart's blood stained frame and surgical instruments, and he'd go take another break.

***

"Hey Bernie. What's up?" Besides tickets to the game, Danny thought.

"I only got one hit on Amanda Stone. From a John Stanton we busted for 2 kilos of coke, he did the Miami-Atlanta route. We turned him around and used him as a CI until somebody found out he was a rat and whacked him. When he first got busted, he was so scared he gave us everybody he ever did business with. Everybody he ever met. Everybody he ever heard about. He was a real wuss. Not all of his stuff panned out, but some of it did." Danny could hear pages rustling over the phone. "We got, one, two, three major busts through Stanton till he met his maker. An occupational hazard in his line of work. We get her name associated with a Kevin, Kevin Jackson, alias Kevin Eubanks, alias Kevin Gothard. APD tagged him for possession of an ounce of crank when he was, twenty-two, ten years ago… got him again three, four years after that, for attempted murder, hmmm... enforcing for his stable, got carried away. You probably can get more stuff on him than I can. Stanton said Jackson dealt crank, coke, ran girls, and when available and easy, blackmail scams on their johns. Amanda Stone was with Kevin Jackson two years ago when Stanton said they were dealing, hooking. He thought by then they'd quit blackmailing, learned too much could go wrong. It's all second party innuendo, but it's what we got."

"Thanks, Bernie. That's the second time we've gotten his name this morning, as Kevin Eubanks. Thank God, it's all starting to come together. Thanks again, Bernie, and don't worry, we'll have good seats, and I'll smuggle in the flask of Jack."

***

Detectives Lester Wallace and Dick Williams were at their third high school, having done one private, one public, finishing with this private school, the most expensive and prestigious in the area. At each school the whole summer school student population would come to the gym and the detectives would go through the same spiel that the students who called it in wouldn't get in trouble, the police would smooth it over with their parents if that was a concern. They were already halfway heroes by calling it in and getting the police to the crime scene, but they could only be real heroes if they stepped forward like responsible adults. They may have seen things that night that could lead to this horrendous murder being solved. They also mentioned if any parkers had been run off by a policemen on Thorn Road, would they please speak up.

The whole school laughed when one couple, holding hands, stood up and said they tried to go parking there but got run off. Wallace asked them to come talk with him. The kids were stirring more in this group than in the other schools, heads were moving as students looked back and forth at each other, and around. The detectives knew they had their phone pals in the audience, or at least kids who knew who their phone pals were.

Williams noticed three fifteen/sixteen year old boys caught up in an intense discussion. Finally one of them raised his hands. The gym got real quiet. Williams thought they had their phone pals. The kid asked if there was a reward. It's always the fucking rich kids who are so concerned about money. Go figure.

"No, there is not a reward at this time. But I'll caution you that if you hold knowledge back hoping that there will eventually be a reward, you would be guilty of obstruction of justice and subject to arrest and prosecution." The kid sat back down, the three began to talk intensely again. Williams watched them, hoping they would do the right thing without any more coercion. "Any more questions?" He scanned the audience.

The one in the middle stood up again. "Sir, we're who you're looking for. We'll be glad to cooperate." They walked on down the bleachers to the police. The student body cheered.

Wallace and Williams took the two lovers and their three phone palls with them, to be interviewed, and have a session with the sketch artist.

***

Tonya couldn't believe her eyes. She had graduated to the top of her industry. Jasmine took her to a five story building right outside the city limits of Las Vegas. Hooking is legal in parts of Nevada, but not inside Vegas' city limits. The bottom two stories were nice businesses, doctors, dentists, CPA's, a health food store, it was NICE. The top three stories were Jasmine's and had their own private entrance/elevator. The third story contained the escort business' reception area and business offices, and a spa, weight room, jacuzzi, classroom, and sauna. And a few private rooms for the customer of specialized tasts. There was also a playschool/nursery, but it was separate, completelty walled off from the rest with separate entrances and exits, fully staffed twelve hours a day. It had great toys and educational stations. Tonya was in heaven. The next story and half the top were where the girls lived. Jasmine had half the top floor, and the roof.

Tonya had a fully furnished two bedroom apartment, with elegant bathroom, complete kitchen, laundry, satellite TV, sound system/entertainment center, everything. She thought she had died and gone to hooker heaven. Besides the day care/play school there was an in-house live-in baby sitter, who didn't hook, or do anything else, but watch the girl's kids all evening and night at the small night nursery on the fourth floor.

Tonya said thank-you more than once during her tour and settling in. Jasmine helped Tonya put Maria down for a nap and chatted for a few minutes.

"You won't go right to work. We have a very, very exclusive clientele. I'm going to let you take a few classes, get used to your new surroundings, make sure you can fit in at whatever level of society a gentleman might take you out to enjoy. You won't have any problems, I'm sure. Are you bilingual?"

Tonya though for a second, not bisexual, bi, oh, languages, "No, only American."

"English."

"No mam, only English. But I'm willing to learn. And I'm good at what I do."

"I'm sure you are Tonya, I'm sure you are. You come highly recommended."

***

"Kevin Eubank's real name is Kevin Jackson, also alias Kevin Gothard. Drug dealer and pimp. I want everything else you can find, any mention of his name, anywhere."

"I've got it all, already." Shaneequa responded to Danny.

"What?"

Shaneeqa looked a little impatient, "He bailed Amanda Stone out twice. Kevin Jackson. We've got his info, and so would the bail bondsman. Pardons and Parole might have his location too. Then again, he might be in the phonebook."

She threw it on his desk. It made a huge WOP! The Atlanta phonebook! There were pieces of newsprint marking the pages. Danny opened it, she had underlined Jackson's address and phone number. There was another sheet. Marking Amanda Stone. Danny looked sheepish. Shaneeqa pressed her advantage. "When do I get *my* gold shield, Danny. I don't see that this stuff is *all* that difficult."

Danny started laughing. "Why would you want to be a detective when you're already the best at what you do, and you work regular hours?" Everybody knew Danny was famous for twenty hour days when he was on the chase. Like now.

"Danny boy, I wouldn't take your job."

She started to walk away. "Shaneeqa, I know you've done great work, and I hate to ask you, but could you…."

She didn't even look around. "Double check and see if there's anything else we might have on Kevin Jackson, alias…." She waved, never looked back. "I want those doughnuts!"

Danny opened the files and looked at the picture. Amanda Stone had the Cyndi Crawford mole and the strawberry blond hair described by Stewart. She was a cross between Julia Roberts and Ellen Barken, or a young Angie Dickinson. She was physically pretty, but there was something tough, sexy, and unmistakably dangerous about this woman. She was good looking, but street-wise good looking, not debutante pretty.

He thought about what he had, Stewart with unexplained blood stains, and two bogus alibis, and now he claims to have been with Amanda Stone, repeatedly linked to Kevin Jackson, alias Eubanks, who may have signed out the victim. He didn't have the puzzle solved yet, but he was laying down some of the corner pieces. This puzzle would come together quickly, if things kept going at this pace.

Danny thought about unwed mothers homes, where indigent or rejected unwed mothers could go to have their children safely, maybe to be kept, maybe to be put up for adoption. Decades ago such houses had been commonplace, but he thought with today's morality, the adoption angle was the only thing that would keep such institutions going. In America, the god Dollar rules.

***

Samantha had to choose, and choose quick. If she left the diary in its place, and he demanded to see what was inside the drawer and the box, and he looked in the book, he would kill her. Flat out, he would kill her. She was certain of it. Also, so much of her plans were intimately tied up with her diary, it was her most precious possession in the whole world. She didn't think she could pull it all off without it.

***

Danny thought about Spooky. Did he need him yet? No, this was all straight cop stuff. All he needed now was a little scientific cooperation, and he'd be mopping up. The phone rang.

It wasn't science, it was more straight cop work. Williams and Wallace had five people to give descriptions of the fake cop - two lovebird parkers who were run off, and the three hell-raisers, who, as anticipated, got run off earlier and came back to take a sunrise look, discovered the crime scene and called it in. He had five for the sketch artists and things were looking up.

***

Spooky lay on his back in his bed. Her head was on his chest, his arm around her, and it was comfortable, like it belonged there. Down Simba, he thought, and drifted off back to sleep.

***

It was one of the biggest decisions of her short lifetime. It was literally, life and death. She unlocked the nightstand drawer, unlocked the box, took the notebook/diary out and placed it between her school notebooks, and put her best jewelry in the box, put the box back and locked it, and went downstairs to eat.

***

Danny did what he often did in any kind of complex or intricate crime. He made a chart. He started with the dead bodies in the center. They were the base. He drew lines up from that to the various names of people he could relate to the body, the bodies, and a smiley face for a fake cop.

***

When Samantha went into the kitchen, it was empty. The coffee wasn't even made. She went on in the living room. Phineas had a half full cognac snifter in his hand as he sat on the floor in front of the fireplace. A fire was burning, odd for the summer. She could smell plastic burning and she saw the remains of her sleep tapes bubbling away on top of some logs in the fireplace. What had she been listening to? The tapes were supposed to give her audial and subliminal sleep suggestions. It had always relaxed her, the sound of the ocean always lulled her to sleep. But if that was all there was, why was he burning them? He seemed absorbed in what he was doing and either hadn't heard her or was paying no attention to her. She came up behind him. He was holding what he called his multi-million dollar pictures. He was burning them slowly, one by one. He had explained them and shown them to her months ago, when he had laid out his plans and goals.

In the picture was a much younger looking Phineas, with a full head of hair and a full beard. You could tell it was him if you looked closely, but the years had not been generous with Phineas. Although it hadn't been more than a decade, you'd have never known it by looking at him now. The pictures showed him and a woman in various sex acts and S&M play, whipping her while she was chained, and paddling her. By today's standards, it was fairly mild stuff. In his divorce a decade ago it had been devastating. He had bought them, and their supposed negatives twice, at $10,000 a pop. When he balked the third time the blackmailers sold them to his wife. Although Phineas and her would have split anyway, he had been charging her with adultery, trying to get out cheap. His sexual tastes had become more exotically extreme in the years after their marriage, and she had pulled away from him. They had both found compatible playmates elsewhere, but she had the pictures. She got millions and maintained a certain standing in the family, while he lost a fortune. She kept their house and estate and he got banished here. One by one he fed the pictures to the hungry flames.

Samantha watched him for minutes. He was oblivious to her presence. He would look at each picture, take a sip, look at it some more, toss it in the fire, and pick up another one, and repeat the process. This hatred for his blackmailers was the strongest single passion she had ever seen him display. Much like the hated she harbored toward her brother/tormentor - intense hatred was one of the few bonds they still shared. Phineas mistakenly thought she was the same person and felt the same way as when she had first found refuge here, but she was entirely different. Samantha concluded their capacity for hatred and desire for revenge was really about all they had left in common.

She had drifted from him philosophically. She'd learned there were other kinds of witches than satanic witches, and she wasn't all that concerned with Christianity one way or the other, and wasn't sure she bought into the whole Judeo-Christian God-Devil deal, anyway. It would never occur to her to do the kind of satanic rites and magical sacrifices which Phineas considered such a cornerstone of his practice. Had she not been able to work out her revenge along with his, she wouldn't have gone along with him at all. She didn't like sacrificing animals, or people. People maybe, if you really hated them like she hated Stewart, but not strangers and never animals.

There were plenty of pictures, he burned them all. It was a big fireplace with gas outlets which he had augmenting the substantial wood fire blazing away. Her tapes had bubbled away to nothing but globs and ash, still he used a poker and played with the fire so that everything was consumed. Finally she let her presence be known. "Phineas, I'll help you go through the house, but I've changed my mind about school, I'm going in for half a day."

Phineas never said a word to her. He reached back with his hand behind her knee, pulled in, bringing her to the floor. He jumped on top of her, ripped her nightshirt up, undid his pants and entered her. It was the closest to forcible rape he had ever gotten with her. She didn't fight him, nor did she encourage him, he just basically had his way with her. She just wondered what kind of kinky games he had been thinking about. Two nights before he could barely get it up, and now he didn't even bother with conversation, just pulls her down and does it. He truly was a pig who deserved the fate that lay before him.

When he was through, lying beside her, she repeated herself, she'd go over the house with him, but she was going to school. She got up, buzzed the help on the intercom, and told him she'd need a ride to school in an hour and a half. Then she went in and grabbed a quick breakfast.

***

It had taken a couple of hours, but Shaneeqa had gotten him all the pertinent files. He had pictures and criminal histories of both Kevin Jackson/Eubanks/Gothard and Amanda Stone. There was nothing that unusual or satanic about their bio's. Amanda was a hooker, a call girl, not a street walker, she had worked bars and conventions, sometimes danced as an exotic dancer, had been caught with small amounts of coke and speed. Kevin was a drug dealer, seller of flesh, not a street pimp, but the "manager of an escort service." One of his customers had cheated and hurt one of his girls. Kevin danced on his skull so much the man was rendered mildly brain damaged. The victim was not a very sympathetic figure in court, having stiffed and beat up a hooker, so Kevin didn't go down all that hard for the attempted murder wrap. But he had done time twice, was street wise, and never gave anybody up, wouldn't rat for reduced time. He wouldn't be easy to break like Stewart would be - once charged, represented, denied bail, and allowed to stew in jail for a while.

He figured Stewart would rat out his own mother after a couple of weeks inside. But there was something that disturbed him about Stewart. When he'd yelled he hadn't killed a single human being yet, it sounded honest. On Danny's internal cop's instinctual truth detector, the kid had passed. Danny wasn't fully aware that his mind and instincts were at odds, but he knew he felt ill at ease about being certain that Stewart was a doer. The phone rang, it was the call he'd been waiting on. The GBI labs hadn't finished the DNA comparison of Stewart's stains and the victim's blood, that would take several days. But they had determined the human blood on Stewart's uniform was the same blood type as that of the victim. The crime lab was also able to determine that on his shoes and on his uniform the non-human stains were the bloodstains of a lamb, a dog, and a goat.

Danny couldn't help himself, he put his hand over the phone and yelled "Yes!" loudly. He thanked them, got off the phone and called the DA. There was no way to explain away the human blood of the right blood type and the blood of three animals on Stewart's uniform and shoes. No way to explain it except that he was there. The DA agreed that after the false statements charges were filed, they should move for no bail, saying Stewart is, at the very least an uncooperative material witness in a murder, if not an active participant. Make him explain the stains. A no bail motion on an obstruction charge would automatically be reviewed in a few days. By then they must be able to move ahead with the murder charges, and move that there be no bail. Horrendous murder charges against someone belonging to a wealthy family with their own jet, constitutes a fairly high flight risk. The DA would make his case strongly at that time, there should be no bail, he should await trial on the inside.

***

The Colonel finally got the parents on the phone. They were on some friend's yatch, visiting and gambling in Monaco. "No, I don't know much about the incident. Only that Stewart went with the Atlanta police and was charged with giving false statements to the police during a murder investigation, and that his clothes and some of his possessions were taken as evidence by the Atlanta police. The arresting officer was Detective Daniel Fagan, yes Fay-gun, of the Atlanta police. Stewart will be in police custody or released to your brother in Atlanta. Perhaps you should call the district attorney. I just felt it was my responsibility to let you know he is no longer with us, but in police custody."

"No ma'am, I haven't called your brother Alpert, I called you first. Yes, perhaps you should call him. Yes, it might be wise to return to Atlanta, it does seem your son's predicament is serious, possibly very serious indeed."

***

I must have been tired, when I woke up I was still flat on my back with her head on my chest. It still felt good, felt natural. I stroked her hair and she made a slight kind of purring sound, "Uuuhhh."

I sat up quickly, forgetting about her head and displacing her less gently than I intended. Actually, it was more like a slapstick comedy, but she wasn't laughing. I was apologizing as I got up, snatched up my jeans, put them on and hit my library. I had forgotten something last night that could no longer wait.

***

Phineas and Samantha went over the house, top to bottom. They didn't change, hide, or destroy anything else. It seemed the pictures and the cassettes were the only loose ends. He did make her unlock the drawer, and her box with the jewelry in it, but he didn't glance twice at her schoolbooks or her backpack. If she was acting unnatural or uneasy, he must have attributed it to his beating her yesterday, and not the incredible risk she was taking.

While in the house she willed herself not to look, to pay no attention whatsoever to her backpack. It worked. The chauffeur was on time and she went to school. On the way there her body went through successive stages of becoming more relaxed, more her real self. She had gone through one of the most intense moments of her life, yet she could not let on, she had no one to share her life with. She thought about the hawk eyes of her newly chosen protector. Maybe one day when her revenge was done and she could wash her hands of these things, she could find someone to share her life with.

Her hallway locker hardly seemed the ideal hiding place, neither was her locker in the music room, but for right now it would have to do.

***

From the five descriptions, the sketch artist had drawn five sketches, and combined them to one drawing that they all agreed looked like the fake cop. A large obese white man, definitely not Kevin Jackson, definitely not Stewart. Danny had a new player, without a clue to his identity other than the drawing. Maybe once Stewart was busted on the murder charge, and denied bail, he'd spill his guts and give up the identity of the fat man. The ADA was on the way over to get with him on the timing of filing the new charges against Stewart when Danny picked up the phone again.

***

"So what's going on?" I asked.

"Everything, absolutely everything. I've got two names, a sketch, and Stewart looks good for a multiple murder charge if he can't explain the blood stains. You get some sleep?"

"Yeah, how about you?"

"*Sleep*, I don't need no stinking *sleep*," Danny said in his best Mexican accent, imitating a famous old movie's line, "…badges? We don't need no stinking badges."

"Well, while you've been busy solving the crime of the century, I was sound asleep. However, I do have one small contribution."

"And what would that be, mister expert?"

"You remember what Samantha called Dr. Faulkner yesterday morning, Uval?"

"Yeah, well?"

"It's the name of a demon. Her pet name for him is the name of a Judeo-Christian demon. According to the old angelic and magical traditions, before he fell Uval was an angel of the order of powers. The old tales say Uval is a great duke in Hell with thirty-seven legions of demons to do his work. One of his main jobs is supposed to be the procurement of love for those who invoke him. It doesn't necessarily mean that Phineas and Samantha are in on the crime, but it surely doesn't make them look more innocent. In fact, it would tend to indicate at least black magic, if not satanic involvement. Tell me how you got the two names, tell me about the sketch, fill me in."

"Yeah, when you get down here. We've got surveillance work to do."

"Should I, or can I bring my assistant Laura?"

"Sure, I'd rather look at her pretty face than your ugly one. Look, the Assistant DA just showed, I've got to go. What's the best surveillance rig you've got? Some of the smarter bad guys have learned to spot some of our stuff. Okay, come in that, see ya."

Assistant DA Diaz sat down and Danny filled him in on what they had, where they were going, what they needed, and what had to be done. Danny didn't say much about Phineas or Samantha, since there was no evidence linking them to the crime. First, charge Stewart with false statements, hold him for a few days without bail and make him explain the blood or charge him with murder and get a permanent no bail ruling. Before anything happens that can hit the press, they needed a judge's permission for wire taps, and they needed around the clock surveillance on Jackson and Stone to be in place. He needed a copy of the last three months phone records for Jackson, Stone, and Stewart to establish links and ties between the doers till he got one to take the deal and burn the rest. He wanted search warrants signed and in place, in case he needed to close down surveillance and move in quickly. A little luck would be nice too, he had to find the fat man and figure out everybody's role in this bizarre business. He didn't want anyone with even the slightest involvement in this crime to skate. Danny wasn't alone in his inability to shake some of the images from the crime scene out of his head. He wanted everyone involved, and he wanted them to go down hard, very hard. Lives for lives. Assistant DA Diaz agreed.

Chapter Ten – Monday

I called Leonard at home, Sarah told me to try his cell, and I got him in his truck on the way to check up on his questers. After I filled him in on the crime scene and my belief that these were serious Satanists he said they'd sent me good energy at the Sweat, and he'd put Danny and me in his Pipe every day until this was over - keep sending more help our way. He reminded me not to lose my temper or give in to the darker side of my nature until this thing was over with. He also reminded me that nobody involved with the investigation should get pass out drunk and he suggested we talk every day. I concured, accepted his advice, and thanked him, then Laura talked to him for a minute before we headed out.

Laura and I went by my office at Triple S Security. Instead of a soul-less modern office we'd converted a large old Victorian house in northeast Atlanta into our headquarters - it's manned twenty-four hours a day, with our radio, all our communications, our vehicle fleet, computers, generator for power outages, etc. For surveillance, we had several work vehicles, we chose the white utilty van. The magnetic signs we attached were for a plumbing company (we had several options), which was fine for this job. We picked Danny up at APD Homicide and he directed us to drive past the house of a Kevin Jackson, alias Eubanks.

It was a common white lower middle class neighborhood, with some trees, mostly pines, among plenty of old one story clapboard houses on the edge of Cabbagetown. Now, even Cabbagetown was going upscale, getting gentrified. Soon the poor people weren't going to have any place left to live in town. We parked up on the street that ran perpendicular into Jackson's, where we had a clear view of his house. It was funny, in that we watched APD's fake phone crew work on a few of the lines - they were starting out with the most basic of taps. Things could get more sophisticated once we knew our targets' routines. The phone van parked about a block up and did some more work. Danny went out the back of our van and got into theirs. Laura reached over, and put her hand on top of mine. It was our first affectionate touch outside the confines of my house or truck. She looked up and smiled with knowing dark brown eyes, then she took her hand away and got out her notebook.

Danny came back with a hand held unit, so we could listen to the tap. Nothing happened. For an hour nothing happened. It kinda made sense, drug dealers and pimps are generally denizens of the night, not your morning or even early afternoon people. After a while, Danny had to go back to work, so we let the phone truck take it till the APD fake water & sewer truck showed up later. We drove by Amanda Stone's house - very similar - less than a mile away. Same deal, nothing happening. We headed back to APD.

***

Stewart woke up for lunch, ate, and found out he'd missed morning court. Nobody seemed too concerned, he'd make it to the afternoon session. Generally an outcasts at most of the schools he'd attended, sometimes he had an occasional fellow outcast friend. Used to being alone, alone didn't usually bother him. But here he was surrounded by dangerous men. He felt alone, and he felt vunerable.

***

We made it back to APD Homicide just in time to witness the positive ID by the two women from Toccoa. Mercifully, only the face and shoulders of the corpse were exposed, but that was gruesome enough. Both women were visibly shaken. Potts and Wilson each took one in tow. The victim was a LeAnn Rutherford from Gainesville. She had been signed out twice before by Kevin Eubanks for the weekend.

"He always looked the same, baseball cap, dark glasses, bushy beard. You really couldn't see him much past that," Ginny, the girl who ran the desk at the home said. We showed her Kevin Jackson's picture with some others. She didn't seem to recognize him, all she'd paid attention to was the beard. "Looked like old Z Z Top."

"One thing."

"Yes?"

"Ginny, do you know what she planned to name the baby?" Danny asked.

"Alex for a boy, Marsella for a girl."

"Thanks." At least now we had names for both victims, LeAnn and Alex Rutherford, death by ritual blasphemy.

***

"She was seventeen." Danny shook his head looking at his desk top on which lay her personal effects from the home, pictures of her, her family. "She was a preacher's niece up in Gainseville, they didn't want the embarrassment so they shipped her off before she started showing. No word on the father. All the poor girl probably ever wanted was for somebody to love her, and look what they did to her." Danny was getting emotional, he had younger nieces and a cop's imagination. "If any of these assholes resist, it would be a pleasure...."

Laura, sitting quietly beside me, studied Danny's face. I sure thought he meant it, I'm sure she did too. I agreed with the sentiment, if you were sure. The whole Stewart deal didn't sit quite right with me. Incredible precision at the scene, and then busted sneaking in wearing blood all over? I couln't, didn't buy that, so I tried not to jump to conclusions, and I'd try to keep

Danny from doing the same. But cops see perps do so many crazy and stupid things - they'll believe anything is possible when it comes to criminal behavior.

***

Stewart Faulkner-Davis finally got arraigned on the false statements charge during afternoon court, but with a complication. The ADA stated to the judge in chambers that Stewart was at the very least a material witness in a first degree murder and detailed the extent of the evidence. The stains meant he'd been there at the crime scene. While here on the first charge he could be temporarily held without bail as a material witness in a murder investigation until he's answered questions about the crime or has been charged with the crime. The investigating team didn't want the press to know they had anybody yet. Stewart got in and out of court before the news hit the press that something was going on with the Faulkner cottage ritual murder. He was simply charged with false statements, but due to complications relating to his charge, he would be held without bail until Wensday at which time a formal bail hearing would be held.

Alpert Faulkner was astonished when he got home and heard Stewart's message. Then he was livid that any relative of his be charged or held, much less without bail. It looked terrible for the family. He called Danny, who directed him to ADA Diaz where he learned there was a bail hearing scheduled in a couple of days. Alpert did corporate law, he needed a criminal lawyer, seemed like he needed a good one. Fast.

Finally, many hours later, Alpert got to sit down with Stewart and discuss the case. Stewart stuck to the Amanda Stone story holding back only two things - a description of Raquel, and a description of her car including its tag number. He planned to hang on to those if the Amanda Stone alabi held up. Raquel said it would, and until proved differently, he would go with what Raquel told him. Despite the unsolved mystery about the ketchup/blood.

"They say they're blood stains, that's what the state crime lab says. There is blood on your uniform, and shoes. How did it get there?"

"Are they sure its not ketchup? Maybe they're wrong, maybe they're lying." Stewart was pleading as much as arguing.

"It's not very damned likely, Stewart, not very likely at all. You better come up with some better answers pretty damn quickly young man, because I doubt they really think you're a material witness, they think you're involved! If they charge you with murder, you better remember something, or come up with something that proves your innocence. From what little I know, this looks very bad, very bad indeed."

***

Danny's team was back to basic police work. Finding out about the victim, tracking her movements and activities the last month, attempting to discover anything about her relationship with Jackson. Looking at Jackson and Stone's phone records to see who they called the most, and who those people really were. After getting the phone records, they would work the DMV records, see what these people looked like, check for a record. Which is how they got the fake cop. He was Kevin Jackson's fourth most called number, Gary Parker. One look at his driver's liscence picture and they knew he was the fake cop in the sketch. When Parker's picture came up on the computer screen, it was screams of joy and high fives at APD Homicide. Now they had another one, solid.

Danny called a meeting of the investigating team to discuss the options for the next step. Continued intensive surveillance to learn as much as possible, or to move quickly, before the rumors about a witness/suspect were blasted all over the media. We had matching blood stains on Stewart, that was a slam dunk. Stewart had vouluntaruly linked himself to Amanda Stone, and she was linked to Jackson who probably signed the victim out, Jackson was tied in with Parker, who seemed a positive match for the fake cop.

Danny looked around the room, finally settled on me. "This is only four people, you said five, what do you think. Are these all our folks, could four have done it?"

I thought about it. Only if the fake cop was the doorman too. I wouldn't have thought that would be enough security to satisfy people doing something this horrendous, but then it didn't make sense that Stewart was caught sneaking in covered in blood. "Danny, I would think five more likely. But if we accept the M.E.'s theory that there were three doers inside, and if there were only four, then the fake cop could have been their only outside security. Yeah, it's possible at a minimum of four, but I still don't think it's likely, but yeah, possible. I still find it highly incongrous; a precision crime scene linked to a bumbling Stewart?"

Danny ignored the last comment and we all discussed whether or not to move quickly. Danny restated his quandary. "We might learn more by listening and watching, but we might lose evidence in place now, that might be destroyed once word about Stewart gets out, and we all know it will get out." Danny was obviously leaning for the blitzkrieg, and I was inclined to agree.

Annie thought about it and asked, "Do we definitely have enough for search warrants on all of them to look for evidence, while we bring them in for questioning? While they're in here answering questions we can bug them, tag their cars, and then, if they're released after questioning, see what turns up. That is, if we don't get enough from the searches or questioning them to charge them. Once we get them all here at once, somebody might give it up for the deal."

About that time Assistant DA Raphael Diaz, who was carrying the ball on this case, a

bright young prosecutor of Cuban heritage, popped in for an update. He got the whole story.
Diaz finally said, "This is going to be plenty embarrassing for Dr. Faulkner, his nephew getting caught doing something like this just as the state and the fed's Department of Justice are reviewing his part of the pilot project."

"The pilot project?" Danny asked real quickly.

"It's a multi-state federally backed experimental project in the southeast. The idea is examining the possibility of privatization of some aspects of our penal system, to see what's most cost effective, public or private corrections facilities, and what types of treatments and training cost the least and produce the lowest rate of residivism. Dr. Faulkner's project has been working with certain classifications of juvenile and young adult offenders during their incarceration, and probation/parole. Through extensive repeated phychological testing he'd pick out those candidates he thought most likely to be successfully and inexpensively rehabilitated. He would also try to pick out those destined for recidivism, and suggest no leniency for them to the Pardons and Paroles Commission. I'm on the governor's panel overlooking the project for the state. Some of his initial numbers look promising. Something like this murder originating from his own family won't look too good for him. Various states and the Feds are looking at possible privatization of almost every segment of the penal system, to make it more cost effective. Pivate prisons may become a huge growth industry, right now there are 38 private penal facilities in Texas. Faulkner's plan was to develop regional treatment centers; save the saveable and three srtike the violently unsaveable - for life."

"Interesting." Danny, like me, was thinking we're always learning something more about the doc, stuff he just never seems to tell us. Well, it's not a crime, just an omission. Danny and Diaz talked for a while, getting it all straight about the warrants. Diaz felt there was enough cause in all cases and he knew which Judge to go to who would expedite the matter. Then Danny, Laura, and I took the plumbing van by Gary Parker's house.

Needless to say, we were absolutely shocked when we first drove by the fake cop Parker's house to see a detective's car sitting in front of his house as big as life. It looked like the ones John the boss bought at auction, most of the hardware APD strips out before auction had been replaced to make it look completely authentic. It looked so good Danny phoned in and rechecked with records to make sure APD didn't have any detective cars stolen recently. The tag was privately owned by some holding company, they were looking for more.

I could look at Danny and tell he was weighing it all out. He had surveillance units at the two other houses, and we were here. Danny called in and got Diaz to send out the freshly signed search warrants along with a couple of uniforms in cars, and a SWAT van with a tactical squad to each of the three locations. Danny's orders were simple. We would move simultaneously at all three locations, executing the warrants and taking the inhabitants in for questioning. The evidence against all of these people was circumstanial and not overwhelming, so Danny didn't want any cowboy shit and end up with corpses of people who turned out later to be innocent. Although he thought to himself, there didn't seem to be many suspects in this case that actually could be honestly described as innocent.

So we sat in the van and waited. I broke out three kevlar vests and two 12 gauge pump shotguns. Danny looked at Laura, "Spooky's at least on contracted, working for us, and is a liscensed PI, with the highest rating for combat shooting. You on the other hand," he held his palms up, shrugged his shoulders, "I'm sorry, but I can't let you in on the raid." She didn't seem too bothered. She might want to see most of the story first hand, but she had seen enough of what weapons can do up close on Pine Ridge. She was uneasy enough as it was being aroun cops and weapons; she didn't mind waiting. Danny and I put on the vests, but neither one of us wanted the shotguns, a little bulky for in house. We both knew the tactical squads would come armed to the teeth anyway. I did leave one shotgun out for Laura, just in case. After having seen the crime scene, these people had to be considered cleverly dangerous.

The only trick was coordinating the three squads to arrive on scene at the same time. It all went off within a two minute time span - at each location it went down the same. The squad cars and tactical van would roll up fast, running silent, with lights on. They'd screech to a halt. Cops poured out of the van and the surveillance units. The yellow door-cannon leads the way. Men yelling, "Search Warrant! Atlanta Police! Search Warrant! Search Warrant! Atlanta Police!" after the boom of the door-cannon. Men streaming in screaming orders.

Danny and I followed the shock troops in. Gary Parker was sitting on his sofa, in two day old boxer shorts and an undershirt, eating day old pizza and drinking beer for breakfast. Shocked would not be the word for the expression on his face. He was stupefied, dumfounded. He sat there with his mouth wide open in utter amazement. Several of the tactical guys yelled out, "Gun! Gun!" and put themselves between Gary and his gun. His entire policeman's uniform was hanging on nails in the wall. The gun was in the holster with the badge and radio lying on the seat of a wooden chair beside his uniform. It was the only nice and neat thing in the house. Gary just sat there with his hands holding a slice and a beer. There were so many guns pointing at him, nobody had to tell him not to move, his survival instinct had.

Danny walked up and made him put down his breakfast and take the search warrant and told him he was wanted for questioning and would he come downtown on his own? Gary was no genius, but he figured if he didn't go voluntarily, they would arrest him for something, and so he agreed. He wasn't handcuffed; under close observation he was allowed to dress, and was taken away. Danny and I began search number one.

The first thing we did was send the tactical unit out of the house and off the property to secure its perimeter. Basically, we just didn't want them in the way. They are great at what they do, but they don't investigate. When trying to be hyper-observant, the less bodies mulling around the better. A squad car took Gary in for questioning. There were four detectives at APD Homicide waiting expectantly for a series of interviews to begin. Very expectantly.

***

Kevin was deeply Asleep because he had partied hard. Friday night he and Amanda and the babe from New Orleans had gotten into coke and ecstasy and partied all night. Saturday night he'd worked and partied after, and Sunday done the lake, too much beer and speed with Gary. He'd gotten home barely before sunrise. He'd crashed out big time. He was sound asleep when the door-cannon went off. He heard the yelling after the door exploded, but through the daze of pass out sleep he was trying to fight his way through to awake consciousness. By the time he had awoken enough to reach under his pillow for his 9 millimeter, there was a 9 millimeter submachine gun barrel at his temple, and several other guns pointing at his face, so he froze, they took his gun away, and they handcuffed him. They sat him on his sofa, and waited for Fagan to arrive.

***

Amanda slept naked, and offered no resistance. She calmly got up out of bed without a stitch on, walked to the bathroom, left the door open, sat down and peed. After flushing she got up, proudly naked, and asked who was in charge. The tactical officer showed her the warrant, and asked if she would come downtown voluntarily. Since they had the warrant, she figured she might as well cooperate. She went downtown with the uniforms in the squadcar, after slowly

dressing - a process everyone involved seemed to have enjoyed.

***

The crime scene unit van showed up at Gary Parker's, the techs came in and photoed and

videoed everything, and we showed them what to bag, and we bagged a bunch. The police

wrecker came and took the fake police car, the techs took his uniform, all his shoes, his dirty

clothes, and I methodically took down and bagged his altar.

Behind a makeshift curtain in the corner of his bedroom, his altar was not impressive.

Gary's altar didn't show much imagination, but one thing for sure, it was a satanic altar, not one

used in the pagan religions of pre-Christian Europe. It was constructed and dedicated to the

service of the devil. Other than the crime scene, I hadn't seen one in a while, I had forgotten

what an odd and sickly repulsed feeling I get whenever faced with a ritual area dedicated to evil.

I had, at a certain point in my shamanic training, been taken by my spiritual teachers to stand on

the highest mountain in the lower forty-eight states and challenged to make a choice of the soul,

where I pledged myself and my life to the side of Light in the war against evil. Had I not taken

the pledge, my training would have ended on that mountain. It was a pledge I took seriously, it

was something... well it was something sacred.

I now stood in front of one of the enemies' outposts. I asked Danny to clear the room for

a second. Looking puzzled, he said okay and cleared it. Laura, who had come in after the

excitment and taken notes for me, and Danny were te only ones who remained. It was weird

enough by police standards what I was about to do; but still better if Danny remained to secure

the chain of evidence. I got out the kit I had packed in the morning, a gift I had been recieved a

little over a year ago, from a friend of mine, Father Murrell, who's a priest in the Liberal

Catholic Church. I got out the beautiful, fully blessed silver cross he had given me and the bottle of Holy Water. I opened the bottle and took the water on the first two fingers of my right hand and crossed myself with the Kabbalistic Cross. Then I took the water on my fingers and made the sign of the cross over the altar, "In the Name of the Father, the Son, and the Holy Spirit." Taking the cross in my right hand I made the sign of the cross three times in front of the altar. "The power of Christ compels all that is evil to go back from whence it came! The power of Christ compels all that is evil to go back from whence it came! The power of Christ compels all that is evil to go back from whence it came! So be it, So be it, So be it now done! By the Name, Power, and Word of God so be it now done! By the holy power of..." I used the Hebrew ineffable name of God, the Aramaic name of Jesus, and the Greek feminine name for the Holy Spirit, "So be it now fully and completely done. Amen." I took the cross and firmly brought my fist and the bottom of the cross down on the altar three times.

After putting up my emergency exorcism kit; I put back on my examination gloves and took apart Gary Parker's satanic altar. He had a poster of the Goat of Mendes in the upside down pentagram in silver on black on the back cloth on the wall. His altar was covered in a black satin cloth, he had two large candles, the left black, the right white, a gong, a black wooden phallic wand, an athame, and a pewter chalice decorated with four devils heads, a flat silver disk with the goat of Mendes in an inverted pentagram, a small whip, a pewter joss stick holder, and some very strong incense which smelled very similar to the crime scene. He had LaVey's books on Satanism, books on Dr. John Dee's magical Enochian language, and some paperbacks on witchcraft and black magic. I took a glance inside his spellbook. He had nothing about the crime scene ritual, seems he had sacrificed his pet cat recently for an unnamed goal. From what I saw, he might be more serious than your average teenage dabbler, but definitely a rank beginner. This was no high priest of a black coven or seriously advanced black magician. A pretty sick puppy if you were a cat lover; but not our head honcho. But we had expected the fake cop/lookout would not be one of the top people, he was just muscle.

The dirt basement floor revealed the recent digging where the cat was buried, but we weren't sure if we should dig it up. Danny said go ahead, so two of the techs exhumed Fritz the sacrifice. Once examined, the food was left in the refrigerator, but that was about it. We left the furniture and some of the clothes, but we took anything possibly of interest. Danny didn't want to do anything half-assed and then find out later we missed something.

When we got back into the plumbing van and headed to Amanda's house, Danny asked me, "I thought you were a shaman, what was all that Christian Exorcists stuff in there?"

"Well Danny, I was raised in a Christian home, I was baptized; just 'cause I'm a shaman that doesn't go away. Anthropologists call what I was taught and do a syncretic religion. I call it Sweat Lodge Christianity. Many Indians kept their own spiritual hierarchy, they just plugged in Jesus and kept going. Lots of tribes already had myths and traditions about a teacher closely resembling Jesus, so when the missionaries came many Indians accepted the main stories about Jesus, without putting much emphasis on the Book which came from the physically and culturally distant Middle East. So I'm a metis - mixed blood - shaman - a Sweatlodge Christian; however when fighting Satanists, Christian symbolgy is the way to go."

Danny nodded like he understood. I doubted he did, I'm not sure I always do, but that didn't matter at the moment. We were fighting criminal opponents who practiced a Christian heresy, a ritual rebellion against Christianity. I'd fight it with the appropriate weapons and symbols, in the appropriate way, at the appropriate time. The cops were solving a physical crime, but there were souls on the line and a spiritual battle being waged here as well. The ancient war between good and evil is as old as the evolution of the human soul and spirit. Usually this war is fought subtely, sometimes insiduiously, often minutuely and mundanely, and sometimes obscenely; but every now and then it is fought openly, symbolically. We were lucky enough, or unfortunate enough to be at the epicenter of one such open combat.

***

When Stewart got back from the meeting with his uncle lawyer, two correction officers gave him a laminated plastic ID with his picture, (taken when they fingerprinted him) name, and number. Then they assigned him a bed. It was cold metal with a thin green mattress and a pull-out locker built in under the bed. He got a pillow case, two white sheets, and a green wool blanket. They told him the meal times, how he had to make his bed immediately after wake up before breakfast, and how he had to learn his new number, and say it five times a day. First thing each morning, last thing each night for roll calls, and before the three meals. If he wanted to eat, he had to say his number. Stewart became 527605. That's who he was now. Not a rich kid that abused his sister and small animals, now he was 527605. His world was changing too quickly and going in really bad directions. Just days ago he'd been happier than he'd ever been, now this. He was in a mental and emotional state of shock.

He was given the bed closest to the deputy's station. To a real con, it's the least wanted bunk, but as a frightened wimp, he figured correctly it was the safest place. Although Stewart was a serious antisocial outcast, the men around him scared the shit out of him. Some of them were just drunks, or deadbeat dads, but some were burglars, car thieves, armed robbers, rapists, drug dealers, and gang bangers. Stewart was no spakling physical specimen, but he was usually the meanest and most ruthless person in his environment. Here, he didn't even rate.

Stewart was sadly lacking in experience dealing with people of other races, classes, cultures, and now he was going through jailhouse culture shock, and culture shock it was. He just kept to himself, watched everything, and tried to figure out how ketchup turned to blood, and how his life had gone to hell. He also hoped his Amanda Stone alibi was going to work out like Raquel said. He wished there were some way he could contact Raquel and he wondered repeatedly about the guys in the white van. Something was certainly happening to him, and he needed to figure out what. He repeated Raquel's license plate number to himself once again, just in case he needed it.

***

Williams gathered the five high school kids while Wallace found men of girth to be in the line-up. The quicker they got overwhelming positive ID, the quicker he would crack, or some other players would crack. The two women cops, Potts and Wilson were taking Gary Parker through his first interview. He was not giving anything up. He would just respond to every question with the same answer, "I can't say."

They got real tired of hearing that. The same questions were repeated: "where were you Friday night?"; "where did the police uniform come from?"; "where did the car come from?"; "who are you working with?"; "who was in charge?"

Gary finally screamed, "I don't have to say notin' but name, rank, 'n serial number." Which made no sense, since he'd never been in the military, and this wasn't a prisoner of war camp, it was a police station, and he didn't even have a serial number. The two women went outside the interrogation room and watched him through the two-way mirror. Annie asked, "What is this boy on, name, rank, and serial number? He's tripping out, or starting early going for the insanity defense."

Amanda Stone's house was different from Gary's in many respects. It wasn't anywhere near as dirty, and she had a huge assortment of clothing, some for normal life, some for exotic dancing, some for hooking, some for sexual role playing. She had clothes in every closet in her house, but one. That's where she hid her altar. It showed a little more imagination than Gary's, with slightly more in the way of aesthetics, but it was still pretty simple - like Gary, she was more than a dabbler, but still a beginner. Her spellbook made no mention of the crime or any animal sacrifices. Just simple selfish candle burning emotionally powered gimmee spells, no big deal occulty. Her altar contained the same items as Gary's altar, had was placed before a Goat of Mendes in the upside down pentagram on a poster.

I got Danny to clear the area like earlier and went through the same process before I dismantled her altar. As we did previously, Laura would take notes. Danny was flabbergasted by the sheer volume of clothing and shoes. Finally, in exasperation, the second time the lab techs asked him what went and what stayed clothes wise, he lost it. "Fuck it! We'll luminol her whole fucking wardrobe here tonight, and see what glows if we have to." Danny went back in the living room, then downstairs, then outside, checking it all out.

Back in the living room on a tray under the sofa APD found three grams of cocaine, four hits of ecstasy, a straw, a mirror, a quarter ounce of pot, a small wooden pipe, and a bottle of muscle relaxers. That gave us easy charges to hold her on, before the lab tests could come through to nail her. She'd been taken away for questioning long before the drugs or altar was found. It was just something else Danny could play with during the interrogation process.

I took the techs aside after Danny left to roam around for a last look and picked out the shoes and outfits I thought might have possibly been used in a ritual setting. Considering the nature of her business and satanic ritual practice, it was not an easy job. At least there were no signs of buried housepets.

She had basically the same altar as Gary, but she had more books, but not a big library. Several of the books I took in as evidence had Kevin Jackson's name written inside the cover.

***

Wilson and Potts watched Amanda through the glass as she nervously smoked cigarettes and drank coffee. Smoking is technically illegal, but it's allowed as an interrogatin tool. Of course, a benefit of that is that the interrogators who indulge can smoke, too. They hadn't really questioned her yet, other than to ask the most basic questions - where was she Friday night? Her story came out quick, and actually impressed the two women cops.

"Thursday night after work I went dancing at the Dungeon & Chamber. I met a beautiful girl there from New Orleans who was in the life, thinking about moving here. We hit it off and we partied. Friday night me, my old man, and her partied at her room at the Ritz Carlton. And did we party, I mean all night long. Kevin told her if she needed a job, she was hired. We had to go to work Saturday night, we left midmorning to go home and crash. I called her later that night, but she'd checked out. Never called us, maybe she didn't want the job after all."

"What was her name?"

"Her stage name, her chosen work name was Honey Delight. I called her Hun, I didn't worry about her straight world given name. She said she worked on Bourbon Street, danced at a club during the afternoon, hooked at night. Yeah, you go find Honey Delight in New Orleans, she'll be glad to tell you where I was."

"You better hope so, your very life may depend on it."

***

Kevin just sat there in the holding cell, stewing. Sure, he had gone for his gun, but they couldn't prove he wasn't so sleepy that he didn't know they were cops and he was just trying to protect himself. His main worry was they would find his stash. He didn't think they'd find enough crank or coke laying on his snowflake mirror to make a serious drug charge. But if they found his stash..... He didn't need this shit, and he wanted another look at that fucking search warrant. He was groggy when he glanced at it, but he was sure it said murder. He wanted to be interviewed like they said, charged or not charged, but he didn't want to sit around in some fucking holding cell all day. He had done real time, and none of this was bringing back good memories. After partying hard all weekend, he really didn't know exactly what was laying around. If it was just little shit, no big deal, but if they found his stash, he was fucked. He didn't think the warrant was for drugs, but murder. What fucking murder, he hadn't killed anyone? Sure, he'd beat some shitheads senseless over the years, but he'd never offed anybody. It's not that he wouldn't, he just hadn't. It wasn't good bussiness.

***

Gary was fourth in line. All of the guys were big, some had dark hair like his, some didn't. Some had facial hair, some didn't. All they seemed to have in common was they were big guys. Some looked like bikers, some looked like cops. Gary had been up on assault charges before, stemming from his work as a bouncer but he had never been in a line-up before. They seemed to have to do the same thing over and over and over again. He was sure it was eleven or twelve times, over what seemed like thirty or forty minutes. One by one they were called, he was fourth."Number four, step forward, turn left, turn right, step back." Pause. "Number four, step forward, left, right, step back." Then a longer pause, then all over again. He was getting sick of it. He was nervous, wondering if his covert employees knew he was here and were going to bail him out, or if this was some kind of ultimate loyalty test. He had to think it all out, not keep

dancing like a fucking puppet on a string for some voice behind a wall.

The high school kids went through one at a time. They looked at the six men one by one

each would come forward, turn left, and right, and step back. They all picked Gary. It was 100%

and no doubt. Annie told the other detectives that was two they had cold, Stewart on the blood

evidence and Gary on six positive ID's and physical evidence. The rest was not as solid but

coming together. The kids were taken back, the people in the line-up were paid or went back to

work, and the four detectives huddled, talking about the next step, and waiting on Danny to get

back. Annie suggested they send for Stewart, that way they could have them all close at hand,

and if one started to crack, play them against each other. Everyone agreed and Stewart was sent

for.

***

\   Kevin's house was vastly different than the other two. It was cleaner, more organized, he

had a large library, and the works were not all of an occult or satanic nature. He had books on

foods, wines, classic motorcycles, ultralight aircraft, and travel. He either had aspirations or was

a serious dreamer. No dabbler, he was also much more seriously into the Black Arts than the

other two. He was a true believer. His spell book, found on his altar revealed that much, with

many workings recorded, over a period of years. The altar was inside a locked room dedicated

for ritual - a one room satanic temple. Yet the altar was bare and and his magical weapons were

not there. None of the primary working tools of his evil art were there. I still cleansed the altar

area and his spellbook as I had the other two. The feeling of evil was much stronger here than at

the previous two residences, even without the his tools being present on the altar. I told Danny

we should check the basement and the yard. He had been at his black craft for years. All his rituals didn't include sacrifice, but some did. Although it made no mention of the crime, it did list the participants at their regular satanic coven meetings. For the last year it always included Amanda, Gary, and sometimes, Beavis and Butthead—obvious nicknames, but for who? Were they involved in the crime? We needed to find Kevin's altar implements and see if he had another spellbook, it could be real important. We found what looked like five possible animal burials in the dirt floor of the unfinished basement. It seemed to be a cemetery for sacrificed animals was all the damp, dark, dank indention in the earth had been for Kevin. The presence of evil was very strong here, as well. I got Danny to give the techs a ten minute break so I could break out the holy water and cleanse it before they started digging. By the time I was through, I felt like I needed a physical and a symbolic bath, at the first possible oppurtunity.

Early on, I had told Danny that this house reflected Kevin was superior to, and much more occultly developed than the other two - much farther along the road of satanic ritual rebellion. Here I saw the evil, organized intelligence and cold ruthlessness I would expect out of the perpertrators of the crime scene. However, I didn't see evidence of the resources or refinement of evil I would expect for the mastermind's home.

***

Gary was taken from the line-up to an interrorgation room. He was left sitting at a table and locked in. He noticed the signs on the walls, that visual and sound recordings could be made at any time, and there should be absolutely no legal expectation of privacy in the room at any time. He guessed the mirror was a two-way mirror. He also figured it was not a room to meet with your lawyers, because they had to be given privacy, that was the law. You watch TV, you learn some basics of criminal law. That's America.

***

As Laura and I were walking through the house (one last time I hoped) before leaving, I heard Danny yell, "YES!" We went running into the kitchen. There was a set of recessed shelves on the kitchen's side wall by the refigerator. The bottom shelf had a gap between the wall and the back of the shelf of maybe a couple of inches, just wide enough to slide your hand in. Danny had done so, found a nail, found a string on that nail, and pulled the string up. At the bottom of that string were securely tied double bagged gallon baggies with what looked like two ounces of cocaine and four ounces of speed. We had Jackson, no matter what. Danny was grinning like a Chesire Cat. "Thanks, Spooky."

"No prob, that's my job."

Laura and I went outside in the sun. It's warmth and brighhtness were welcome. I leaned up against the back of a pine tree and closed my eyes, relaxed and did the yogic cleansing breath for a while. Finally Laura, who was resting against the hood of a squadcar asked, "All right, what was he thanking you for? I didn't see you do anything."

I opened my eyes and looked at her.

"I mean anything he should have been thanking you for."

"Oh." I kind of grinned. It wasn't like I'd been idle all day. "Just something I told him the first day at the crime scene. Kind of out of the blue. He just remembered it and it paid off."

"Well?"

"Drugs. I told him to always look for drugs. To do something as evil as our perps, a certain numbing of the soul must take place. I won't get into whether people are necessarily inherently good or evil, but I don't think your average person could easily become this desynsitized. I'd look for heavy herion, or cocaine, or speed use previously or currently by at least some, if not all of the participants. I warned him that any warrant written should always mention drugs that could be used in satanic rites. If we came here on a murder warrant, and he's not guilty of murder, and we find the drugs but didn't mention drugs on the warrant there's a good chance at the trial or in subsequent appeals, the evidence would be thrown out. I also warned Danny that the more organized individuals might have ingeneous hidng places. Danny remembered and all our warrants include drugs as one of the items we're searching for. With this guy's record, I'm sure Danny would have included drugs on his warrant, anyway. But maybe not all the warrants. As to ingeneous hiding places, they're criminals and Satanists, their lives and practices demand a certain amount of secrecy, the smart ones should have hiddens stashes they have easy access to but are well hidden.

Annie Wilson and Potts went into the interrogation room with their coffee mugs full. They were being nice, friendly, letting her smoke, even had another styrofoam cup for Amanda. The two detectives were talking about the Braves, their chances to win it all this year, which player had the cuttest butt. All very friendly. They gave Amanda the coffee, dropped baseball, and got down to work.

Annie looked Amanada in the eyes, made sure she had her full attention. "Girl, we got a problem. New Orleans police don't have any records of a Honey Delight. They said they'd check on Bourbon Street but I doubt it'll be a high priority for them. We need something more. You got to give us something solid to establish your alibi."

"I partied all night Friday night. I know where I was and who I was with. I shouldn't need an alibi." Amanda was confident, hanging tough.

It was time to start shaking the tree and see what would fall out. "That's funny, because we have another suspect in a murder case that says they partied with you all weekend." Annie used 'they,' wanted to hold back as much as possible. Maybe Amanda preferred girls, maybe she didn't. It might have some bearing, it might not. Better to keep it back.

"Then they're fucking lying. Who says I was with them all weekend? I know I can prove that's bullshit!"

"Amanda, girl face facts, you're a hooker, even if you were with other people, you think they'll come forward? Your best chance is cooperating with us, telling us everything you know." Annie stayed on her.

"Ask Kevin Jackson, he manages the legitimate, tax paying escort service I work for. I was with him Friday night along with Honey at the Ritz, and I was with him Saturday night at my house after work. I had two Joh... escorts Saturday, an afternoon party and a late dinner date. We always get credit card numbers. It's a security thing, of course the bland name of our company doesn't match our services, to protect our customers. If this gets to be fucking life and death, the service I work for will be able to come up with the customer's credit card numbers and ID them for you. But if you do that, be discreet, it's really, really bad for bussiness." She stubbed out her cigarette, drank some cofffee, and lit a new one.

Annie's instincts told her the girl sounded awful sure of herself and might be telling the truth. If so, then Stewart was without an alibi, but then where does that leave Amanda and Kevin. Danny called in with word that drugs were found at both their houses. They weren't going to be going anywhere anytime soon. APD had time to sort it all out and connect the dots

"Maybe we'll hear from NOPD, they will miraculously find Honey and she will clear you. But another hooker and your pimp aren't great sources for alibis." Annie and Potts got up to leave.

On the way out, Amanda said, "He's not a pimp. He runs an escort service. A damn nice legitimate one, too." The door closed, the lock engaged.

***

I left Laura with Danny at his office. It seems everybody had gotten used to her quietly being around, which was good for all concerned. Danny thought I was crazy, but I went down to the to the locker room and took a shower. It was a physical, as well as symbolic cleansing, I quietly intoned the pranavah, the "OM/AUM sound, and certain specific Tibetan cleansing sounds. There was nobody in the shower, but I still chose discretion. Then I almost silently sang a Cherokee song to my animal spirits. I borrowed an undershirt and Danny's APD sweats. At least they were clean, thank God for his wife. She loved him and had the patience and understanding of Job. I figured she needed it. By the time I got back, there was no one in Danny's office. I found them in the room where the task force had first met. Danny was at the chaulk board with the names of the four suspects written out.

"Okay, we've got the blood evidence against Stewart, he was there. We've got the eyewitnesses and the fake police car, we know Gary Parker was there. We've got Amanda Stone and Kevin Jackson on drug charges, so we'll have them all for a while no matter what. So what's their story?"

Annie spoke out, "She claims that she, Kevin, and a New Orleans hooker named Honey Delight partied all Friday night at the Ritz. NOPD has no Honey Delight on its computers. Amanda says she had two escorts Saturday, and partied with Kevin late Saturday night. So far their alibis are unconfirmed except by each other. We haven't had time to check, just got the info."

Danny nodded. "And Stewart claims her as his alibi, did you bring up Stewart's name yet?"

"No. I said somebody used her as an alibi, but didn't say who. Didn't even say what sex."

"Good. Good. We don't have any physical evidence linking Stone and Jackson yet. Any chance their alibi is real?"Annie hesitated. Both Potts and she thought the girl told her story with a lot of conviction.

"She sure sounds confident. If she's lying, she's good. But she's a hooker. She should be a good liar." She imitated a southern bell in a real sexy voice, "Oh my gosh, I'ts so BIG!" She laughed, "I'm sure she's a good liar, it's a neccessity in her chosen field." Everybody had laughed, but the women laughed longer.

Danny went on, "So Kevin Jackson knows nothing except he pulled a gun on the police while we were serving a warrant. He doesn't know about the drugs we found, neither does Amanda Stone. Keep holding that back, once they know they're busted, they'll ask for a lawyer. Let's get everything we can before the bloodsuckers show up."

Everybody nodded. "Wallace, you get on the phone, no physically go to the labs, push them for something, be nice, take pastries, or be obnoxious, whatever you must do, get bs something to use in interrogation. Hang around, be a pain in the ass, but get me something by tonight. We need traces of blood on Jackson's and Stone's clothes, we need evidence, now! Williams, you go to Toccoa and search that girl's room. Bring back everything. We'll return what we can to her parents as soon as possible." Williams didn't look too thrilled as he left.

"Has anybody lawyered up yet?"

Wilson spoke up again, "Only Stewart, and he's already seen him this afternoon. We've brought Stewart up here, but we haven't questioned him or contacted his lawyer. Stewart hasn't asked to see him again, so I doubt he will, since he just did. But he is here for others to see, or for him to observe them"

"We know Gary Parker and Stewart were there, we don't know yet about Stone and Jackson but we'll have Mr. Jackson for a few years no matter what, this is his second drug bust with weight, and third major felony. He's screwed no matter what. Who's in the studio?" It was the in-house nickname for the high tech surveillance room. Miked, videoed, two-way mirror, and with big signs saying there is no expectation of privacy. In there, what a prisoner or suspect said to one another was fair game for the law.

"Parker." Annie said quickly.

Danny smiled, "Move Parker out, put Stewart in, leave Amanda where she is for now. Don't let any of the suspects see each other yet. Until I say so, and we can watch."

***

Kevin Jackson finally started raising hell in the holding cell downstairs, he wanted to be interviewed. Interview him, press charges, or let him go. He was yelling through the open bars, raising a ruckus, pissing people off. They called up to Danny, said he was a pain in the butt and wanted to move him to the jail, hold him in isolation, or kick his ass. Danny said to send him up in handcuffs. They asked where, Danny said his office. He got up, motioned for me, Laura, Potts, and Wilson to follow, and we headed for Danny's office.

***

They put handcuffs on Kevin, after they told him to calm the fuck down, he was on his way to an interview. Confident he wasn't connected with any murder, he wondered if one of his competitors was trying to fuck with him by giving him up for something he didn't do. He figured if they had found his stash, they would have arrested him by now; he was growing more confident, maybe this was all going to work out. Maybe he'd snorted everything that was out, and they had nothing on him at all. Maybe they foun nada and he was going to get an apology. He knew some of his books and posters might seem strange to the cops, but none of them knew shit about the occult. And freedom of religion is guaranteed legally. The cops were clueless. But it was a damn good thing he'd moved his altar stuff up to the boathouse.

***

Potts was dispatched to the Ritz with pictures of Kevin and Amanda to see if anybody remembered them. That left Annie, Laura, and me, with Danny in his office. I wondered if Danny shared the opinion of Annie that I did, that she was head and shoulders above the rest of the task force when it came to brains and cop's intuition. Schultz barged in for a minute. He was carrying all of Danny's other work load while we went 100% at this case. You could tell he felt left out, following up on mundane stuff, making dull court apperances on solved cases while he missed out on solving the glamor case. He was definitely sullen, not the normal Schultz. He got some files and headed back to court.

Danny sat a lone chair directly in front of his desk to face him. He pulled up a chair behind and to the right of his desk for Annie. Laura was quiet, leaning in the corner, but I noticed she had a perfect view of the interrogation chair. I sat on the back left edge of Danny's big desk. I didn't think he was thrilled about it, but there wasn't much room.

A uniformed cop brought Kevin Jackson to the door. He was in the clothes he'd woken up in, jeans and a tee shirt, assumably he'd passed out or was too tired to undress the night before. Unshaved, uncombed, he looked rough, real rough. He was muscled, probably from a prison weight room. He had a faint all black jailhouse tattoo on his right shoulder, a rough skull and crossbones, like the old pirate symbol. He wasn't that tall or massive, under six feet, under 190, but I wouln't have been eager to take him on. I'd gone through the same finishing school he had -the Georgia penal system, and I came from a strongly military/martial arts background, I knew I could have taken him, but I wouldn't have been eager to. He would be a dangerous opponent - it was in his eyes.

Danny told the officer to remove his handcuffs. Jackson hadn't been charged with anything offically, although he had tried to draw his gun on cops serving a warant. It was a conscious and intentional move on Danny's part, but still, I thought somewhat risky.

Kevin Jackson didn't have the dead eyes of many criminals, crackheads, junkies, alchoholics, his eyes were bright, intense, fierce - feral. He looked at Danny, suspect to cop, briefly glanced at Annie, moved to look at Laura, whom he eyed up and down. That bothered me in some real deep primal way. Then he looked at me. Our eyes locked. In two seconds I felt he was cold, ruthless, evil. If he hadn't commited the blasphemy at our crime scene, he would produce something similar someday. In the war I had pledged my soul to, I recognized one of the evil ones before me. Not a master, not an adept yet, but not a dabbler, his soul was as committed to his side as mine was to the Light. We stared at each other for what seemed like a very long time. Danny slapped his hand down flat on the desk, WHACK! Kevin slowly turned his head and looked at Danny, the eye-lock over, the interview begining.

"Kevin Jackson, your name has come up in a murder investigation. In connection with that investigation we secured the warant I showed you when we searched your house. We know of your previous drug and attempted murder convictions, we know you run call girls. Let's not bullshit around. The best thing you can possibly do for yourself, right now, is account for your whereabouts all weekend. It may be you have been implicated falsely and we can resolve this matter amicably."

Amicably. Were this guy not a Satanist, I might have grinned at how thick Danny was laying it on, but there was nothing funny going on in the room at all.

"Sure cop, I seen you on TV, but who are your pals here, not everybody here smells like a cop? And what murder are we talking about? I had a busy weekend, but I sure as hell didn't off anybody, never have., it's bad business."

"Yeah, you're a model citizen Jackson, up for the key to the city. I'm detective Fagan, this is detective Wilson, this is detective Mosby, and Miss Star." Danny forgot or didn't understand her name was Laura Red Star, a two name last name. But what the heck, I'd just as soon this scumbag not know her name. I noticed I was already getting in that macho "protective over my woman" mode. It didn't take long. Danny also didn't put private in front of detective for me. I didn't worry about it, it was Danny's show, let him run it. "The murdered victim's name is a matter of police bussines. Let's find out where you've been all weekend."

Kevin looked around, quickly, then settled on Danny. "Friday night I played with my girlfriend and a girl from New Orleans at her room at the Ritz. Saturday night I worked at my escort service office, and played with my girlfriend after work. Sunday me and my bud Gary went to the lake." He knew Gary wasn't smart enough to ad lib, so he'd stick to the truth concerning him. If they charged him, he'd call his business partner to get a lawyer for him and clean out his houseboat. She knew he played around with the occult, but she didn't really know anything about his practices, especially their satanic aspect. She'd only been on the houseboat a couple of times, and the altar wasn't even set up there then. He'd work it out with her later. The thing right now was beat the bullshit murder rap and try to get out of this without getting busted. "It could be one of my competitors is trying to set me up, so he can put me out of business, and while I'm inside, steal my girls."

"That's entirely possible, very plausible." Danny was still laying it on thick, very smooth, no hostility. "What room at the Ritz?"

"Fuck, I don't know, somewhere on the sixth floor. My girlfriend set it up, I don't know if I ever even heard the fucking room number."

"Look at it our way Kevin, you're a violent pimp and a convicted drug dealer. We need solid alibis to clear you of this. Surely you understand your hooker girfriend and some girl from the Big Easy we can't find doesn't give you a very credible alibi. We need things we can verify. Think." Danny sounded really concerned, like it was a matter that needed to be cleared up for Kevin's own good. Not like we were trying to nail his ass for murder.

Kevin did something strange. Something I'd never seen before in a police interview. He brought his feet up off the floor and sat cross legged in his chair, Indian/yoga style, and closed his eyes. I could see he was relaxing and doing deep breathing. My opinion of this opponent went up. Danny looked up at me, turned his palms up, and mouthed the words, "What the fuck?"

I shook my head, and lifted my finger to my lips. I thought let him remember what he can remember, or figure out what he could. A worthy opponent is a good thing in many warrior cultures. He was evil, but he showed signs of being disciplined, strong.

Finally, after about a minute of Kevin's quiet, eyes closed relaxation and deep breathing technique - the whole time being stared at relentlessly by cops, Kevin said loudly and with great confidence, "Juan Valdez!"

I didn't know about anybody else, but I couldn't figure out what the hell old Columbian coffee commercials on TV had to do with our double homicide.

"Juan Valdez. Room service, sixth floor, late Friday night, real late. Valdez isn't his real name, but it's something close. That's what Honey called him. We got a fifth of Absolut and a fifth of Chevas. He was half drunk on the job, we let him have a drink with us. I thought his eyes would fall out. I'll tell you why I know he'll remember us. Besides the fact we were nice enough to let a drunk bellboy have a drink with us, he won't forget the tip." Kevin was smiling, he looked supremely confident.

"Why?" Danny was dropping the nice guy sound.

"Because I gave him a choice. A cash tip or a double flash. He took the flash, both girls opened their robes. I thought his tounge would hit the floor. Finally I had to tell the girls to cover up and walk him to the door. Looked like he wanted to stay. Check it out. I know he'll remember us. At least the girls."

Danny leaned over, talked quietly to Annie for a few seconds, then she got up and left. I assumed she was going to contact Potts, and get her to run down the Juan Valdez angle on site, and check the names of all the guests on the sixth floor.

"Just a couple of more things for now, and maybe we can resolve all this in a short while." Danny paused, opened and looked over a file, I didn't know if it was about this case or if he was just using it as a prop. "How long have you gone out with LeAnn Rutherford?"

"Who?" Kevin was quick, no sign of recognition. "She's not one of my girls. Does she have a street name or a stage name?"

Danny shook his head.

"No. I don't have any LeAnn, never have. What else can I do for you, or can I finally get the hell out of here. I've been here all day long. I've been cooperative. I was asleep this morning, dead to the world, I didn't realize they were cops at first. And I sure as hell didn't kill anybody this weekend. Now, can I go?"

Danny went back to being nice. "Not yet, there are a couple of things we've got to clear up. I'm going to have to ask you to wait a little while longer. I'll put you in an interrogation room nearby. Have you eaten?" I thought Danny was being overly nice.

"No, I'm hungry as hell Anything you got worth eating,throw it my way."

Danny said, "Okay, I'll take care of it." He took Kevin to an interview room without handcuffs, but locked him in. He came back and we all went to eat a late dinner. Danny brought back Kevin and all our suspects some burgers. Considering the nature of the crime and that he paid out of his own pocket, it was extremely considerate. Food service is dependable in jail, not so in the APD's holding tanks, and nonexistent in the interrogation rooms.

Annie had talked to Potts, gone to eat, talked again with Potts, and gotten the word. Danny wasn't thrilled with what he heard from Annie.

"There is a Juan Martinez, who did work the sixth floor Friday night. At 3:30 AM he delivered fifths of Absolut and Chevas to a room on the sixth floor belonging to a Holly Delight, who paid in cash. Martinez was drinking on the job, was so drunk, in fact, they fired him early Saturday morning at the end of his shift. His friend Mario works the day shift and told Potts that Juan had gone to Panama City, Florida, where his sister is the day or night manager of some high rise hotel right on the beach. Mario was pretty sketchy, didn't know which hotel, what part of PC, or the name of the sister."

"Damn," Danny sighed. The phone rang. "Hello."

Wallace said, "Sorry it took all day, but I've got good news. We've got blood on a pair of shoes and clothes taken from Jackson's closet and blood on one of Amanda's outfits and a pair of shoes that Spooky picked out for the techs this morning. You can still run your luminol test and you might find more, but we've got blood, human and animal."

Chapter Eleven - Monday Evening/Night

We had four suspects in holding cells and interview rooms, and night had fallen on a long and exciting day. Were it not for the adrenalin, everyone would be dead tired. Adrenalin is a wonderful thing, but even it has limitations. Danny told everybody they could go home. Nobody wanted to. Everybody wanted to watch the next step. We went to the small viewing room which lets you watch through the two way mirror of "the studio."

There was no interrogation, so we needed no lawyers. We simply left Stewart in the studio, and brought Amanda in. The studio had one table, six chairs. Stewart had been left there all evening, by himself, with the exception of being fed. The remains of his hamburger wrappers and empty Coke can were still on the table.

The officer opened the door, led Amanda in, and said, "You'll wait here for your next interview. Remember…" He pointed at the sign and launched into the same speech he gave Stewart. "In here you have no expectation of privacy. Everything said and done in here can be recorded or videoed. Think of it like there's an officer in here watching you and listening to everything you say. You both understand?" Stewart nodded vacantly and Amanda eyed her environment, said "yeah," and sat down. The door clicked shut as the lock engaged.

They had no legal expectation of privacy. We had the video camera recording, the volume up, and we watched every move.

***

Stewart had spent his idle hours thinking, but he still didn't know what was up. He has the best time of his life then gets caught sneaking in. He gets caught lying, he gets arrested, he's got blood on his uniform, and his uncle says he's in serious trouble. What was going on? Of all the things he had actually done which society might frown on, no mention, but a murder? Sure, a person such as himself, with his uniquely dark proclivities has wondered what it feels like to take a human life, fantasized about it, often. But he knew damn well he hadn't done it yet, so somebody, somewhere, was making a big mistake. He needed to find out if Raquel's friend was going to come through and give him the alibi he needed.

He kept thinking about the white van. Raquel took his uniform, he knew that. It came back with the ketchup stains the cops say is blood. So something happened in the van; who were those guys, and was Raquel involved? If she was, he always had what he'd held back. But he was still hoping she was his ally, not his enemy. In his evil heart of hearts, he was in love.

The door opened. A cop led in a pretty young woman with light red hair. He was sitting at one end of the table, she stood at the other. The deputy told her to wait here, pointed at the sign about no privacy, gave her and him the same speech he'd been given before and left. Once the cop exited they looked at each other. Stewart nodded, she said hi and looked away. He noticed she was in street clothes, not a jailhouse jumpsuit like his.

After sitting for a second she got up and paced back and forth trying to figure it out. All they had to do was find Honey, and everything was cool. But what if they couldn't find Honey? She needed something, these assholes were talking murder. MURDER. She was a hooker with a record. A jury would see her good for any crime if the DA was slick enough and she had no alibi. She had partied hard Friday night, sex, drugs, booze, it was a long orgy, and Honey was good, real good. Why hadn't she called the next day; she'd had a great time? Why'd Honey dissapear? Lots of things here didn't make sense. Why the fuck was she picked up on a murder charge and who the hell claimed her for an alibi? She needed some answers, damn quick.

Stewart would watch her butt as she walked away, look down as she walked towards him. She was attractive. Something about her reminded him of Raquel. Not that they looked alike, but there was something similar. Stewart didn't know much about body language or attitude, Stewart didn't know much about women. He thought about some of the things he and Raquel had done. He closed his eyes as he thought of Raquel while he heard the quick steps, pacing back and forth.

"Yo. Kid. How long you been here?"

Stewart opened his eyes and looked at her. "I've been here all afternoon and evening. They finally let me eat. I was starving. I'm still hungry."

"What's your crime?" Stewart looked at her, puzzled.

"What's your crime?" She said it loud and slow like he was deaf or retarded. "What were you arrested for, or do you like wearing jailhouse whites or maybe you trick-or-treating a few months early?"

Stewart looked down at his uniform, "Lying. Giving false statements."

Amanda laughed. "Sweetie, if everybody who got caught lying was arrested, the whole world would be in jail. They'd be nobody on the outside."

"Well, the charge they said in court was giving a false statement to the police during the course of a murder investigation, obstructing justice. Something like that."

Amanda looked at him, scrutinized him. "What murder?"

"A Miss Jane Doe. I guess that means they, like don't know the dead lady's real name." Stewart noticed this woman had a Cyndi Crawford mole. She also had light red hair. Stewart knew what he'd said for an alibi, but he couldn't judge height or weight.

"When did this murder take place?"

"Friday night."

She looked at him again, hard. "What'd you lie about?"

"I said I was at my uncle's, then I said I was camping. They found out neither was true."

"Well, what were you doing?"

"I was in a hotel room." He said it with a devilishly wicked grin. Amanda began reassessing.

"You have fun?" She looked him in the eyes, knowingly.

"All weekend long, most fun I've ever had." Stewart kept looking at her, at her mole. He looked over at the sign. "Do they really listen in and tape things?"

"Sure they do, sweetie, they're cops. They have no honor. I didn't do what I'm charged with, so I'm not worried. How come your girlfriend hasn't saved your butt?"

"I'm hoping she will. Real soon."

"What's your name, honey?"

"I'm Stewart Faulkner-Davis, what's yours?" Stewart had a bad feeling about what he was about to hear. Sure enough.

"I'm Amanda, Amanda Stone, never used a stage name much, like most of my friends do, thought it was a hassle."

Stewart had a sinking feeling, like the physical world around him and below him was melting away. Reality was no longer solid.

"Hey Stewart, are you okay? You look like you seen a ghost."

Stewart's world was spinning. If this was his alibi, and she didn't know his name, then Raquel never called her.

He sat there looking straight down. He never answered her question, it didn't even register.

Fianlly he asked in a very defeated voice, "Amanda, do you know a woman named Raquel, maybe work for her husband?"

"I only know one Raquel. She's a man that dresses like a woman and gives blow jobs down on Eighth Avenue. Is that who you mean? I've sure as hell never worked for, or with him/her."

"My," he hesitated, he didn't know what words to use, so he used Amanda's, "girfriend, Raquel, said she was a rich man's wife and couldn't tell me her real name, said she had to protect herself. She said she had a friend, an Amanda Stone, who would provide me with an alibi if I needed one. Maybe she knows another Amanda Stone."

Amanda looked at the mirror. She was beginning to smell a setup. She probably should be mad as hell, but this kid didn't seem responsible - didn't seem smart enough to be responsible. He was probably easily manipualted. I was told somebody used my name as an alibi in a murder investigation. So that would be you?"

"I guess so. I said what Raquel told me to." Stewart was honest.

"Which was?"

"Amanda Stone, five foot six, one hundred and twenty pounds, strawberry blond hair, and a Cyndi Crawford mole over the left lip."

Amanda's world was starting to get shaky, she had a sinking feeking in the pit of her stomach. Somebody was fucking setting her up. "What did this Raquel look like?"

"She was short, thin, had blond hair, and great nipples." He said it without thinking about it, it was how he thought of her.

"Was her pubic hair blond?" This kid didn't look like any genius.

"She didn't have any. It was shaved off."

"Shit, a bald beaver, her hair could be any color." Over the years she had met hundreds of girls in the life. Which one would set her up. And why?

***

Danny was spellbound. "If that's acting, they should get the Academy Award."

I spoke out without thinking. "That's not acting. Those two have never met. But what about the blood? How can all the suspects be linked by evidence to the crime scene, but yet these two don't know each other? Hell, he's the one that implicated her. Who is this Raquel? I know I could be wrong, maybe they are acting, but if so, forget prison and send them to Hollywood."

***

"Stewart, you better tell me everything about this Raquel, every little detail, because baby, she set you up and she set me up. Jurors don't take kindly to people like me, a good setup could work because of my past, especially if the cops and DA are under pressure and need a quick fix. They might not have much motivation to work through the setup to find the real people. A good setup means they have to work twice as hard, and man, cops are lazy. Murder can mean a life sentence or the killer needle, so we're in deep shit and you better tell me absolutley everything."

"Maybe that explains the blood." Stewart blurted out. He didn't want to believe Raquel had set him up, but here was Amanda Stone saying they had both been set up.

"What blood?"

"Raquel took my clothes with her Sunday morning when she went to get breakfast while I was still asleep. Later she said it was to make sure nobody saw me, that she had to protect her image as a respectable married woman. She came back in a white van with two guys in it. When she brought my clothes back, they were badly stained. She said it was ketchup from spilled hash browns. The cops say their labs have proved that it's not ketchup but blood. My uncle's a lawyer. He says they think I was like, in on the murder. But I was with Raquel all weekend." By the end he was whining more than talking.

"I was busy this weekend too, but if I can't prove it, I'm screwed. And so are you."

***

As the night wore on Wallace, Willams, and Potts went on home to rest. Danny, Annie, Laura, and I watched and listened for an hour. Annie's niece watched her kids after school and was going to stay late, freeing Annie to work past her norm. She reminded me a little of Danny, she was on the chase, enthusiastic, driven.

Amanda made Stewart stand up and show her how tall Raquel was and describe her body type. She made him describe the weekend. She was interested in what Raquel wore, what games they played. She was interested in the van and the two guys, but Stewart hadn't seen what they looked like. Finally Stewart shocked us with something we wanted.

"I saw her car and I got her tag number." Stewart told her what he'd held back, waiting on his alibi to come through.

Annie left to go call the South Carolina Bureau of Investigation. We needed to know who Raquel was, and if Stewart's story was true. All along we knew they could be acting, but it sure didn't look like acting or anything prepared. But there was blood on Stewart's, Amanda Stone's, and Kevin Jackson's clothing. That's stronger evidence than a subjective impression that someone is telling the truth.

The crime scene techs called in with the luminol results from the three houses. There were traces of blood on the floors around Parker's and Jackson's ritual areas, presumably from animal sacrifices. But that was about it, nothing else out of the ordinary. Annie came back with the info, the tag was a rental car. It belonged to a small local rental agency not far from Stewart's military school. They'd have to wait until the morning when they opened for anything further.

After getting as much as we could, we finally took Amanda out and interviewed her again. It was short and sweet. She knew where she was Friday night, she didn't do it, and the guy that fingered her did so on his girlfriend's orders and he didn't even know her. Amanda had just talked to him and she pointed back to the interview room. We asked her about the blood on some of her clothes and on one pair of shoes. She said she was being set up. Danny charged her with possession of controlled substances. Amanda wanted to know what we'd found, the weight, were the charges misdemeanor or felony? She had three grams of coke and four hits of ecstasy, muscle relaxers without a script, and a quarter ounce of pot - the coke alone made it a definite felony.

Danny put handcuffs on her, read her her rights and had an officer take her down to be offically charged, photoed, fingerprinted, and jailed. Danny called down to the jail to make sure the four prisoners he was about to send them had no contact with each other at all. It was extremely important that there be no possible contact, in jail or at court. Danny had to talk to the supervisor, to get it all straight. There were definite logistical problems, some might have to be farmed out to other institons.

Kevin Jackson started raising hell again in the APD holding cell, making a huge fuss. So we interviewed him again, his song remained the same. Danny asked him about the blood on his clothes. Kevin said there wasn't any, we were bullshitting or crazy. At the end of the short interview, Danny placed him under arrest for violation of the controlled substances act, possesion of a firearm by a convicted felon, and interfering with the execution of a search warrant.

Kevin's first question, "Not that I'm admitting it's mine, in fact, you guys probably planted it, but what do you guys claim to have found, what kind of weight are we talking about?"

"Six ounces Kevin, you're fucked." Danny said. "I found your stash myself. Not a bad hiding place, Kevin, but not good enough." I think Danny really enjoyed saying it. "Who knows, maybe if you come clean on the murder charges, we'll drop the drug charges. We won't be greedy, murder one is fine."

"I didn't kill anybody, and you guys know it. I want a phone call and a lawyer, now."

"You'll get your phone call. We've got to process you, put you into the system, and get you arrained in court, but you'll get your phone call." We sent Kevin on down with an officer to be entered into the system. It's not like Kevin didn't know his way around the system, this was way too familiar to him.

We moved on to Gary Parker. He still wouldn't say anything. He could have been charged with murder and conspiracy to commit murder. But if we did that it would become public - part of the court record, then the word would be out, and the press would be a bigger pain in the butt than they already were. They hung around outside all the time and watched Danny and followed him around as it was. It was amazingly lucky Stewart had been run through court without notice, but that happened only because the charges were minor. If murder was part of the court record, word would get out. So we charged Parker with felony possession of forged government documents, possession of an unlicensed firearm, and impersonation of a police officer. We shipped him off in handcuffs. The ADA would make sure none of these four got bail without a formal hearing that wouldn't be held until Wensday, since at the very least they were material witnesses in a murder investigation. Hopefully, they could be charged for murder, and then permanently denied bail. As long as that could be done in as short a time as possible it was practical. If the suspects had decent lawyers, they would appeal the initial no bail ruling and move strongly for bail. The clock was ticking.

***

Stewart was sorry to see Amanda leave, he liked her and she seemed capable of figuring out what was going on. He wasn't making much progress by himself. Two cops he recognized and a dark skinned woman with long black hair came into the room.

"Stewart, how's it going? We understand you've been holding out on us and want to come clean." Danny said it almost like he was kidding.

Stewart looked at Danny, he was starting to figure the truth was much better than what he was currently facing - murder. He started to launch into the whole story he had just told Amanda. Danny waved him off, "You can tell us tommorow. Go get some sleep, kid."

"Can I have more food?"

Danny gave the officer who escorted him back a couple of dollars to stop at the vending machines. Danny had a heart of gold, or was playing Stewart. I kept thinking about Stewart the amatuer surgeon. I didn't give a damn if that the little shit went hungry one night. As much pain as he'd probably inflicted on helpless little animals, let him go hungry one night. He'd be getting his three squares a day for the rest of his sick life - if he was in on our crime.

***

Laura and I had to drop the van off and pick up my pickup. It's a hobby and a ride, my '52 Ford, cherry red, reconditioned with chrome mags and a good sound system. We headed straight home. Although we had been around each other almost the whole day, it was seldom private, and we really hadn't gotten to talk much. The ride home was quiet however, windows partly down, letting in the warm summer night air, sometimes carrying the sweet scent of honeysuckles. As the wind blew through her hair, she reached over and put a hand on my thigh. I thought that the wind was good, let it blow away the dust from where we'd been today, blow us clean from what we'd seen and felt.

Once we got home, we had a late snack and I suggested the hot tub. The moon was still over half full reflecting in the pond, the lightning bugs were out, and a little relaxation wouldn't hurt either one of us. We took a bottle of wine, glasses, towels, and my pipe. I often did this, letting the day go, after reviewing and clarifying it. I was glad to have her beside me. Her presence was a positive good, on a day where I saw and touched the negative manifestations of evil. I didn't understand it. There are so many beautiful symbols of a benign and beneficent diety, there are so many different pantheons, various gods and goddesses, both light and dark, across the space and time of human cultural experience, and there is the spiritual reality of the Light, why would someone choose to serve evil - the Judeo-Christian Satan? I just didn't get it, I never did, never would.

Sitting in the clean bubbling, steaming water, with our backs to my house and the lights down low, the fireflys were putting on a sparkling show. When the jets went quiet, the sounds of the crickets and tree frogs, a natural choral chanting along with the healing of water brought rest and reflection.

"How do you like your new job? You're working long hours, and the pay is not good?"

"There are a few fringe benefits." She smiled. "I like Betty and the horses." She smiled again, looking directly into my eyes, she was truly beautiful, just pulling my heartstrings. "It's much prettier down here than I would ever have thought. It's fertile, lush." She paused, "So what do you think?"

She caught me off guard. "About what?" She could have meant the South, us, or the case.

"The case, what everybody's saying. Have Stewart and Amanda never met, or are they laying the groundwork for their defense? The only one we have eyewitnesses on is Gary Parker, and he doesn't seem like that important a player. Kevin Jackson seems strong, but you said you weren't sure he had the resources to pull it all off. Kevin and Amanda say the same things, pretty convincingly. But are they lying? Is Kevin the head Satanist here? Is it possible Amanda and Kevin are being set up in some daring move of a prostitution war?"

I shook my head, starting with her last question. "I don't know. I wouldn't think their escort agency is big enough or so profitable that it would entice someone to risk so much scrutiny for such a small stable. Whoever moved in on them would be such an obvious suspect. Kevin may move medium weight blow and speed, he might have jealous competitors, but I doubt anyone would go to the extensive efforts required in an intricate set up. If it were a drug or whore war, they'd just kill them flat out. A set up can always lead back to its point of origin. An unregistered and filed down .357 lying on the bottom of the Chatahoochee River tells few tales. There is certainly a lot of blood evidence against everybody except Gary and the labs won't finish his car until tommorrow, and he's the only one we're sure was actually there. So far the circumstancial evidence is strong, and all their alibis are uncorroborated. The DNA test will be conclusive about the blood, but that's still days away." She didn't comment, so I kept going.

"I've always been bothered by the percision of the crime scene and Stewart sneaking in with an obviously bloody uniform. For one thing, it's just too stupid, the second thing, a military school uniform is not the kind of garment that would be appropriate for this kind of ritual. The only reasonable way the stains got on his uniform at the crime scene would have been after the ritual, folding up and moving the tarps.

"Another thing, a ritual that elaboratle would have a definite purpose, a specific goal that its performance would ritually accomplish, magically ensure. So far we have no motive, there's certainly not one evident yet with our current suspects."

"What do you think?" I asked her back. I figured she'd spent all day watching and taking notes. Sometimes the quietest observers are the most proficent. Not to mention she was a reporter by trade.

She looked at me for a while, like she was thinking whether or not to say what was on her mind. Finally she did, "You keep talking about the precision of the crime scene, about resources, organized intelligence. Well, isn't that just what it would take to frame somebody else for what the real perpetrators did? Why didn't Gary Parker get rid of the evidence, unless he was planning to use the car and uniform again, or he had no idea about what he was participating in? If so, were other rituals planned? If this is an elaborate set up, would the perpetrators be betting that the state, local, and city power brokers would want this solved so quickly there would be a rush to judgement? Or the strong probability of a forced speedy and swift conclusion?"

"But there is the other side," she continued, "if Kevin and this bunch were the perpetrators of the crime scene, might setting up a seeming frame help strengthen their alibis or possibly even serve as part of a plot to set up others as the perpetrators. Maybe they've set up somebody else to take the fall, and they just haven't given them to us yet, it's still too early. Maybe they are good, really good actors, and they're playing us."

I said nothing, just nodded, then Laura said, "We saw the BIA frame lots of people on the Pine Ridge Rez. The Bureau and the GOONs had more resources than your average criminal, still, if you could pull off that ritual on the nice part of town on a Friday night, near a popular lovers lane, you should be capable of framing someone else for it. Are the actual perpetrators framing this crew we've got in custody, or is this crew acting framed, creating reasonable doubt, and possibly setting up somebody else?"

I poured us another glass of wine and lit my pipe. She made some good points. We watched the lightning bugs do their mating dance. It was a good idea. Mating. Earlier Danny had said he'd call me when he needed me tommorrow, that I could have the morning off, probably. That was good, cause I needed to think for a little while, and then I needed to lie down with the exquisite woman beside me and make passionate love with her and please her, and be pleased by her. Repeatedly.

Life is good when you get what you need.

***

Chapter Twelve - Tuesday Morning

Danny called early and told me not to come in unitl around two p.m. While on the phone I noticed Laura and I were both smiling. Me on the phone listening to Danny, and her in half sleep snuggled against me. Then he hit me with the bad news. "The story's broke. Not all of it, but the TV crews must have raised the money being offered for info. Obviously a few people cashed in."

I was still sleepy, but my smile was fading. "What do they have?"

"They know it was a mother and child ritual sacrifice, and that three animals were also sacrificed. That came from the M.E. or CSU offices most probably. But the really bad news is they know we've got four potential suspects in custody who are definitely related to the murders, being held on other charges and they know Stewart is one of them by name. That probably got leaked from the court or the jail. TV crews are swarming everywhere, and following me around whenever I go outside. No offense, Spooky, but I don't want them seeing us together, unlesss it's really neccessary. They'll start asking questions about you, probing your background. They could make you look bad and the city look bad for hiring you. In fact, call me around two and let me update you, and see if I need you in today at all."

"Cool."

***

Stewart sat there at the table in the interview room looking at Alpert and a skinny and alive Jerry Garcia. This guy had long white hair in a single braid down the back - longer than the undercover cop/detective's. He didn't look like any of the lawyers he'd seen with Uncle Alpert before, this guy looked like a muscian. His uncle introduced him, Lief Wilmington, criminal defense lawyer. "He's represented some of the most famous..." Alpert paused.

Lief spoke up, "clients, not criminals."

Alpert continued, "of course, some of the most famous clients in the state, the whole nation. You're in good hands." Alpert let Lief take over.

"Stewart, I know you're innocent. All my clients are innocent. Now, we just have to prove that, or at the very least create a reasonable doubt concerning your guilt. Thank God we're in America, in France, a case like this, you'd hang." Lief smiled a big smile, let's see if the kid's got a sense of humor.

Stewart didn't smile. "All I can tell you is the truth, the whole truth. Also, there's a woman here, I think she got arrested, Amanda Stone, who can help us. You've got to get me out of here, and maybe get her out. We're being set up for something we didn't do. She can figure out by who. Uncle Alpert, they don't give you enough to eat in here, I just had breakfast and I'm starving. I stay hungry all the time."

***

Danny sat at his desk, mulling over the case. Every speck of physical evidence pointed at the suspects in custody. At least Gary Parker isn't claiming he's been framed. He did ask one of the deputies during breakfast if there was some way he could contact the FBI and CIA, to let them know where he was, just in case. The deputies had special orders concerning the four suspects, to pass along any tibit or rumor, immediately. Parker would let the feds know where he was in case of what? Danny had three suspects claiming they were framed and some wanna-be James Bond just begging to be included in somebody's conspiracy theory about something.

Danny had sent Potts and Williams back to the Ritz to get more information on the alibi witness Juan Martinez. Juan's best friend Mario, who worked there, had some pictures of Juan, but couldn't remember the sister's married name or which hotel it was. Just a high rise, on the ocean, in Panama City. Which is where Williams and Potts were dispatched to, posthaste. They copied Mario's pictures of Juan, distributed them at APD, and hit the road. Danny wondered about his own wisdom - he had two detectives on the road, looking for a recently fired heavy drinking Hispanic male, who may or may not provide an alibi for Stone and Jackson, to whom all the blood evidence pointed. If Juan was drinking that night, his memory would be open to question and attack in court. But Danny couldn't ignore it, either. Jackson knew the drink order, the floor, and the man's name. It was a lead that had to be followed. To do otherwise would be a dereliction of duty.

Danny could only imagine a realistic lineup for Juan to establish Amanda's alibi. Give Juan three of four shots of Tequila, line up Amanda with some fellow hookers or strippers in robes, and let them flash Juan. If he knows Amanda's the girl, that lends her story more credibility. Danny laughed quietly to himself, like that would ever happen.

Juan would have to pick her out of a normal lineup. He also needed to establish that the suspects didn't know Martinez from before. Maybe owe them money, or a favor. Hookers - hotels, it's certainly possible that their paths had crossed. Juan would also have to pick Jackson out of a lineup. If he could pick both out, would Juan take a lie detector test to prove he's not involved with the suspects? Would the suspects take a lie detector test?

Danny worried about the Faulkner's influence. It was significant. If they got Stewart up in front of a sympathetic judge, a high bail might be set. The Faulkners might be very willing to give up a million in bail and fly Stewart by private jet to some country without extradition treaties with the US. Where he could live comfortably the rest of his sick life.

Danny wanted everybody involved in this crime to go down as hard as possible. He didn't want anyone to escape, sadistic little rich kids especially.

Lester Wallace and Annie Wilson came in. They had more evidence pointing at the suspects. The car Stewart described was rented by none other than Kevin Eubanks. Exact same signature on the fax from South Carolina as that on the sign-out sheets from the Toccoa mothers home. Exact same description. Could easily be Jackson, or possibly not - hat, sunglasses, bushy beard. Basic Z Z Top, could have been anybody in the basic size range.

Annie was constanly astounded and annoyed at her fellow man's stupidiy. "Get this, Danny, the car rental place has a security camera, we'd have the man and woman who rented the car on tape, but there was no tape in the machine! Seems the Einstein owner knew he needed a new tape and had been meaning to get one, but thought the presence of the camera was deterrent enough until he got around to it." She shook her head and changed subjects. "If Kevin Jackson is so eager to prove his innocence, maybe he wouldn't mind giving us a sample of his handwriting. Having him write his names and aliases would be a nice place to start. He says he's being framed, how willing is he to prove it?"

***

Lief answered both of Stewart's questions. "We'll get your doctor to verify you need more nutrition than you're presently getting, some kind of pre-diabetic condition or something, we'll work that out. We'll get you some more food immediately. We will also put money on the books for you in the jail store. You'll have snacks in addition to your regular meals, I think it's up to twenty-five dollars you can spend a week in the jail store. You fill out a form and they'll bring you your goodies once a week. Keep them in your drawer-locker under your bunk. We'll get you a lock and a key and some food today and get you as comfortable as possible until I can get you out of here. That all depends on the bail hearing and any other additional charges that might be filed. But of course, we'll move to get you out on bail immediately. They're trying to hold you on minimal charges, when, in actuallity, they're really detaining you as a suspect in a crime you haven't been charged with. I'll rattle their cage. They might be able to get away with it for a few days, depending on what they've got. But it won't stand up indefinitely. Now, tell me about where you were this weekend, what you were doing, who you were doing it with, who Amanda Stone is, and what role she can play in proving you innocent. Don't be embarrassed about anything, don't hold anything back."

Stewart looked at his lawyer, over at his uncle, back at the lawyer, and then shrugged his shoulders slightly. His lawyer picked up on the obvious, and turned to Alpert. "Alpert, why don't you leave me and your nephew alone to get down to it. This might take hours. I'll call you at your office and update you this afternoon. It'll be okay." Leif patted him on the arm, and nodded. Alpert said good-by to Stewart, rose, walked over and knocked on the door, where he stood and waited to be let out.

***

Betty called over at ten to twelve to see if we were up and gonna watch the news. She said there had been short reports about our case, but at noon they'd go into detail. We slept in but had been up since 10:30, watching CNN and drinking Jamaican Blue Mountain coffee. CNN didn't mention it. Normally I'm not a big breakfast eater, but it seems Laura was. She took over my kitchen, and I guess I had more exercise during the night than normal, because it turned out I was starving. I cook, but I seldom do pancakes, bacon, eggs, and toast at any one time. Or maybe any one week. Pancakes almost never. So we pigged out and watched the local news, flipping back and forth during commercials. The media sharks were in an absolute feeding frenzy now that the rumors had been confirmed, that it was a satanic ritual sacrifice of the most horriffic nature. The TV reporters were drooling and wetting themselves, they were so excited. It was pathetic. Four people in custody, one a member of the ultra wealthy family which owned the estate where the abandoned cabin was located. More as the story develops....

"So much for us doing our job quietly, privately, and efficiently. Danny doesn't want me being in the public eye on this case. I'll have to work surreptitiously. That's cool. Maybe we get the whole day off, or you can check in with the Unity Convention folks. When does the convention start?"

"Tommorrow. But there are a lot of parties and mixers over the next three or four days. I'll have to go to some, I need a job. My friend and colleague from San Francisco, Mai Li, helped set the convention up and has a double room comped, so I can stay with her as much as I like. But I don't want to miss out on anything big in the case. I've gott my cell phone so we can stay in touch and you can keep me updated."

***

Amanda had to go see her lawyer. She was in her jailhouse jumpsuit, now a numbered part of the system. She'd been here before, she was plenty tough, so her attitude was no big deal. What she didn't know was that she had a lawyer. She better check the guy out damn well, he might be part of the setup. What better way to make sure the setup holds? She sat at a table in a very small and simple interview room. No windows, one table, four folding chairs, a locked metal door with a small wired glass window.

A deputy led "her" lawyer in. The deputy told him to knock when through and locked the door. He walked over, sat down, opened his brief case, and took out a pen and a yellow legal pad. She took one look at his long white hair, his face, and she knew immediately she'd seen him on TV before. He was big time.

"I'm Lief Wilmington, I'll be representing you in this matter." He held out his hand and they formally shook hands.

"Yeah. I've seen you on the tube. Who's paying your salary?"

"Alpert Faulkner retained me on behalf of his nephew, Stewart Faulkner-Davis, who last night requested that I represent you as well. Stewart sees your role as crucial, as absolutely central in discovering the truth at the bottom of this situation and exonerating you both. I've heard his story. Now, Miss Stone, let's hear yours."

***

Danny thought to himself he was busier than the proverbial one legged man in an ass kicking contest. He couldn't stop himself from relentlessly moving forward nor control the outside flow of information. It all came pouring down on him like a July thunderstorm. The news buzzards were circling ever closer. Political and social pressure was boiling over. The black mayor had called the black lady chief of police, who called whitebread Danny. The chief told him the mayor's complaining that she'd just as soon have rednecks and Confederate flag controversies costing the city convention dollars than satanic homicides. Who, besides ritual homocide enthusiasts wants to come now? Assistant DA Diaz had called Danny twice already, saying that big money and big time lawyers might get some of our doers out on bail, we needed charges - homicide charges - NO BAIL charges. The clock was already ticking, time was precious. With the Faulkner's money, fucking Johnnie Cockran might show up, and get all four and the devil found not guilty while he crucified the APD. ADA Diaz was a worried man, so was his boss, the DA.

Danny still had only the one slam dunk. Parker had been unanimously identified by the eyewitnesses, and the labs had reported in, human blood stains had been found in his "police" car's trunk. He was gone. Done deal. The only thing that determined whether he got life or the needle-sleep was whether or not he actually committerd any of the murders. He still wouldn't talk, kept asking if anybody had come forward to represent him. When told no and asked if he wanted a public defender, he'd say no again. Dumbass.

Confirmation came in on the three other suspect's human blood stains as being the victim's correct blood type, also the animal blood stains on the conficated clothes of Stewart, Kevin Jackson, and Amanda Stone were confirmed as being that of the correct three animals. The physical evidence against the suspects kept stacking up. Convincingly. All that was missing from the lab were the DNA results, and hopefully that was just days away.

Nothing of interest had been found in the victim's belongings, so Danny directed they be returneded to her bereaved family by Lester Wallace. So far the victims' names had been withheld, but Danny knew that that wouldn't last forever. Before Wallace hit the road Danny told him to prepare the parents as best he could. Their lives had been changed forever in a terible way, and it was about to become even worse, whenever the victims names got out and they lost their privacy. Wallace was a compassionate man in his own way. He came from a large family and had a large family. He could only imagine....

***

Phineas told Samantha as soon as she woke up that he was calling in to her school that she was sick, they were taking the day off. Tommorrow was her birthday, but he had to work tommorrow and she had to leave with her school orchestra Thursday afternoon. Her school orchetra had been chosen among hundreds to do two performances, one at the Kennedy Center, during a three day visit to the capital. He told her today she could play hooky and celebrate her birthday. Which was fine with Samantha, her diary was safe at school, she had plans for tommorrow, and she wouldn't have to endure Phineas that much longer anyway. Her torso still hurt a good bit, and she could use a day of rest.

She and Phineas were drinking Mimosas in front of the TV set. Phineas had recorded the noon news on two differeent channels, he was so happy he was almost giddy. He was replaying the news, and they were toasting success. Phineas didn't have a clue how far off his picture of success was from hers.

***

George and Bobby Sanders ate some burgers and drank some beers on their lunch break. Then it would be back down the road a couple of miles to the combination junkyard/scrap metal business where the brothers worked their day job under their own legitimate names. Geoge had two other part-time night/weekend jobs, under two other legitimate names of men now desceased, while Bobby just did whatever George told him to. It all worked out.

George was paying close attention to the TV news while they ate, so Bobby did too. Even he knew what they were talking about. Bobby had never made the news before, not that he, by name had really made it on the news, but kinda, sorta. He felt part of something big.

***

Amanda was waiting to have her second meeting with her new lawyer. She had talked to him in depth and then he had told her to wait there, knocked on the door, and said he'd be back within 45 minutes. It was more like an hour and five or ten.

He was let in, locked in, and sat down. Lief launched right in.

"I've seen assitant DA Diaz, I've talked to the DA on the phone, I talked to two reporters outside, and I've just left cheif investigating officer Danny Fagan. Here's what I know from my conversations, and what's on the news. There was a ritual crime with two human victims, a mother and her baby, and three animal victims Friday night on the Faulkner estate. Stewart was caught sneaking in Sunday night. He had stains…"

"Yeah, I know about the stains, I talked to Stewart for hours, tell me what I don't know." He might be big time, but it was her ass on the line and she was impatient.

"Four people have been arrested on various charges, but no murder charges have been filed. I know about Stewart, your friend Kevin Jackson and you, my information is sketchy about the fourth, other than he's been identified by eye witnesses as being on the scene, and things were taken by the police when they searched his house. Stewart gave your name to the police as an alibi, just doing what he was told by his companion, Kevin's name has been linked to the victim, how, I don't know yet. There is blood evidence on Stewart's, your's, and Mr. Jackson's clothing which gives them a direct link between you three and the crime scene. The warrants so far seem valid, drugs were listed on all the warrants, so you and Kevin face serious charges however the murder charges go. Of course, you haven't been charged with murder yet, but it seems almost certain you will be. Kevin Jackson's drug charges are much more serious than yours. Your substance violations and Stewart's obstruction charges are serious, but certainly bailable charges. Eventually they will have to charge you and Stewart in the murders, or set bail. Kevin is difficult, a twice convicted felon, with an illegal gun, resisting, and six ounces of narcotics. He's an obvious three time loser now, and he won't be getting bail, period. Flight risk. No matter what, Mr. Jackson will inevitably be going away for a long time. You need to think about yourself now. To a great extent, his situation is beyond hope on what they already have on him."

"You and Stewart, if not charged with murder, will get bail within a few days. If not at the first hearing, definitely by the second. Definitely within a week. Stewart's family has powerful friends, among them judges. We will try to come before a sympathetic ear. If they haven't charged you with the murders yet, it's possibly because they're waiting on the DNA tests to make it absolutely conclusive. I think the blood evidence is damning enough already, you must come through with convincing alibis, now! But, just as importantly, you must figure out who has framed you, and why. We may be spending a significant amount of time together Miss Stone. The answer most probably lies somewhere in your past, or Mr. Jackson's."

"How about Kevin, Stewart, and I take lie detector tests. That'll show we didn't do it. Case over." It made sense to Amanda, but in the back of her mind something told her it wouldn't work.

"Lie detector tests are not considered reliable and are inadmissable in a court of law. Although willingness to take a lie detector test, and then passing it, may prove to be powerful weapons in our attempt to persuade the police and DA's office that you've been framed and deserve bail. As long as we can limit the scope of the questioning, the three of you offering to take a polygraph is an avenue we may soon persue.

"We have the two other avenues we must pursue. To solidify and document your alibis, and figure out who's framing you. Someone would have to possess ample knowledge about you, or hate you intensely, or both, to go to this much trouble to frame you. Planning and committing the crime, the planting of evidence, this is all very complex. Your innocence will be hard for a jury to believe without convincing evidence on our side. I'm looking to you for serious help on both the establishing your alibis and determining the identity of those who perpetrated this crime and framed you for it.

I try not to know any more than I have to about the details of the drug or prostituion trades where my clients are concerned, but I am not ignorant of these practices. However, I am not well versed on the occult, nor do I have any knowledge of satanic rites. It seems out of the four incarcerated, only Stewart is not linked to satanic practice by the contents of their possessions seized during the searches. If you and Mr. Jackson are invovled in satanic practice, that would make you perfect scapegoats for a crime such as this. It will also make you very suspect in the eyes of the jury, and they will be heavily prejudiced against you as soon as you admit to satanic activities. No matter what they say, this is still Georgia, and you're a Satanist with prostitution and drug convictions on record. Whoever framed you knew you were involved in such activities. That is certainly one area to explore. I must know what you may have done to someone to elicit this much hate, and who they might be. Please keep no secrets. Do not let shame or embarassment put a needle in your arm. You, Kevin, and Stewart, together or separately, at least one of you has a very serious enemy. A serious and extremely dangerous enemy. We need to know who and we need to know why."

***

Laura took my truck back to the convention, with enough clothes for a two or three day stay. It was good she was a tough girl who grew up on the rez, the three speed on the column and and stiff clutch didn't phase her at all. She said she'd try to come back, but just didn't know. Usually when a new lover is with me constantly and then leaves, it's a relief to be by myself again. I didn't feel that way about Laura.

I grabbed my small blaster, put in a shamanic drumming cassette, and then I took the long deerskin pouch in which I keep my Sared Pipe off the peg on the west wall and headed out to the pond. It was a bright, warm day, rapidly on its way to being hot. There were scattered puffy white cottonball clouds drifting east across a brilliant blue sky. The day felt good to my skin - bright sunshine with a light breeze, but my heart was heavy. I had been so busy playing detective and expert I hadn't *acted* as a shaman. As the only person of spiritual office on the scene, I had a responsibility I had not yet fulfilled. It's not like there had been any wasted liesure time since the call early Saturday morning, but still, I had wanted to do this as soon as possible. The day off gave me an oppurtunity to catch up.

Barefooted, in old jeans and a tee shirt, I sat down comfortably at the edge of the pond on lush green grass, positioned myself cross-legged, and slowly emptied the contents of my pipe bag in a sacred manner. After pulling up the flap, I pulled out the pipestem, thirteen inches long, made of cottonwood, wrapped in a red cotton cloth. Beside it I pulled out a single eagle feather, its base addorned by leather and red threads, and laid it on my lap. I slowly unrolled the pipestem, and spread the large rectangular red cloth on the ground before me and then set the pipestem upon it near the top, and placed the eagle feather on the right. Next out, wrapped in red silk, came the pipe, large and red, carved out of Minnesota catlanite - Pipestone. It had taken me many days to carve the stone into a pipe and carve and burn out the stem, all done by hand, without power tools of any sort. Those are the medicine rules, by your own hands, with no power tools, all natural.

Next out was a fairly large leather pouch, with a leather thong drawstring at the top. I pulled the thong loose and emptied the pouch's contents: a bag of American Spirit tobacco, a large box of wooden kitchen matches, a long thin spike from a Joshua tree, a long sprig of sage, and a small piece of rough pipestone which resembled the sideways view of the talons of a bird of prey. I arranged the contents of the bag upon the cloth with purpose. From the bottom of the pipe bag I drew out a geode, a hollow half rock three inches in diameter and placed it before me next to the sage. I rested my hands in my lap, straightened my back, relaxed my body, and refined my breathing. I considered the sacred objects before me and the task I needed to accomplish.

Before me on the center of the red cloth was the pipe. Below it, the symbolic rock talons; to the right the matches, and my eagle feather; to the left, the sprig of sage resting on the geode. At the bottom of the cloth rested the joshua spike, at the top, the pipestem. In Christianity the Holy Eucharist is held with ultimate reverence. When done correctly, according to the theory of divine substantiation, the wine and unleavened bread *become* the body and blood of Christ. Christ being one of the three aspects of Divinity - God as Christ is symbolically consumed in a sacred manner and one achieves an unction with Divinity, the Creator. The Indians have their own spiritual hierarchy, an ancient spiritual conception born of a continuous shamanic spiritual tradition possibly 90,000 years older than the Judaic-Christian spiritual hierarchy, yet the same concept as that represented in the Holy Eucharist is found in the Sacred Pipe. All of Creation, absolutely everything was created by the Creator, and when the Sacred Pipe is filled and smoked in a sacred way, the one praying symbolically loads all of Creation, as well as the Creator, into the Pipe. By smoking the Sacred Pipe in the saced manner, one becomes symbolically at one with all Creation, and sends a voice to the Creator - a voice to and with all of Creation, a voice to and with the Creator.

The Sacred Pipe's importance in Indian religion is seldom understood by non-Indians, long led astray by Hollywood's concept of a peace pipe. The Sacred Pipe would be smoked before a peace treaty was agreed to, thereby consecrating the promises made. Supposedly, this would ensure the honesty of the participants by the performance of a sacred ritual; in the long run that theory didn't work and the Holy Eucharist of Native American theology became known as the peace pipe. We innocently played cowboys and Indians with toy six shooters, bows and arrows, and plastic peace pipes but when we played knights and Crusaders with the toy plastic swords and shields, they never came with a plastic eucharist kit. Our cultural misunderstanding of, and demeaning of, the Sacred Pipe is indicative of the way the dominant western European /Anglo culture treated the conquered Indian cultures in general, and their spiritual practices specifically.

The area where the pipestone was mined by the Indians was always considered sacred and holy. Even when wars between Indian nations were being waged in that area, the Pipe's homeland was always a place of peace.

Before me lay a serious task. A truly horrible thing had been done to two undeserving humans and three animals at a time when powerfull evil forces were being invoked. The responsibility of spiritually cleaning it up was mine by default. Quite simply, there was no one else. Only police had access to the crime scene and knowledge of the events.

I took the matches and lit the sprig of the Owens Valley high mountain desert sage, got it burning and let it burn for a second, then, with a sharp percussion of air from a cupped hand extinguished the flame. Although the flame was out, the sprig smouldered like incense and I waved my eagle feather above it and got it smoking thickly, and then laid it on the geode so the smoke could rise, and put down the feather. I asked outloud that the Great Spirit might be with the smoke, that it might bless, cleanse, and purify. With cupped hands I brought the smoke up to the top of my head and then down the front of my body, then repeated the action behind, and on either side of my body.

Then I picked up the pipestem and held it above the smoke, one end pointing up to the Sky, the other to the core of the Earth. I lifted it up an inch towards the Sky. "Great Spirit bless this, that I might send to You a voice." I moved it an inch down. "Earth Mother bless this, that I might send to You a voice." I pointed and moved it east, south, west, and north and asked the Power of each direction to bless it, that I might send a voice.

Although not all Indian nations have the exact same spiritual beliefs, spiritual hierarchy, creation myths, ritual practices, sacred dances, sacred songs, witchcraft, sorcery, or magical traditions, they all have the powers of the four directions or elements, although the ascribed colors and symbols may vary.

The way I ritually work the six directions or planes or aspects of reality and being is: the Great Spirit Mother Father Creator of all life - above, the Mother Earth - below, the Powers of the four directions - east, south, west, and north, representing the four elemental worlds, or fundamental dimensions of human reality. Each of the four Powers in the Indian spiritual hierarchy represents a series of symbolic associations, including aspects of the outer physical world and the inner human realm, between certain aspects of human existence and the associated element or fundamental aspect of reality. Each Power is associated with a cardinal direction, as well as the symbolic wind from that direction, and the time of day, the season of the year, and the stage of life associated with that direction, etc. In Judaic-Christian mysticism, the four directions are associated with four Archangels - Archangel Raphael in the east, Michael in the south, Gabriel in the west, and Auriel in the north. The Bible also mentions the four beasts (beings) before the throne of God. For me, as a metis or mixed blood shaman, the Power of the East represents the element of Air: the human mind and the power of human thought, the dimension of mind and thought in human reality and throughout the universe, it is associated with dawn, sunrise, spring. In Revelations and Ezekiel, the corresponding "animal" (being) is the angel. The power of the South represents: the element Fire, spirit, will, Life Force, miday, the summer, and the biblical lion. The Power of the West represents: the element Water, love, emotions, desires, the subconcious mind, dusk/sunset, the autumn, and the biblical eagle. The Power of the North represents: the element Earth, the physical body, midnight, winter, the power of physical manifestation, and the biblical bull. By this scheme, humanity finds itself at the center of, and participating in, these six worlds – planes - dimensions—aspects of Life. We come from the Divine, the godhead of which at one point can be represented as a central Divine Spiritual Sun, and all immortal created beings have a spark of that Divinity within. We live and breathe and have our being on Mother Earth, and we all have minds, wills, emotions, and bodies. We are little co-creators, an evolving divine spark, creating in our personal worlds, in our own small spot in this magnificent universe. The way our Creator, the Great Spitit, brings things into being and the way we humans bring things into being may be similar in all but scale.

When looked at from the point of view of the six sacred directions, the individual - the person, an immortal created divine spark/spirit, in human manifestation with a soul, intuition, mind, emotions, electromagnetic energy field, and physical body - is at the center of those six directions, thus is the seventh point. But there is a seventh Power in my metis hierarchy not represented in the six directions, but mentioned later with the healing grandfathers. In the Christian heritage of my European ancestors, and in the Christ-like legends of the native peoples all over the Americas (long before the Europeans showed up) there is the persistent legend that the Creator had a special son, who walked among us telling us that God was love. In some of the Paiute, Arapaho, and Miwok Sweat Lodges he is called the Star Child because a star announced his birth on Earth. Because the Indians had the legends already, well described in the book *He Walked the Americas* by L. Taylor Hansen, many accepted the main stories told them about Jesus, but felt no strong inclination to learn and study every word of a holy book from the

Middle East. They accepted Jesus - the Star Child - as a special child of the Great Spirit and powerful healer and added him to their pre-existing (by 10,000 to 100,000 years) ancient spiritual hierarchy.

After moving the pipestem in the six directions I laid it down and repeated the prayers and movements with the red stone pipe (pipe bowl). When finished I put stem and pipe together and laid it on the cloth. Then I took every object on the cloth and asked that it be blessed as I moved it towards the six directions over the smoking sage, bathing each in the smoke. After everything was blessed, I placed the Pipe so that its bowl sat on the red cloth directly in front of me with the pipestem resting on my crossed legs. I opened the bag of tobacco and took a pinch of tobacco out with my fingers and held it up to the Sky.

"Great Spirit, Mother Father Creator, there is a place for You in this Pipe, I send to You a voice." I put the pinch of tobacco in the bowl. I took another pinch and touched it to the earth. "Mother Earth upon whom I live, and breathe, and have my being, there is a place for You in this Pipe, I send to You a voice." I put it in the bowl and took out another pinch and held it to the east, "Power of the East, Power of Air, mind, and thought, Power of the sunrise and springtime, I send to You a voice." Another pinch in the bowl, another lifted, "Power of the South..."

I went through the four Powers and continued, filling my Pipe with the constituents of the universe as well as its Mother and Father. I filled my Pipe with that which is mineral, vegtable, animal, and human. With all beings that fly, those that walk on two legs and on four, with those that crawl, and those that slither, and those that swim, with all life on Planet Earth I filled my Pipe. With all who have smoked with me, and with those loved ones who have passed on before me I filled my Pipe. With my animal spirits and all the healing spirits, and all the Grandfather Spirits I filled my Sacred Pipe. I filled my Pipe with Mother Earth, Father Sun, Grandmother

Moon, Grandfather Sky, all the Star People (each star is considered an individual being), and the power of the Star Child, called Jesus the Christ. With all that is good, holy, and healing, I filled my Sacred Pipe.

When filled with all that is, I lifted the Pipe with both hands above my head, and held it and myself as a silent offering. Then pointing the pipestem towards the sky I traced a clockwise circle towards the sky and spoke.

"Great Spirit, Mother Father Creator of All Life, I send to You a voice." I brought the Pipe down, placed the bowl on the red cloth in front of me, put the stem to my mouth and struck a wooden match and lit the Sacred Pipe. As I inhaled I looked up and spoke again, "Great Spirit, I send to You a voice." I blew the smoke up, that my prayers might rise to the Great Spirit as the smoke rises upward. I inhaled and blew the smoke down to the Earth, "Mother Earth, I send to You a voice." I inhaled and blew to the east, "Power of the East, I send to You a voice." I inhaled and blew to the south, "Power of the South...."

After the four directions, I sent a voice to all that is on earth and in the heavens. I recognised the four elements, the rocks, plants, animals, and humans, the Earth, Sun, Moon, Sky, Stars, the Star Child, the Healing Grandfather Spirits, and my own personal animal spirits (it is my association and work with my animal spirits which makes me a shaman). When all the healing forces were recognized, I once more turned to the Creator.

I would inhale, blow smoke upward, pray out loud, then inhale again and send the smoke to the sky, and pray some more. "Great Spirit, Mother Father Creator of All Life, I send to You a voice. There was a horrible event on the Faulkner estate Friday night, the foul death and desecration of two of your human children, and three of your animal children. I ask that all made the transition through death to the world of Spirit and ask that they be blessed on their paths as they evolve. Inhalation, holding, blowing out of smoke. Great Spirit, may LeeAnn Rutherford and Alex Rutherford be blessed by your Spiritual Light, Life, and Love and may they be healed in all ways, surrounded by and immersed in your Divine Love."

The work here was to make sure the souls/spirits of the mother and child made it fully into the Heaven World of Light. Due to the extremely traumatic circumstances of their deaths it was important to make sure that no aspect of the psyche/soul or human consciousness shattered, causing a seperation or hiving off of some segment of the soul.

Mystical and occult traditions suggest that most "ghostly" phenomenon is caused by one of two circumstances. Most commonly, a ghost or wraith exists when some kind of shocking death occurs and there is a shattering, a splintering, a splitting off of some segment of the personality, generally thought to be a part of the subconscious mind and the instinctive being. Due to a traumatic or horrendous death, what becomes the wraith hives off and associates itself with some physical place or structure and often a repetitve behavior. Secondly, ghosts occur when a soul/spirit refuses to leave the earth plane because of some very strong attachment. The soul/spirit wants to stay here on the earth plane of existence, near the loved one(s), and chooses not to make the transition to the spiritual plane of Light to continue on their path.

In the first such case, the work is to send the wraith, the hived off subconscious segment, into the Light to reconnect with its larger self. In the second it is to convince the earth-attached being to go forward into the Light, to continue on its own personal path of evolution.   In this case there were even deeper concerns for the health of the victim's souls, due to the actions and invocations of the murderers. In some cultures there exists traditions of the magical capture and enslavement of a sacrifical victim's soul, or some specific component of a victim's soul, to afterward work magically for the sorcerer who thus enslaves it. However, this practice is not one associated with the satanic phenomenon. Nevertheless, powerful evil forces were being invoked, putting their souls at risk, by the tenets of several spiritual traditions.

I do not claim to be clairvoyant, clairaudient, or a psychic. However the training to be a shaman does neccessarily sharpen and develop the intuition. Training to be a shaman, I experienced many meaningful, what Jung called numinous events, experiences of a deeply profound spiritual nature. One's dreaming may occasionally become more symbolically significant than normal dreaming, but most such profound experiences I have personally undergone happened during a Sweat Lodge, while fasting and praying in nature, while smoking a Sacred Pipe, or while performing a healing ritual. Sometimes I lose the sensations of my body and experience what seems to be the sensations of a specific animal when I achieve a union with one of my animal spirits. At such times I work in whatever way and place is appropriate in the form of my animal spirit. At other times, I may somehow percieve or experience things which are relevant to the spiritual work being undertaken, but which have occured in reality elsewhere at a previous time. In such instances, I perceive events as though I was floating slightly above, watching and hearing what transpires. Sometimes in my shamanic healing work, the causes/events/situations that brought about the dis-ease of the patient which subsequently became the medical condition are revealed in this manner. Because of these experiences and the training, I wasn't too surprised or disturbed when something similar began to happen while I prayed for LeeAnn and Alex Rutherford.

I was smoking my Sacred Pipe, maybe two-thirds of the way through, when my inner vision was filled with a very bright white light. This light was not the highest spiritual Light, as in the Bible. In the entire Bible divinity is only described by three words. God is Light, God is Love, and God is Spirit. This was not that Light, but the light which is the higher spiritual plane of the astral light. After a few moments of my inner vision being filled and surrounded by the illumination, I heard a small low sound, kind of a pop-whoosh. Then I was there, witnessing as in the present, the blasphemous ritual as it happened some 86 hours earlier. I saw LeeAnn Rutherford lying down, tied with restraints, naked, and very pregnant on a satanic altar. Because the eternal now transcends the space/time continuum, I immeditely began praying for the protection of her soul and the deliverance of her spirit as the dark ritual proceeded. My conscious experience was that of being a hovering point of consciousness above the roof of the cabin, yet seeing right through it as though it wasn't there. My perception was centered on LeeAnn, and suddenly I was no longer only floating above, but was in soul empathy with her, somehow slightly sharing her conciousness. Her liking a freindly man and a desire to no longer be lonely had made her vunerable. After a few dates, *this* - she knew she had been tricked and drugged, having come into moments of conscious awareness, but remaining mostly unconscious. The drugs caused a lethargy and a compliance even during those rare monents when she was not so heavily sedated. She had been kept with animals and treated like an animal, dazed, she knew that much. Drugged again before being moved to this location, upon arrival she had be given extremly strong drugs - sedated and anethetized - she was numb and paralysed at that point and time, and she knew the situation was beyond bad, past horrible, she was living a nightmare but it was real. She did the only thing she could manage to do, she closed her eyes, retreated within, and prayed. She started with the Twenty-third Psalm and the Lord's Prayer. Over and over. She could barely maintain consciousness, drifting in and out, but while conscious, she prayed. As time passed she could no longer recite the Twenty-third Psalm and the Lord's Prayer, so she simply started repeating the name Jesus, or Jesus Christ, or Lord, sometimes, in her last conscious moments she thought of her baby, "Lord protect us and be with us."

She had been stripped and tied down, arms by her sides, legs spread, knees up. Her eyes were closed when through several veiled doors of perception, she felt the pressure which was the begining of her C-section delivery. She lost consciousness of her body, and at that point she seemed to be suspended, floating in an ocean of light. I lost my sharing of her perceptions then and was once more hovering over the scene, but I was not alone. I percieved them as powerful sparkling points of light, which every now and then shimmered in my mind's eye in the translucent forms of traditional Judeo-Christian angels. (On that etheric/astral level beings whose true higher spiritual nature might ultimately be percieved as points of light, may appear in human peception - in the mind's eye - in ways that the observer can understand, which reveal the beings' inner nature and intentions. Such perceptions may be shared by many, or may be unique to an individual.) In the midst of her horror she had called out and been heard. Like me, they hovered above. Although I sensed that they radiated down a spiritual blessing, they did not yet draw beside her physical body.

Below me I watched as the baby was delivered by C-section, had its bottom slapped and Alex cried out his first sounds of life. The baby was laid upon the bleeding mother, its umbilical cord cut and tied, and then the tall figure in a dark robe with cowl did the most unexpected thing. He produced a cross and holy water from a pocket in his black robe and baptized the infant in the Name of the Father, the Son, and the Holy Spirit. At that point the angels rushed down engulfing both child and mother in their radiant brightness. The angels then lifted the shimmering astral/etheric double of each up above the cabin, souls now linked to the physical bodies only by shimmering etheric cords attached below the navals, their biblical silver threads.

The Satanists were calling out the infernal names of the devil, one of them held the crying baby as another cut LeeAnn below her bottom left rib. She had her heart pulled, ripped, and cut out. Her heart's liquid contents were poured into a chalice. The child, sedated by the mother's extended periods of sedation, was placed upon its now lifeless bloodied mother, while the participants drank from the chalice. The High Priest offered his infernal prince the sacrifice of the woman, the animals, and now that of a sinless Christian child. The mother's and child's silver cords from their souls to their physical bodies dissolved simultaneously as the child died with the first stab by the High Priest. Both mother and child, released from their bodies, were freed to go with the angels up the rising tunnel of light into the Light Beyond - lifting quickly into the Heavenly Light. After watching them float into the radiant white light I returned my attention to the dark ritual being finished below me, but my vision clouded and I returned to my body in the pasture by the pond to the sound of that distinctive pop/whoosh.

My Sacred Pipe was out. I relit it and said my thank-you prayers. The mother and child had made it wholely into the Light. Despite the dark circumstances of their deaths, they had cleanly departed from the land of sufffering, their souls/spirits were safe in the Light, **experiencing** in a way seldom known incarnate, that God is Love.

***

Amanda ate her McDonald's appreciatively. After two days in stir, fucking McDonald's was steak, Burger King would have been filet mingon. But she wasn't complaining. The lawyer was bringing her food from the outside, and giving her almost everything she wanted. Using the same interview room, which was rapidly becoming a second home, she had the legal pads and pencils she'd requested. Leif was going to put money on the jail books for her like he had Stewart, which was great. So far he wouldn't budge on helping Kevin, saying that both Amanda and Stewart needed to distance themselves as far as possible from Kevin, who was going down hard no matter what. A three time loser, it was a done deal, his previous life was over; he would probably never get out of jail. She and Stewart could still salvage theirs. Lief chose to cast

Stewart as a pawn of the mysterious Raquel, and cast Amanda as the hooker with a heart of gold

- a good soul gone bad under the Svengali-like influence of Kevin. He offered to bring her a

Bible, a conversion to Christianity as soon as she was no longer around Kevin and under his

influence, would definitely help her with the jury. Of course, only if it was "sincere."

On several pages of one of the pads she had three names, Kevin's, her's, and Stewart's,

with lines drawn down the page seperating them. On the firstpage under Stewart's name all she

had was Raquel - short, thin, small breasts, nice nipples, mild S&M. Under her and Kevin she

listed all their joint ventures over the years, and other stuff she knew Kevin had done. Kevin had

hurt people physically for infringements with the girls, he had cut his dope more than he should

have at times, and they had blackmailed some of the richer players in the early days. Trouble

was, the more she worked on it and though about it, the longer the lists got. She made it to page

three, Kevin had page four to himself. She and Kevin had plenty of potential enemies. All it took

was one whacko who seriously held a grudge.... The streets are full of whackos who want

women or drugs, just full of them. Not to mention short girls with nice titties, she knew a town

full.

***

Having finished my prayers, said my thank-you's, and closed, I took the joshua spike and

cleaned out the bowl, pouring its charcoal contents on the sacred Mother Earth. I seperated the

pipestem from the pipe bowl, and blew through each four times to keep them clean. Once more I

lit the sage, which had smouldered and gone out during my trance, and cleansed and blessed

every object in the smoke to the six directions. As I began to put away all the contents of my

pipe bag, I heard the scream of a raptor and looked up, to see above me the red-tailed hawk circling, who often comes when I smoke my Pipe. He circled above for minutes as I put away my sacred tools. I have three spirit powers, animal spirits, one of which is a red-tailed hawk. It's not that I believe the physical hawk which flies above me is my animal spirit, it's not. But there is some kind of spiritual asociation, kinship, clanship, synchronisity, something between the incarnate physical animal and its animal spirit cousin. When you love, respect, and relate to the Mother Earth and all her children, spiritual relationships are established which are seldom understood by western science - relationships possibly over 100,000 years old in human experience. The very concept of human/spirit power relationships is often ridiculed by a science which is often clueless to the underlying spiritual nature of reality. After I put away my Sacred Pipe, the hawk quit circling above me and flew away. The crows had left him alone this time. Sometimes they do, other times their mock combat ensues with his arrival.

I have never heard, nor read, a decent explantion of the nature of animal spirits and their relationship with the shaman. It may be a spiritual mystery beyond rational exlpanation. When I first tried to explain it to Danny, I told him the Judeo-Christians had angels and archangels as part of their setup. The Indian's angels appeared to them as denizens of the natural world. While an animal spirit might be the equivalent of a guardian angel, a Grandfather Spirit would be the equivalent of an archangel. In the realms of consciousness or the collective unconscious where humans interact with deeper spiritual reality, those beings which humans are able to percieve will often have the apperance that is traditionally ascribed to them in their cultural background. Both the beings of Light and the creations - creatures of evil will be percieved by the beholder in some way that he or she can understand.

The crows began cawing in the distance. I love the hawks, I love the crows, so I don't take sides in their running war. Each will potentially eat the other's young, and crows feel duty bound to run away any hawk they see. Since the tribe of crows and the pair of hawks share much territory in common, it is a long standing war, with no known causualties.

Having seen and experienced much while I smoked my Sacred Pipe, I did not choose to consciously analyse my perceptions at this point. What I had seen was clear in my mind. I would not forget. I placed my pipe bag to the side and played the shamanic drumming cassette tape on my blaster. I had prayed with the universe to the Creator on behalf of two souls. Those prayers had already been graciously answered, before I even asked. Now I was going to do what I could as a man, as a human, as a shaman. It was time to go forward and fight the good fight, or at least to go do some basic reconaissance so that I could fight the good fight victoriously. I knew what I had seen of the evil ritual as it occured days earlier, now I needed to see where things stood at the present.

I crossed myself with the Kabbalistic cross three times, said the Lord's Prayer, and put on the complete armor of God as described in the sixth chapter of Ephesians. I had known from the beginning, to some extent, who we were fighting. Now I knew in much greater detail. This was a modern derivation of the apostate Christian ritual rebellion of classical Satanism, not a pure decendant of the seventeenth century incarnation, but rather a more mongrel, ecclectic, and hopefully unique version. What I knew for certain, in terms of spiritual realities, was that it was serious, it was evil, and it was not without determined intention. These, in the shamanic sense, were worthy adversaries. There was evil before us that needed to be defeated, and one or more souls which need to be redeemed. Very possibly there were souls here were capable of being redeemed.

In the Owens Valley where I underwent most of my shamanic training I was taught to call all birds of prey, even crows, eagles. The crows were called the little black eagles, so my hawk would be called the red-tailed eagle. That's how I learned it, so that's how I thought about it. As the cassette played, the drumming beat out the rhythm of life and I turned up the volume, then sang a song to the Great Spirit, a song to the Earth Mother, and then I sang a Cherokee eagle song. Over and over, as the rhythm of the drumming became more incessant, I sang my song, and went into what the anthropologists call a trance, and then a deeper trance. This was made all the easier and faster by my having already entered an altered state of consciousness smoking my Sacred Pipe just moments before.

I don't know how long I had sung my song when the transition happened. One moment I'm in my body, centered in my head, singing, the next moment my entire being is my head, and my head becomes a bird, and I'm a red-tailed eagle, flying, flying, flying. At first, flying at what seemed like a natural speed, then flying higher and more rapidily in white clouds and then down, in a moment, at the destination.

I landed high in a pine tree overlooking the "murder cabin." I had the double sensation of both being one with my spirit animal, and having 360 degree perception of everything happening around my animal spirit. The cabin was dark and silent, the lone police car was stationed where Thorn Road ended. Nothing was happening, so I flew up and over the pines, then oaks, over the estate's inhabited dwellings, which I flew over in high wide circles.

All the houses and structures looked normal to my animal spirit/eagle eyes except for Phineas' house, which seemed shrouded in a mist, a sometimes shimmering, sometimes dark grey shadowy mist. A mist through which I could not percieve. A mist which meant occult protective measures had been taken. Functioning as I was, at one with my spirit animal, I was a red-tailed eagle in that glowing nether world - where the physical world meets the astral world, where the electromagnetic energy fields of life are etherically visible. A world in which willed thought can be instantaneously creative. A world in one way like a dream, and in another way more real in essence than the "real" world this one gives rise to.

After several rotations I glided in to settle down at the top of an oak tree near the edge of the dark mist and take a closer look. No sooner had my talons come to grip the branch when SWOOSH! The snake struck out from out of the grey mist with fangs exposed, going for my heart. I lifted and pushed down powerfully with my wings as the snake's head came towards me and was almost upon me. I beat my wings again quickly and raised both talons, kicking out, and knocking away the snake, ripping away some slimy skin on its head, making it tumble down to a lower limb. It looked like no earthly snake, but a bad creation of a B horror flick, a scaly snake, black, with a komodo dragon face, a split tounge, and huge fangs. What I called a subdemon, or by the intentionally belittling term - an astral beastie.

No sooner had I begun to fly up and away, between the oak and the mist when up from the house's dark mist without warning came another beast. This one with wings, bat-like wings. It was about the size of, and looked something like, the flying monkey demons from *the Wizard of Oz*, except the contenance of this creature was really evil. A monkey's hand with long black nails like shapened claws reached out, tried to grab my talons and pull me down. I pulled my talons up out of reach and beat my wings powerfully and rapidly, rising above the beast's grasp. Then I did something I didn't know until that moment that I could do, and had certainly never done before. But this was a highly unusual situation. This beast was bigger than I was, and could fly. Instinctively, I wished to change the situation in my favor. So I expanded. I willed to be larger, and instantaneously was, three times the size of a normal red-tailed eagle, and a whole lot bigger than the butt ugly Dorothy beastie. I flew up quickly, very high, and then turned and dove, at full speed, screaming as a giant raptor, down at monkey boy where he hovered at the edge of the mist. I hit him in the chest with both talons, and tossed his trick or treat ass back into the mist from whence he came. Then I headed home, I'd seen all I needed to see. The enemy was formidable. Either those were his personal beasties - his own personal little sub-demons, or they were sent there to watch over and protect him by the dark forces he invoked. Neither explanation was thrilling, none too thrilling at all. Flying away, I heard the wail of a wolf.

***

Stewart waited expectanly on his bunk, as much as possible keeping to himself. He reviewed his day. During his second meeting with his lawyer just after lunch, Stewart was surprised to see his doctor walk into the interview room. Stewart underwent a basic examination. The doctor and lawyer had a long, low talk, the doctor wrote some stuff out and left. Lief went out and called two judges whose campaigns had recieved generous Faulkner family donations. The judges called the APD Chief, who called the jail supervisor, and Lief got everything he wanted. Lief found it neccessarty to let Stewart go back to jail so he could personally take care of everything. He'd patted Stewart on the shoulder and told him not to worry, that it was all going to be all right. "Your family has lots of money and influence, this Amanda Stone is no dummy, she will help us figure out who's responsible for all this, and remember, all my clients are innocent. And you really are."

Kevin had gotten his phone call and finally gotten arraigned. He called his legitimate business partner, she said she'd clean up and hide or throw away whatever was in the boathouse and get him a lawyer. She didn't sound too thrilled, but she didn't tell him to go to hell either. She asked about bail, he told her about the bail hearing on Wensday, she promised to have a lawyer there for him. He felt a little better, but not much. If they had blood evidence against him like they said, and they had him good for a murder, either the cops were setting him up or someone he knew or who at least knew about him was setting him up. He had to figure who, and why, and had to establish a fucking alibi. He wanted to talk to his lawyer as soon as possible, he needed a legal strategy, he needed advice.

I flew high and fast went into white and then came down over the pasture, saw my slumped body, and pop-whoosh - I was me again, back in my body. I fell over sideways and stayed down for a few seconds. I righted myself, turned off the tape, and laid back, straightening my legs. I was sweating profusely.

I thanked my red-tailed eagle spirit for its help, and thanked the Star Child, and the forces of spiritual Light, Life, and Love, I thanked the Great Spirit, and the Earth Mother. Then I lay back, without conscious thought, breathing deeply, recovering my life force.

***

Amanda sat there with her pencils and pads, thinking. It had to center around Kevin, not likely her, not likely the dorky blob. She had helped Kevin during the blackmails; she'd been the one injured that he had enforced retribution viciously for, once. She wasn't responsible for any drug deals gone sour, but she might have been around. Whatever happened to cause someone so much anger that they would go to the trouble to set them up, it was Kevin's deal, not hers. She needed a one on one with Kevin, or maybe a two on one, her and Lief interviewing Kevin. Lief was due back sooner or later. She had to make him see it her way, one way or another.

***

I came fully back to aware earthly conciousness and took my pipe bag, my blaster, and dragged my fatigued butt back inside my house. The ceiling fans were going, so it was nice and cool when I stepped inside and replaced my pipe bag on the west wall. Then I went in and washed my hands with spiritual purpose, opened and downed half a Coke, then took a warm shower. I don't take cold or cool showers, warm was as cool as my showers ever got. Still, it was invigorating. I went to my kitchen, poured the rest of the Coke in a glass filleed with ice, sat down, and let it all sink in.

Chapter Thirteen – Tuesday Afternoon and Evening

The cell door opened from the outside and in walked Captain Barrnett, the jail supervisor, and Lief, and another officer, a lieutenant. The corrections officer inside went from around the guard's desk to greet them.

There was a general stir throughout the fifty man cell. What was going on was highly unusual. After a few minutes of what looked like light-hearted banter, the whole group made their way over to Stewart, who hadn't taken his eyes off Lief and the brown paper grocery bag cradled under his arm. If Stewart had believed in anything, good or evil, he would have prayed. Instead, he wished and hoped, real hard. His eyes followed the bag as it made its way to him. He said his "hellos" and listened as best he could, but he wasn't all there until Leif poured out the contents of the sack on the bed. There was a combination lock, a yellow legal pad, some pencils, and there was food - honeybuns, candybars, bags of chips, packets for hot chocolate and soup, and a thermal plastic mug with top. Considering the situation, Stewart was about as happy as he possibly could be. Leif told him again about the jail store, that the guards had been alerted to his medical condidtion and if he felt ill to let them know, he would come back again tomorrow...."

Stewart listened somewhat, happy that for now, at least his most basic need was being met - he had food.

***

Dick Williams had called Danny on their lunch break on the way down to Panama City Beach, Florida. He and Potts had been thinking, they had an idea. Danny had made a few calls, when Williams called back he gave him the go ahead. They were going to offer Juan expense money for his time, $100 a day. They needed something to get a Mexican who may or may not have a valid green card to voluntarily come forward to help in a police investigation. There were

a limited number of high-rises on the beach, under twenty-five, hopefully the expense money and

a no hassle guarantee would make multiple visits to the same hotels unneccessary. With at least

some carrot on the stick, Potts and Williams went foreward in search of their potential witness.

***

Sitting at my kitchen table, I looked out the sliding glass doors at the pasture where the

horses grazed. It was very peaceful. I had written out the barest outline of my two OBE's (out-

of-body-experiences) and what they meant to the case. I had gathered many relevant perceptions,

absolutely none of which could or would ever be considered as evidence in a court of law.

Nevertheless, I felt I *knew* things very relevant to the case. I knew who our primary enemy was

now, without doubt, and I'd seen shadows, outlines, and faint images of the other two

performing the blasphemous ritual with him. I hadn't seen the doorman or the fake policeman,

but I had sensed them. I knew we faced an opponent who practiced a very rare form of evil

indeed, he practiced aspects of classical Satanism - the baptism of the infant before sacrifice, and

he practiced a ritual magic form of Satanism - Invoking not demons or archdemons, but the devil

himself. His ritual work was self-styled, it involved ritual rebellion against Christianity, but it

was not the precise ritual inversion of the Christian Mass, nor the magic of LaVey or the other

public Satanists. The ritual remains were left to be discovered because what the satanic priest

desired involved working in the public domain, serving his own and presumably his dark

master's goals.

Feeling a great sense of relief concerning the victims, I also felt a strong sense of dread

concerning my opponents. The kind of spirit combat just engaged in was a very rare, extremely

rare phenomenon indeed, at least in my experiences. The changing size while working as my spirit power was a unique and new experience for me, brought about only by the neccessity of the moment. But now that I knew I could do it... It's one of the things I love about shamansim - although it is mankind's oldest and original form of religion - shamanism is never static or bound by expectations or proscriptions, it is always fluid, an ever renewing fountain in the spiritual waters of Life.

***

Stewart left one honey bun on the bed and put away the rest of his treasure locked up in the drawer under the bed. He ate the bun, went and peed. As he started walking back to his bed, he felt very uneasy. There was a group of tough looking young black men hanging out between the guard's desk and his bed, and back behind his bed standing like a giant, was the biggest black man in the block, probably the whole jail.

Not knowing what else to do, he went back and sat on his bed. He hoped all the black men weren't near him all of a sudden for a reason, but they were. Stewart had no idea some of these men were nearly his age, some just a few years older. Their knowledge of the world, at least the streets and the gang world, put them light years ahead of Stewart in these surroundings.

The shortest of the black youths hanging out came forward. To Stewart's inexperienced ears it sounded something like: "Yo. Home. Ya know, we all seen da big man come down here ya know, wit' ya mouthpiece, you know 'n all da goodies. Now ya know ya gonna need sum protection heah, someun ta watch ya back. Dat would be us, da Double Duece." He held up two fingers across his chest. Opened and closed them and then twice, hit his chest and turned them down to the ground. Stewart had never seen a gang sign before and didn't have a clue. "Itz on' gonna cost ya, ya know, one third of ya goodies every week, can't get a bettah deal dan dat. Double Duece got yah back, nobody fuck wit you. Nobody."

"One-third?"

"Only one third, an' we got ya back. We down fah you." He pointed both forefingers at Stewart. Stewart felt like they were trying to make him feel important and scare him into compliance at the same time. The scare part was definitely working.

"One foth." The black giant standing behind Stewart spoke low, but loud enough for Stewart to hear him. "Wezen' down for one-foth." Stewart had no idea the giant was saying Westend, identifying his gang. But Stewart damn sure knew this man was huge, and one-fourth was a better deal than one-third. Greed was something most of the rich learn at an early age.

The young man spoke directly to the giant. "Ol' man. Don' be fucking wit' da Double Duece, Wezen' nothin' but a few ol' time'ahs, 'bout due for da ol' folks home. All y'all dead or in da pen, ya know. We got da juice heah, not a bunch of ol' men has-beens."

The giant had drawn close behind Stewart, he made Stewart feel safer, so Stewart went with the giant. Stewart looked back way up over his shoulder at the giant, asked again, "One-fourth?"

The giant repeated, "One-foth."

The deal was done. The Double Duece were not too happy about his choice."Yo man. Ya dissing me, ya know, ya dissing da Double Duece, ya made a large mistake, a very large mistake. One ya goin pay fah, fucker, and ya goin be fuckin' sorry ya turn us dowm. Ya got da word of the Double Duece on dat." The tallest one behind the leader made a gun with his hand, cocked back his thumb, and symbolically, silently, shot Stewart. He smiled, they all turned and sauntered away, acting like they didn't care, but they were obviously pissed.

The giant introduced himself and two of his "Hommies." The giant was Littl' Bob, his sidekicks Willie and Twotone. Just like the Double Duece they didn't mention money on the books or other help they'd want later, for now it was one step at a time.

***

Kevin looked at the papers before him. "Are you serious? I haven't used either of these two since the last time I got out. That would be stupid, to use aliases that I know you knew about. Then it wouldn't really be an alias, now would it? I don't do things that stupid."

"Well, look where you are right now, is this an indication of your true genius?" Annie couldn't help herself. This smug fiend served the devil, doer or not. He was guilty of exploiting women in prostitution, dealing, and selling his soul.

"You keep saying you're innocent and want to prove it, here's the best way to start. If somebody has used your old aliases trying to set you up, and their writing doesn't match yours, your alibi is looking better. Of course, if it's your signature, that's just one more piece of damning evidence. And the evidence sure is piling up." Annie kept talking. This was her idea, Danny just took it easy for a few minutes and let Annie go. At the top of each page were the names she wanted him to write, she wanted him to do it quickly, without thought or attention, repititiously. So Kevin wrote his name, and Kevin Eubanks, and Kevin Gothard over and over and over.

***

Contemplating it all, I stayed at my kitchen table, drinking purified water, writing notes, and thinking. I now knew things that could help guide the investigation. Guide being the operative word. Danny was pretty accepting of my ways, but he wouldn't fly in the face of physical evidence on what he would call my hunch. I understood. To prove that what I had just experienced was vastly different than a nightly dream of inconsequence would be a very difficult task. I had to be subtle. I might have more insight than before, but even in my own mind, far from all the questions had answers.

***

Tonya had already been assigned etiquette and language classes and her daughter's nursery school was great, the best she'd ever had. Her daughter and Jasmine's were instant buddies. Tonya could not keep from being anxious, she kept an eye on CNN. Her life style and living standard had taken a dramatic leap up and she was thrilled. But she had a bad feeling about what George was up to. Asking around she'd found out who else had just worked in Atlanta - Deseree. They had an initail general conversation concerning Atlanta, but nothing heavy. Tonya would just keep watching, hoping she didn't recognize any names or faces on the news.

***

Samantha had let the bald pig have his way with her one last time. She hadn't always despised this man, and he had given her the oppurtunity for her revenge, which were the thoughts she'd used to rationlize it lately, and in a few days she would give herself the gift of freedom. She guessed it was the exhiliration of the moment, why the S&M preliminaries hadn't been neccessary the last time. He was obviously getting off on the news casts, and in pulling it all off. She still wondered about her "sleep" tapes he had been so determined to burn. She had always had trouble getting to sleep, and had been plagued by vivid, disturbing dreams throughout her life. He had made some tapes combining wave sounds from a beach, with direct suggestions, subliminal suggestions, and the timed heartbeat/percussive sounds of a metronome progressively mimicking deeper levels of relaxation and brain wave activity. Except for a few recurrent dreams that showed up every so often, she had been able to go to sleep easier, and she slept much deeper when she listened to the tapes. However, for months she had never been able to resist any direct command Phineas gave her while in his physical presence. She knew he sometimes used hypnosis effectively in his practice. What was on those tapes? All of her manipulations were done subltely, planned away from him, he always seemed in control when they were together. But all she had to do now was stay calm and keep it together. She only had a few more moves to make, mere hours to get through, and she would be away.

***

Kevin had written the names until his fingers were sore and the muscles in his forearm tired. The last few pages got real sloppy, then they told him to stop. As he stood up Kevin put out his best idea so far. "Look, I didn't do this ritual murder thing. I'm no angel, you've got my record, but I didn't do this. Once I meet with my lawyer, if he agrees, and y'all won't ask me about anything but these charges, I'll take a lie detector test. I didn't do no murder, this is bullshit."

***

I got up and answered the phone. Danny sounded a little worried. "I want you to come on down, but ride the Harley, look rough, come in the back door, use my locker and clean up. I don't want the press on you. We've got 'the most eager to take lie detector tests' suspects I've ever seen. All three are adamant they didn't do the crime. Jackson gave us all the signatures we wanted. These folks are too willing to please. If they're the doers, I don't get their strategy, unless they refuse to take the lie detector tests at the last minute. Anyway, besides all that, Stewart's lawyer is going to let us interview Stewart, no holds barred, in an attempt to get our nod on bail. Ride fast, if you get a ticket, have them call me, I'll square it, but haul butt, then low profile."

***

Phineas dismissed her like a servant, told her to pack and get ready for her trip to Washington, D.C. She went about her packing, and after he was absorbed with his work in his study, made her way quietly to Alpert's. Between the cops and the private security the family felt the property was secure and the houses still weren't locked during the day. The maid was somewhere about in one of the houses doing her cleaning. The gardner/gatekeeper was cutting the grass. Samantha made her way to the phone in Alpert's kitchen. By the phone was the number of the security firm. She called their main office, identified herself, said the Mosby brother with the long hair told her to call him if he could help, and she was calling. Samantha was depending on the weight of her family name and the importance of the case to smooth over any obstacles and she was absolutely correct. She was patched in to his home phone. She looked around one last time to check, she was all alone.

***

Tonya thought she would pee her pants. There on CNN was Pugsley, his picture, his real name - Stewart Faulkner-Davis, in jail, held for false statements, suspected in a ritual murder, and every bit as rich as he said. She didn't know if a brutal death, or the oppurtunity of a lifetime, lay before her. She had her daughter to think about. And Deseree to talk to. Then Jasmine.

***

I didn't mind Danny's suggestion, I'd been meaning to ride my scooter more. It's a twenty year old Harley, not showroom, not fully outlaw chopped, somewhere in the middle. Danny gave

me license to speed, which meant a fun ride. I got my gun, badge, APD Special Services ID,
notebook, and headed to get my work clothes and backpack when the phone rang. Surprise is a
mild word.

"This is Samantha Faulkner-Davis, you said you were at my service, that you would help me.
I'm holding you to your promise."

"What can I do for you, Samantha?"

"Come to my school's back entrance tommorrow, the one for the student parking lot.
Once you enter, the first door to your left is the orchestra room. Be there at 10:00 AM. Show
your badge to my teacher, the conductor. I'll leave with you. Our band is leaving for Washington
D.C. tommorrow. I'll have my bags, we'll take them. I'm putting myself in your protective
custody. I'm trusting your promise, I'm trusting you; you will fiercely protect me, won't you?
Because what I can tell you will put my life in danger. And yours. You acted like a man of your
word, are you? I can't talk long, yes or no?"

"Yes."

"Word of honor, now, for a few days at first, for reasons I'll explain to you, this has to be
between just me and you, not the whole police force, just you. Yes or no? And hurry, this is life
or death!"

"Yes. At least for now."

"See you tommorrow at ten." Click.

***

The handwriting expert, Danny, and Annie looked at the signatures. All of Kevin's and
the car rental form and the unwed mothers home's check-in/out sheet.

"That's the best you can do?" Danny asked plaintively. "Is it or isn't it?"

The expert repeated himself, almost word for word, again. "It is either the same signature, or a studied and well executed duplication by a skilled forger. It is not the work of some punk with a stolen credit card. It's Jackson's or somebody who has studied and worked on exactly replicating Jackson's signature to the point it is natural and flowing."

***

Wallace headed home and thought about the last few hours. They hadn't been easy. Thirty years ago the idea of a black policeman dealing with or comforting a white family in such circumstances was unheard of. These days, most folks didn't think anything about it. Now, it was just people and people, policeman and civilian, in this case, one church going Christian to another. How do you comfort someone whose daughter died in such a manner? How do you prepare them for the heartless and exploitative media? How do you return her personal items after you're one of the ones who examined them?

There in the police car, speeding down the highway, something happened to Wallace that hadn't happened in a long, long time. He'd shed tears five times in his adult life. The marriages of his son and daughter, the death of his parents, and the death of Martin Luther King, Jr. This was the sixth. He would see the faces of her poor parents. He continued driving, ignoring the tears that rolled intermittently down his cheeks. He just kept driving.

I'd gathered the tools of my trade and put them in my backpack, then put on my denims and rode. It was a clear hot day, good visibility, perfect road conditions. I concentrated on making time, the mental issues at hand were too complex to deal with at speeds sometimes nearing 100 MPH.

***

Samantha snuck back inside Phineas' house without notice. She had one more life-risking task to undertake tonight. Once it was done, she'd be counting the hours down until ten AM tommorrow when she'd be safe. She'd be in control. Hopefully for the rest of her life, she'd be in control.

***

I pulled in the back and parked my scooter near the door. There was no press back here, and if any interested observer thought anything about me, it would be undercover cop, confidential informant, undercover DEA, it might be anything but a specialist working on the highest profile case in the region. Once inside, I took off the denim jacket and sleeveless shirt, secured them in Danny's locker, put on one of our security tee shirts, slid my badge on my belt, grabbed my notebook, and headed up to see Danny.

As soon as I walked in Danny got up with Annie close behind. "Stewart and Wilmington are in interview three. Let's hear what their offer is, and what Stewart has to say." Danny stopped cold in his tracks, "Y'all go on, I'll be there in a sec."

He came in right after we did, with the suitcase from Stewart's house of horrors, fresh from the lab.

It was a small interview room, nobody was behind any mirrors, no tape recording allowed, this was all face to face. There was Stewart in his white jailhouse jumpsuit, with Wilmington, solo as always. He was one of the few high priced bloodsuckers who worked alone. The prevalent theory was he didn't want to share the decision making or limelight with anybody at all, even an underling. He had a secretary and two paralegals, but they never left the office. Wilmington had an offer to make; we had an interview to conduct. Danny sat in the middle, Annie on his left, me on the right. Danny set the suitcase on the floor and I laid out my notebook, Annie did the same thing.

Wilmington launched straight in, "Gentlemen, Stewart has agreed to answer any and all questions you have for him. But we have certain propositions for you. If Stewart takes a polygraph test given by your people, and passes it, you will agree to bail for Stewart. We ask that you let us bring in a sketch artist for Stewart to help in creating a picture of his alibi witness Raquel and for Amanda and Kevin to come up with a sketch for their alibi witness, Honey Delight of New Orleans. We would like to put forward a reward for Raquel and Honey or anyone who can tell us the whereabouts of these two, so that they can come forth and clear my clients and hopefully help point us in the right direction of the actual perpetrators. Amanda is willing to take a lie detector test to improve her chances of getting out on a low bail. She may be a recreational drug user and a prostitute, but she took no part in any murder and I truly doubt the whole satanic thing for her is anything more than a lark, or going along with her boyfriend. Kevin's not my client, but after the sketches are done, I would like to get Kevin, Amanda, and Stewart together to see if they can figure out who's framing them. Of course, you would be present at that meeting, perhaps together we can figure out who really is behind this. Once we have the sketches, and if Raquel and Honey are found, we may be able to expose this complex frame-up for what it is and identify the perpertrators of this horrendous act. So you see gentlemen, we all have the same goal here, finding the real perpetrators."

Danny listened, while Annie and I wrote down notes. Guilty people seldom offer to take lie detector tests. Some do, out of arrogance or bravado, but most don't. Psychotics, sociopaths, yogis, and some people on certain drugs can beat them, but it's not common. Our Special Forces Operators and CIA spooks train to beat them. Some people also seem to give conflicting results, but that might be due to the proficiency of the tester. Before anyone said anything, Lief had an addendum. "We propose that the reward situation be handled by the police or DA's office. We, the Faulkner family, will put up the reward money as well as pay the city back every cent such

an operation costs. But if some law enforcement agency doesn't handle the reward situation and

the interviews involved, the DA's office will never believe it, and neither would you."

Danny didn't need to confer with anybody on this. It was his call. "The sketch artist idea

is fine, if these people aren't the doers, fine, I want the ones responsible. I'm not here to give the

death-needle to scapegoats. We haven't even had the first bail hearing on the lesser charges, the

murder charges haven't even been filed yet. Some of what you're asking is premature."

Lief jumped in. "Whatever bail decision is made on the lesser charges, you could always

charge my clients with murder as soon as the first bail hearing is over, before they even walk out

the door. We don't want to string this thing out and you can avoid the embarrassment of falsely

charging my clients. We both know they've already been charged in the court of public opinion.

My client's family is less than thrilled and would like Stewart cleared as soon as possible."

"Fine." Danny took over. "First things first. I agree to the sketch artists and the lie

detector tests. If both pass the tests with flying colors, we will then deal with all your other

propositions. How about this - we postpone the bail hearings from Wednesday to Friday, and we

do the polygraphs and sketch artist tommorrow? If that goes as you're certain it will, we will

discuss the other matters. However, I've got to say rewards are offered for the capture of bad

guys normally, not the procurement of alibi witnesses. I doubt the DA will touch it. The up-side

of the postponement till Friday for your clients is we hold off on the murder charges. If they're

cleared by Friday of the murders, they can help us find the doers."

"My clients and I will confer on it, but I feel favorably towards such a proposal. Now, if

there are some questions you'd like to ask Stewart."

So we asked. At first we went over the same stuff we heard through the looking glass on the previous evening. What he told Amanda then and what he told us was coherent and consistent. He took us through his whole weekend, from the time he went to the convenience store to the moment he got caught by the Colonel sneaking in. Danny told him to keep going. Stewart described waiting, recieving the warrant, us searching his room.

Danny lifted the suitcase off the floor and threw it on the table. He undid and flipped the top open and dumped the contents on the table. Danny was as sickened by this stuff as Annie and myself, he wanted some accounting. "The lab tells us there's no human blood on this stuff, only animal blood. The blood of many animals. What do you have to say about this Stewart?"

Stewart and Lief had spent some time on this one, Stewart didn't hesitate. "I'm interested in biology and anatomy. Those are my dissection tools."

I couldn't help myself, this little monster wasn't (in my mind) one of the doers, but he was a serial murderer in training. "Jeffrey Dalmer liked biology and anatomy just like you do. Is he one of your heroes?"

"No." Quietly. Maybe Dalmer was this kid's hero.

"Where'd you get your victims Stewart?"

"Roadkill."

I couldn't help it. "We know from the lab reports of blood spray that most of these animals were still alive when dissected. How did you sedate them, drugs in baited food?" Stewart looked at Lief, he nodded. "With my slingshot."

"How?"

"I'd hit them in the head with a rock or round steel pellet, stun them. I'm a good marksman with a slingshot or a rifle. Once they were down or slowed and dazed I'd hit them in the head with another rock. I only pulled back halfway, so it didn't kill them."

"No," I said, "you wanted that pleasure, slowly, and at your fingertips." All the world needed was another sadistic homocidal maniac that was a great shot. Jeffery Dalmer as a sharpshooter. They'd had that once in Texas, it didn't go well.

Lief said to Danny, "We are cooperating. Can't we all be more civil." Danny looked over at me, then he took over the questioning.

"Stewart, we know you've killed cats, squirrells, rabbits, what we're worried about is that people with your..."

Danny stalled, so I threw in the word, "Proclivities."

"proclivites often graduate to other things like abusing children - sadistically or sexually, or torture and murder, or serial murders. Did you know that in the locality of every school you've attended in the last three years, there was an unexplained rise in the number of dogs shot. Shot specifically by .22 rifles, the kind often used for target practice in military shools. You did all the dog shootings, didn't you? Snuck a weapon out at night and hunted domestic dogs because you enjoyed killing them. Didn't you?"

Stewart looked to his lawyer, who was having second thoughts about letting his client answer any more questions, despite the deal he had just struck at Stewart's insistence of innocence in the ritual murders. Stewart had filled Leif in some, but not completely. Lief was getting very nervous about where this was going.

I couldn't help myself again and jumped in. "How long have you enjoyed your hobby Stewart? How about sadistic and sexual abuse of your little sister growing up? She would certainly have been your most available potential human victim?"

Lief stood up and screamed, "That's enough. Stewart offered to answer any questions you had pertaining *to the murder in question*! He did not agree to a general inquisition. You know our offer about the polygraph. You can ask him any question relating to the ritual murders. I wasn't prepared to go into these other areas, I'll need more time to confer with my client. Perhaps if we prove Stewart was not involved in the ritual murders, we can plea bargain Stewart out of a guilty charge on false statements for a no lo contendre and a few years of intensive therapy. Maybe a few months in-house, then lots of out patient therapy. Court monitored."

Lief was packing his briefcase. His no holds barred interview had come to an abrupt halt. His last statement was certainly indicative that he recognized his client was a dangerously sick young man in need of therapy. I wondered if any therapy short of a final solution could stop someone as disturbed as Stewart from riding that dark road from chilhood sadism to adult mass murderer. In a totalitarian police state, you would either let Stewart work for your secret police, or kill him. Western governments are too humanitarian for such solutions, and are currenting wrestling with the problem of repeat sex offenders. Do we let them go free at the end of their sentence to repeat their crime, or condemn them to mental institutions? It won't be solved easily. In our society, we wait for potential killers to kill, then if found guilty at the trial and appeals, we either kill them or jail them. Better to kill them if there is clear DNA evidence, take them out of the gene pool, no chance of escape, or parole, or political pardon. Leif stood there, aware that he was breaking his word, and still hoping we'd keep ours.

"I just need to talk to my client about some of these areas I haven't discussed with him before. I can't just let him answer.... That's standard. But anyway, I have a sketch artist outside. If we agree to postpone the bail hearings till Friday, can she come in now and start with Stewart on the sketch, and we'll do the polygraphs tommorow? Then after Stewart and I confer more, we'll have another open discussion and try to resolve any remaining concerns."

Danny was pissed about the abrupt ending of the interview, but happy about the postponement until Friday and the lie detector tests. Getting two main suspects to volunteer for the test was great. If there was a setup, he needed to know now, and not look stupid later. So Danny agreed, and the sketch artist came in after Stewart conferred with Lief about his current situation. We went back to Danny's office. Things were getting interesting.

Kevin just sat there on his bunk, going through his life in crime, trying to figure out who would hate him this much, know him so well, and how could they hate him so much without him having a clue who it was. Kevin had cut some of his drugs too much, but he didn't see this perfect a setup as revenge for cut drugs. And he didn't see this as a grand scheme/complicated setup to take over his escort business. Business was good, but there was plenty to go around. That left revenge for an ass kicking, or for one of the blackmail scams he ran early on. The trouble there was that it was when he was just beginning his criminal career. He wasn't disciplined, hadn't learned many lessons yet, he was heavily into coke and speed back then, drinking too much and on the job, sometimes tripping on LSD, sometimes smoking opium, and to sleep he'd crash on morphine. His memory of that time was far from clear, practically all one big blur. He made some quick money, but blackmail was just too much hassle. Working the girls, selling speed and coke, that was easy money in a low maintenance, low risk, low exposure enterprise when compared to blackmailing professioanlly. Blackmail was just too much: too much could go wrong, way too much exposure, too hard a fall for the rewards. It had been years since he last ran the pictures scams, six, seven, eight, a long time back; he needed a time-line on his on career and pick out the most viable candidates. Who would wait that long, and who would know so much about him?

***

We were in Danny's office when he got the call from Potts, she was ecstactic.

"It was at the fifth hotel, his sister is the day manager. Seems Juan and her hubbie had a huge row last night, because Juan was drinking day and night. Once I crossed myself and swore to God it was no arrest, that we'd pay him $100 a day and her $50 for putting him in our hands, and that we'd get him sober because he was an important witness, she led us to him. He was shitface, and came quietly. We paid the lady cash and got a reciept."

"Good work. Hurry home." It might be good work, but what if most of the perps in custody weren't the doers. He'd have to find a whole new set, ones he presently knew nothing about. But Gary Parker must know, and Parker would eventually break. Despite his stupidly stubborn resistance so far.

It was hard for me to sit on his desk, while working for him, and not tell Danny about the unexpected call, but I had given my word. I'm not saying I don't lie when I'm undercover, I do. But I've never lied to Danny, yet Samantha had asked me for my word, and I'd given it. Annie immediately wanted to know what Danny had just been told. "Has Juan identified our people, remember much about them, what?"

Danny knew that yearning, to know every piece of the puzzle, instantly, as soon as that piece comes in. "Naw, right now he's drunk as a skunk, and they're bringing him pronto. We'll have a line up late tonight if we're lucky, more likely tomorrow."

***

The sketch artist felt more like a pornographer than a professional. The kid had unbelieveable recall of the woman's body, which she sketched naked from different angles, but he had more problems with the face, she wondered how much the kid had looked at his supposed lover's face. Definitely not as much as he had her body. She had a lot of trouble getting it just right. The kid was never quite satisfied, but couldn't articulate what was wrong to fix it. He kept saying sexier, but nothing she did made him say she'd got it. All he'd say about the final drawing was that it was close.

When the artist was through she tapped on the door, a guard came and walked her to Detective Fagan's office, where he took all her drawings as Lief had agreed, and told her to take as long a break as she wanted, then the guard would show her to Amanda Stone for her next sketch.

"Can I go eat dinner first?" she asked in a rather demanding voice. Danny said fine, told the deputy to take Stewart back, he'd get Miss Bowen to Amanda after dinner. There was a decent diner within walking distance. Danny was hungry, so he offered to go with her. His covert desire was to learn if Stewart was playing make believe, or describing a real person.

There had been nothing left for me to do, so I'd gone home. I was drained on several levels, and looked forward to some rest time back at the nest. After dinner Laura called in, described a full itenerary, and I told her I'd call her if anything earth shattering happened. She told me she'd see me in a couple of days, three at the most, which was fine, considering the new Samantha development which I didn't, couldn't tell her about, yet.

The phone rang again, it was the in-house ring from next door. "Where's your beautiful new girlfriend, where's your pickup? You haven't run her off already, have you?" Betty was kidding, laughing as she finished.

"Well Betty, she's not my girlfriend, at least not yet, and yes I did lend her my wheels."

"Sounds like love to me."

"Or being a good host. What's up?"

"First off, I want my husband back. He's doing your job and his. I don't see him much anymore, do you?"

"Not much." I had to admit. I missed him too.

"And you know I don't want him working those titty bars, that's your end, not his."

"Yes Betty, but he's not doing the clubs, he's just finishing up on some of his stuff, and some of mine. It'll get more normal soon."

"I doubt that. Mosby's Rangers are due here this weekend. Four of those loonies, in the lake cabin. I asked him to cancel, you know what he said?"

"No fuckin' way."

"No fuckin' way." She said it with a resigned accepttance. "Well don't let them see Laura, they'll go nuts. I won't have them behaving like adolescent maniacs. They're grown men with gray hair still acting like they're twenty and refusing to grow up, but hey, that's just my opinion." She paused, "It's not like I don't love those crazies, but we've got kids now."

"When do they get in?" It would be nice to know, especially if Samantha was here. They could be potential guard dogs - let loose the dogs of war. Shakespear got in right for these boys, they were dogs, and they were warriors.

"Thursday afternoon, evening. You know I love those guys, but all that gunfire, and the explosions, it scares the little ones. Think you could get them to hold it down some this time?"

"I'll try." Which is what John and I say every time. "Betty, the only time those boys ever get real quiet is when you out shoot them. Why don't you challenge them all, and if you win, make them babysit the whole weekend. That would keep them busy."

"Just because I can out shoot you and my old man, and I got lucky once and beat Gordy and the rest of those loudmouths, doesn't mean I'll always beat Gordy and the two snipers. They are snipers, you know their mentality, their slogan says it all - one shot, one kill, no remorse, I decide. And they train, I don't even practice."

"Yeah," I agreed, "but what have you got to lose?"

She laughed, said "Later," and clicked off. Come Thursday night my brother and I would have the most skillfull, most deadly people I've ever known in my checkered life, as a private army. Not neccessarily the sanest group, but definitely the deadliest.

***

Leif had come and brought Amanda dinner while she and Miss Bowen worked on a sketch of Honey Delight. Then he left. Kentucky fried, a ton of it, with all the fixins, for her and Stewart both, who was in a holding cell nearby. Something was going on. Leif had an investigator on the case, who learned her real name was Holly Delight, at least in the hotel's records. All that really meant was she had an ID with that name on it. The police had found no records of a Holly Delight of New Orleans either.

Miss Bowen was finishing the sketch of Honey, getting real close. Stewart was already through with his sketch, and Leif was dealing with the Assistant DA.

"That's it, Miss Bowen, you've got her. That's Honey Delight." Amanda was pleased, it was a good likeness.

"Great." She'd had a long day spent around some wierd people. Home, her cat, and a cup of herbal tea, seemed like an oasis of serenity and sanity.

As Miss Bowen walked out Leif walked in, pissed.

"Damn. I'm sorry Amanda, it seems every time I make progress this bull headed Fagan gets in the way. He won't let you and Stewart see each other's drawings, or talk to each other. Not yet. The ADA won't cooperate fully, either. They say we're welcome to go public trying to find Raquel and Honey, once they give us the nod. But even if we do, it won't seem very credible to those inclined against us, and it can always be cast in a bad light - cash for an alibi. Fagan will release the drawings to us tomorrow or the next day, after the lie detector tests and after you, Stewart, Kevin, and I have a sit down with Diaz, Fagan, et al. Any questions? I have to rush, Stewart's parents are here back from Europe."

"Not this second, but thanks for dinner. You got no idea how bad the food here can be."

Lief shook hands with Amanda and left. Lief, who had been a dork, dweeb, nerd, geek growing up hadn't really had that much of a social life until after law school and some early successes. He made eye contact with Amanda as he always did. She was rough around the edges, but undeniably sexy.

***

Danny watched Lief Wilmington and Assistant DA Diaz get Mr. and Mrs. Faulkner-Davis past the corrections officers with the most desultry of searches he'd ever seen. The guard glanced in her bag, and looked them over, and they went in. Who says wealth and privilege can't buy a different form of treatment in our legal system, Danny thought to himself – well, almost no one. No one with any sense.

Back in his office, Danny thought about his first impression, the kid's parents were fruitcakes. Wealthy people, shallow at depths, who thought the high life was one big party for the elect who paid others to do everything, and did nothing but satisfy themselves. Glitzy Americans mixing with Eurotrash. Aristoracy wannabes. They were not an appealling couple, but what mistake did they commit to breed such a monster? Apathy? Danny wasn't going to solve the nature/nurture debate that he and Spooky kicked around sometimes, so he went back to his desk and looked at the sketches. Nobody he knew. He was more than curious to see how the lie detector tests would go the next day, and what Juan Valdez had to say.

***

ADA Diaz left them in interview two and went to talk to Fagan. Lief settled in next to Stewart across from his parents. Alexi Faulkner-Davis was a beautiful woman, Lief thought to himself, or at least had been at one time. Years of too much alchohol, prescription pills, late night or all weekend partying, and exposure to too much sun had taken its toll. She and Biff had that George Hamilton tanned to the bone look. They were still attractive at a distance, good looking, well mannered, sophisticated, but up close, it was a different story. Life in the fast lane, for way too long.

The guard left the room and locked the door. Alexi reached out and grabbed her son's hands. "Stewie, are you all right? We came as fast as we could. How did you get yourself in such a mess? You've misbehaved before, but you've never been locked up. Is it our fault, I always wondered if maybe we shouldn't have travelled so much? But we got you the best nannies money could buy. Stewie, tell your Mummy everything's going to be all right, and that this is all just one big mistake."

Stewart had sat there the whole time, didn't even try to get a word in. What would be the point? When his mummy finally came up for air, he mimicked her words. "It might end up being all right. I didn't do what they say, but we've got to find our alibi witnesses and figure out who is behind it all. I'm being framed, so are Amanda Stone and and Kevin Jackson. Amanda has been, like, a lot of help."

Alexi looked at Leif, while Biff was wooden and quiet, staring down at the table. Leif met Alexi's eyes. "Stewart's accessment is accurate. He will take a lie detector test tomorrow which will go a long way towards establishing his innocence in the DA's mind. We've got sketches of the alibi witnesses, we've got an important meeting set up for tommorrow or the next day, and by Friday, Stewart's innocence may be apparrent and he may never be charged with murder. We can plea bargain the false statements charge down in exchange for some court ordered and monitored therapy. You and Biff will have to be patient, just as Stewart must be. Because of your family, we are getting much more cooperation than is normal. If we are patient and a little lucky, this may all work out for the best." By that Lief meant getting his client out of trouble and into therapy. Much, intense, long-term therapy.

***

Williams and Potts called in and told Danny they weren't going to make it in time to do anything that night. Juan was starting to bitch about wanting a drink, maybe changing his mind about cooperating. He said he could definitely recognize one of the two women in a line up, and could probably identify pictures of either one. But who knows, he's a drinker. They stopped, bought a six pack and some Tylenol PM, got a room, and would be in by midmorning. Danny told them to make sure they didn't lose Juan, but also make damn sure he was sober in the morning.

***

At 11:45 PM Phineas went into his bathroom and began his nightly thirty minute shower. Unless he had specific other plans, or was drinking, he was a man of habit. It was what Samantha had depended on. All night she had tried to stick to her routine, behaving as normally as anyone could who's a day shy of fifteen, takes part in ritual black magic, and has incestuous sex with her sado-masochistic uncle - an uncle responsible for one of the most horrendous and public crimes in state history. Yeah, she though to herself, I'm acting as normal as could possibly be expected.

She went down the steps sockfooted, silently. She went to the bookshelf to perform the routine she had practied many times when he was away. But there was a problem. The sound, would it be audible in his shower, would it cause vibrations in the house that he could feel in his shower? The inital unlocking sound, and the final closing sound were more than just sounds, they generated vibrations that could be felt as well as heard throughout parts of the house. If he caught her, he'd kill her. Blood simple. If he caught her, she was dead.

She was glad Phineas was not the sensitive or intuitive kind. He might fancy himself a satanic high priest, a ritual black magician, but he was certainly no psychic. He had explained to her that magicians commanded spirits and forces, whereas psychics sensed and felt things. Traditionally a magician would have a sensitive or two to work with, but Phineas didn't think it was neccessary, or hadn't found the right one yet, or was grooming her for the role. Whatever, she was glad he wasn't psychic. All she had to fear was the sound and vibrations when the electric locking mechanism unlocked or engaged.

She could hear him singing when she'd gone by his room. Hopefully he was still singing opera at the top of his lungs. She stood there in the libray, gloves on both hands, her backpack at her feet, with her hand on the tail of one of the decorative wooden griffins which adorned the library's mahogany shelves. She listened one last time and heard nothing, held her breath and pulled down on the griffin's tail with her left hand and reached into the lowest shelf's corner with her right. Her index finger found and pressed up on the small circular indention and the lock released, seemingly one of the loudest sounds she'd ever heard in her life. It sounded like a huge explosion sending out earthquake like shock waves as the lock released and the complete section of the wall, floor to ceiling opened inward about eight inches. She pushed in with her gloved hand and opened the wall/door. With her other hand she reached down and grabbed her backpack, pulled the pocket flashlight out, turned it on, put it in her mouth, and moved inside.

She couldn't risk the smell of candles or the time they required. The electric lock which secured

the chamber was the only thing electric near the ritual area, all light inside was from real flames,

real candles, as tradition dictated. The ritual chamber was all black, with a small ante room

leading into the ritual area. She walked quickly to her altar, covered by an old ornate fringed

shawl.   Her heart pounded wildly as she removed from the

her backpack a large plastic thermal coffeee mug, a long kitchen knife, a small cardboard box,

and a foot long stick, a straight pine branch from outside. All of which she had repeatedly wiped

clean of prints. She lifted the shawl that served as her altar cloth off her altar. Her altar was to the

left, Phinnie's to the right, both facing a wall sized goat of Mendes in an upside down pentagram.

She put her chalice, athame, pentacle, small gong, and phallic wand in her bag. She had already

wiped off the altar and the candelabras in an earlier forray. She had not dared to remove her

magical weapons until the last possible moment. She arranged the cup, knife, box, and branch on

her altar so that with the shawl upon it, it would have the same apperance as before. She looked,

once, twice, the third time, then quickly walked out. She pulled the griffin's tale back up, the

wall closed with a huge noise. She walked as silently and as quickly as possible to her room, and

ditched her backpack. She laid down on her bed and read a school book. Five minutes later

Phineas looked in toweling his bald head and asked if she'd heard anything.

"No, why?"

"A couple of times while I was singing, I thought I heard something, some kind of noise,

but when I quit singing and listened for a few seconds, I didn't hear anything. You're sure you

heard nothing?"

"Maybe it's the water pipes or water heater, something in the plumbing. I've been lying here reading for a long time, haven't heard a thing."

***

Stewart lay there in his bunk with Littl' Bob on the bunk to the left, with Twotone on the bunk above him, and Willie on the bunk at his feet. He couldn't understand half of what his new friends said. They spoke in street talk, eubonics, a kind of language he hadn't been exposed to at private schools. He knew ax meant ask, other than that, he was about lost. He wondered about his decision. There were probably eight to ten Doubleduece to the three Wezenders. Would his new bodyguards really risk their lives to save his, for less than ten dollars worth of food a week? Stewart was in a world he knew nothing about. His lawyer would probably tell his parents everything, and at the very least, he'd end up in therapy. However, therapy at an exclusive pyschiatric treatment center seemed much preferrable to his current residence. He figured he could pass the lie detector test, and now that they had the sketches, maybe Raquel would change her mind and come rescue him.

***

Chapter Fourteen – Wednesday

At the first sound of music from her radio alarm clock Samantha sat straight up in bed, wide awake. She had drifted into a light sleep off and on during the night, but hadn't really ever gone into deep sleep. Today she was about to become free, and put herself in the hands of her new protector. She glanced over at her backpack and her packed suitcase. She was ready. All she had to do was not alarm Phinnie for an hour, have the chaffuer pick her up, and she was done, safe, free. She had been very lucky the whole Washing D.C./summer school/ concert thing came up. It was her perfect way out.

It was still early when I woke up and made my coffee, looked out at the sunrise over the pasture, and thought about Samantha and the secrecy she'd asked for. How could I work for Danny and hide Samantha at the same time? I'd give her maybe a day, maybe 24 hours to tell me why I couldn't tell Danny, and John and Betty were bound to know. There were logistical problems - it's hard to be in two places doing two different things at the same time.

***

After breakfast, correction officers came in and read the roll for morning court. Kevin's name was on the list. He still didn't know if he had a lawyer or not, he'd find out in a few hours. They marched off everybody on the court roll to a holding cell, to wait for the bus.

***

John rolled down the walkway to my house as I poured my second cup of coffee. I opened the door and he rolled on in. "Long time no talk, little brother, what's up with the glamour case?"

"You want the physical evidence side, or my opinion on the spiritual/what the insane fuck really happened side?"

John hesitated a second and thought about it. "Physical first."

So I gave him a breakdown on the suspects and the evidence.

John thought about the four suspects, the mountain of evidence, about Parker not talking or wanting a lawyer, and the other three wanting to take lie detector tests.

"Weird, even on such a weird case, Spooky. What's the spiritual angle?"

"I think we've got the wrong folks. Three out of our four suspects weren't even there and the one that was is the fall-guy. But the setup is solid, the fix is tight, they might all go down for it, doers or not. They're well chosen, not the kind of people who'd generate much public sympathy - hookers, dealers, Satanists, sadists. Except for the Faulkner family, who'd give a damn if these folks got railroaded?"

The phone rang. I started humming "Danny Boy" on the way to the phone.

"What's up Danny?"

"Everything. We've got the Juan Valdez line up this afternoon, and two, maybe three lie detector tests, too. Nothing happening for you this morning, so come in around one, same low profile as yesterday."

"See ya."

I called Leonard, thanked him again for his work at the Sweat Lodge and smoking his Pipe for us every day. I gave him the details of the spiritual skirmish and hearing his wolf spirit howl as I flew away victoriously. He said I'd done the right things so far and to keep the faith. He had my back, spiritually.

Samantha thought about her normal routine and tried to do everything like it was just another morning. Her suitcase and backback waited for her by the front door. One look by Phineas inside her backback and she was wormfood. She thought about how studying

Shakespear had actually changed her vocabulary, then thought, whatever. Coffee, OJ, English muffins with jam, bagels with cream cheese. She and Phineas ate quietly. In his mind they had celebrated her birthday yesterday. He didn't mention it this morning. As the car pulled up, Phineas, still sitting at the breakfast table, wished her good luck at her performances, and said he'd see her Sunday night.

As she put on her backpack and pulled her suitcase out the door, she silently wispered her good wishes to Phineas. "Good luck in hell, asshole." The driver came to get her bag as she closed the door. On that chapter of her life.

***

It was difficult and very frustrating to not tell John about Samantha, but I would as soon as possible. We caught up on our shared workload, all of which he was now doing. We talked about Mosby's Rangers coming.

John was adamant about not cancelling. "Those guys can entertain themselves, I don't know what Betty's worried about. They only come one to three times a year, stay in the cabin, but she freaks every time. A couple of times they got carried away, but I told them two years ago no loud explosions. She still complains. It's the same thing every time."

"Who knows, John, with this crazy case, they may come in handy."

He was in a hurry, so he didn't ask what I'd meant. "The Cheetah II and III both need extra off-duty cops, can you make the calls this morning?" I assured him I would and he was off to work..

***

Kevin sat in the holding cell in the courthouse with the same group he'd ridden over with in the bus. They were all shackeled - handcuffed with the footcuffs chain running up through the handcuffs resulting in small shuffle steps. Most of them considered it overkill, the police and court security didn't.

A small dark man with curly black hair, a little portly, came with a cop and stood in front of the cell. "Kevin Jackson, Mr. Kevin Jackson."

"Yo. I'm Jackson."

"I'm Gary Goldstein, your attorney. They're going to give us a few minutes to go over your case."

The deputy opened the door, let Kevin out, and led him, shuffling slowly, and Goldstein to a bench across from his desk. The deputy said, "Talk quietly, this is the best privacy I can give you under the circumstances." Assistant DA Diaz had called down and instructed the deputies to let Jackson meet with his lawyer. So they were, Diaz didn't say how or where, that was the deputy's call. This was safest and easiest.

"Mr. Jackson, they're going to arraign you on drug charges, 6 ounces of narcotics, and a gun charge, illegal possession of a firearm by a convicted felon, and interfering with the execution of a search warrant. They are not going to charge you with murder today. They will give you the oppurtunity to take a lie detector test, and they will allow, possibly even assist Miss Stone's and Stewart Faulkner-Davis' lawyer, Lief Wilmington, to search for the two alibi witnesses. I've talked to Assistant DA Diaz, several reporters, and Lief Willmington. You won't get bail this hearing, because you're an obvious candidate for the three time loser law. Your hope should be that you will not be charged for murder, and that you get bail at the next hearing. Possibly I can find some procedural flaw and get you off on a technicality at your trial."

"Tell me everything you know about this case quickly." Kevin was tired of not knowing.

In no time at all his head was reeling. "Fatboy" Gary Parker was the fourth one suspected in the murder. That explained all the weird shit Gary told him at the lake. Gary was set up, too. Whoever this Stewart kid was, Amanda seemed to be working with him, hopefully to clear them all. By the end of the conversation some things made more sense, but not enough. He needed to meet with Amanda, he needed to see the sketches. "So, what're they offering again?"

Goldstein went over it slowly. "They will not charge you with murder at this time. They will let you take a lie detector test. They will let you work with Wilmington's sketch artist. Then they want a grand inquisition. All four of you, represented by counsel, with ADA Diaz and the police task force. If you all pass the lie detector tests and can come up with composite sketches you all agree on, and can establish your alibi, they want your help finding the real perpetrators. Doing that could help us get a reduced sentence on your drug and weapon charges."

Kevin wanted the real perpetrators too, wanted them six feet under, after they suffered some long and arduous hours. Somebody was fucking with the wrong person, and they would *pay*.

***

It was just one small suitcase on rollers. She wouldn't let the chauffer bring it into the school for her. He understood. Samantha went directly to the orchestra room and left her suitcase and went on to her homeroom with her backpack still on. After checking in, she and the rest of the orchestra members destined for D.C. were given their homeroom time free to hand in work and get assignments for the days they'd miss.

Samantha's last stop was the art room. She handed in three drawings due Friday. On the way out she stopped at the big round garbage can. Most rooms had trash cans, only the cafeteria and the art room had large garbage cans. The can had paint, clay, broken frames, tons of half sketches, all the debris generated by two hundred young artists and goof-offs a day. She opened her backpack, took out some wads of paper and threw them in, then a brown crumpled up grocery bag. She pushed it in, under the paint and gooh until only the top inch of the bag remained exposed. Then she went back to her homeroom.

After homeroom, the students going on the trip went to the orchestra room for one last rehersal of both shows and then the packing of their instruments. At 9:30 she got up, spoke briefly to the conductor, and left. She waited at the parking lot door, standing just inside the building, looking out the wired glass window of the back door. Two boys from the art class brought the garbage can out past her and dumped it in the dumpster. Six minutes later the four cans from the cafeteria were rolled out by two janitors and dumped into the dumpster. It worked just as planned. She'd interviewed the head custodian, supposedly for a report on waste management, and gotten tons of unneccessary information, and a few vital pieces.

She would watch out the window in the band room for the truck that would soon come, empty the dumpster and take her problems away. As she watched the truck drive away twenty-three minutes later, she felt an incredible sense of relief. She breathed out, fully, not even aware she'd been holding her breath while she watched the truck lift the dumpster over the cab and pour its contents in with all the other trash. Relieved, she turned her attention back to the music.

***

I didn't bother with a parking place, I just pulled up by the curb. I rode my scooter to our lot and traded for one of our city auction detective cars. Judging from the SUV's, beamers, and Porshes, this was the student parking lot for this affluent private school. I knew nobody would bother a cop car. Which is just what this one had been before we bought it, and replaced the equipment the cops stripped. In fact, this car and the one Parker manned at the crime scene were very similar.

I put my gold badge in one of my many leather cases, this time across from my APD picture ID I have for access when working there. Her teacher was much more likely to let her go with a cop than a PI. It wasn't totally dishonest, I currently was working for APD, but to the untrained eye, I would appear to be an APD detective. I would do nothing to dissuade that impression. I had on my gun and handcuff case, so I looked the part of a detective who sometimes does undercover work - with my hair pulled back in a ponytail. If worse came to worse and I got busted by the teacher, I'd just call Danny and try to square it. But that wasn't neccessary.

I found the orchestra door following her intructions and looked in through the glass. The scene was chaotic, students moving around with instruments and cases. I just walked on in. As soon as I did Samantha walked up quickly, grabbed my arm and lead me to the conductor.

"Mr. Allison, this is the man I told you about, can we talk in your office?"

We walked over to a small office in the corner by the door. I noticed all the glass was closed off with curtains. She introduced me to Mr. Allison as Detective Mosby. We shook hands, he seemed very nervous. I noticed a slight tremble to his hand, a crack on the edge of his voice. If he was a suspect in an interrorgation room, I'd have tagged him as guilty on sight.

"Samantha has told me that this involves witness protection circumstances and must be hush hush, but if you don't mind, I'd like to check your ID and at least have a contact phone number."

That seemed reasonable, but Samantha looked pissed off by it. I flipped open and handed him the ID and badge, he looked at it and wrote down my name.

"If any friend or relative contacts you to speak with her, no matter the circumstances or story they tell, even if it's a close relative, you say she's with another chaperone and it'll take some time, and you take their number."

I took his pen and paper and wrote down a number. "This is my cell number. I usually keep it in my vehicle and don't leave it on, but under the circumstances it will be with me and on. You call this number, and you will reach me immediately. Then Samantha can call whoever is looking for her back. It is imperative to protect her cover during the entire trip. APD or GBI will take over openly afterwards. We appreciate your cooperation, this is an urgent and dangerous matter."

I handed him back the paper while Samantha just looked more and more impatient. As soon as he looked down at the phone number and nodded she said forcefully, "That's it Phillip, it's time for us to go. Now!" She turned and walked toward the door, throwing her backpack on one shoulder. He flinched a little when she spoke, seemed scared of her, of me, offf something. I looked once more at the shaky and in my mind rather sketchy conductor and headed out the door to catch up. I walked quickly, pulled up beside her, and opened the school's back door and pointed to my car.

She looked at me, still pissed about something. "You didn't have to give him all that information. I own him!" Samantha got in the front, dropped her backpack on the floorboard in front of her, I put the suitcase in the trunk, got in behnd the wheel and headed home. It was the safest place I could think of for her, besides my office, but there she'd be way too visible.

She repeated herself. "You didn't have to tell him all that."

"How do you own him? I'm prettty sure slavery is illegal."

"He's married, he's a teacher, and I have a video, a very sexy video. He's one of the stars."

"And you're the other star." I didn't ask, I asummed. She looked over at me, no longer so hostile, more at ease, like I understood.

"We live in an evil, predatory world." She said it as a statement of fact, way beyond her years. It seemed a complete explanation about her, the conductor, and the video. I let the subject go. We had other fish to fry.

I glanced sideways over at her. She was wearing black pants, a short sleeve white blouse, and a black vsest. Some fourteen-year olds look twelve, some twenty. She was the latter. Including my school days, she was the most fetching fourteen, almost fifteen-year old I'd ever seen, except for one. I imagined she was quite the high school femme fatale. If I'd been a teenager who knew nothing about her and saw her on the street, I'd have been interested; but thankfully, I was old enough to be her father.

"Samantha, what I'm doing here in secret may not be so good for my career. I'm investigating the crime I assume you have some information on. If our current suspects don't pan out, who knows, you may be a suspect. You see where I'm going here. You're fourteen..."

"No, I'm fifteen. Today. Today's my birthday."

Things hadn't been very friendly so far, I'd try a little charm."Well happy birthday, Samantha." I meant it. She might be mixed up, she might be crazy, possibly even partly evil. But she was still a child, at least somewhat, and I didn't have the visceral reaction to her I had with Kevin. If she was a lost soul on the side of evil, I didn't sense it was a done deal. But I've been wrong before. Oh man, have I been wrong before.

She smiled at me. It was the sweetest expression I'd seen on her face so far, and it was genuinely nice. She said, "I have a whole bunch to tell you, but I can't at once. I've got to trust you first, know that you'll protect me. Know that I can trust you more than I ever have anyone before in my life. Do you understand?"

"I do. But how do I know that I can trust you, that you'll tell me the truth?"

"You'll have to. I'm the key to solving your case."

***

Kevin was denied bail. Goldstein asked if the bail issue could be addressed again Friday. ADA Diaz was all for it, so the judge agreed. Kevin went back on the bus, relieved he had a lawyer, that his business partner was standing by him, and anxious to see Amanda and Gary, check out the kid, and work with an artist on Honey's sketch. Not to mention take a lie detector test. He had a full dance card to be on the inside.

***

We didn't talk about the case on the way home. Mostly she asked personal questions, how long had I been a PI, did I like my work, was I married, did I have a girlfriend, why was I a specialist for APD, what exactly was my specialty? She was full of questions, which was okay, it made the ride fast, and if she was in danger like she said, and I believed, she had a right to know something about who she came to for protection.

The only problem I had was with the girlfriend question. It was too early to say it yet, but it was on the way with Laura. I told her no, but I had recently started seeing someone, but it hadn't gone that far yet. It was the only answer that seemed to displease her. Which worried me some.

***

Detectives Potts and Dick Williams showed up at APD with Juan Martinez sober, but there were problems. He didn't know if he could recognize both girls' faces, but he could recognize the shorter one's body. They went around and round with that one until Juan cleared it up, a little. He had been drinking some that night, had a drink with the three of them and then the two girls disrobbed as his tip. They walked him to the door. He remembered Absolut and Chevas, their order, knew there was a man and two women, one taller woman and one shorter, and there was something, a birthmark or some moles around one of the shorter one's breats, something that reminded him of Mexico, Texas, something, he'd know it when he saw it.

Danny thought about how he jokingly had pictured the line up. Juan drunk with naked hookers to recognize. His joke was closer to the truth than he liked. A line-up of women willing to show their breasts in the cause of justice. He didn't know, but he shook his head just thinking about it. He'd call Spooky on that one.

***

Annie Wilson and Potts went into the holding cell at APD where Amanda had been brought from jail. They exlpained to Amanda what was up. She erupted with happiness when she found out Juan was in the building. Then they asked her if she would take down the top of her jumpsuit and expose herself, if it would help in verifying Juan's story. Since nudity was part of her professions, no bigee, she skinned down. Both Wilson and Potts looked closely at her right breast, and there was a birthmark on the lower side of her right breast. Amanda took her hand and lifted her breast, showing off the red birthmark roughly in the shape of Texas. Not perfect, but damn close.

"What, I showed Juan my birthmark, I forgot, but yeah, I always show it to Texans, Mexicans, anybody from the southwest." She yelled "Yes!" and bounced, then seemingly circulated her nipples to the left and then the right; exhibiting an amount of control of her breasts that both Potts and Wilson would have just as soon have not witnessed.

***

I didn't know how to tell Samantha I couldn't watch her all the time. Not every minute. She seemed fixated on me as her protector, but I had work to do for APD. Although I believed her when she said she could crack the case; I still had to do my job. I'd give her twenty-four hours before I'd tell Danny, but John the Boss and Betty, they'd have to know.

I'd made a point of showing her our security gate, the first fence and razor wire and the inner electric fence. When we went in to my house I called Betty to let her know I had a guest and was concerned for her safety and was about to switch on the fence. I also asked her to okay it with me before she buzzed in anybody. Either house could be buzzed from the box at the security gate so that a button could be pushed in either house to open the gate. I went to the box on the wall next to the door and turned on the electric fence. Every time it turned on, ten seconds before the charge flowed, a warning horn blew loudly four times.

I hadn't gotten to the say the part about having to leave her when the phone rang. Danny told me about the three lie detector tests, the huge meeting with everyone involved if they passed the tests, and that he needed me to pick up five strippers to bring in for a line-up. I looked at Samantha, she was watching me like an owl. So I called Betty back, asked if her oldest girl could watch the kids for a second while she came over, and would she bring her Berretta with the silencer.

"Look, it's simple, Samantha. You know what my job is, I work for Triple S which provides security for your family and I'm Under contract with APD as a technical expert. Chief investigating officer Detective Fagan needs me and expects me right now. I have a contractural obligation to go. No other human being on this planet knows where you are. Nobody. I have to go to work for APD, for a few hours. I could take you with me to APD Homocide, but you'd be recognised, have your picture taken by the press, something would go wrong. Not to mention my APD boss not being told about you yet, which might get me fired. I could leave you at Triple S headquarters, but I really think you'd be safer here, and I'll come back as soon as possible. I'd like to leave you here, with all the alarm systems on, protected by my sister-in-law. I trust her as much as I trust anyone in this world, and she's one of the best people I know. I wouldn't think of leaving you here if I wasn't totally confident about your security. Now is not the time to worry, if I can't tell Fagan about you sometime in the next day or two, and the bad guys start missing you, then start worrying. For now, it's cool."

Samantha did not look pleased. Betty knocked, I introduced Betty but didn't give Samantha's name, which Betty immediately picked up on. I grabbed four beer cans out of my recycling bin and headed outside. I stood them up about fifty feet from the women, walked back and asked Betty to shoot them.

"Which way do you want them to jump?"

"Two up to the right, two up to the left."

I'd seen this trick too many times to have much doubt.

She checked and made sure the silencer was screwed on tight, flicked off the safety, and jacked one into the chamber. Samantha watched, intensely. Starting with the right outside can, Betty shot, puff,… puff, the first can jumped two feet high to the right with the first shot, she hit it in midair with the second shot, making it fly backwards. Again, puuf, puuf, the inside right can jumped and was popped midair. The outside left and inside left, puff, puff, puff, puff. Every can launched and hit midair. Launching the can is hard enough, but hitting it in midair, too! It was impressive, I sure as hell couldn't do it. I do fine in combat shooting, way above average, but not small target and trick shooting. Hell, Betty could be in the circus, or go back to competeing nationally and internationally any time she wants to. She's got a wall full of trophies and medals, but she says she's just too busy with the kids and all, and that she really doesn't miss it.

Betty swiched the safety on and slid the gun in the holster on the back of her belt. She must have known I wanted her to impress the unintroduced stranger. "Betty, I've sworn to protect this young woman and right now nobody on Earth knows she's here, not even John or Danny. She's made me promise it would be that way until she tells me her story. I've got to go right now and work for Danny, it's imperative, Danny wants me to do a hundred things, immediately. I feel she would be safer and lower profile here than anywhere. Nobody knows she's here. Nobody.

"Betty just smiled and said, "Sure. But she stays with me and the kids."

"It's her birthday. The kids can have fun with that." I threw in.

"Sure, my seven year old loves to bake, and the twins and baby love to eat, we'll have a birthday party. That settles that. "

I stood directly in front of Samantha, put a hand on each arm and looked into her eyes. And let her look into mine. "I wouldn't leave you here if it wasn't safe. I'll be back in two or three hours, four at the most, and then I won't leave your side till you've told me your story and we decide what to do."

She wasn't happy, but she sensed a genuine concern. She did something surprising, she kissed me on the cheek. "I'll wait here, you go do your job, but come back quickly." The kiss, of course, bothered me, but she was a kid, and scared, so I smiled and began to leave.

Samantha joined Betty, who took her by the arm and guided her towards her house. Samantha still had her backpack on. Betty looked back at me and called out, "I expect you to explain all this to your brother, that's not my job. And no hesitation, you need to tell him."

"Yes, Ma'am."

***

The lunch crowd had thinned out at the 24K Club so I talked to my friend the manager. The day shift would pick up and get busy again at happy hour, but the lull until then was serious. I asked him to talk it up like an adventure and fulfilling a civic responsibility, while at the same time it might also help clear a fellow exotic dancer from being wrongly charged with a serious offense, and $25 each. He did a great job, then I had to find five girls with some kind of birthmark or mole, or any oddity around the breasts. Some had to remove copious amounts of the body makeup they use to cover up just the kind of imperfections I was looking for. I've had worse jobs. I settled on the best five, one with a small birth mark under her right breast, one with a large birthmark to the side of her left breast. One with three small moles forming a triangle between her breasts, one with a heart tatoo on her left breast, and one with pierced nipples and gold nipple rings. I asked them to change into their street clothes. Five girls in a cop car, so I pulled around back, the reporters staking out the front door would have been blind not to notice my companions if I'd gone in there.

Danny hadn't succeded in keeping the line-up a secret. When I walked the five girls through the major crimes section, the men applauded and screamed their approval of the girls' sense of civic responsibility. Some of the cops were awarded a wink or a psuedo-flash for their ovation. I brought the girls to the back, Danny was waiting, pissed at the noise and attention, but he tried to be nice.

"Ladies, we appreciate ya'll coming down and doing this, I'm sure Spooky told you when you're through the city pays you each $25. But I need to remind y'all that this is serious, real serious. You girls are all professsional performers. Your performance during this line-up is to act serious, because the stakes here are really high. Whether or not someone is charged for murder is being determined here. That's as serious as it gets. Detective Potts will tell you what to do."

Danny and I left to go watch Juan Valdez look at titties and see if he remebered Amanda. What a country.

When we got to the viewing room, Williams and Martinez weren't there yet, but a crowd of cops sure was. Annie Wilson hadn't even tried bulling her way in. She was waiting by the door, arms crossed, tapping her left foot impatiently. Wallace and Schultz were in the back, jammed in by lots of folks not on the case. Danny went off on them.

"EVERYONE NOT ON MY TASK FORCE HAS THREE SECONDS TO LEAVE THE AREA BEFORE DISCIPLINARY ACTION IS TAKEN! ONE! TWO! THREE!"

Not everybody made it out in time, but they were moving quickly enough that they were all gone seven seconds later. Danny motioned with his hand for Annie to go in, ladies first and all. Potts showed up a few seconds later, having left the line-up to a female uniformed officer, she just missed the commotion. She was wearing her APD sweatsuit. Nobody had let Amanda put on the clothes she went into the system with, they'd brought her straight over. It would be a little too obvious if only one girl wore jailhouse whites. So Potts gave up her clothes. Williams brought Juan Martinez into the viewing room, Danny took the mike, and the show was on.

For the first time in days the whole task force was together. It was too bad Laura wasn't with us. She missed a fascinating piece of modern police work. All six came in, and opened their tops. Amanda was fourth of six. Danny had each one come to the mirror, do a left turn, right turn, frontal, and lift each breast by hand. Juan looked intensely, with no show of humor, he was serious. He kept looking over at Amanda. When she walked up he started nodding his head, when she lifted her breast and he could see the birthmark, he yelled. "That's it, she has Texas under her titty. I remember now, Texas under her titty. He had to look at the other two girls, and look at all of them in a lineup, front and left and right, but Juan knew.

Danny knew things were getting complicated. This would never be used legally, for anything, this whole show was just to prove to Danny that at least Amanda, and probably Kevin might actually have real alibis. He decided the city was compensating Juan for his time by the day, so he should take a lie detector test, to prove Juan didn't know any of the players already incarcerated. Danny was beginning to believe there might be a whole other set of players out there, who had set these doofs up and were trying to fool him. Satanic murderers who assumed they could manipulate and play APD. Danny would get these fuckers. And may God have no mercy on their souls.

I needed to talk to Danny alone sometime soon, I hadn't had much chance to sublety guide anything since the two O.B.E.'s, and there was the Samantha issue I had to lay the groundwork for.

***

Samantha had not spent any time around people like Betty, and she liked what she saw. She felt a warmth in their family setting that she had never known as a child. It made her sentimental over what she had missed. Katey, seven, the two and a half year old twins Hunter and Hudson, and the baby Rachel, were all quite excited over their new friend Sam's birthday. (Sam was easier for the twins to say.) Betty was busy making a cake while the older three were making birthday cards and decorations, and in general a mess, which didn't seem to bother Betty at all. Rachel started crying in her high chair, Bettty wiped her hands, picked up Rachel and depositied her in Samantha's arms. The baby smiled at Samantha, made eye contact and gave her the happy baby look. Something happened in Samantha's heart at that moment, she felt something hard in her crack, like a dam bursting, and a flood of emotions overcame her.

Emotions she had not experienced before in this lifetime, a love of that baby, a love of all babies,

a love of humanity, a maternal love of life. A feeling that began in her innermost primal instincts,

but reached to her highest spiritual virtue.

She thought about the last time she was around an infant, and tears began to roll

down her face. She held the baby on her chest and walked her around, patting her back gently,

the baby looking over her shoulder behind her, so Rachel wouldn't see Samantha cry. After she

walked the baby around a few minutes, tears quietly pouring from her eyes, weeping silently, she

heard the baby snore. Sure enough baby Rachel had gone to sleep. She laid her down in the

playpen in the livingroom, then just stood there, looking down on the baby, weeping. She began

shaking, still crying quietly, but harder. Betty noticed while the kids were still busy. She didn't

want Sam to scare the kids, so she took Samantha by the arm and walked her out the sliding glass

door into the side yard.

Betty walked her through the flower garden to the white gazebo and sat her down

on the padded outdoor sofa. Betty sat down beside her, put her arm around her, patted her gently,

and let the girl cry. Not since she had been a young teenager and watched so many boys she'd

known come back in body bags from Nam, not since those days outside the V.A. hospitals, not

since then had she seen any human cry their eyes out like this poor girl. Every now and then she

murmered things, some of which Betty got, some she didn't.

"I've done some terrible, terrible things... I didn't want to, I had to...only way to get my

broth...really terrible, horrible things...I couldn't...he pushed my hands...gave me drugs... guided

my hands but I didn't stop...didn't run...didn't seem real...had to get my brother ba...."

After several long minutes Betty was starting to worry about the kids when she realised the girl in her arms had quit crying, and, emotionally exhausted, had shut down and gone to

sleep. Just like a baby, Betty guided the child down to let her keep sleeping, then went back in

the house.

***

Before I drove the dancers back, I told Danny I needed some one on one time, real soon.

He told me he hadn't had lunch yet and was going to take a break, then it was lie detector test,

test, test, test, then the big meeting. Break time was it, and he didn't even have time to go out. I

dropped the girls off, went by and got some Zesto's burgers, and headed back to APD.

Danny closed the door behind me when I walked in. Grabbed his food, "What's up,

Spooky?"

"It depends. It depends on whether you like our current suspects, or want to go back to

some of our original suspicions. If you like our current batch, you may be in for a long and

disappointing day. My intuitive…hunch is that Gary Parker was there, if he actually knows

anything or was just set up as a fall-guy, who knows yet. I doubt he knows anything, seems

perfect for a dumdass patsy. My intuitive hunch is that Amanda isn't one of ours, I despise

Jackson but I doubt Jackson is either, I'm not sure about Stewart yet. I feel there were five perps,

of which Parker was one. Three on the inside doing the ritual, a doorman, and Parker on the

street. Whether any of the remaining three we have in custody were involved, I have my doubts,

serious doubts."

"After what we just saw in the line-up I don't consider that earth shattering insight at this

point. But you think this why?" Danny was curious.

"You could say I had a vision, saw it in my crystal ball, whatever, I know it's not

evidence, I don't expcect you to understand or believe, but at the end, we'll be looking at the not so good doctor again. Did you ever get the list of inmates he's worked with, details about the project ADA Diaz talked about?"

"Not yet, things got so busy with Stewart Sunday night, and all the rest on Monday, it went to being on a back burner."

"It might need to be moved up to the front some time soon."

"Okay, that is noted and taken under advisement. Let's go see another line-up and watch the lie detector tests."

Juan was not so exact with Kevin as he had been Amanda. He narrowed it down to Kevin and the guy that most resembled Kevin. "I never paid no attention to the hombre, juz' the weemen." He did even worse with a sketch line up, Honey's sketch thrown in with some from the sketch artist's portfolio. Looking at the sketches, Juan didn't have a clue.

But Juan aced the lie detector test. He was ranked as completely truthful – he did meet Amanda, and a taller woman, and a guy in the hotel that night on the sixth floor. He did not know Kevin Jackson, Amanda Stone, or a Honey, Holly Delight before he met them that night, and hadn't seen or talked to any of them again until today. Danny watched each question, watched the tester make his red marks on the printout of galvanic skin respones, heartbeat, and respiration. He talked to the tester after each test.

Kevin worked with the sketch artist while Juan and Amanda took the lie detector tests. Amanda breezed through it. She was at the hotel Friday night with Kevin and Honey. She was not at the Faulkner estate. She had never been to the Faulkner estate. She didn't know Juan until Friday night. As far as she knew, Honey worked in New Orleans. No, she had never killed anyone. No, she had never ritually sacrificed a human being. No, No, No, she was not involved.

Kevin finished with the sketch artists and aced most of the test. He was clear that he had been with Amanda and Honey all night Friday. He was clear that he had never been on the Faulkner estate. But when asked about ritual sacrifice and murder, the answers weren't so clear. He had some guilt about something, probably not the crime at hand I guessed, but something. I knew he had ritually sacrificed animals and almost beat a man to death. Maybe he had killed somewhere, sometime, or thought he might have, but didn't do this ritual murder. Afterwards the tester told Danny he'd like to rephrase some questions, test Jackson again tommorrow, see if they could clear things up. Which is what he said about Stewart's test results. Stewart was real clear about where he was that weekend and with whom he'd been. But his answers about murder and ritual sacrifice were not clear. But he was judged truthful when he denied being on the estate that weekend. As they all had been.

***

Samantha woke up, at first didn't know where she was, then remembered. She sat up, scared at first to be alone, then relaxed, taking in the peacefulness of the setting. From the gazebo she could see the horses grazing by the pond, with a few cows, and seven or eight deer, grazing at the edge of the pasture where it met the woods. There were a few puffy white cumulus clouds moving lazily overhead on an otherwise bright sunny afternoon. She stretched out, feeling better at that moment than she had since she began her dark journey with Phineas, better than she had in a long, long time.

***

Jeff Mundy, public defender, had never been called in under circumstances like this before. To represent someone who hadn't asked for an attorney in an open discussion between cops, suspects, an Assistant DA, and defense attorneys, deciding whether or not to charge the suspects at hand with murder, it was all very strange, highly irregular. He looked down on his legal pad, Gary Parker, evidence looked strong, five eyewitnesses, fake police uniform and ID, fake car in front of house, bloodstains in the trunk. Unless there were some major procedural flaws, slam dunk, good-bye Mr. Parker.

ADA Diaz was waiting outside the door; showed him the players. He pointed out his client Gary, in prison whites; Lief Wilmington with Stewart Faulner-Davis and Amanda, likewise in whites; Kevin Jackson in whites with his attorney Gary Goldstein; Detectives Williams and Potts with material witness Juan Martinez; Detectives Wallace and Wilson, and they were waiting for Fagan and Mosby. Mundy was listening to Diaz explain why it was in his client's best interest to come clean and give up any information he had. If his client had some information, Mundy thought, it should buy him some consideration. Reduced sentence, something.

Danny and I went to the big meeting after our quick lunch. Everybody was there. Danny sat at the table facing everybody, I sat to his right, Annie to his left, Wallace remanined standing back behind Annie. Williams and Potts were around Juan, out of habit I suppose.

Danny opened his briefcase. Diaz moved his chair behind the table, back behind mine. Watching the reactions on someone's face can be very revealing, very revealing. You only have one moment sometimes, to catch the look of guilt, surprise, whatever.

Danny took out the sketches, the lie detector results, the lab reports, lots of files. When he put his opened briefcase on the floor he covertly switched on his micro cassette recorder. Just as he started, both Wilmington and Goldstein raised their hands and tried to speak. Goldstein let Lief have the floor. "Before we start, I'd like to go over the ground rules so everybody's clear on them. This is not being recorded, nor adversarial, or formal at all, we're all gathered here voluntarily and informally to share information that may keep the defendants here from being charged with murder and allow them to be released on bail. Is that correct Detective Fagan?"

"Yes. So let's get on with it."

I couldn't help but wonder how many recordings were being made of this non-recorded session. I'd seen Lief's hand move in his briefcase, and Goldstein's too. There would be no formal legal record, but what was said here sure wasn't going to get lost.

Danny kept going. It was his show. "Every defendant here is guilty of what they've been charged with so far. I know that some of you may think the lie detector tests prove you're innocent and protects you from any pending charges of murder. They don't. They are totally inadmissable in a court of law. Gary Parker," Danny looked directly at Parker, "you're going down at the very minimum on the current charges AND conspiracy to commit 1st degree murder. I've got five eyewitnesses put you at the scene, I've got the car in front of your house with your fingerprints all over it and with blood stains in the trunk, the uniform, ID, gun, everything. Son, you are going down hard and have no chance of bail. Your only hope is to tell us something we don't already know and try to buy yourself some leniency with cooperation.

"Kevin, you're a three time loser now, not even considering the murders. You're going down on drugs too, Amanda. Now, concerning the murders, there is a mountain of physical evidence against you all, and all you've got is inadmissable lie detector tests and the word of a drunk Mexican who doesn't remember a whole lot and who got fired that very shift. No offense Juan, but by your own statement you were drinking heavily that night."

Juan agreed, "Si, that's for sure."

Your other alibi witness is still a figment of your imagination by legal standards. Your alibi, too, Stewart, at this point also doesn't exist. Listen up, folks, cause I want you to understand this. Fired drunk bell boys and party-ing hookers do not make believable alibis, right, Mr. Diaz?"

Assistant DA Diaz nodded, "It's true."

"Neither do paid alibis."

Diaz agreed, "That's certainly true."

"In fact, I could charge you all today with the murders and ADA Diaz would probably get guilty verdicts on all of you, easy. If I charge you right now for the sake of political expediency; we'd win on the physical evidence and predjudice against your lifestyles. I have blood from the crime scene on the clothes of a satanic pimp/drug dealer and a satanic druggie hooker. Oh yeah, the jury's gonna love you two. Parker, you're toast, Stewart, too. Don't think we won't. This is a high profile case with financial and political considerations in a city whose economy is convention dependent. Dependent! The 'powers that be' want this thing solved. If you folks think you've been framed, you damn sure need to explain why and by whom. And make it good. We don't want twenty different versions, get it right."

"That's why we need bail. Now!" Kevin wasn't going to let a bunch of legal leeches fuck up his life. He could damn sure speak for himself. "I sure as hell can't find out who's setting us up in a jail cell, now can I?"

"Well, Kevin, why don't you ask your buddy Gary here who set you up? We've got eyewitnesses who put him there. We, at the very, least know for a fact he was there." Danny put it to them, let them work it out. They hadn't seen each other since being arrested, none of the suspects had, except for the manipulated Stewart-Amanda meeting.

Kevin didn't hesitate. "I already know his story, he was set up, too. He thinks the CIA or some CIA entity, or some Mafia family has recruited him. He probably thinks his silence now is the final fucking test. Gary's got a big imagination." Kevin turned and talked directly to Gary, "Shit man, this ain't *Soldier of Fortune!* You've been set up, just like me and Amanda, by the same people and you don't even know it yet. Get out of fantasy land, man. We gotta nail these fuckers, or go down for murder. Fucking Murder!"

Gary sat there, silent. Kevin kept going. "I know how they recruited Gary, he never saw a soul, just got letters he had to burn on his porch. I know how they set up Amanda and me, the fucking honey trap, oldest game in the book. What I don't know is who orchestrated it or why. I'll tell you if you let me out on bail. Amanda too, so we can find out who did this."

"That's not too likely," Danny responded, "it'd take a miracle unless you give us something major that's rock solid."

"Tag me like a migrating animal, put a collar on me, a radio transmitter, whatever, I don't want to rabbit, I want to find out who. Probably worse than you do."

Danny took back over. "That's what we police do. You tell us who, we find them. I've got all your sketches here. I want honest answers. Kevin, do you know this woman?"

Danny held up the sketch of Stewart's Raquel. I thought I saw a flicker of recognition, something, but Kevin didn't hesitate. "I don't know her, she might resemble somebody I've seen around town in the life, but no bells, I don't know her. But if she's in the life, and you let me out, I'll find her."

Danny held the picture towards Amanda, who had been watching Kevin and checking out the picture. She just shook her head, then looked over at Kevin. Danny held it towards Gary too, who shook his head no. Kevin was glad Gary didn't know his stable. Gary was extra muscle on a drug deal, but he kept him away from the ladies.

Danny held up the two sketches of Honey, no recognition from Stewart or Gary. Danny shook his head, laid the pictures down.

Kevin spoke back up. "I can tell you why, I think, but not who."

Danny simply jestured with open palms, encouraging Jackson to enlighten us. Goldstein warned Jackson to ask for immunity if he was about to publicly admit to any past criminal behavior. Better to speak hypotheticaly. Which is what Jackson asked for and was granted, the right to talk about hypothetical crimes. So he talked hypothetically about a young entrepenuer in the pleasure trade who saw and took advantage of certain cinemagraphic oppurtunites. Where one party or their spouse might greatly benefit from the possession of such cinema it was sold. Sometimes sold repeatedly.

"Do you know the names or still have any pictures of these hypothetical people who were hypothetically blackmailed?" Danny cut to the point. "Who were they?"

Kevin shook his head. "I was... hypothetically, the person who did out these things was doing a shitload of drugs some of the time, he can't remember any specific names, and he destroyed all links to the people so there would be no evidence to link him to blackmail. It was five or six times over the space two or three years; seven, eight, ten years ago. But I feel like if I can just get back out on the street and find out who hired our two alibi lovers, I can find out who's behind this. Whoever hired the hooker sent to Stewart and the hooker sent to me and Amanda set us up. I can find out who that is, but only on the streets, I can't locked up here."

Stewart looked down on the floor. He had accepted that Raquel was in on the setup, and probably wasn't married to a rich bussiness man. Somehow it had never hit home before that she was a lowly prostitute.

***

I sat there and watched the spectacle unfold before me, without a word. Having an instinctive antagonism towards Kevin and the evil he served, I didn't like my aura and his even being in the same room, so I'd used the chest high circle of white Light for Protection. Then thought rationally about what he was asking. He had much better access to the world we were interested in than we did. He lived in that world. We might not get to the bottom of the problem any time soon unless we shook the tree. Shaking the tree in this case might mean letting Kevin and Amanda out. I wondered about the flicker of recogonition on Kevin's face. If Kevin and Amanda had recognized the girl, Amanda was following Kevin's lead in saying she didn't recognize her. If they knew her, following them might be the easiest way to track her down. If "poorly funded during hard times" APD didn't have the right equipment, we did.

Wilmington and Goldstein took their best shots at convincing us to let their clients have bail. Danny finally decided that if Kevin and Stewart were lie detector tested again tommorrow and they passed, bail and not filing murder charges were definitely under consideration for everybody but Gary. But they hadn't given us much help so far today. Wilmington stood up. "Detective Fagan, we still haven't addressed the alibi witness issue. We have sketches of the two women. You should allow us to go public. If a reward brings them in, they can tell us who hired them, and lead to a resolution of this matter."

Danny said, "Fine, you go public with these two sketches. Offer any reward you want. You know damn well if you pay these people much money, no jury will give much credence to a word they say."

Wilmington wasn't giving up on his best chance. "If they come in on their own accord, money or no money, will you give them a lie detector test, or at least check out their story for accuracy. We know they exist, and we know someone paid them to do their jobs. If we can find out who hired them, this crime is solved."

Danny paused, he hated the idea of a media circus, but this already was one. Any arrest in this case would draw intense public attention. But if he charged the wrong people with murder he'd look bad, and the city'd look bad. "Okay, I'm going to release the sketches to you, Wilmington. You know damn well if you offer enough money, people of low caliber will come out of the woodworks to claim the reward, willing to tell you anything you want to hear. But go ahead, if Raquel and Honey really exist, I'm eager as hell to interview them. You go right ahead. We'll wait on the bail decision until after the retests tommorrow. No bail on Parker, he needs to tell his story. The rest, we'll wait and see."

Wilmigton said thank you, Goldstein looked happy, and Mundy asked if he could confer with his client. Danny agreed. It wasn't all we may have hoped for, but it was something. We may have finally arrived at the why for the setup.

Wilmington asked if he could hold a press conference immediately. Danny didn't see why not. He handed all the lawyers copies of the two sketches and wished them good luck. "We just want the real perpetrators." He looked at the innmates, "But if we let any of you out on bail, it will be like intensive probation. We will put a radio transmitter on you. If you take it off, bail is revoked. Gary," Danny looked at Gary again, "son, if you know more than Kevin said, you better have a long heart to heart with your mouthpiece. If you're the only one we have on this, you'll go down for the max. Any questions? Okay, we'll see how things go tommorrow. That's it."

Ever since she found out about Pugsley, Tonya had been obsessed with CNN, MSNBC, any news she could get, well, anybody but FOX. She might be a prostitute who didn't finish high school, but she thought the announcers there were stupid, total idiots. She had asked Deseree if she'd seen the news, her answer was negative. Tonya didn't want to act until she knew what to do, so when she wasn't taking classes, she watched the news. When she saw the press conference live with Wilmington, Goldstein, and saw the sketchs of her and Deseree she called Jasmine, and gave her the skinny. Jasmine got Deseree, and before the press conference was over, all three women were in Tonya's room, watching.

Deseree was dismayed, but Jasmine was pissed, really pissed. "That son of a bitch told me it was no big deal. A simple job. Murder is not simple. Carl, George, whatever the fuck his real name is, has screwed with the wrong woman. Pack your bags, ladies. NOW!"

***

Wilmington was emphatic, Stewart needed a bath. If he passed the lie detector test tommorrow, he'd get bail, by that night or Friday. Stewart needed to be ready to meet the press. The real reason was Wilmington couldn't take it any more, the kid stank. So when Stewart got back, he went to his bunk to get his bodyguard before showering. Littl' Bob and Willie were playing hearts with two other innmates, so Bob told Twotone to be Stewart's escort to the shower. Twotone said in a minute. Stewart looked around for the Double Duece and saw one of them nearby and a few of them scattered around. The one near them walked away. Stewart didn't see all of them, but Twotone told him to hang on he'd be ready in a minute.

It wasn't a long walk, away from the bunks, take a left, into the bathroom area, past the lines of toilets, (no stalls in jail) and into the showers. They never made it that far. As soon as they rounded the turn into the bathroom area, out of sight of the lone guard at his desk, the whole world went to hell. Twotone went in first, followed by Stewart. As soon as they entered the bathroom, two Doubleduece grabbed Twotone, three grabbed Stewart. They had blades - slicing shivs - the kind made by melting a razor blade onto the shaft of a toothbrush; not much for stabbing, but an excellent slicing weapon. One man threw Twotone up against the wall, the second held the razor shiv to his throat. "One word, home, you dead. You wanta die fo' whitey?" Twotone shook his head.

Stewart also had a blade at his throat. The small leader, the tall one, and a scarfaced one had Stewart. The tall one had the blade at his throat, the short one stuck a sock in Stewart's mouth.

"Time da pay, bitch. Dhat sock come out, we slit ya throat."

The two with Twotone walked him to the back of the shower. One kept him there with the blade at his throat, the other came back to have fun with Stewart. Stewart had dissed the Double Duece, rich kid or not, he was about to pay. One way or another, it was his ass. They had street cred to protect.

They moved Stewart forward to the next to the last toilet, with the blade at his throat the whole time. Stewart had been scared of the cops, scared shitless by this whole deal, but this was different. He had never been so scared - this was primal fear, fear of pain and torture, fear of immediate death. He had no choice, they moved him at will. They unzipped his jumpsuit and pulled it down around his knees. They laid him on the top of the toilet's water chamber, chest on the top, bare butt in the air. Each arm was held down on his back, while one kept a blade at his throat. The boss of the crew moved behind him. Stewart had an idea what was about to happen, but he had no idea of the pain and humiliation until the boss entered him. It hurt, real bad, each arm was pinned behind his back, and there was the sock in his mouth and an everpresent blade at his throat.

He'd been nicked a couple of times already and was starting to bleed some. His biology at school and his own pursuits with a scalpel gave him a clear understanding of what a razor slice of the neck in the right place meant in terms of immediate massive blood loss. The boss grabbed handfuls of his flesh as he raped him, fingernails biting in, tearing his skin. The gang bangers knew the percussion of a hard hit would make a distinctive sound, make too loud a noise, so the ones holding his arms refrained from punching him, instead they would grab chunks of his flesh and twist it with their free hand.

"You my bitch, now, motha fucka, you our bitch, now."

Once the boss climaxed, he switched places with the one holding Stewart's left arm, Scarface, so he could have his turn. He didn't take that long, when he was through, he switched with the one on the right arm, the tall one. They kept pinching and twisting chunks of his skin, quietly taunting in obscene wispers, insulting and belittling him. For a moment Stewart thought about his sister and all the animals he had tortured. He wondered if they had felt like he felt now. The tall one raping him took a long time, so the one who had a blade at his throat got impatient.

"Bitch, ya make one sound, ya dead."

He unzipped his own jumpsuit, took the sock out of Stewart's mouth and attempted to replaced the sock with his erect penis. Stewart kept his mouth shut; thought he would puke. But the guy was pulling at his hair, starting to hurt his face. Then, Stewart figured in desperation that he was about to die anyway, so what the fuck. Stewart took it in his mouth and then bit the man's penis harder than he'd ever bitten anything in his life. He could feel his teeth tearing in, further, and further, as he shook his jaw side to side like a shark biting hard, harder, until he bit right through it. He could hear the man screaming, loudly, the most ear shattering pain wrenched scream he'd ever heard. Then he pulled his head back and forth like a scavenging jackal with the tip of the banger's penis in his mouth; then he spit it into the last toilet's bowl directly in front of him. The injured man had fallen yelling and sreaming, then was writhing on the ground, bleeding profusely. The two holding Stewart and the one raping him forgot about sex, and instead, concentrated on beating Stewart to death.

They no longer worried about noise, they pulled him up and down, slammed him onto the porcelain, beat him, then ran him, ramming his head into the water tank of the last toilet, giving Stewart the one oppurtunity of total revenge. During the blows and bleeding, Stewart's left arm got free momentarily. He flushed the toilet. With the one eye he could still see through, he watched the tip of the man's penis get flushed into the Chatahochee. Stewart knew he was dead anyway, about to lose consciousness, but he had his one moment.

***

The officer at the desk, everyone in the cell heard the most blood curdling scream they had ever heard. The deputy knew he had a situation and called in on the walkie-talkie. "We have a situation, code red. I need backup, Block B–code red, now, code red, code red. This is not a drill, Block-B, code red, Block B….

***

They dropped Stewart down on the floor, amidst the blood and the water leaking out where Stewart's head had cracked the water chamber of the last toilet. They kicked and stomped the shit out of Stewart while their gang brother lay screaming in agony, bleeding profusely. Stewart's head was kicked and stomped, his body was kicked, they stomped him unconscious and kept stomping and kicking him, until the red squad took them down, with excesssive force.

***

The Emergency Response Team came flying in, in riot gear, with plastic shields, billy sticks, helmets, gas masks, and pepper spray. The deputy pointed to the shower and ran with them. They found three young black men kicking and stomping the seemingly lifeless body of a young white male, while a black man lay four feet away, bleeding profusely from his crotch on the floor. They pepper sprayed the three blacks and beat the hell out of them with their billy sticks. The guards felt their lives were endangered by such incidents, so they took it out on the perps. They also found Twotone and the man who had just tossed the shiv in the back. Twotone pissed as hell, yelled who had done what. Stewart was rushed out on a stretcher immediately. Nobody exactly rushed to get the bleeding gangbanger medical aid. They called it in, however, while they carried Stewart out.

***

The jail supervisor called ADA Diaz, who freaked. They took Stewart to Grady, the best emergency room in Atlanta. Diaz called Wilmington, told him the situation, and that the Faulkners had his permission to rush in specialists and take Stewart anywhere they wanted him to go.

***

ADA Diaz went to Grady to supervise the situation. When he got there Lief Wilmington was there, so were Stewart's parents. Diaz called a judge and got Stewart a conditional bail of $1,000 that was verbally agreed to by Biff Faulkner-Davis. When Stewart was gurneyed out of the emergency room where they prepped him for surgery the prognosis was very bad. He had multiple skull fractures from multiple head traumas, the brain damage was massive, if he survived. He had seven cracked ribs, a broken left arm, broken right leg, his entire body was battered and bruised. He was immediately stabilized and prepped and went from the ER to surgery to reduce swelling on the brain. Ater the surgery and stablization he was moved a few miles up Peachtree St. to the Shepherd Center, a hospital specializing in spinal cord and brain injuries, one of the best in the world. There he was fully stabilized, and they were cautiously optimistic about survival, but the doctors feared the massive brain trauma may render a comatose or near brain dead state. All Diaz could do was think lawsuit and promise the parents that the perps would be punished to the fullest extent of the law, for rape and attempted murder. It wasn't much consolation.

Jasmine and her daughters, Tonya and her daughter, Deseree, and one of the Mexican women who worked in the nursery flew into Cancun and checked into a four star hotel with satellite TV. Jasmine had called her lawyer before leaving, told him the basics, and that she'd call him. She didn't say from where. He didn't want to know. Then she'd made one last call, and sent by courier an envelope with a large fee for a specialized service.

I'd asked John the boss to meet me for a beer after work at Moe's and Joe's, an old hole in the wall beer and burger joint, popular long before the Virginia-Highland area became so trendy and gentrified. We ate some mojo burgers with cheese as I tried to figure out how to tell him who was waiting at our place. I'd have liked to told him why, but I didn't really know that yet either, I hadn't heard her story. But I couldn't let him go home and find Samantha there without any warning. He'd have gone off on me - something he hadn't done in a while, and something I would pretty much avoid at all costs. My brother had killed with gun, knife, and hand in Nam, and chair or no chair, it was better not to piss him off. Not that he would ever hurt me, family meant everything to him, but still, it was a wise policy not to piss him off.

Our cell phones went off at the same time. We knew something was wrong somewhere. I called Danny's home number, and he let me in on the details. Thank God Stewart was stone cold guilty with multiple witnesses on the false statements charge, or the city and God knows who else would be sued to high heaven. Hell, the city might still get sued, badly. Any way you looked at it, this was not good. A high profile case, local rich kid, stomped senseless while in jail in a street gang beat down. Danny was not happy, nobody with the city was.

After our phone calls, we discussed the news. "Well, now might not be the greatest time for this, but I've got some news, too."

John just looked at me, "Well?"

"Samantha Faulkner is at our place, waiting for me to come back."

"What?"

***

John and I left at the same time and arrived home together. We both went to his house, mine was dark.

Betty was drinking white wine. She'd told Samantha she wouldn't offer her any, that would be illegal, but she could help herself to whatever was in the kitchen. Betty had been out of the kitchen when Samantha had helped herself to a small glass of wine. Phineas had always treated her as an adult, so she drank coffee in the mornings, had wine with dinner.

Samantha had never held babies, put children down at night, read bedtime stories, or been in such a love filled home. All of it was new, and let her see a part of life she hadn't known before. Betty had not mentioned what Samantha muttered while crying. They talked about mundane things, about general life stuff - the kids, hopes, dreams. Betty had figured out Samantha seemed new to so many things that were common, normal, natural in a healthy family setting. She felt sorry for the kid. Rich or not, her life had been impoverished in many ways.

When we came in, Betty got up like she always does and gave John a big hug and kiss. Unexpectedly Samantha was right behind her and tried to give me a big hug. I hugged her for a second, but then pulled back.

"We all better sit down, there's a lot going on."

John grabbed a beer out of the fridge and threw me one. I couldn't say what was different, but Samantha seemed different than earlier - younger, older, happier, I didn't know, but definitely different, in a good sort of way. Knowing what I knew about Stewart, and what I suspected about Stewart, I wasn't sure how she would take the news. Still, she had a right to know.

She didn't cry over her brother, or show much emotion, or any remorse. She just wanted details, so we told her everything we knew. Her reaction was not that of someone shocked or saddened by an outrage perpetrated against one's beloved family member. She wanted to know if the brain damage was severe and permanent. I guessed from her reaction that what I had suspected about Stewart was true, his sister had been one of his victims, for God knows how long. I told her her parents might have more details, but she seemed ambivalent, if not apathetic about her parents. If Stewart had abused her, she would blame them, too, for letting it happen. And so would I.

After a long discussion John yawned a few times, so did Betty. I asked Samantha if she would she like to stay with John and Betty or at my house. She chose me. I wasn't surprised. I wanted to soak in my hot tub, drink beer, smoke my pipe, and think about this case. I told them of my intentions and Samantha said it sounded great. That was a problem. Usually, I soak nude, and I had no bathing suit for Samantha. Betty said she had an old one piece that Samantha could use, and went and got it. As we left Betty told me to give her a call before I left for work tommorrow. She wispered in my ear, "Let her unburden her soul." I said sure and then

Samantha and I went back to my house. If Samantha did anything too improper, I'd call Betty

immediately, get her to stay over there.

***

I wasn't unobservant and had noticed Samantha was showing an attachment to me as her

protector that could be very problematic down the road. Especially if some of my suspicions

were confirmed. At the same time, if her brother had abused her and her uncle had manipulated

her into a sexual relationship, her desire for a protector was understandable. Also, I desperately

needed to know what she knew. She needed to trust me, to feel secure with me, but the kiss on

the cheek and the hug had me worried. I had to build her trust but not lead her on, or do anything

that might be considered any more inappropriate than what had already transpired.

Considering the circumstances, I figured it was CYA time. I asked Samantha didn't she

think she ought to formally hire me as her bodyguard. It might offer me some flimsy legal

protection if everything in this case came out in court. She agreed to pay me one dollar cash now,

and the rest of the fee when she turned twenty-one and got her first trust fund. We wrote out and

signed a simple contract. It wasn't much, but it was the best I could think of in this situation,

especially if all this was going where I thought.

I sat there in my cut offs next to her in the hot tub, smoked my pipe, and realized sitting

with her in the hot tub was bad enough, Betty letting her drink wine was bad enough, having her

at my house without parental or guardian approval was bad enough, I just hoped I hadn't crossed

any lines yet that would get me fired, have my licence suspended, or make me look like an idiot

in court and blow the case. In my mystical vision of the obscene ritual, Phineas was the only one

I saw clearly, but I felt she was there, with another man we didn't yet know, but that needed to put away, or down.

I closed my eyes and laid my head back, letting the pounding water relax my body, sinking into a lucid level of relaxation. I jumped about half a mile when she put her hand on my thigh. Let's face it - she was young, beautiful, looked twenty, and was a very attractive young woman. But my mind was in control, not my body. I put my hand on hers and moved it away.

"Samantha, you're a very attractive young woman, but our relationship must be professional and platonic." In my cynical mind I also thought, until you're at least eighteen.

She looked hurt, but I held on to her hand, "I'm here to help, to protect, to be your friend, and to listen to your story."

She glanced over at her backpack, a few feet away.

"What's in that thing Samantha, you act like it holds all the treasures in the world."

"Not treasure, just the truth."

"Do you really know everything I need to know?"

"Yes." She left it at that.

***

John and Betty were lying in bed talking. John was worried. "I just hope Spooky doesn't do anything real stupid."

"He's your brother. You ought to know him better than that."

"I do know him. That's why I'm worried. Remember that thing a year or so ago, that couldn't have been much more of a disaster. Sometimes he thinks with his heart, not his head. So what do you think about Samantha?"

Betty hesitated. "I think she hasn't had a very good life, rich as heck, but not loved right, not brought up in a loving environment. I think..., I think she's a basically good soul with a bad past and a few dark corners in her mind. Sometimes she seems like a wise old woman, other times like a child. I wouldn't be surprised if she has a bad temper, or is vindictive to those that hurt her. She might need, no, definitely needs some therapy to get beyond her past."

"Any chance she was in on the ritual murders?"

"I wouldn't want to say, that's Danny's and Spooky's job. I'll leave them to it." She knew some of what the girl had mumbled, but nothing conclusive, and had also seen the extent of her anguish. "But I certainly don't think she's any danger to the kids or me. Spooky wouldn't have brought her here, he's too intuitive, and I'd have felt or picked up something. She's fine here, this might be just what she needs."

***

Jasmine, Deseree, and Tonya stayed at it long hours, looking at the players they knew, the risk, and the potential financial reward. After that, the various possibilities: wealth, fame, notoriety, scandal, being made tabloid trash, public ridicule, humiliation. If they went into the public eye and implicated people as dangerous as Carl Lewis/George and Bobby Sanders, what would happen if they both didn't get the neddle sleep and ever got out of jail. The financial rewards must be high, very high, to take such a risk. But Jasmine was really pissed that she had been lied to, used, exploited, and manipulated involving murder by a sometimes lover. She was livid. Then Tonya dropped the bombshell—that Pugsley wanted to marry her.

***

I didn't ask her to tell me about recent events, I asked her to tell me about her whole life. Early childhood, nannies, pets, her first horse, her favorite teacher. She had an affinity with cats, horses, certain animals, she felt best outdoors riding her horse, walking through the woods, or playing with her cats. It was plain in some ways she preferred her animals to people. She told me about the first time Stewart terrorized her, waking her up with a fork inches from her eyes, after she'd told on him when he'd killed one of her kittens. She told of a lifetime of abuse, her hatred of Stewart was deep, she had little warmth towards her parents, whom she saw as basically unconcerned with, or burdened by, their children.

She told me of childhood dreams and nightmares, of shadow memories, of feelings that she was sometimes older, more somehow, than she was at other times, feeling that she may have lived before. It was these things, she claimed, that had brought her to her uncle's attention.

We finally got to the heart of the matter. Samantha moved to the present.

"Phineas reached out to me, I confided in him, and he talked to my parents without going into detail, just that it was a better phychological situation for both children if we were kept apart. So he kept Stewart away from me, threatened to have him institutionalized if he ever came near me again. But Phineas is into some very wierd things. Sexually, S&M; he calls it philosophy, but he's into magic and Satanism."

I interjected. "You do know those two aren't the same things?"

"Yes, but I think they are to Phineas. That's how he went from would-be Episcopal priest to satanic high priest. You were either this or that, and Phineas decided in his heart he belonged with the devil. He used to tell me what he said was an old saying, he'd rather be a ruler in hell than a servant in heaven. I think he really believes that."

"So Phineas recruited you onto a satanic path?"

"No." She looked down into the bubbling water. "He tried, but failed. He has a cohort, George, and he manipulated Stewart into joining. He lured him with the prospect of animals being ritually sacrificed. Stewart, George, and Phineas do their black magic together."

I pondered this. I'd found plenty of evidence of Stewart's sickness, but nothing that indicated that kind of involvement. It didn't match with what I'd seen and sensed during my OBE's

I had to remember that this was the fifteen year old who had earlier told me she owned her music teacher. She was certainly not above manipulation of her new protector. But I let her tell her story, listening to details, and every time Stewart was mentioned, I wondered it it was Stewart, or someone much closer at hand, substituting Stewart for herself.

***

Before pulling a Cherly Crow and leaving Las Vegas, Jasmine had communicated with a Vegas P.I. who was a surveillance expert and electronic wizard. The note said she would be doing some out of country communications with a lawyer, and didn't want it traced, could he work it out. She'd sent him an envelope filled with cash along with the note. By messenger, he sent her back a phone number to route all calls through, a cell phone, and the number of hours to wait before the sysem would be operational.

The three women talked for hours before deciding what was a reasonable figure for them to come forward. Obviously, Stewart's parents were willing to pay something for the truth, but they wouldn't understand the risks for them, considering it meant personal danger of the worst kind, and that the scrutiny and exposure of their personal lives would be embarrassing to them and their families, put them in the scandal tabloids, as well as ruin them professionally. They all wanted immunity from prosecution. Jasmine would probably have to sell her business and retire. She wouldn't take less than six million for all the inconvenience this was going to cause. She would ask for sixteen million, ten for her, three each for the girls. After negotiating, they wouldn't come down to less than six mil for Jasmine and two mil each for the girls. (Tonya was still interested in getting married to Stewart, and then moving to California, to later sue him for divorce and get half. But that was her gig, and not part of the negotiations.) Everybody lives happily ever after, as long as ALL the bad guys DIE. That was the problem. The quality of American justice. Sometimes the heinously guilty go free. OJ's out playing golf. They were risking their lives to do the right thing, 10 mil total was reasonable. If the Faulkners didn't want to pay, someone would - for the book and movie rights.

Jasmine waited past the set number of hours and then called her lawyer from Mexico, using the bounced around secure path set up by the P.I. She woke him up to let him know serious negotiations were about to begin early in the morning. The stakes were high, public scrutiny would be intense, the risks serious. Lives would change forever. And three women might be reaching retirement early. She mentioned she might be selling her bussiness, also, so he should also look very discreetly for buyers.

***

Samantha continued the line that it was Phineas, Stewart, and a man named George, last name unknown. I'd seen the lie detector tests. I doubted Amanda, Kevin, and Stewart were all lying about where they were last weekend. I believed them when they said they weren't on the estate. So every time Samantha mentioned Stewart, I kept plugging her into the picture. She was obviously reticent about telling what she knew. I grew sleepy, I understood I couldn't expect complete trust in one day, so I gave her something to think about.

"I told you I work as a shaman. I had a vision of the dark ritual performed on the estate. In my vision I saw someone your size and shape, not Stewart's, assisting Phineas in his version of the Black Mass. If they find Stewart's alibi witness, I hope the truth in your backpack will stand up under close inspection. If it's a writtten record you have, I hope it will mesh with reality, when the truth is finally revealed, and eventually it will be. Count on it."

Samantha sat and thought. I just wanted some sleep so I started getting out when she surprised me.

"I want to see my brother tommorrow. No parents, no lawyers, no cops. I want you to sneak me in. I want to see what kind of shape he's in. Alpert says doctors are often wrong, and they sometimes exaggerate the severity of an injury to protect themselves and so they look that much better later. I want to see Stewart with my own eyes. Then maybe I'll tell you more of what you want to hear."

She looked tired, exhausted. I was afraid she was going to try to say she was too scared to sleep alone in my guest room. At which point I'd call Betty, but she went quietly, almost as eager for rest as I was.

***

Chapter Fifteen – Thursday

Phineas was aware he had tossed and turned all night as he finally rose to consciousness in the morning. The elation of the first days had long since worn off, replaced by ever growing anxiety. That night he had some drinks and had taken a pill to sleep, he had no memory but of the early morning dreams, and that memory was in glimpses. All he remembered was combat, between the two subdemons who had peopled his dreams since he had ritually committed his soul to serving evil and some gigantic bird that was red and brown, glowed gold and brilliant white. His troops seemed to be taking the worst of it, something he had never seen before. In his previous dreams they had always gone unchallenged. He rubbed his hands over his face and bald head, trying to make it to the conscious world, and leave the astral world behind.

Leif got into his office at 8:30. His phone rang at 8:35. A lawyer in Las Vegas, representing the parties he was looking for, informed him it was time to begin the negotiations. After five minutes, Leif knew it was going to be a long day. The Vegas lawyer knew the lovers' nicknames - Pugsley and Raquel - which had been kept secret. Only Stewart, law enforecement personell, and he knew their nicknames. This lawyer knew other things that could have only come from the woman Stewart was with. It would be an interesting, maybe productive, but definitely long day. He had three alibi witnesses with totally unrealistic expectations concerning the price of justice.

Danny had thought about it drinking coffee alone in his office. The DA was pissed, so was the chief and the mayor. Stewart getting stomped into mush, possibly brain dead was not good; the bad publicity just wouldn't go away, the city powers wanted this case over and done. Off the news and out of the papers. Danny needed to find the real perps, not have a rich young sadist who didn't do the crime get killed in custody. He called up Diaz, early. He wanted warrants to bug everything Kevin and Amanda have or had ever touched. Houses, vehicles, whatever, and he wanted to tag Kevin and Amanda like migrating whales, so he knew where both of them were at all times. Then he called Spooky, who sounded sleepy.

"Yeah, yeah, call Abe down at our shop. He gets in early. He'll tell you what we got and how to use it. Our stuff's more sophisticated than what you've got. Of course, you'll have to get inluded in their bail conditions that if they mess with the equipment, bail is revoked automatically. And they have to pay to replace it. They do, or the city does, if it gets damaged. Okay, Danny, this is expensive gadetry."

"Sure. No prob."

"Have you gotten the info on the Doc, patients, criminals, sadists, Satanists?"

"No, but I'm going to put Annie on it today. I'll get it."

"What time are the retests?"

"9:30. You coming?"

"Naw, I'll sit it out, I think the results this time are predictable. Kevin, although evil as hell, didn't do this ritual murder. Neither did Stewart. Danny, you know Kevin will try to find and kill whoever set him up. It's down to strect justice now, he's not gonna wait on us."

Danny knew. "If no innocents get hurt or killed, worse things could happen. But we need to stay close, listen in, and let him lead us to the perps, then we take him and the perps before any bloodshed."

I hoped Danny wasn't being overly optimistic. "I have the perfect crew to help in the surveillance. Not that some of your guys aren't good, but with something this big...."

***

George Sanders did something he almost never did, he called in sick to work. He sent Bobby on, he'd fectch Bobby if neccessary. He'd seen the local news. He doubted Tonya or Deseree had, and he didn't think Jasmine would be paying attention to Atlanta news either. The sketches were far from perfect and the news of a reward for coming forward would bring out every greedy asshole stupid enough to think they could con their way to the money. And if the women in Vegas did put two and two together, surely they should have enough fucking sense to be scared of him and keep their mouths shut. Tonya and Jasmine both knew what he was capable of, that should be enough to insure their silence. However, he was getting rid of anything that might possibly link him to the crime. Obviously, that meant the destruction of at least two of his magical weapons, his athame and his chalice. Both would have blood residue that couldn't be washed off. But he also had to destroy the rest of his regalia, blood scattered everywhere during the ritual, so it all had to go. His black silk altar cloth may have been contaminated by contact, possibly all his magical tools. In terms of ritual tools, he would have to start over again. Maybe here, if it all blew over and the frame held, maybe somewhere else. The setup might still work, but the frame might just as well come unraveled so he had to be ready, stay ahead of the game. He checked his four other identities, the two he was currently using at his two part time jobs, and the two he saved for emergencies.

If neccessary, George and Bobby Sanders would fall off the edge of the earth, never to be seen or heard of again as themselves. But that might not be neccessary, they just had to be able to go at a moments notice. He checked his supply of hair dye, fake mustaches and beards, sunglasses, clear glass glasses. If neccessary, they would dissappear, no problem. He didn't want to break parole and give up his family and friends forever - if he didn't have to. He'd keep an eye on the news.

Kevin wasn't smart enough to figure it out on his own, but if the hookers came in for the money and went public, it was time to go.

***

Once I woke up fully, I tried calling Danny back, but he was observing the retest of Kevin. Stewart's retest was put off indefinitely. Thank God he was guilty of what Danny busted him for, and there were plenty of witnesses. I got Schultz on the phone which was even better. I told him I had to go by and take a look at Stewart. It was no big deal, but he needed to let the cop on duty and the doctor know. He was used to my ways, he didn't even ask why, just said he would and that was that. Easy peasy. We went on my Harley, dressed rough so as not to catch any media attention. I doubted they'd be camping out at the Shepherd Center to see if Stewart could remember who he was when and if he woke up, but they are the media - no scruples, no decency, no common sense, vultures by trade and nature, they just might be camped out. We went up high in the parking deck, went down the elevator and through the tunnel the back way. The ABI - aquired brain injury unit of the Shepherd Center is a secure section of the hospital. The APD cop was on the inside at the nurses station, overseeing the coming and goings. I'd been told the name of the officer on duty, who had gotten his orders to let me in. I showed him my APD ID and told him he could take a break. He went off like a bolt.

Samantha had quietly followed behind me. We went to Stewart's room where she immediately walked directly to Stewart and looked down. He was hooked up to monitors, his heart was beating regularly, if slowly. He was one continuious bruised, cut, bloody mess. His face, what little you could see under the oxygen tubing and the dressings, was swollen and grotesque. Stewart had taken a serious hard core g-style beat down. His body had survived, amazingly, considering the amount and intensity of violence inflicted upon it; but his mind hadn't. The nurse that came in to check on him told me he was unconcious most of the time, but not in a full coma. When he was awake his eyes were dull, and he couldn't speak. Physically he might still able, but his brain was so damaged speech was gone. There really wasn't a whole lot that Samantha could see. After the nurse left, she turned to me and told me, "Next we go see his doctor. I want to know..., I want to know." Then she leaned down, having noticed Stewart had opened his eyes half way. He opened them more fully as her face got near his, but they were not aware eyes that showed any sign of recognition.

She said what she had to say, not loud, but with intensity. "You fucking monster. You have made my life a living hell for as long as I can remember. Suffer now, suffer bad, then burn in hell you evil bastard. Burn in hell. You and Phinnie can rot there together for all time." Then she made a symbolic (nothing much came out) spitting action on her brother's face, stood up straight, and headed for the door. From the intensity of what I had just witnessed, I was glad she hadn't whipped out a machete and cut him up into little pieces. I could't imagine growing up a victim of abuse. My family was large, loud, and interactive. Sure, we had some sibling rivalry and fights, and we got switched and spanked by hand, and by the belt when we really misbehaved, but we grew up surrounded by love. They way kids should.

Here was Samantha, rich as shit, but abused, too scared to report the abuse, with absentee disinterested parents too oblivious to notice. It explained a lot, maybe not everything, but a lot. I walked with her to the nurses station where I had earlier shown my ID to the cop, and asked to see Stewart's doctor. They said it would be a few minutes. The APD cop came back, then went to check on Stewart. We waited there a couple of minutes and Stewart's doctor showed.

I asked for privacy, he looked around, then lead us outside the secured double doors of the ABI unit, to an empty lounge where we all sat down. There was no one within earshot. I explained Samantha as a relevant witness and left it at that. "Doctor Pear, I need some analysis of Stewart. Will he recover? Will he be himself again? Will he talk, walk, think? What?"

The doctor shook his head. "It's incredible he survived that kind of trauma to the head and body. Without the immediate medical attention he recieved he would have died. The brain damage is massive, extensive, and irreparable. How much brain function will he have left? It's too early to tell. A couple of times nurses thought he might be responding to his name, which is something. He does not seem to be completely brain dead, nor comatose. We haven't had to do a tracheomtomy and insert the respirator tube into his throat. That's the first positive, no trache. His next step would be to be weaned from the oxygen mask and start breathing on his own. Then take it from there. He can't talk, I doubt he will ever be able to. At absolute best he may be capable of simple tasks, not walking which is very complex, possibly he can get rudementary control of an electric wheelchair, but that is doubtful. He is incapable of complex thought now, and will remain that way, he will never be himself again. If he can recognize people he knows, feed himself, or use the bathroom by himself, he'd be doing extremely well, much better than we expect. He may become capable of simple communication, I doubt in words, but he may be able to indicate yes, no, good, bad. That's about the best you could possibly hope for. The absolute best. It could go either way, he might backslide, where we have to trache him, where the machine breathes for him and he's basically brain dead. His reality may be life in bed on a respirator, in and out of a coma like state. The latter prognosis is more likely than the first, it is not encouraging."

"What's the worst case scenario?" Samantha asked?

The doctor looked at me, so I nodded, and he answered her. "Death, he could still die. He could easily end up in an almost brain dead state. He seemed to recognise his name, that might be as good as it gets. Worst case: total coma, more likely he's incontinent, has to be fed, cleaned, basically is like a totally helpless infant in an adult body, in need of constant care, with no hope for improvement. That's what's most likely. Best case, he'll be able to heal and improve to function at a level similar to a one, one and a half year old. Anything past that would be a miracle."

Samantha looked at the doctor and spoke with certainty. "I wouldn't be expecting any divine intervention in his case." She briskly stood up, turned, and walked away to leave. Dr. Pear looked confused, not knowing what to make of her comment. I thanked the doc and followed after her.

***

I caught up with her, and we walked back to my Harley together, without conversation. When we got to the bike, I put on my helmet and climbed on, then so did she, still no words. After I started the bike, she leaned up and yelled in my ear, "Take me back to your place, I need to go over my diary and think. We can talk tonight. Fully." I nodded and we headed back home.

***

Betty said she'd be glad to have Sam around for the day. Samantha said she felt safe with Betty, that it was peaceful inside our electrified compound. I told her she should feel safe, nobody in the world knew where she was, but me and my family. Samantha, with her ever present backpack, headed off to sit by the pond, think, and read. She had some decisions to make. I checked my machine, there was a message from Laura, saying the convention was going great, she had several good prospects for jobs, and would be back Saturday or Sunday, that she'd call later for an update. Leonard had called, said he'd thought about our conversation and felt good about what I was doing and what he was doing, but if necessary he'd call for an emergency

Sweat. For now he thought our combined animal spirits and prayers were enough, and he'd put me in his Pipe every day. Then I roared on off on my scooter - time to go work for Danny.

***

Kevin had passed the second lie detector test. The tester said he was 99.9% sure Kevin had never set foot on the Faulkner estate, and did not participate in any ritual on the Faulkner estate that weekend, or any other time. The tester told Danny, "He may be a bad guy, but he's not guilty of this crime."

Although Danny knew psychotics, people using certain drugs, and some specially trained people could falsely pass lie detector tests, he doubted all three of *these* suspects could. The results were the straw that broke the camel's back. With Juan Valdez's statements and the test results, Danny finally accepted it in totality. There really was a whole other group of Satanists, who had done the crime and set up these scumbags as patsies. Somebody had been using him, from the beginning, manipulating him and his investigation, wasting his time. These people had to pay. Big time.

When I went into Danny's office, I came in on a three person debate. Danny was trying to make the final decision on whether or not to let Amanda and Kevin out on bail, for the purpose of following them, letting them lead us to the real perps. It was not an angry debate. Everybody was trying to look at it from every angle. ADA Diaz, Annie Wilson, and Danny all were leaning towards letting them out. But they all had reservations. There were some bad possibilities: number one, they escape; number two, they can't find the perps and lead the task force on a wild goose chase costing valuable time; number three, they find the perps and instigate carnge and mayhem in a public setting and innocents get hurt or dead; and number four, while we're out following Kevin and Amanda on a wild goose chase, the tabloids or *Hard Copy* find the alibi hookers and solve the case publicly to our humiliation.

I hadn't heard any news. "Any word from the lawyers? Has the reward worked yet."

Diaz answered, "Not a word so far. Lief called me to reaffirm the hookers will get immunity from prosecution if they weren't involved in the murder. He's picking it up in writing from my secretary any time now. What if anything they've heard, they haven't told us."

"All our previous suspects but one is boggus, we have to generate new suspects, immediately." Danny looked over at me for a sec, then stated, "Spooky and I have observed some behavior at Dr. Faulkner's house that have made us suspicious that Phineas and his niece may be involved in the occult, possibly satanic black magic, and incestuous sexual relations." He handed Annie a file. "Go to records, make the calls, find out everything about the Doc and his treatment of crimals, and his involvement in this," he looked over at Diaz, "experimental pilot program in privatization and penal reform. We need to know if he has worked with any sadists or satanists." What was said during treatment may be covered by the doctor patient priveledge, but who the doctor treated and their criminal records was not.

Diaz spoke up, "I'll make a call, and get my assistant on it, too."

Diaz whipped out his cell phone while Danny and Annie went over what he wanted and then Annie told Diaz how his assistant could help and headed out. Danny took the lead. It was still his show. "I want to have another long heart to heart with Jackson, Stone, and their lawyers. If they cooperate and tell me everything I want to hear, I say let them out on low bail. We let them snoop around while we watch and listen. I've already had their vehicles bugged and transponded and released from impound. In a tax records search we found Kevin has a boathouse at Lake Lanier, it's now bugged. We'll know where those cars are and what's said inside. We'll hear everything said in their houses and on their phones. They'll wear the electronic homing ankle bracelets that let us track their whereabouts. They'll be tracked using GPS - the global positioning satellite system. We'll know exactly where on the face of this planet they are within twelve feet." He paused, he almost mentioned another feature, but since Diaz was there he didn't. Within a certain range, using certain equipment, the ankle bracelets with our modifications allowed us to hear what was going on immediately around the targets. Legally, it was dark grey when it came to expectation of privacy, but it wasn't going to be used to make tapes to be played in court, just track the targets, who hopefully would lead us to the perps.

He continued, "If the lawyers bring us the alibi hookers, fine, that's one area to work. The doctor is another. Working on Gary Parker, or what Jackson can tell us about Parker is another. These people were selected - chosen to play the role of patsies. They had to be well known to be set up. Or known about and studied. Kevin has suggested the possibility of previous blackmail victims. We need to know who knew enough about our fall-guys to set them up. And who had the motive. It may be someone very close to them, that was jealous, or had a grudge. It would be far easier to set up a fellow criminal than a total stranger."

Sometimes you hear a phrase that triggers something and all of a sudden you're looking at something from a different angle and it hits you, wham! You're glad you looked at it different, but you feel dumb you didn't think of it before.

"Cellmates!" I kind of just yelled it out. It definitely stopped the flow of conversation. Everybody just looked at me.

"The first place I would start looking for somebody that set up Jackson, Stone, and Parker would be a cellmate of Jackson's. Or a jailhouse friend that became an enemy, or an enemy with resources. There's not much to do inside. People talk, tell stories, trade ideas and techniques.

They don't call prison the graudate school of crime for nothing. There's no guarantee, but it's a place to start - a cellmate with a grudge, a friend who became an enemy, maybe someone he raped in the shower. We need to know where he did time, who he did time with - cellmates, friends, allies inside, enemies on the inside - we need to see his prison records and interview his old cellmates still in the system. What we need to look for is the link between Jackson and the Faulkners. Jackson's crew and Stewart were set up together. Who knows them both? Stewart and the location were not chosen at random. There has to be a connection."

Danny wrote some notes down and said he'd put Potts on it. "All right. If the inquisition with Jacksdon and Stone goes well at three o'clock the surveillance teams will meet and discuss techniques, strategies, and work out the schedule for 24 hour babysitting, cause we're staying on top of these folks. We can't lose them and we have to be able to move in with overwhelming force whenever neccessary. As long as I get all the right answers, we let them do bail, conditionally, reviewed every week, one week at a time. We'll get the right judge, it will be done secretly, we'll let them out and see what they do."

***

I called Abe after the decision was made and he told me he and Danny had already squared away most of the details about surveillance equipment - what APD had, and what we could help augment or provide, but he agreed to come to the meeting at three o'clock when I asked him. I figured techical questions might come up that he was better suited to answer. Danny had asked the big bosses for money to spend, and gotten it. It was bad enough for the city - the publicity of the crime, now the near death of a suspect who gets beaten and maimed while incarcerated. The Atlanta jail already had a troubled reputation as it was. The pressure to solve the crime, and get it off the airways and front pages, was ever increasing.

The Faulkners weren't talking lawsuit yet, but the city was running scared. I talked to Danny after the meeting, once Diaz was gone. Diaz was a nice guy, but he was a lawyer for the DA's office - different perspective. I told Danny what else I thought APD needed from us to make sure the perps didn't successfully rabbit. Danny agreed. The money was there, so I made the calls. I called in the calvalry. Time for the flying "onnies" to ride again for the sake of truth, justice, and the American Dollar. In truth, mostly for the thrill of the chase.

***

Samantha sat by the pond, read her diary, and took notes. The diary was two years old, but all the fictional parts were less than a year old. She was writing a separate addendum - a sheet of corrections. She had decided she trusted the man with the raptor's eyes. She would tell him, and only him, the truth. Her brother had finally been punished for his evil. Finally. It was time she faced her own.

Phineas had always given her drugged wine before the rituals. It had rendered her calm and compliant, and made the experiences seem like dreams, unpleasant dreams. Nightmares she lived through and acted in, but which weren't really real, not part of her normal daily world. Her behavior during thoses drug induced states was disassociated from her self image. She knew in her heart of hearts that she would never have done those things on her own - would never had imagined doing things like that. But that didn't change the fact that she had done them. She had participated. To free herself and punish her brother she had let Phineas lead her to witness and participate in absolutely revolting behavior. She had no love of the satanic path. That was all Phinnie.

Samanth was drawn to what she had read about the old religion of Europe and some modern day witches and was disgusted by animal sacrifice. She could not stab an animal or a human - Phineas had taken her hand in his, every time, and made her do the stabbing - she had been there, willingly participating. She had not run out, or away, and she had mouthed the words. Phineas had told her it would be over a year, maybe two, before she was fully trained and initiated as a Satanist. Although some of the cold selfish logic of the satanic path reflected what she'd experienced, and how she felt the world worked, she had never committted her soul to evil or the devil, never considered herself a Satanist down deep. She went along with Phineas driven by her overwhelming compulsion to rid herself of Stewart. He was gone now, in all practicality, and he would never again be a threat to her, or anyone. She would follow Phinnie's path no longer. In her mixed up mind, the only religious figure she identified with was the woman in her dreams - the wise woman that the preist and mob would burn to death.

She sat by the pond and looked into the water, filled with regrets, wishing she could go to sleep and wake up with no memory of what her brother put her through, or what she'd done with her uncle. Samantha wished she could start over with a clean slate. She also knew she couldn't.

By whatever name they knew him, his employers knew he was a competent, hardworking, intelligent, valuable employee. Because he always kept the same secrets and told the same lies, he would tell all three employers the same story. Although he almost never got ill, he had come down with a virus, might be out for days. And to complicate matters, his mother in Florida was critically ill, and he might have to go at any second to take care of family matters. He called his printing shop boss and his animal shelter boss and game them the line, then went and gave it personally to his junkyard/recycling center boss, acting as ill as possible, warning that he and Bobby might have to take off suddenly. He found Bobby, and without explaining why, he and Bobby got rid of every ritual item that might possibly link him to the crime, all his magical weapons and satanic regalia, crushed inside a junked automobile until it was part of a small compacted steel square, on its way to be smelted. His magical weapon's fate was to become untraceable slag - leaving him temporarily magically incomplete, but free of any physical link to the crime. He believed himself smart enough to create reasonable doubt in any jury, if there was no physical evidence, and now, there was none.

He was selling the van that afternoon at the biweekly auction in Loganville. Even though he'd been extra careful on their roadtrip in South Carolina when they'd picked up Tonya, and cleaned it thoroughly, repeatedly, it was better to get the vehicle in someone else's possession. After that, there would be no possible physical link left. George Sanders was not about to go down for one of the most infamous crimes in Georgia's history, or be paraded in handcuffs in front of the world on the evening news. It just might be time for him and Bobby to go. But he was not about to panic and do something stupid. Always respected for his cool and calm, he wouldn't lose that now. The only people that knew shit were in Vegas and were probably not paying attention to the news. It was *Vegas*. And if they were, they should have enough sense, or fear, to keep their mouths shut. Even if they didn't hear about it through the legitimate news, they might see it in the tabloids at the grocery store or on TV tabloids. He figured he should call out there later, just to check on things.

But the three working ladies weren't in Vegas, they were spending the morning in a Cancun hotel room, haggling over money. For such a rich family, they thought the Faulkners and their lawyer were a bunch of cheapscates.

***

"Okay, Kevin, a few more questions, and you're looking good for bail. Who are Beavis and Butthead?"

Kevin started laughing.

"Not the ass wipes from MTV, the ones in Amanda's spellbook. They did rituals with you four months ago. Who are they? Any chance they are involved in the crime or in setting you up?"

"Naw. They're two lightwieght dabblers in a heavy metal band. They think the satanic thing is part of the heavy metal gig, like Ozzy Osbourne and Black Sabbath. They're touring with Death Shriek in Europe, have been for the last three months. It should be easy enough to check."

"What's the deal with Parker, is he really crazy or stupid enough to think the CIA or Mob has recruited him?"

"Definitely. If you guys had put me in with him, I could have got him to talk in a few days, maybe a week, but I think I know pretty much what what he knows."

"Okay, Kevin, tell us again what he told you, everthing in detail, about his recriutment and the night of the crime. Be complete, this is your ticket out."

***

Phineas couldn't believe the frame might be falling apart. He'd seen the two sketches and snippets of the news conference on the local news. He hadn't handled that part of things - that was George's responsibilty. Was George not as capable as he thought? Had he overestimated George and put himself in peril? Phineas still believed the physical evidence was too overwhelming for the police to ignore, and even if the hookers came forward, what jury would believe them? But Phineas felt more anxious and worried than ever before, even more than when he was being blackmailed years earlier which started all this in motion. He could lose everything. Maybe it was a test of faith from his dark master. He had done the "public" sacrifice in honor of Satan. Surely he was protected. He hit the intercom, and had his secretary send in his next patient.

Alpert Faulkner, Alexi and Biff Faulkner-Davis, and Emmett and Gretta had been in Lief's office since mid-morning attempting to work out the agreement. The Faulkner position was clear, as the five executors and lawyer of Stewart's trust, the 20 mil due him at twenty-one was what they had to work with. Despite his present state of health, they wanted him cleared of all murder charges, and to plea bargain or pay a fine on the false statements charge. They wanted the family's involvement with this public spectacle ended immediately. Lief thought Diaz would go for time served on the false statement charges, it would be over once the cloud of murder hanging over Stewart dissappeared with the capture of the real perpetrators. They would be buying the hookers cooperation, and silence, but they weren't coming cheap. Alexi was horrified that this sordid affair might become a movie of the week, a mini-series, or worse, a feature film.

The family had mentioned suing the city, but Lief put it in perspective. He gave them a brief run down on Stewart's hobbies/proclivities and what the police had in their possesion of Stewart's. If they attempted to sue the city for Stewart's current condition, those activities could be made public. They had money and standing in the community, and the family had already been hit with more bad publicity than it ever dreamed of.... The subject died.

The family reiterated their position that the best thing to do was use Stewart's trust fund money to get Stewart out of this mess immediately, pay any medical bills not covered by insurance, and set him up with good home health care or in the best institution. They didn't talk about future trust funds, only the one due at twenty-one was discussed. Stewart's 20 mil would pay for the lawyer's, doctor's, and any uninsured health care bills, as well as the reward. These harlots certainly weren't getting any sixteen million. The family made the situation clear to Lief. They were at an empass.

The Vegas lawyer let them know the women were out of the country, location unknown, and couldn't be coerced to come forward. Although, if and when they did, they would exonerate Stewart, Amanda, and Kevin. They haven't begun to take bids on the rights to their stories in Hollywood yet....

The Faulkners understood the womens' needs for compensation, and maybe protection, but not any 16 million. The highest the family would go was 2 mil. For their cooperation and the exclusive rights to the story - 2 mil for no murder charges for Stewart and total silence. The women wanted more. They said the tabloids or a movie or book company might give them more, probably a million each, in which case they didn't have to go out of their way to help Stewart or make his family look good. Things went back and forth. Finally, Jasmine told her lawyer to ask about offshore accounts. Possibly part could be paid openly in the US and part could be paid discreetly in the Grand Caymans. That broke the ice, and after three more hours of negotiations, the deal was finally settled. Jasmine would get 5 million dollars, 2.5 mil in the US, 2.5 in the Grand Caymans. Tonya and Deseree would each get 1.5 mil, $750,000 in the US and $750,000 in the Grand Caymans. Monies to be delivered to accounts as soon as the three women were deposed, passed lie detector tests, and signed away the rights to their stories to the Faulkners, agreeing to never discuss the subject or the settlement, if they did, the money would be forfeited. Jasmine negotiated her lawyer's fee privately

There were logistics to work out. The solution was made simple by the Faulkner's corporate jet. Leif, his secretary, the security/lie detector expert ADA Diaz recommended, Alpert, Emmet and Gretta, and Alexi and Biff would leave for Las Vegas where they'd pick up the prostitutes' lawyer. Phineas wasn't an executor for Stewart's trust, hadn't responded yet to the message they'd left on his machine and with his receptionist so he was left out of the loop.

The pilot of the jet would learn their ultimate destination once the Vegas lawyer was aboard. The depositions would be taken, the lie detector tests administered, story rights signed away, and total and absolute silence ageed to and signed. If everything held up, the funds would be transferred. The women would have to turn themselves in to the police, but if they were only guilty of prostitution, Diaz had promised them immunity. When Lief picked up the ADA's signed offer on the way to DeKalb Peachtree Airport, he told Diaz nothing, except he'd talk to him later.

***

Phineas kept watching news between appointments, but nothing changed. He had heard his two messages but when he got around to calling Alpert and Lief for an update, Alpert's secretary said he had tried to get Phineas earlier, but was now away on business, and she didn't know where. Lief's secretary wouldn't say anything, except that he wasn't available and she'd take a message. Both reported that their bosses said they would contact him later if he was to call. Phineas was not happy. This was not S.O.P.

***

Betty had yelled to Samantha who was still out by the pond to come in and eat lunch: BLT's, pork and beans, potato chips, and iced tea. Samantha hadn't even realised she was hungry, or how much time had passed as she worked. Betty couldn't help but think the girl still looked troubled. "Has Spooky mentioned his friend Father Murrell?"

Samantha drew a blank and shook her head.

"Who is Father Murrell?"

"Father Murrell is a good friend of Spooky's. He's a priest in the Liberal Catholic Church. Spooky calls it a branch of esoteric Christianity - some of the same people who led the Theosophical Society, a kind of an occult philosophical group, around the turn of the last century took over an offshoot of the Church of Holland, which supposedly had a valid apostolic sucession, and began their own very mystical Christian faith. They teach that Jesus taught an esoteric, hidden wisdom to his initiate desciples as well as the exoteric outer teachings he taught to the general public.

"Father Murrell was born in Europe, been in the States for over a decade, walks with a limp from childhood polio, and uses a cane. He and Spooky train together in martial arts. I've seen them work our. Father Murrell can use his walking stick as a lethal weapon, but he's really a very kind and compassionate man. He's my confessor. I didn't grow up Catholic, but I believe confession of one's failings and mistakes is very therapuetic. It's a kind of inner cleansing, and it's good for the soul. Would you like me to call him, and see if he'd be free later on this afternoon? He's a wonderful father confessor and counselor. Or just a kind person willing to listen."

Samantha nodded her head in assent. In her recurring dream she experienced dread, fear, and hate when she saw the preist. However, she instinctively trusted Betty and sensed her genuine concern. Samantha also knew a priest couldn't give her up, confession is legally protected, and the priest is sworn to secrecy. She had a lot to get off her chest. It was like a physical weight she wanted lifted off her, so she could breathe freely again. Confesion might be ideal therapy. After being around Betty and the kids, her immediate past made her feel dirty inside. Every time she thought about the things she'd seen, and done, what she had participated in, she wanted to be cleansed, to feel clean and new, to start over. The desperation to rid herself of Stewart had driven her to the point of willingness to do almost anything…

***

All four of the "flying 'onnies" showed up together five minutes before Danny's meeting. Inside were the task force, the FBI liason, some undercover cops, the SWAT team people, our expert Abe, some uniform brass, and some police technicians who worked with the surviellance equipment.

Before walking the "flying 'onnies" in, I had to prep them a little. "Look, folks, some of the cops in there are not going to be thrilled about outside help. That's like saying they can't do the job. I'm going to make a big deal about your racing experience and your machinery. I think it will make this go over better." I led them inside. It's hard to know what the cops thought about the 'flying onnies' -three young men, short, thin but muscular, wiry, they looked like motorcycle racers do all over the world. So much for Donnie, Johnnie, and Ronnie. Lonnie, on the other hand was a tall thin redhead with a magnificent body. She raced quad runners where size didn't matter as much, the guys raced moto cross and TNT, where it does.

Everybody knew everybody but my crew. Danny asked me to introduce them, which I did, as well as mentioning in which events they held national titles. They all had at least one national title. Johnnie had five. He spent half his time in the air, one of the best jumpers in the business. "These are the best surveilance technicians we've ever had. Their bikes can stay on the road, go off road, they're fast, they can jump, and they've been specially muffled so they are the quietest racing dirt bikes you'll ever not hear coming. All they'll be doing is trailing the targets at a distance and giving chase if neccessary. They just add a dimension that cars and street bikes don't have. They'll be miked, so if the targets do give us the slip, everybody but one of them, they'll just call in. They're not cops or P.I.'s, they're not armed. However, they are bonded and insured part time employees of Tripple S Security. What they are is insurance. Kevin's got a bike, so he might be able to lose a car or a large police Harley, but not very likely a bike like theirs." I looked around, and the cops seemed to accept it okay. It's hard to complain about national champions with specialized equipment, so Danny went on with the meeting.

It was a good plan: police working in three eight hour shifts; a SWAT team and van ready around the clock; three undercover teams; and one of the 'onnies' on each target in 12 hour shifts. We had the police command vehicle in which they could take turns slepping while the targets slept. The targets would be electronically tagged, we would know instanly if the ankle bracelet was cut and removed. We had transponders in Kevin's car, truck, and chopper, and in Amanda's car. The houses and Kevin's boathouse were totally bugged. APD's large rolling command post/communication vehicle would be used by Danny – it was an old UPS truck painted white and kept dirty on the outside. Danny had thought things out.

"Now, if these were normal folks, the busy shifts would be the day and evening shifts. But these are night people. They know we'll be watching, they'll prefer the cover of darkness. We must be prepared for all possibilities. They may truly help us - search for the identity of the perps and when they find out, tell us. More likely, they might already suspect, maybe have figured out who the perps are, and try to take them out themselves. If so, we must let them lead us to the bad guys, and then move in with overwhelming force. Above all else, we must contain any and all problems so that no innocents are put at risk. The lie detector results were inconclusive concerning whether Kevin knows who set him up. The lie detector expert thinks

Kevin may know the identity of one of the two girls. He says he doesn't, but we sure as hell hope he does."

***

Joseph Smith, the lawyer, not the Mormon prophet, got on the corporate jet in Vegas and introduced himself to everyone. He walked to the pilot, handed him a flight plan, and told him he'd filed it with the tower. He went back to the plush environs of the lounge and accepted an expresso. He was going to make a nice piece of change on this, and get a little notoriety too. Not bad for one day's work. It was all in the nicknames. One of his client's made up the nicknames which Stewart had confided in his lawyer, and the nicknames had never been made public. It was all he had needed. At least in establishing his bona fides in a moment. Lief and he knew the same graphic story of sex and more sex, outfit and game, by outfit and game.

Lief was even more excited than Joseph Smith. He felt terrible about what had happened to Stewart, although he had totally forgotten being the person who ordered Stewart to shower that night. He had a personal gift for unconsciously selective self-induced amnesia. Many lawyers do. He was excited about getting to know it all. After days of hearing this bizarre thing, and that perverse thing, and everybody's stories, he wanted to know - just like the cops, the press, and the public - who, what, why, all the reasons and the rationalizations. He thought he was about to.

***

The anxiety was driving Phineas crazy. He drove from his office to a convience store and used their pay phone to call George Sanders. He wanted to be reassured that George's end wasn't going to bring them all down. He called George's house forst and surprisingly, George answered the phone. After the basic amenities things heated up quickly.

"This was your responsibility. You guarnanteed me no problems from your end, yet I see two problems every time I watch the news."

"Look, man, this whole thing was your idea, not mine. I could have gotten *my* revenge on my own, in a much less elaborate way. But don't worry, the two women know me too well to do anything stupid. They really aren't the type to do much news watching. Anyway, they're a thousand miles away, and are probably oblivious to what's going on here. But I'll call out there, and make sure everything's cool."

"I'll call you back in half an hour. I hope you have reassuring news by then." Phineas headed for a diner where he could drink coffee and think about his options. He called in and cancelled his remaining appointments.

Sitting at the diner, Phineas tried to look at all sides, all options. Having an arrogantly high intellect, although he had planned out contingencies for all the possibilities, it never really occurred to him that things might go wrong with his plan and the cops would look past the obvious solution, despite so much physical evidence. If the cops got the two girls, and the girls gave them George, the trail could concievably lead back to him. Possibly George would give him up for a reduced sentence, if caught. The dream of his subdemons losing their pitched battle left him unsettled. His chosen master was supposed to be lord and prince of the physical world and he had done the rituals correctly. He should be protected. So why did things look so bleak right now? He needed to know the two women would stay silent, or George would have to go kill them. That might be the best solution, just send George to kill them. Phineas felt better. It was time to call George back.

They checked out of the hotel and went to the airport. Rosalina was given the daunting task of flying with the three children back to Vegas. Both mothers wanted their children far away from the circus in which they were about to star. After getting special permission to escort their daughters to the gate, the mothers hugged and kissed on their kids and reassured them before they boarded. Tonya's daughter had only flown twice before, and that very recently, from Atlanta to Vegas and Vegas to Cancun. But since Jasmine's girls were cool, Tonya's baby girl didn't even cry.

Once the Faulkner's corporate jet landed in Mexico, arrangements were made to park the jet in a private hanger and the three women boarded. After living conditions in the plane were put on automatic, the pilot, co-pilot and lone flight attendant got off the Faulkner's jet. The crew streched their legs in the hangar, walked outside in the brightness and warmed in the sun for a few moments, and then walked to the concorse.

Jasmine had made sure the women wore respectable business attire and that neither girl's make-up was too heavy. Jasmine wanted a good first impression and a business like setting. No street talk, no sexual innuendos. Serious money was going down, and their lives were being permanently changed, and if George or Bobby ever got loose, their lives would be in immanent peril.

Gretta Faulkner was thinking it was the first time she had ever been face to face with such fallen women, such harlots. Alexi, on the other hand, had never been knowingly face to face with any female that had been intimate with her son; but she had no illusions and knew that many of the women in her circle of friends had similar values to these women. They might not sleep with a man until he gives her a diamond bracelet, takes her to Tahiti, whatever, but it wasn't that different. What she didn't know was how many of the second, third, or fourth wives in high society, had previously been thousand dollar a night callgirls.

The ground rules were laid out. There would be three lie detector tests proving Tonya was with Stewart, and Deseree was with Kevin and Amanda last weekend, and that Jasmine knows who hired them. At that point the monies are wired to the banks in the Grand Caymans and Vegas and held, waiting to be deposited. Then the women tell their complete story in detail, followed by the second set of lie detector tests to confirm their story. If all three pass again, and they sign away the story rights and sign total non-disclosure agreements, the money is deposited into the accounts set up by their lawyer at the Cayman banks and in the Vegas bank. Jasmine agreed. The stenographer typed up this initial agreements in a couple of minutes, every one signed, and the process began.

***

Kevin and Amanda walked on two thousand dollars bond each levied against Kevin's property - on his signature. They each got a shiny new thick and heavy left ankle bracelete, and had to sign a bunch of forms. If they tried to take the bracelete off, bail was automatically revoked, the bond forfeited, and they would pay for damgage to the equipment. Part of the agreement was that they would call in every day, and tell us what progress they were making. Nobody really expected their cooperation. We all figured Kevin would find out, or make sure who set them up, then try to hunt them down and kill them. We just wanted to interupt that process, and send everybody where they belonged. Kevin and Amanda would go back to jail and we'd have the real perps on multiple murder charges.

APD had towed Kevin's bike and Amanda's car back to their houses after processing and being tagged with transponders, and had Kevin's tagged car waiting for them at the back entrance of the courthouse. They weren't complete idiots, they knew we were watching. From their conversation, they knew we were probably listening. Since both undercover surveillance teams, the command truck, and Johnnie and Lonnie were all following the same car, it was a little too much like a parade. Danny wanted me in the command truck with him. I'd have felt better on my scooter, but he wasn't having any of me on my Harley - I was riding with him. I was also in touch with the two 'onnies,' who weren't on the police radio band, but on our company channel.

***

The first lie detector tests were short and sweet. Name, address, date of birth, the known answers used to calibrate the results, then were you with so and so on the weekend of..., or did you arrange to send Deseree to Atlanta and did you arrange to accept Tonya…, three short tests and it was done. The expert believed their short answers so far. They were who they said they were, were where they said they were, with who they said they were with, and Jasmine knew who hired them. The funds were transferred to the banks, not deposited in the lady's accounts yet, but transferred awaiting those final instructions. It was time to tell their story in detail, all to be recorded, then the retests, the final signing of contracts, then the deposits. Nobody was going anywhere any time soon. The girls weren't heading El Norte until the money was in the banks. The lawyers didn't want a basic summary either, they wanted the whole story I detail. The pilot and flight attendant came back; he checked everything, she served everyone, and then they left them alone again. The pilot was thinking that Mexico and New Orleans had much in common. Nobody rushed about nothing. He ambled off.

***

Father Murrell had full curly dark hair, just starting to grey at the temples. He was a fit man, healthy, exuberant, with one bad leg, but it didn't slow him down much or distract him. He exuded a general feeling of benevolence, an aura of caring. Samantha immediately felt at ease with him, despite what she was about to let him hear. When she thought of that, she tensed up a little, but he was like a spiritual fire, and she was warming herself in his healing prescence. After the introductions, Betty gave them iced tea, and sent them off to sit in the gazebo, to talk alone.

Kevin and Amanda drove staight to Deacon Burton's, a bastion of down home country soul food, where they ate like ravenous wolves. The food in jail almost always sucks, unless you're on one of the prison farms like Reidsville. Wherever the innmates grow their own food, the food is better, more plentiful, and the cooks take more pride in their work. The food in most county jails, however, really, really sucks. Before they even got their food they borrowed a pen from the waitress and wrote on napkins for a long time. Every now and then one of them would say all right, or okay, or yeah, but that was about it for verbal communication of import.

After food, they headed home, Kevin dropped Amanda off. They were verbally quiet at home, active, but no phone calls. However, they both turned on loud music. They took out the old garbage stinking up the houses, they opened windows, they took baths. Amanda left the curtains open, always the exhibitionist.

***

George was getting pissed. He knew the receptionist, and she was blowing him off like some john. "I'm sorry Mr. Lewis, but that is all she told me to say. She's not available and I will be glad to take your message and pass it on." He got the same run around when he asked for Tonya and Deseree. He didn't like what he was hearing, at all.

"Look, this is Carl Lewis, you know I'm a close personal friend of Jasmine's. Cut the horseshit and tell me where they are. This is important. Hell, I just sent Tonya there, at least let me talk to her."

"Miss Jasmine was very specific…." George Sanders was getting desperate and starting to lose it. "Liz, I'm the last person in the world you want to piss off, I have a very long

memor...."

Click.

She had an armed mountain of a man a buzzer away. Carl Lewis knew damn well she

was only following orders.

***

George was starting to break out in a cold sweat. He felt a single drop of sweat trickle

from his armpit down his side. The AC was up, but the pressure was coming down on him, big

time. Either the two women had gone into hiding - left the country to avoid involvement,

possible prosecution, or they were taking the deal. That would mean immunity for them and a fat

reward from the Faulkners. But if they did that, they had to know he or Bobby would take them

out. Would they really risk their lives? He had cousins and uncles, too. Would they really

endanger their lives and publicly expose themselves as hookers for the reward money? He sat

and stewed. They might for really big money, and the Faulkner's definitely had big money. The

phone rang.

Before they really got going, Joseph Smith, the lawyer, asked if they could have a typed

and notarized copy of the depositions before the women turned themselves in to APD in Atlanta.

That was no problem, Lief's stenographer would transcribe and type the depositions during the

flight back. He was a notary, too. It'd be done by Atlanta, he was very fast.

"Let's begin." Lief was ready to get the ball rolling.

Tonya spoke out, "Before we start, I grew to care about Stewart during our time together,

I'd like to know how Stewart is doing, the reports say stable, but are vague." She had looked at

the parents, but Lief responded. "His life seems for the moment to be out of danger. Stewart is stable but has been very severely beaten, has cracked ribs, broken bones, multiple massive skull fractures, probably severe and irreversible brain damage." Lief felt uncomfortable saying it in front of his mother. It was factual, if sugar coated, but no parent wants to hear their child has permanent brain damge. He didn't know how much denial the parents were in. Tonya looked sad and concerned, like she really cared. Yeah, right.

Then Tonya raised an objection. Everyone had been introduced. Tonya now knew who Pugsley's mother and father were. She was a mother herself. She'd told cops what she'd done before, pled guilty, and paid a fine. It was bad and humiliating but part of the business. That was one thing, but she'd never had to talk in front of a young john's parents about her activites. Especially his mother. So she asked, "In front of his momma?"

Alexi had a quick reply. "If this is costing my family 8 million dollars, and what you have to say will help explain why my son is in the position he's now in, I'm going to hear every single incredibly expensive word."

Tonya just looked down and nodded her head. It was her money, her son. The depositions began with the normal swearing in procedures. Lief knew they knew what he needed to know, so he intended to ask broad leading questions, and let the women talk.

"Who should I start with?"

Jasmine answered authoratively, "Begin with Tonya, she has a history with two of your suspects in Atlanta, and with who set them up. Then Deseree, then I'll fill in the pieces. If you want the complete story quickly, that's the way to go."

***

George slowly and deliberately picked up the ringing telephone. Now was a time for complete control, not panic.

"Well?" Phineas wanted to be reassured. He would not be.

"I cannot get through to either of the two parties or their new employer. This has me very concerned. They have either fled to avoid involvement, or done something stupid they will live to regret. Trading common sense and loyalty for money is a lethal mistake. Scarlet, definitely scarlet." George hung up.

Scarlet was their code word for full cessation of contact. Everyone must destroy all possible links to the crime. Of course, Phineas no longer possessed any physical links to the crime that were not of a ritual nature. Now the ritual regalia, all his cherished magical weaponry had to be destroyed. George made a quick call to Bobby at work.

Phineas, despite his arrogance, had planned out all contingencies, although he never thought he would need them. It had been a mental exercise. George had prepared a box full of scrap metal kept at Phineas's house that would fit into the trunk of his car. Phineas was to put his and Samantha's magical weapons, his cherished athame, chalice, Phallic wand, gong, small whip, incense burner, silver disk with the inverted paentagram, the altar cloths, spellbook, the wood altar itself broken into pieces, everything in with the scrap. George had showed him to hide it among the bottom of the box of scrap, how to cover it. He would take it to the scrap metal/junkyard/recycling center and Bobby Sanders would make sure it was crushed inside a car into a small steel square which would be smelted until it became steel and slag. Unrecognizeable slag. Then all physical ties between him and and the ritual would be broken. Having his satanic tools, altar, and spellbook destroyed was difficult for him, but he had to do what he had to do. Plausible deniability was more important, but it was like destroying a part of himself.

Bobby acted like he'd never seen Phineas before, took his load, wieghed it, paid Phineas, who left. When no one was looking, Bobby placed it inside an old wrecked Ford Galaxy 500 and crushed it. As soon as he was through, Bobby called George and said, "Hello. Okay, I'm ready to come home as soon as I get off. Everything here is done." Bobby went back to work. Half an hour later, George called the boss and told him their mother had taken a turn for the worse. Would he please send Bobby home, they needed to immediately head for their sick mother in Jacksonville, Florida. The boss had been warned, said all right, and it was done.

George had sold the van early in the afternoon, before the auction, for a low end price to a quasi-used car dealer who worked the auctions. Riding his Harley home George was thinking that all the physical links were gone, now all they had to do was change identities and start over, if neccessary. He wasn't sure yet about giving up his real identity forever, until he knew for certain that the women had come forward. He'd wait and see. The three women might just be hiding out till the whole thing is over, maybe in Mexico, the Caribbean, Rio. Jasmine knew how to live well - she might be playing it safe. Everything might still work out okay. But George had no idea about the panic gripping the doc. Or that he had mistakingly only thought in terms of the women fearing him; not from the perspective of a woman who had quit needing men, or lived in no fear of them. He had not fully considered the consequences of decieving and pissing off a strong independent woman like Jasmine.

Phineas hadn't let on to Bobby about the state he was in, or told him or George that he had just discovered Samantha's ritual tools were missing, their absence camouflaged. He was agitated, upset, and he wanted some answers. First off, was Samantha really on the school trip, and why had she stolen into his temple, taken her magical weapons, and substitued them with objects of similar size? Had she destoyed them herself from fear of getting caught, taken them with her on her trip, what did it mean? She wasn't supposed to go into the ritual area without him. He didn't know she even knew how to get in. Not only had she covertly gone in, but had taken her ritual weapons and then disguised their dissappearance. This did not bode well. It was a lack of respect for him, and his rules. What were her plans? Why take the ritual tools unless she planned to destroy them?

***

"This whole story may break down into a conflict of male egos," Tonya began. "Big surprise that male egos could lead to murder. It's a story of jealousy, envy, and revenge between supposed friends and allies."

Tonya paused, "Have the names of George and Bobby Sanders come up in the investigation yet?"

Lief simply said, "No."

"But you guys do know about Kevin Jackson, and they've got him and Amanda in custody?"

"Yes, that's correct, along with Kevin's friend Gary Parker."

"Well Kevin and Amanda didn't do shit. They were set up."

"So they've steadfastly claimed," Lief said.

"Well, believe them, they didn't do crap, George set them up, and Pugsley, I mean Stewart, too."

"Why?"

"Well, give me time, it's a long story." Tonya took a drink of her iced tea. Jasmine had said no drinking till the business part was all over.

"I should begin with the fact that I grew up in Cabbagetown and the Sanders boys grew up three houses away. They were a big family. There were Sanders all over Cabbagetown, that whole side of Atlanta. The Sander's men were either ministers, or printers, or both. The women were almost always religious, very religious. The Sanders men had a reputation for forgery all over the state.

Except for the preachers, all the Sanders families would go through these cycles where they had lots of money, lived high on the hog, then the man or men would go to prison and it'd be hard times again for the women and kids. It was a cycle I watched growing up, over and over.

"So I grew up with George and Bobby Sanders. George was the smart one. Bobby was big and dumb, almost retarded, but he looked normal enough, he was just mentally slow. George always looked out for his brother, and Bobby would do whatever George said, and I do mean whatever. George pretty much ruled the neighborhood growing up. If anybody ever screwed with George and Bobby, they always had lots of badass relatives to call in. The Sanders might be outlaws, but they were big on family. George was my first love, popped my cherry and everything, but he was never big on romance. It just really didn't seem to matter much to him. His whole life, all he wanted to be was a criminal genius. Hell, his favorite character growing up was Moriarty, the guy Sherlock Holmes was always after. George followed in his father's and uncle's footprints - he became a printer, a master forger, but he always had criminal ambitions to be more. He made fake ID's in high school, but never directly, he made his minions do the public work, but everybody knew George was behind it. He also got into selling drugs.

We went to Towers High School, the school next to us was Grady. There was interschool dating, drug dealing, and fighting, I'm not sure when Kevin Jackson and George Sanders became aware of each other, probably about tenth grade. Anyway, there were some big fights, George busted one of Kevin's friends skull with a tire iron, but George and Kevin never squared off until jail. But each one, by the eleventh or twelfth grade, was considered the ultimate badass at each school. I know they did some drug business in high school, because I dated George some, and I also one of Kevin's friends at Grady. But they didn't know each other well until later, when they did time. Are there any bikers involved in the investigation, any bikers come forward to give Kevin an alibi?"

Leif shook his head, he hadn't heard any mention of bikers.

"I'm surprised, Kevin has a biker club that will do anythinyg he says. Well, not what Kevin says, but what the president of the Midnight Riders says, and he'll do anything for Kevin."

Since she paused, although it didn't seem relevant, Lief asked why.

"Because he went to jail instead of squeal."

"Who?"

"Kevin. Kevin went to jail instead of ratting out and because of that, Randy, head of the Riders, owes Kevin big time."

Leif didn't see where this was going or how it was relevant, but he rolled with it, better too much information than too little.

"Randy was one of the kids a few years younger that looked up to Kevin at Grady. When he grew up, he started the Midnight Riders, which became one of Atlanta's largest outlaw biker gangs. Kevin did drug bussiness with the Riders. Nobody suspected it, but there was a DEA plant in the Riders. Kevin was heading towards the Riders with a methamphetamine shipment when the cops tried to pull him over. It was a case of mistaken identity, Kevin was driving a car exacly like one just reported stolen in that area, and he matched the general description of the thief. Of course Kevin didn't know it was a mistaken stolen car bust and he wouldn't pull over for the cops, thinking he was getting busted for drugs. He ran and started dumping meth out the window. Once the chase was on, lots of police joined in and one of the units eventually forced him off the road. He didn't have much weight left by then, but enough meth was scattered on him and around the car for a decent bust. They had him for possession and all the car offenses -

speeding, not pulling over, reckless driving, endangerment, resisting arrest. They had enough to put him away for years.

"The kicker was that the DEA was really pissed, they went through with their bust and got the weapons but very little of the drugs they were expecting. When the DEA found out what happened, they offered Kevin a deal. They had long time surveillance, all they needed for their case was for Kevin to roll. He wouldn't do it, did a five spot instead. Served the whole five years. By not ratting he saved Randy and some of the Riders from serious time. I'm surprised they're not involved trying to help Kevin somehow. Maybe they don't even know he was busted."

"Anyway, that's where Kevin and George got to be buddies, enemies, whatever they are, in stir. George had gone down when a drug dealer he made fake ID's and passports for got busted. He turned George in as part of his deal. The guy died mysteriously years later when he left the witness protection program after six years of boredom and came back to Atlanta. George, or somebody else whacked him, he'd ratted out way too many people to keep breathing.

"Anyway, George and Kevin were cellmates at Riedsville. It's where thay put all the young badasses. They knew each other a little from high school and had similar backgrounds, although Kevin was not a forger. They'd both dealt drugs, were outlaws by nature, and by then both had small escort services.

***

Samantha cried so hard sometimes it was difficult for Father Murrell to understand everything she said. She had started off calmly and rationally, detailing her brother's abuse and her fear of him. She wanted Father Murrell to understand the reasons why she had done what she'd done. Betty had given him the barest of details - who she was, what being a Faulkner meant. He knew what he'd seen on the news, but he was deeply shocked by what he heard. Sadistic and sexual abuse by the brother, incest and satanic practice with her uncle. It was not your normal confession. But when she described the ritual she had participated in, she fell apart. She would cry convulsively, get a few more sentences out, then become hysterical again. She made sure he understood she'd been drugged (with what sounded like the date rape drug or something similar that made her compliant) and that her uncle had taken her hand with his and made her do the stabbing motions. She couldn't do it, even on the drugged wine. Yet she had witnessed and participated in the utter horror. She had chanted, performed her parts in the ritual at the proper time, she had not gone running, screaming, into the night and away from the evil madness, but stayed.

Father Murrell was both revolted and compassionate. The satanic rite was absolute ritual blasphemy, but the pitiful girl had been abused one way or another her whole life. There was no doubt she regretted what she had done and felt tremendous shame and guilt. Once her complete story was finally told, she told him she didn't believe she could ever be forgiven, by God or man. Murrell very patiently told her God was Love, and one truly seeking forgiveness would be forgiven. But she must change her life. He had assumed she was a Christian, but when asked she shook her head. He explained there were many kinds of Christians, many denominations and sects. He was a mystic, an esoteric universalist who believed God revealed Divinity to humanity in many ways throughout space and time.

Murrell explained as an esoteric Christian, he believed the Love of God was universal, was the Light all religions talked about and this universal Light and Love was what Jesus taught to his disciples in secret. He said the man Jesus became the Christ when the Holy Spirit descended upon him as a dove at his baptism. At that point, Jesus the man became one with the Christ Light, the ominpresent Love of God. Jesus had become one with the God within, and that same divinity awaited discovery in the heart of every man and woman. He said the path of Jesus was the same path every human should tread, the realization of the divine self, in the kingdom of heaven within, although that process usually takes many lifetimes.

She had not enjoyed the couple of times she'd gone to church with friends and she'd hated the religious crap she'd seen on TV. She was suprised and intrigued by this priest who believed in reincarnation, in a mystical form of Christianity she had never even heard about. She wanted to hear more.

Amanda got in her car, and drove to Kevin's house. APD tried to keep the parade as discreet as possible, but that didn't always work, with so many people and vehicles involved. So when Amanda showed at Kevin's so did the other half of the surveillance team, joining the half sitting on Kevin. So far, so boring, was all I could think, but I doubted it would stay so boring. It didn't.

***

"Do you guys know that Kevin is into Satan?" Tonya paused.

"Yes."

"Well Kevin was into it a little bit before he went in, but he got most of it from George, George is into Satan, big time. It might be because his dad and uncles were such outlaws, while his mom and aunts were so religious. Whatever, George said society thought people like him were evil, so he might as well live up to it. Gerorge is committed to a life of crime, as a philosophy. I've talked to him about the Satan stuff, he's for real. He said there were two sides in life, and he had enough sense, self-knowledge, and courage to know which side he belonged on.

He really believes he's one of the Devil's own, something special."

***

Danny, the driver, and I sat in the van and listened to what was going on at Kevin's, which was very little. Finally he and Amanda got in his car and drove to the Dirt Shack, a rough biker bar on Memorial Drive where it croses the edge of Cabbagetown.

We parked in the parking lot. Our people covered the entrances. Our driver was an undercover cop wired with a hidden mike and a earphone that looked like a hearing aid. After he left to go in the bar, Lonnie and Johnnie knocked on the back door and came in. They were bored shitless.

***

"So George went down for forgery and went to jail about Kevin's second or third year in. Because Kevin had refused to rat out the Riders - he got no probation or parole. But that way, once he got out, he was free. No parole officer looking over his shoulder for him to run afoul of the law. So, anyway, George ended up being cellmates with Kevin at Riedsville. Like I said, they knew of each other before but weren't close. I've heard both Kevin and George talk about those times. They had one fight at the begining, but they needed each other, with so many black innmates and racial tensions, they needed each other too much to be enemies.

"I don't know many details about the fight. It was one of those macho who's the boss bullshit things. But what I do know is Kevin won. He'd been a regional wrestling champion in the tenth grade, and would have won state the next year, but he chose to raise hell, drink, smoke, party instead of be a rah-rah athlete. Kevin said it was close quarters inside their cell, and Kevin is larger and stronger than George; although George is probably meaner. George is not the kind to fight with his hands. As a kid he would always use something, a stick, a rock, whatever was there, as a weapon. George enjoyed hurting people. He would have beaten two or three kids to death if Bobby and others hadn't pulled him off. The truth is both men are mean as snakes. Cruelty comes easy to both of them.

"I know George, he needed Kevin as an ally in the big house, but he was just biding his time until the oppurtunity for revenge presented itself. You see, George had never lost a fight in his entire life, it was a point of personal pride. Losing that fight, to him, was an unforgivable humiliation. This whole crime/setup deal was probably orchestrated just so George could make Kevin pay for that humiliating ass kicking - some sweet revenge for the first fight he ever lost in his life."

***

Our driver went into the Dirt Shack and pretended he was on the pay phone while he described what was going on. Kevin and Amanda sat with a couple of bikers at a table and shared a pitcher of beer. Again, conversation was very limited, but Kevin was writing his ass off. He'd write, they'd read. They'd write, he'd read. It went on for over an hour. The cop would drink a little beer, pretend to make a call, drink a little more beer, make a call, all the time talking to us on his hidden mike, listening to us through his "hearing aid." Finally, it seemed everything was worked out. Everybody hugged each other and left at the same time. The bikers got on their choppers and rode away. Kevin and Amanda went back to Kevin's house, followed by our covert parade, where they made put on some loud classic AC/DC and made love, loudly, and repeatedly. Every now and then yelling "Fuck the cops!"

***

"Kevin got out of prison before George did. George called me from jail, told me and the rest of the girls who had worked for his escort service that when he got out he wouldn't be working girls, so we should all work for Kevin; which most of us did. That's when I met

Amanda Stone, Kevin's number one girl and semi-girlfriend. I'd still see George every now and

then, but I've worked for Kevin for years. Then a month ago, George called me from out of the

blue and told me he had a once in a lifetime oppurtunity for me." Tonya took another sip of her

second iced tea. It was a long story, telling it made her thirsty, she wanted a real drink, but knew

she had to wait.

Father Murrell had spent a long time revealing his philosophy. It was unlike anything

she'd ever heard before. "So you see, although many Christian denominations approach this

from many perspectives, from the esoteric perspective the whole Christ event, the crucifixtion

and resurrection was a way all who believed could find forgiveness - like you and so many

countless others throughout the centuries who thought they were unforgivable and undeserving

of Divine Love. Through believing in his sacrifice they could become open to recieve God's love

and forgiveness, His Grace. Jesus' life given willingly as a ritual sacrifice, as the pure sacrifical

lamb of God, provided a belief mechanism for all those in tribes, cultures, or societies where the

belief in their inherent guilt and sin blocked them in their mind from reaching the Divine spark

within. The Christ event happened so that all who seek love, forgiveness, and mercy from God

could believe in it and by believing in it, open themselves up to and recieve it. Although some

denominations see this very exclusively, this Love of God, this Christ Light is an aspect of

reality, part of Nature. We believe that when Jesus said 'know ye not that ye are already are as

the sons of God' he was referring to the Divinity that dwells in eyeryone's higher self. Much

like when he said the entire kingdom of heaven is within you."

***

"The deal was simple. I did everything George said, exactly like he said, and I'd have a new and better life for me and my baby girl in Vegas."

Tonya described the quality and amount of drugs he gave her, the reconnaisance they did when he showed her who Stewart was, told her Stewart's schedule, told her where she'd pick him up, the story she would tell, how scripted it all was.

She told it all, the car rental, the pickup, the weekend, the van ride, the staining of Stewart's clothes and shoes. She told how close to her own death she felt several times when being questioned by George during the "staining" van ride and on the ride to pick up her daughter. "If I'd said it wrong, played it wrong, I'd be dead and ya'll woulda' never found my body."

Father Murrell didn't push her, but he asked her *could* she believe. She wasn't sure, but she thought she wanted to. "Can you believe Jesus died in the fashion that he did so people such as yourself could come to God's mercy and forgiveness?"

"Yes, I can believe that," Samantha said. And she did. It was not the huge leap of faith some people make, but it was enough for Father Murrell.

"You have confessed your sins, will you take Holy Communion with me?"

"Yes." She had taken part in the blasphemy, the ritual rebellion, the inversion and perversion of communion. But she had never taken holy communion before.

"Now, Samantha, for the good of your soul, I'm going to ask you one more question before we take Communion. Think about this, and mean it if you say it. Will you renounce Satan and all his works?"

"Yes."

"Then do so, now, verbally."

Samantha took a long breath. She knew the beliefs her uncle had and all that he had taught her. It had made sense to her at first, the law of survival, every man for himself, eat or be eaten, strength and selfishness as the only truly honest path. But she was sickened by where those beliefs had led.

"Yes, I renounce Satan and all his works."

"Samantha, will you now open your soul to the Divine Love of God through the sacrifice of Jesus Christ?"

"Yes, I will."

"Then recieve the body and blood of Jesus the Christ. Reach union with the Christ Spirit, the Lord of Love, and the Prince of Peace."

***

Deseree really didn't have that much of a story. A friend of Jasmine's, Carl Lewis, the same man Tonya called George Sanders, came to Jasmine with a request. He needed a special gift for a special client. He looked over the whole stable and chose her. Deseree flew back with Carl/George. He showed her Amanda from a distance, gave her a ton of coaciane, paid her a lot of money, told her what story to tell, and told her what to say and do to pick up Amanda and get to Kevin.

The plan worked - she got Amanda and Kevin in her room, partied all night, did everything that Carl said, then got on an airplane and flew back when the job was over.

She'd had fun, partied hard, and was well paid.

***

Samantha took the wafer in her mouth and swallowed the wine. She kept her eyes closed. They were outside in the gazebo on a sunny day, but a different kind of light began to radiate, to shine, back between her eyes towards the center of her head, she experienced Light. Light, like she'd never seen or known. Light that somehow *was* compassion, *was* Love. Light that filled her awareness completely. She was lost in that Light for what seemed an indeterminant period of time. After experiencing the Light it faded and she returned to her normal consciousness and opened her eyes to see the kindest smile she'd ever seen. She felt like heavy chains fell off her chest and shoulders - an oppresive weight had been lifted off her body. She felt renewed, reborn. She could not remember feeling that good before, ever. It was as though some part of her inside had been in cold darkness her whole life, and for the first time, had come into the sunlight.

***

Jasmine had known Carl Lewis/George Sanders for years. They had been introduced by one of her customers and they had become lovers. She knew Carl was a gifted forger, that he was involved in the drug business, and had worked women before, but was no longer in the life.

"Unfortunately, I'm something of a sucker for a really hard man, and Carl is strong, cruel, ruthless. For some reason, I find that very attractive. Believe me, it is not my most productive trait. Carl/George came to me looking for a woman for a special job. I asked him what kind of job, he said no big deal, just entertaining a couple. I call ritual murder a very big deal and would have never sent Deseree, or taken in Tonya for him, if I'd known murder was involved. Carl lied to me, manipulated me, and underestimated me. That's why we're going to help you make sure these guys get the death penalty. And these guys better get the death penalty. If not, and they ever get out, we three are dead. And that's as honest a statement as any cleared by your lie detector."

***

Samantha asked Betty if Father Murrell could stay for dinner. Of couse he could. Betty was thrilled Samantha had taken to Father Murrell. Samantha looked happy – radiant - like a diferent girl than the one who had arrived days earlier. The fact she had cried long and hard was obviously written around her eyes. That, too, was a good sign to Betty. She knew how tears can help wash the soul clean.

***

Lief was pleased, they had the real perpetrators and the reason for the setup. It was all clear, except for two things.

"Why was Stewart set up, and why was the Faulkner estate chosen as the site for the ghastly ritual?"

All three women were quiet. They had thought, until that moment, they had all the pieces to the puzzle, but quickly realized they didn't. Jasmine thought fast, she didn't want to blow the millions, but she had to tell the truth or she wouldn't pass the test. "There must be someone else involved that we don't know about. George was working out his revenge, and maybe also someone else's. To find out the answer to that question, the police will have to follow the Sanders boys, George and Bobby, wiretap them, whatever. We've told you everything we know.

"George is not a talkative person by nature and is professionally very secretive. Anyway, our information will break the case wide open and lead to the answers to those last two questions. It may be the only person that knows the answer to those questions is George Sanders. But it's certain he will know."

Lief was dissappointed. He wanted to know it all, but they were right, they had broken the case wide open. He would provide the police with most of the missing pieces, and Stewart would be fully exonerated, which was what the family was after. That and the public silence of these three.

One by one, they took the lie detector tests. Same simple questions, then the big one, was the statement you've just given the truth, the whole truth. They all passed. The contracts prepared by Lief and Alpert were signed and notarized, the calls were made, computers put in motion, and the money deposited. Finally, after literally talking all day long and into the night, the crew came back on board, the captain had filed the flight plan to Atlanta and they departed immediately. Jasmine wanted her lawyer with them every step of the way. He didn't mind. He was making a bundle.

Father Murrell said good night, hugged Betty and kissed Samantha on the forehead. They had arranged for him to come back in a couple of days to spend another afternoon counseling Samantha.

As Father Murrell drove away, he wondered what had gone wrong with America, with the whole modern world. Now the children had guns, took drugs, treated sex as unimportant, killed with reckless abandon, had no respect for the sanctity of human life. Every day he read things in the paper or saw stories on the news that horrified and sickened him. In his conversations with Spooky, Spooky sometimes used the phrase - Rome is burning. Well, Rome was burning, and nobody gave a damn. Nero just played on his fiddle and watched the world self-destruct. Murrell knew he could only work on one soul at a time. That was good, because he didn't think he could stand to hear too many confessions like Samantha's.

Betty explained to Samantha that John had left for Savannah to attend a security conference, and asked her wouldn't she rather stay with them than in Spooky's house alone.

"God only knows when he'll be back. It will be lika a spend the night party. We'll make popcorn and watch a movie."

Samantha readily agreed, she liked the warmth of the house, she liked hanging out with Betty and the kids.

***

Night had become near midnight, our two targets appeared to be sleeping after marathon sex. Everybody was bored. Johnnie and Lonnie were in the command truck, drinking coffee with Danny, the driver - Peter, and me. Every now and then we'd look out the tinted windows APD had installed on the old UPS truck. Danny had SWAT watching all sides of the house wearing night vision goggles that pierced the darkness. All we had heard for hours was snoring. After midnight we heard the alarm clock go off and radio music began playing suddenly, very loudly. Finally, something was about to happen. Johnnie and Lonnie rushed back to their bikes.

***

George and Bobby had been busy since Bobby came home. Bobby had been sent him down in the crawl space under the front corner of the house to dig out the lock box filled with cash and ID's. George had gone to the bank and cleaned out his safety depoit box, which also held cash and ID's. Then George had gone out and bought a van at Carmax under a name he'd never used before - he had the totally legit papers of a dead man. It was good to read the obituaries back in the day. He was glad he was farsighted. The orbituary path to a new ID was closed now, but he had taken advantage for years and had numerous available idebtities. George had decided that he and Bobby were going to have to dissapear for a while. If the frame held up, they'd come back quickly and be themselves again, resume their lives. If not, they would never come back and never use their real names again, or see their relatives, unless it was done very covertly.

They were going through their whole house, deciding what to take or leave, preparing the house for a long absence, packing what they'd take in their new van. CNN or the local news was left playing on the tube depending on the time, trying to find out if there were any new developments. At the first rumor that the girls were coming in to cooperate, it was time to book. So far, nothing had changed. The hooker's sketches were still being shown along with Lief's appeal for them to come forward every half hour. George figured the news hounds would be on top of any recent developments and the whole world would know immediately.

***

Wilson and Potts had gone to the various jails and made copies of the hand written and typed records of Kevin's and Amanda's incarcerations, and they also had finally gotten the lists of Phineas' penal clients and information on his treatment programs from Diaz's secretary who likewise had worked incredibly hard for the info. They were spending the night looking for anything that would tie the doctor in with Kevin and Amanda. Annie's sister was again watching her kids. Annie owed her sister some kind of present for all she'd done lately. She knew she was pushing it, so it'd have to be something nice.

***

The police radios were crackling, there was music and movement coming over the bugs in the house. It sounded like people showering, getting dressed, preparing to leave. They wispered a few times but were mostly mute. After twenty-three minutes, the two came out and got on Kevin's outlaw-chopped Harley. He had on blue jeans, a black leather jacket with colors - a denim vest over it reading Midnight Riders in large letters on the back. Amanda had on jeans, a black leather jacket, and a red scarf around her neck. They took off, and so did all of us.

The parade followed Kevin and Amanda at a distance, back to the Dirt

Shack. It looked like a biker convention, there were choppers everywhere, and tons of men wearing colors, and every denim vest was like the one Kevin wore.

Like before, our driver Peter went in to report. Ronnie and Lonnie came back to the truck, for a minute, to drink coffee and see what was up. More and more bikers kept pulling in, many with women on the back. Lonnie was the first one to notice the obvious. We expected the male bikers to look alike, they all had on their colors over their leather jackets. Lonnie brought to our attention that all the women were dressed alike too, blue jeans, black leather jackets, with red scarfs. After a quick cup, they went back to their positions, Johhnie in front of the place, Lonnie in the back.

Danny had undercover people positioned watching the front and back doors, so he sent in a couple more undercover cops to join the one already inside to observe what was happening.

***

Phineas had called the school's headmaster earlier during the evening and found out what hotel the band was staying in and called there, trying to reach Samantha, or at least establish whether she were there or not. The front desk told him which room Samantha was assigned, and who her roomates were, but offered the knowledge that the band was giving a 9:00 PM concert and going out for food afterwards. The desk said they would be glad to leave a message for Samantha, but the chaperones had informed them they'd be in late. Phineas told them it was very important Samantha call home, there was a family emergency. The desk promised to pass the message on to the chaperones at the first oppurtunity. There was not much for Phineas to do but watch the news and worry. He took a sedative, had a few drinks, and fell asleep in his recliner with the TV on.

***

The trouble with sending undercover cops into a biker bar is the bikers know the regulars and are suspicious of anyone they don't know. Extremely suspicious. The cops might as well had on their dress blues or daylight floresent orange, they were that obvious.

***

Jasmine and her girls felt like celebrating, they had just become millionaires. Tonya was undecided about what to do concerning Pugsley and his proposal. The time hadn't really seemed right so far to broach the subject. Maybe if she impressed the family by being devoted to him while he was recovering, she could still pull it off, but there was so much animosity from the family…. She was already now a millionaire, so it didn't seem all that important at the moment. So why worry about it. She knew where Stewart was, if she was so inclined, she could visit him at the hospital. Anyway, if he was a vegtable, there was no possibility for a marriage.

Jasmine already had a large net worth, but not millions in cash. The hookers and their mouthpiece sat in the back lounge section. The Faulkners, Lief, et al were in the front section. The bathroom and a flimsy door seperated the two sides. The two lawyers had talked, and decided that since they would be flying into the morning, they would go straight to the Atlanta's DA's office, where the women would turn themselves in. After a few drinks, the women and their lawyer went to sleep. The group up front did the same.

***

Still more Midnight Riders kept coming to the Dirt Shack, and everybody was wearing the same outfit. We couldn't hear much off the mike in the ankle bracelets, except all the loud music, the background voices, and occasional snatches of short and insignificant conversation.

Danny had people watching Kevin's bike, and the three undercovers inside were watching Kevin and Amanda. I got out and walked around circumfrence of the Dirt Shack and did some quick math, and did a quick walkthrough of the bar. I had counted over fifty choppers and at least eighteen women wearing exactly the same outfit. Danny had asked our driver through his earphone about the women, and already been told everyone inside had on the same clothes.

Kevin and Amanda sat at a table by themselves and shared a pitcher of beer. Every now and then a Rider would come by, shake hands, say howdy, but that was about it. Randy knew exactly what Kevin wanted, and when Randy gave the high sign, everything would go down. All the bikers waited.

***

I climbed back in the rear of the command truck. We had undercover cars watching both doors, and Johnnie was on top of Kevin's bike in the front, Lonnie had the back. I told Danny how I felt. "Danny, I think we have problems, there are too damn many of them, and they're all wearing the same clothes, that's no accident. If all the bikers split at once, create some kind of diversion, what we have here is not enough, we could lose them. Easy."

Danny got on the radio, and asked for all uniformed officers and undercover officers in the zone, not working a major felony, to converge on the Dirt Shack. We were outnumbered, and needed reinforcements. Danny didn't know it, but it was already too late.

***

Randy - long time and only president of the Midnight Riders, came with a waitress carrying a tray of nine shots of Tequila. He sat down with Kevin and Amanda and distributed the tequila among them, three shots each.

Randy lifted his glass, "Here's to brotherhood." They toched glasses and all shot their first shooter, slamming the empty glasses down. "Here's to paying a debt of honor." They shot and slammed the second one. "Here's to good hunting." They touched glasses for the third time, and drained the glasses and slammed them down in perfect unison. They got up and hugged. Randy hugged Kevin first, then Amanda. "You've always got friends," Randy said. Then he tapped on the table, loudly with his shooter glass, five times. Amanda picked up her helmet and headed to the bathrooms, with Kevin right behind her. In fact, every biker couple headed toward the bathrooms at once, all carrying their helmets. At the same time, ten bikers moved closer to the two undercovers standing together, and five headed towards Peter in the phone booth.

***

Peter was watching, as thirty-six people headed toward the johns and lots of big badass mo' fo' bikers gathered nearby, giving him the eye.

"Yo, Danny, whatever's going down here is about to happen, and we're outnumbered, and you know at least half theses guys are packing, if not all of them. I could use some backup about now. Before now. Hurry!"

"We've called in everybody in the zone, hang on. Tell me what's up."

"All the couples are heading to the john, carrying their helmets and most of the solo bikers are hanging out near me and our other two. It doesn't look good. I have a bad feeling about...

***

Kevin and Amanda, along with the seventeen other couples headed into the rest rooms or waited by the door. In the men's room helmets and keys were exchanged. Then one of the biggest bikers pulled a lock cutting tool out of a stall where it had been waiting for hours. Snip, snip, the ankle bracelts went off. Eighteen couples went running full speed out of the johns, motorcycle helmets already on, keys in their hands at the ready. Kevin and Amanda were in a throng heading towards the back door, opposite from the bike they rode in on, following an unrelenting human wave.

***

We were in the truck waiting for the requested reinforcements, when we heard Peter almost finish his sentence, "... about this situation."

We heard another voice say, "Hey, no fucking Hell's Angels in here, mother fucker."

Then the noise of what sounded like a massive head blow, as the tracking alarms in the truck went off, indicating that both braceltes had been cut off. Bikers came pouring out of the club in massive human waves. You could hear the noise of Peter groaning as a rain of blows came down on him from God knows how many assailants. Bikers with helmets on were starting bikes everywhere. The couple that got on Kevin's bike was about the same size and shape as Kevin and Amanda, but who could be sure. But not just the couples came out with their helmets on, so did about half the club. The others were inside kicking the shit out of the three undercovers. Danny was freaking, there was no way to follow everybody, and three fellow officers were getting beaten half to death inside, and needed have help.

***

Peter, nearly unconscious, tried unsuccessfully to get his .38 out of his ankle holster. But there were too many thugs on top of him, all he could do was yell out for help, cover himself as best he could, and experience pain.

***

Danny yelled, "Thank God!" as three squad cars came rolling into the parking lot at high speed and slid as they hit the brakes. On the radio he yelled. "Officer down, officer down, inside!" The uniformed cops got out with shotguns at the ready and ran inside. All the chase team could do was pick out the most likely candidates who were probably Kevin and Amanda, and follow them. It was chaotic and frantic on the radio. Some of the couples had anywhere from one to three solo riders escorting them, all heading out in different directions. But on my headset that picked up only Johnine and Lonnie, I heard Lonnie with crystal clear clarity say, "I've got her!"

***

Danny got in the driver's seat, but wasn't sure which way to go, all his people were trying to chase somebody, but nobody sounded confident. I yelled at Danny, "Lonnie says she's got them!"

"Is she sure?"

"Lonnie, are you certain?"

She was giving chase, talking on the mike in her helmet. "Yeah, I studied her ass on the way in, she's wearing Guess Jeans. I know I've got her, believe me."

"She's sure. Nobody else is. Let's go." I yelled. I couldn't give Danny orders, but there was no time for diplomacy. Danny understood and went with it.

And go we did, racing east on Memorial, following her descriptions as she gave chase. We took the fourth left, started winding through the neighborhoods as she desribed her route.

She was following the couple, escorted by three solo choppers. She was going too fast to always give the street names, but she counted roads and gave street names when she could.

Danny's radio kept crackling, everybody reporting in on who they were chasing. I heard

Danny say under his breath, "Great, just fucking great, I've got my career on the line during the biggest cluster fuck in APD history." All I could do was hope and pray Lonnie was right, and my friend Danny was wrong.

Our truck was no speed demon and since Peter had been busy fighting/getting the shit kicked out of him on the floor, Danny had taken the wheel. I had the feeling it had been a long time since Danny drove a truck. That is, if he'd ever driven one.

Lonnie called in, "I'm gaining, getting close." Then I heard, "Oh shit, they've seen me."

Then, "Oh shit, he's got a gun." Followed by the unmistakeable sound of a bike skidding on pavement.

***

The last two of the three escorts kept looking back, and spotted a chaser. The biggest, badest of the two bikers slowed down while the rest kept speeding. Then he hit the brakes, skidding, swerving. He almost laid the bike down, but managed not to, as he drew his .357 long barrel. He saw it was a chick. He raised and aimed, as he thought to himself, "Damn, she's fine."

***

Lonnie hit the brakes in a controlled skid a hundred and fifty feet away, she wasn't getting paid enough to die. The biker pointed the gun straight at her. She accelerated with her back wheel sliding and screeching into a side street. She then tried to guess where the bad guys were going. She didn't see them, but checked back in, letting us know in what direction they were heading, where she'd lost them. She'd keep looking; they couldn't have gotten that far away.

Danny got on the radio, and attempted to order every available car into the area. The problem was that every available car was already involved in a chase or trying to calm the disturbance at the Dirt Shack. Most bikers aren't intimidated by cops, and aren't afraid to fight. Especially when together in their group.

*****

Four blocks northeast of where they'd lost Lonnie, the bikers came to a stop at a white van. Amanda got off the chopper, opened and crawled into the back of the van. The driver of the van got out, and as Kevin got off the bike, still running, the driver got on in his place. Kevin handed him his helmet and said, "Tell Randy thanks," and got in the van's driver seat and took off. Kevin knew exactly where they were going, but nobody else besides Amanda did. Amanda stayed in the back to check that everything they'd ordered was there while Kevin drove.

"We have two five gallon jugs of gasoline. We have two semi-automatic twelve gauge shotguns. We have two nine millimeter semi-automatic pistols, with two extra clips each and four boxes of shotgun shells. Is that it, baby?"

"That's it, baby, everything I asked for. It's payback time."

*****

We made our way towards Lonnie following her directions, as she scoured the side streets to no avail. When we met up, all she could do is say where they'd been and where they were going when she lost them. She looked at me and said, "I'm sorry, boss, but he levelled that magnum at *me*, and you don't pay me enough to die."

I responded, "Don't worry, Lonnie, nobody pays that much." And meant it.

In my mind all I could think was that it wouldn't take long, somebody will hear the gunshots sson enough. I said so to Danny, and was right. BFD.

***

Kevin knew where George lived. In his line of business, it pays to know everything. Besides, he had been there twice, after all, George gave him half the girls that made up his stable. So Kevin had paid George back with some sweet prices on coke. They were cellmates, he had thought friends. He didn't know the motherfucker hated him and was crazy. George must have never gotten over the ass whipping he'd given him. It was the only possible source of resentment Kevin could come up with. Their business dealings had always been fair and worked out okay. They drove to the street parrallel with and behind George's, to a dark area that gave them access to a small wooded spot next to a creek, past which was George's backyard. Kevin was certain Amanda knew how to shoot, because he'd taught her. They took off their leathers. It was too warm for them, unless you were riding a bike. "Okay, honey, just like I laid it out, you remember it all?"

"No problem, baby, I know what to do."

Kevin put a nine millimeter in the small of his back, the extra clips in his back pocket, threw the twelve gauge on his shoulder supported by the strap, and shoved a handful of extra shotgun shells in his front pocket, then picked up both five gallon jugs of gas.

Amanda threw the other twelve gauge over her shoulder, put the nine millimeter in the front of her jeans, put the extra clips in her back pocket, grabbed some of the extra shotgun shells, and then put them in her front pockets. Then she added a few more.

"Smart, baby, but hopefully, we won't need them.

It was late, still of the night time, but all the lights were on at the Sanders' house. There was a van in the driveway, halfway in the carport, and a sedan in the driveway nearer the street. They watched from a distance, hidden in the dense foilage by the creek, then made their way along the

Sander's backyard to the neighbors side yard and hid behind bushes. The white clapboard house was a simple two bedroom, on a slight hill sloping towards the back and the small creek. They could see two window air conditioners, running full speed, making lots of noise as they made their way. Observing Bobby take a couple of loads of stuff to the van, it seemed the Sanders boys had decicided to go on vacation. Kevin was committed to making it permanent.

Danny looked at the map, there were commercial buildings past a certain point. He thought he knew the general neighborhood their targets must be in. But it wasn't a small area.

The police radio reported the Dirt Shack was under control. There had been no gunfire exchanged. The first police had come in, screaming loudly, pointing shotguns, and gotten almost everyone's attention. Nevertheless, there was some resistance. Many more squad cars showed up. By then, the Riders had accomplished their goal, no use getting in any more trouble than neccesssary. The job was done, the debt was paid. But they were bikers, some refused to go down easy out of principle.

More and more units had rolled in, some of the police hopped out of their cars running with riot 12 gauge shotguns ready, some with pistols, other relied on nightsticks. The good thing was no biker pulled a gun or a knife. The police radio reported mass arrests, for assaulting police officers, resisting arrest, weapons violations, and drug charges. Many of the Riders also had outstanding warrants. All the uniformed cops on the scene thought they were damn lucky no shots had been exchanged, considering how many weapons they confiscated. There were so many arrested, they had to bring in a corrections bus to take them all in.

Kevin and Amanda watched Bobby head back in, he left the carport door open.

***

Bobby stood a few feet inside the open door and yelled at George, "That's everything but the stuff on the kitchen counter." On the counter was a lock box with the cash and fake ID's. George had gone through the house, and brought almost everything he wanted to take with him to the kitchen, where Bobby loaded it into the van. Beside the lock box on the kitchen counter was the Sanders' collection of guns, an M-1 carbine with a thirty shot banana clip, a sawed off twelve gauge double barreled shotgun, loaded with double aught buckshot, and two semi-automatic pistols—a Smith and Wesson 9 milimeter and a 1911 .45 caliber.

George yelled back at Bobby, "There's one more duffel bag in here. Close the door, the mosquitos are getting in, and bring me a cold one. CNN says there's a new development."

So Bobby closed the door, went to the frig, and got out two beers, and joined his brother in the living room watching TV.

****

It was a very basic clapboard two bedroom with a side carport. There was a basement door which went into a small unfinished basement, really just a dirt floor and crawl space with a door and stairs. The carport door led into the kitchen. From the driveway, there was a small concrete walkway which led to the front door, with two short steps up to a small landing.

Kevin moved quietly with Amanda behind him to the front of the van. She levelled the shotgun at the middle of the closed carport door, resting her front hand on the sloping incline of the van in front of the windshield. Kevin left her, moving to the back of the house with the gas cans. He set one down and began to pour the other one along the back wall of the house and then left the half empty can in front of the basement door. He went back, got the second can, and he worked his way around the house, poured a trail on the concrete walkway, and left the half empty can in front of the front door. He went back to where the trail began on the walkway, and got out an old Zippo lighter, the kind that only goes out when you close the top.

Bobby stood besides George, sitting in his recliner, and watched the late breaking story. The correspondent reported that a reliable source in law enforcement had told them that two of the primary suspects in the Atlanta satanic ritual murder case who were being held on unrelated charges, had been released on two thousand dollars bail, which must mean they were no longer considered suspects in the ritual murder.   "Mother fucker, time to go!" George told Bobby to take the remaining duffel bag sitting beside him out to the van while he unhooked the VCR , DVD, and the thin wide screen TV. That and what was on the counter was all that was left. "Move quick, Bobby, it's really time to go."

Bobby took the duffel bag headed outside and opened the back door.

***

Amanda stood there, with the semi-automatic shotgun pointed in the middle of the door. Kevin had told her if anyone came in her sights, to shoot twice. The door opened, Bobby started to walk out, dead center in the middle of her sights. She fired. The double aught buckshot ripped a huge hole in Bobby's chest and threw him back on the floor. Amanda wasn't sure if she meant to shoot twice, or if it was an accident and just happened. The second shot blew a hole in the carport's ceiling, right above the door. But she had seen Bobby's chest explode, she knew he was dead.

***

Kevin threw the Zippo on the gasoline trail a split second after he heard the blast. He didn't even watch the trail of fire circle the house in less than four seconds, he was running to his position at the back of the van, where he could cover both the front and carport door. He did hear the two small whoosh-explosions, as both gas cans blew apart, covering the front and basement doors with flames.

***

George jumped up at the sound of gunfire. In his subconscious mind he was aware of the sounds of a first and second gunshot and of the two whoosh-explosions of gas igniting moments later, but his conscious thoughts were of his brother. He ran into the kitchen at full speed, towards Bobby and the weaponry. As he passed the counter he could see out the open door, and a rifle pointed at him and a female head above it. He dove back behind the counter as the refrigerator on the other side of the counter to the right took a direct hit, its door shattering in the middle to the unmistakeble roar of a twelve gauge. He had caught a glimpse of Bobby before he dived behind the counter. His chest was a bloody mess, and his body was shaking in convulsions, like many humans and animals do as they're dying. He got out of the line of sight of the door, reached up and with one sweep of his arm brought almost everything on the counter top down around him. Out the kitchen window over the sink he could see flames leaping up. He took the safety off the sawed off double barreled shotgun, and one of the 9mm's. He also pulled the M-1 near him, and took the safety off and jacked one in the chamber. Then he pulled the lock box near him. He threw the box in an arching motion over the counter towards the door, the refrigerator took another blast, its door, what was left of it, flew open. He inched his way towards the edge of the counter. He had seen where Amanda was, he didn't think she would move. He knelt by the edge of the counter, said "Hail, Satan, prince of this world," leaned around the corner on one knee and fired both barrells of the .12 gauge. Amanda's head exploded like a dropped watermelon, her body flew backwards. The right side of the door frame was splintered by a gunblast in response. He knew Kevin was out there, too, and now he knew where. He grabbed the M-1 and ran into the living room. He generally kept the cutrains closed, now he reached up and pulled them down. It was a bad angle but he could make out where Kevin was, although at the angle he could barely see him behind the rear of the van, and would have to shoot through the glass and window panes, and through the rising flames to get him. George aimed and began firing, ten shots as quick as he could pull the trigger. He saw Kevin fall sideways, there was no doubt he was hit, but where and how severely he didn't know.

What he did know was his house was on fire and all his money was in the lock box he'd thrown at the back door.

***

Kevin had seen Amanda take the hit and he fired at the door. He had seen her face, her whole head fly into bloody fragments. She was gone. Seconds later, as he watched the carport door a hail of gunfire came at him from his right, and he got hit in the hip. He fell over and then quickly crawled under the van, trying to figure out George's next move. Kevin pulled himself along, towards the front of the van, where he could have a better shot at the back door. He figured the flames at the other doors made it the only viable exit. He had to push Amandas lifeless body back to get into firing position. With shotgun aimed at the lower half of the back door, bleeding and almost numb on one side, he waited.

George ran towards the open back door, kicked the lock box out the kitchen door and into the carport, and jumped to the side out of sight. No one fired. Maybe Kevin was dead. The house was begining to get hot, qucikly filling up with smoke, he had to get out. He shouted "Hail Satan, prince of this world," and ran full speed out the backdoor with the M-1 already pointing towards the back of the van. As George came out firing, his lower half came into Kevin's line of fire as he waited behind the front left tire under the van. Kevin shot at George's pelvis with the twelve gauge. George was hit in the left upper thigh and crotch and went down immediately. But George fell on his right side, rifle towards Kevin, painfully aware of the origin of the blast. For a milli-second they both saw each other lying on the concrete floor of the carport. For another milli-second, they looked, recognising each other over the barrells of their rifles as they both fired. George put the bullet through Kevin's nose into his brain. Kevin blew George's head apart with the shotgun blast. Both died instantly.

Danny had radioed in, to be alerted to any distrurbance in our part of town. We were following Lonnie to see if see could lead us back to our targets. The radio crackled with the report, gunfire, multilpe shots fired at 618 Hagan Way, with the house on fire. We went as fast as the truck and Danny's driving would allow. He called in every car in the zone not tied up at the Dirt Shack. Things there were under control, the corrections bus was filled with bikers, so more squad cars headed our way at full speed, as did those still following after the decoy bikers.

We were the first on scene. Lonnie hung back, and Danny and I got out with pistols ready. I slipped my badge on my belt, I didn't want any late comers confusing me for the perps - that could be very dangerous. But all we saw was a house whose walls were burning at the bottom with flames rapidly moving upward and three bodies in the carport covered in blood. We were talking carnage here, not a solo homicide. One body, faceless, that definitely, most probably was Amanda. The one next to it missing the center of its face was probably Kevin. We cautiously moved forward, made our way past one more body,shot in the head at close range and pulled the large guy with no chest out of the kitchen so his body wouldn't be consumed by the flames. Danny ran back and called to make sure AFD had it, but it, like the gunshots, had already been reported to the appropriate sources, and the fire trucks were on the way.

Although it seemed unneccessary, we checked pulses, there was no need to call an ambulance, just the Crime Scene Unit and the meat wagon from the coroner's office. No one survived this confrontation.

More and more police cars showed up, as did the rest of the surveillance team. We closed off the two roads, after finding the van Kevin and Amanda had probably used, just to keep the reporters away. We needed to make sense out of what happened and identify the unknown corpses. Which wasn't that hard, in their wallets they still had their real ID's, quickly verified by our computer check. We also found the lock box, filled with cash and multiple high quality ID's. The good news was no innocents appeared to have been hurt, or involved at all, and we had to assume that these were the perps in the ritual murders. Why else would Kevin and Amanda have come here to kill these people, if they weren't the ones who had set them up?

It was too bad about the fire, we didn't know what would be destroyed, or if any damning eveidence might be saved. Danny and I probably scared the first fire crew on the scene. We still had our guns out when we ran up to the first firetruck as they arrived, asking them to be aware we had a crime scene to save. But we had to holster our guns and assure them all the bad guys were dead before they got to it.

When the Crime Scene Unit van came pulling up, Danny wanted whatever pictures and videos could be taken, in case the firefighting effort destroyed the crime scene. They thought Danny didn't seem to get it that the place was on fire and filled with smoke.

***

Danny and I watched the firemen, the CSU team, and everybody else do their job. Danny was not hesitant to deliver instructions. I asked the firemen how long before it would be safe to go into the smouldering house once the flames were extinguished. They said many hours. With the whole area secured by APD, there was nothing for me to do until I could go in. I asked

Danny if I could leave right as one of the officers came up with an urgent message. Annie had called in, we went to the radio in our truck.

***

Chapter Sixteen – Friday Morning and Afternoon

"I've found three names of people that did time in jails with with Kevin or Amanda who were seen by Dr. Faulkner, but one is more likely than the other two. He was Kevin's cellmate..."

"George or Bobby Sanders?"

"George Sanders," Annie replied, bewildered. "How did you know?" She had been in her office most of the night, combing through files, not listening to the unfolding events of the evening.

Danny was tired, "Because Kevin and Amanda and George and Bobby Sanders just blew each others brains out. They're all dead." It was descriptive, if not totally accurate, Bobby still had skull and brains intact over his doughnut chest. Lonnie gave me a ride back to the station and my bike, I was due for my bed and some Zeezz.

***

The lawyers and the three witnesses got off the Faulkner jet and went from DeKalb Peachtree airport straight to ADA Diaz's office, having called from the plane. Diaz called the station, they patched him through to Danny. Once Danny was satisfied everything was secure and the way he wanted it, at what he now thought of as the resolution crime scene, he drove to Diaz's office, ready to hear some explanations.

***

Phineas' bladder woke him up from his pill and alcohol induced sleep in the recliner. After he did his business he groggily checked his messages, there were none. Despite his acheing back his survival instinct began to kick in and woke him up. He called the hotel in Washington, D.C. and raised hell with the manager, who assured him the conductor's message light on his phone was blinking, as was the message light in Samantha's room. Phineas demanded to be put through to the conductor's room immediately and was.

The private high school conductor Samantha called Phillip was sound asleep when the phone finally woke him up on the twenty-third ring. After a long night, once the kids were safe in their rooms, he and another teacher had downed some strong drinks in the hotel bar, which at the time seemed to have closed way too early. A lightweight drinker, he hadn't gone by the front desk, noticed his flashing telephone, much less gotten undressed other than having kicked off his shoes, nor had he turned off the lights. Asleep, exhausted, still drunk and embarrassed by the fact, hyper sensitive due to his vunerable position because of Samantha, whatever, Dr. Phineas Faulkner shocked and scared the feces out of him.

"If you do not get my niece on the phone within a five minute time span, I will sue you, sue the school, and make sure you never teach or conduct again in a first world nation. Do I make myself perfectly clear?

Phillip, extremely fearful and not quite himself, told the truth.

"She didn't even come on the trip, she's in protective custody with the Atlanta Police Department, with a detective..." He tore his wallet frantically apart and found the name, "Detective Mosby, Singelton Mosby. I have a contact num..." Phineas slammed down the phone. It was a sad age when you couldn't count on your own centurions. Were these guys the hired help, or a Brutus in their midst?

***

The sun was rising into a new morning when I punched in the numbers at the electronic box at the first gate, was let in by the inward opening double electric gates, rode the small flat stretch and then down the long hill to where the pasture flattens out, between the pond and John's to my house. On the door was a note from Samantha, saying welcome home and that she was spending the night at Betty's. I went in, grabbed a beer, and hit the hot tub for twenty or thirty minutes. After that, I planned a warm shower and a long sleep, knowing Danny would call me when and if he needed me. Probably as soon as the latest crime scene was safe to enter. I'd get what rest I could. Whatever it is that drives Danny relentlessly onward doesn't get to me. I'm human, I need my sleep.

***

Phineas didn't know what to think. He threw on some coffee, turned on the local news and found out there had been a fatal gunfight and a fire in Cabbagetown last night on Hagan Way. Rumors were rampant but unconfirmed that the shootout was related to the satanic ritual murder case. Unidentified sources close to Atlanta law enforcement said that two of the previous suspects who had been exonerated in this infamous case were involved. All that was known was four were dead, no survivors. Fatalities being three men and a woman. Relatives were being notifyed, the investigation was underway, the names and details were being witheld. Phineas didn't know if it was good news or bad. If everyone who knew of his involvement was dead, that was good except he had lost two of his satanic coven. If the frame fell apart, there was no evidence or potential confessions that could lead the investigation back to him - other than Samantha, she was the only weak link, and he knew where she (most probably) was. Before Emmet, Alpert and he decided on Triple S Security, John Mosby had them come out to his house, their family compound, to see various security systems in a working environment. Phineas didn't have the directions, but Alpert did in his Roladex. Phineas went and got his spare key and let himself into Alpert's house. Alpert was still gone, Phineas wondered where. He found the Roladex, found Mosby, and found the directions on the back. He tore it out and went back to his house.

Phineas grabbed his short barrelled .357, the one the salesman said was a guaranteed kill, or minimum severed limb when shot, and even if he missed, the incredibly loud noise would scare anyone to death anyway. He checked and made sure it was loaded, with the hollow point bullets the salesman recommended, took the safety off, put on the leather shoulder holster, slid in the pistol, put on his blue blazer over his white polo shirt and grey slacks, and headed for the Mosby's. He hadn't thought through what to do once he got there, but with George and Bobby probably dead, Samantha was the only vunerable opening in his armor that could bring him down. He needed answers. He needed her in his custody. He was her legal guardian in absence of her parents, who were somewhere around but couldn't be located, just like his brothers. He had every legal ground to stand on. Although her parents had come back to Atlanta, with Stewart's crisis, they had paid scant attention to Samantha, who was supposedly away with her school orchestra.

***

At APD homicide Danny got the materials Wilson and Potts had gathered through a long day and night, scanned them, went to Diaz' office, scanned the women's signed statements, and then began asking questions. None of the women knew who else was involved, but they acknowledged the fact they didn't understand the Faulkner link. Why set up Stewart, why have the ritual at the Faulkner's estate? All other questions were answered. More and more, it looked to Danny like Spooky was right, the only possible missing link was Dr. Faulkner, or through Dr. Faulkner. He must be involved. Danny knew Dr. Faulkner had many private sessions with

George Sanders in his prototype program, but that didn't explain anything. Why Stewart, what was the link?

***

I got into my shower, turned up the heat, lathered everywhere trying to loose that house fire nasty stinky smoke smell all over me. The hot tub had helped but didn't complete the job. I just wanted to lose that stink and get some sleep, hopefully for a meaningful time span.

***

"Mosby's Rangers" had driven through the night, since they were already a day late. They would have been on time yesterday afternoon but the water pump in their RV went out. It was an unusual RV, a very long one with room for four, an arsenal, equipped with a motorized wheelchair lift in the back, and a souped up engine. They were an unusual group to say the least. Two of the four in the RV were part of the Special Forces A-Team that John had commanded in Nam. Coming back in a Huey after a long range search and destroy mission leading mountain warriors whom they had trained, while less than three miles from their base camp, a VC with a shoulder held Russian heat seeking missile had downed their chopper. Help had arrived quickly, which was why all three were still alive.

John was a captain at the time, Gordy was his leiutenant, and Sanchez was a master sargeant/E7. After the crash, Sanchez was a mid-thigh double amputee and got shipped home to the VA. Sanchez was an odd combination, a sniper/medic - a cold blooded killer and a healer. In the old A-team system, in each six man unit would go out among the isolated villagers or tribes and win their hearts and minds, and trained the locals how to fight their own fight – this was before Pacification, CIA control, and Project Phoenix - each soldier had double duties.

Gordy was a weapons specialist and demolition expert, but his natural shining glory was tactical urban combat. He made it through the chopper crash with just broken bones and a missing left eye. Stubbornly, he stayed in country and kept fighting. Gordy lost his left foot, his left testicle, and his left pinky and ring finger years later as a Captain targeted during a motor scooter civilian grenade attack in Saigon. That was long after he had helped clean the streets of Hue. Which was where he revealed his true expertise, urban combat. Fighting in the streets, in close fighting, in single/multiple dwellings, in residential/commercial/industrial, block by block, he was the ultimate expert. In fact, that's how the four remaining active "Rangers" made a living. After the war and their rehab they'd formed a security and training corporation in North Carolina near Gordy's home town. Early on they'd taught at Quantico and on the Farm, way outside Langley, they'd given seminars to FBI, CIA, ATF, and US Marshalls. Urban Combat Inc, had taught SWAT teams all over the nation, some had come to them at their training grounds, sometimes they'd travel. Although to a man, they had stayed in top condidtion, now that they were grey and aging they mainly supervised the teachers they'd hired; many of the places they originally taught now had their own courses and instructors. Over the years they had taught whomever whatever, as long as it came down approved through proper channells, including Contras, South American anti-drug squads, besides half the major SWAT teams in the US. They taught urban tactics, in-house fighting, bombs, bobbytraps, demolition, and sniping. They were your full service special weapons and tactics instructors. In any safe environment, they were happy to share their expertise with what they hoped (and most of the time were) the forces of good. After working some groups sent them by their intelligence community and military contacts they sometimes doubted their own government's widom, but all they taught was the control of violence through violence. They didn't do politics, torture, or population control. The School of the Americas at Fort Benning had taught that stuff.

Oddly enough, John later sustained almost the same injury as Sanchez, but his legs were taken by an incoming mortar shell two tours later. John had made it to major when he got shipped stateside to the VA.

Besides Gordy and Raul Sanchez, Moose and Walter were also in the RV. Moose had always been as been big as an ox, and as some kids he grew up with would tell you, twice as dumb. It was somewhat true, Moose was six foot eight of brawn and not brains; he only beat the Army's minimum IQ requirement by one point. The shrapnell that found its way inside his skull, brain, and neck for which the doctors could find no way out, probably didn't help. But Moose's Mom and Dad had been strong and wise people, who'd taught him right from wrong and to respect authority that behaved correctly. Moose had done fine. He had made it into the military, had been a good soldier, made it to corporal, and had stayed out of trouble. During the war he was an M-60 machine gunner with the 101st Airborne for four tours in country. He was big enough and strong enough to shoot any weapon from the hip. His physical strength was immense, and he could break down, clean, and reassemble any semi or automatic weapon as quick as anyone. He had been a near miss for a mortar shell explosion on his way back from the showers at his base camp. The shrapnell killed the two boys standing beside him, and got him in the side, head, and neck. The shrapnell in his side came out.

Walter Hunting Elk, another master sargeant/E7, was the fourth in the RV - a low t-12 level injury/highly functional paraplegic had been a highly successful sniper and was full blooded Lakota from a long line of warriors. His confirmed kill count was 65 when his team was picked up at the completion of an assasination mission for Project Phoenix, and made it halfway home, at which point the copter was downed hard by a shoulder held heat seeking SAM.

***

One day, years earlier, the original seven who made up the now aging and mellower "Mosby's Rangers" were sitting around, drinking beer, shooting a few targets, taking it easy, when they tried to figure out what they had in common. They had all been in Nam, they had all been wounded, they had all been decorated several times, and they all possessed a confirmed kill count over twenty, some over fifty. Other than that, they were a diverse bunch of hard partying dogs of war who had linked up doing rehab in the VA system. Now they all were married, and divorced/single or remarried, with kids running the gamut from grown and working to three years old. Two had left the company for other jobs and only showed up every other year or so. John had gone stable, too - but he always provided the cabin and a safe haven for these loonies to let loose. Something the Rangers still needed, although the hard partying days were mostly long gone. Now less than an hour away, they were happy to be approaching one of the few places they could really let their hair down and be themselves.

Hudson's eyes fluttered open. He was only two, but he was very aware. He listened to the noises. His twin brother Hunter, in the bed pushed next to his, was sleeping. Mom and Dad had figured out the twins did best in close proximity to each other. It was a twin thing. Hudson didn't hear his older sister up yet and the baby wasn't crying. He heard no adult or parent sounds. Hudson listened to the calm a few more moments and quietly let himself down off the bed feet first, holding on to the covers. His feet landed noiselessly on the floor. The pull-on diapers, which he now wore only at night, being mostly potty trained, were dry, not that he would have cared. This was his time to explore the world. His twin Hunter was bigger, stronger, more aggressive while Hudson tended to hang back and watch. And then explore on his own terms, like now.

His feet quietly padded down the hall towards the kitchen. Momma and Daddy talked about how the house was baby-proofed. It wasn't fun proofed. He tried to open the lower kitchen cabinets, they still wouldn't open. Then he noticed a chair had been left in an unusual place, below the talk and button box. Every so often the lights would light up and Daddy or Mama would talk to the box, and hold one of them up to push the red button. Then, in a little while, a visitor would appear. Some, like Grandparents, brought presents, candy, toys.

Hudson began to climb up into the chair. He didn't get to look at the talk box much, or get to do anything but push the red button when his parents held him up. With the chair there, he could finally check it out.

***

Phineas followed the directions down I-20 east and off on the secondary roads through new suburbs till he was out in the country. He kept going until the pavement ran out, and he continued down a gravel road that looked somewhat familiar. After a few off and on doubtful miles he came upon a group of mail boxes and a driveway at a double fence and electric gate that definitely looked familiar. There was a camera monitoring the gate, so he held back, put the car in park, he needed to formulate a plan.

Phineas thought about his priorities. So much had happened so suddenly that it was hard for him to collect all his thoughts. Had Samantha destroyed all her ritual regalia? Was she scared of getting caught and gotten rid of them? He hoped so. Had she run away because he had punished and beaten her? Hopefully. Had she told anyone anything? He certainly hoped not. Phineas needed to have her in his possesion and under his control, and maybe leave the country for some time - tell his sister it was for her therapy, rat out Stewart as her tormentor. Then if it was necessary, commit her. Maybe in Zurich, maybe in Rio, to a very expensive, vary exclusive sanitarium. If necessary, move her to a country with no extradition treaty with the US. If there were no physical links left, it would be her word against his, if she *had* told anyone. But why would she tell anyone anything? It would incriminate her as well.

If she was considered insane and institutionalised in a foriegn country, her word wouldn't matter much, for no one would hear it. He was considering burning his house down when they got home, just to be sure, concerned about fibers, trace evidence. No sacrifice was too great to continue his freedom and the status quo. He might have to postpone his grand plan, but he was still hoping his dark master would provide; although he was beginning to have doubts, since the evil one hadn't helped George much, and they'd done the same rituals. He called the airport, instructed them to have the jet ready for a trip, and was surprised to be told it had just returned and might be scheduled for another flight and that he needed to talk to Alpert. Whatever his siblings were up to was not a priority, Phineas might have to commandeer it. He told them to have the jet ready.

Phineas needed to get Samantha now, before her parents wanted to see her, one quick trip home for passports and cash, then leave the stove on with paper and trash nearby, and everything might work out. Something like that, oe kill her.

***

Most people don't generally sleep that deeply in an unfamiliar bed. Samantha felt perfectly at ease with Betty, and had slept unusally well. However, when the baby started crying and Betty got up to tend to her, it awakened Samantha. She got up and sleepily trudged on in to the bathroom.

***

Phineas pulled up to the gate. He decided the best way in was logical and legal. Absent her parents, he was Samantha's legal guardian, and he had every reason to demand to see his niece, to insure her safety. If that didn't work, he would consider other more drastic methods. But if memory served him correctly, the inner fence was electrified, and if he tried ramming his way through, he might get hurt and all kinds of law enforcement might show up. Better he schmooze his way in.

Without hesitation now, he drove up, stopped in front of the panel and hit the appropriately labelled button that would let him announce himself. "This is Dr. Phineas Faulkner, I would like to see my legal charge, my niece Samantha, immediately."

Hudson couldn't believe his luck, as soon as he pulled himself up on the chair and stood up, the machine started talking to him, too bad the TV part wasn't on. The blue light was flashing. All he had to do now was press the red button. Maybe this person was bringing presents or candy like his grandparents. It was a long reach, and the chair wasn't really close enough, but on his tip toes, reaching and stretching, he might be able to press the red button. He did, but lost his balance and child and chair went tumbling over. He saw a flash of light where his head hit the floor.

As Samantha came out of the bathroom, and was debating whether or not to go back to bed or ask Betty if she could do anything, she heard the crash. Furniture and child hit the floor, the child reacting immediately and loudly. Samantha went running, and yelled at Betty in the baby's room, "I've got him."

She ran to the kitchen, and there was a chair turned over and Hudson sitting on the floor, holding his hand to his forehead and crying loudly. Samantha didn't know she had sat in that chair and then put it where it didn't belong earlier during the night when she drank some water before retiring.

Samantha scooped him up and settled him on her hip as she'd seen Betty do. "Does Hudson have a boo boo?"

Hudson just nodded and lifted his hand off. There was a definite red spot, but it wasn't bleeding and didn't appear to be swelling. So Samantha tried something she'd seen on the movies and TV. "Do you want me to kiss it and make it well?"

Hudson nodded. He had put his hand back on his forehead but took it off and let Samantha kiss it. Samantha was glad it worked. He was still sobbing, but not as much. She guessed her nannies didn't think kissing boo boos was appropriate. Her own parents were never around, not that she could remember. She'd had lots of boo boos that went unkissed. Poor little rich girl, she thought to herself sarcastically.

During the previous evening Betty had told her that Hudson loved picking blackberries, although Hunter found it excruciating torment. She looked where Betty had pointed out her leather gloves and a big red Tupperware bowl.

"Would Hudson like to go blackberry picking down by the pond?" Still sobbing a little bit, he grinned and nodded his head. Samantha yelled to the back of the house and Betty, "I'm taking Hudson out blackberry picking. We'll make a pie later." Betty had told her it was Hudson's favorite food. With the baby still crying loudly, she barely heard Betty say, "Great, ya'll have fun." Samantha picked up the gloves and bowl, opened the door and took Hudson out into the bright new day.

Leonard Wounded Face was sleeping out in the open, near the questers tents on Black Mountain, fifteen miles east of Big Pine in the White Mountains. In one of the (several) local

Paiute creation myths, this was the only dry spot when the world was covered by water. Hawk and his uncle Fish Eater (crane) had lived here surrounded by nothing but water. One day Hawk was shaking a rattle while they sang and dirt began to fall out of the rattle. They sang all day and night and dirt kept coming out of the rattle and the water kept going down. Once it was all the way down they made the Sierra Nevada's to hold the water back. Hawk decided to live on rabbits and Fish Eater on fish, and it was finished.

Leonard was exhausted when he finally went to sleep. Although busy with Personal Quest, he'd been smoking his Sacred Pipe every day to send Spooky, Danny, and the investigating team spiritual protection and help. Leonard had smoked his Pipe on Black Mountain, once they'd hiked up, gotten their camp set up, and the questers were busy preparing dinner. It had been a long, hard hike to get to this place and set up camp but teenagers are teenagers and they still stayed up late.

Leonard was sleeping but came into awareness, lucid dreaming awareness, but he was in his bunk at Reidsville, not on Black Mountain. Spooky was shaking him, trying to wake him up. Spooky kept shaking him saying that the Hyatt's are coming, wake up, we're in danger. Leonard was sure he was dreaming, because they'd killed the Hyatts, he'd watched them die. Then in absolute terror Spooky yelled, "They're gonna kill Hudson, wake up, I need you!"

Leonard jumped in his sleeping bag, going straight from lucid dreaming to being awake. Although part of the dream was non-sense, Spooky's call for help rang true. He grabbed his flashlight, went over to the smouldering fire, found the coffee pot from last night, shook it, it still had a cup or two left, and put it on the hottest coals and began stretching. It was still night, the first light of dawn hadn't reached the mountain yet. He scanned around with his flashlight, found

484

a cup, then kept stretching, then started running in place. He had to have clarity to do good work, and he needed it now.

Leonard blew out long and hard on the coals, added a little wood and got the fire going again. After the coffee reached boiling point, he poured himself a cup. He blew on it, drank some, and went and got his Sacred Pipe. The kids were all asleep, he'd smoke the Pipe here by the fire.

****

Both gates opened and Phineas pulled inside, past the inner gate. He had expected some kind of verbal reply, but gotten none, just the gate swinging open. He drove to next gate and it opened.When he was here before the gates had closed a short time after John had driven past the second gate. This time the gates did not close. He found the intercom silence and the unclosed gates curious phenomenon, but couldn't make sense of it. He drove forward in his car very slowly, the sleek new silver Mercedes sports coupe pulling up close to where the hill dropped off running down to the flat pastures and the pond and houses below. After putting it in park and getting out, well out of sight of anybody down on the bottom land, he crouched down and inched himself to the edge. He couldn't believe his eyes. There was Samantha, still in her nightshirt, carrying a child in diapers towards the pond. He looked back, the gates were still open and couldn't believe his luck. Maybe, despite George's death and his seeming setbacks, his dark lord was helping, and he would still win the day. He watched as Samantha and the child stopped near the pond at some bushes and started picking berries and putting them in a big red plastic bowl.

****

Samantha did what Betty had told her about the night before. Wearing Betty's thick leather gloves she would bend the branch close to Hudson, and he, very fastidiously, would pick the dark berries and drop them in the bowl. For a child his age, it required patience, concentration, and coordination to not get scratched by the thorns. She found it very endearing to watch the focus in his face as he went about his task.

***

Phineas watched to make sure his arrival had gone unnoticed, then he got in his car and accelerated enough to get to the crown of the hill and over. Then shifting the Mercedes into neutral, he let it roll down the hill at its quietest. Samantha and the child were hidden from view by the blackberry bushes during his descent. They must not have heard him coming for a long time. He was already down the hill and placed his car directly between the pond and John's house when he saw Samantha, with child in arm, come into view as they peered curiously around the bushes.

***

She wasn't wearing any panties, just the nightshirt, so on the edge of her consciousness she was aware she didn't pee on herself much at the sight of Phineas, just the grass, and where her feet got splashed, but that was just a little. She had never been so shocked and scared to that point of intense physical reaction before. There was Phineas' Mercedes and there was Phineas, getting out of the car. As he walked around the front of the car his blazer opened, and she could see a very large pistol strapped under his arm. Samantha didn't know whether to run, scream, or be cool. So, she didn't do anything besides look over at Spooky's, but his carport opened on the far side so she couldn't tell if he was even home or not. An eternity passed in seconds. She knew if she ran, Hudson might get hurt and she couldn't risk that. Not knowing what Phineas knew other than how to find her, not knowing what he wanted, she thought she should find out. All she had to do was stall until Betty or Spooky saw what was going on. She just had to be cool.

***

Phineas was anything but cool, his eyes seemed wider open than normal, with a wild, crazy look. "Samantha, come here and talk to me, now." He ordered, not loudly, but forcefully.

She thought about just chancing it and running for the house, but decided against it when he drew the gun. He didn't point it yet, but the threat was obvious. When she got near the car, he was standing in front of it. He told her to lean back against the car while they talked, she didn't need to run or go anywhere, just explain. She held Hudson and leaned back against the passenger door. Although such a position would only slow her down a second or two if she did run, she couldn't outrun a bullet. Sometimes as he talked he gestured with the gun, sometimes pointing the gun at her, sometimes in the direction of Hudson. She just had to be calm and talk for a long time, somebody would rescue her. He was irratic, but still seemed somewhat logical. At least he was not drunk.

Phineas, not much more than ten feet away, pointed the gun loosely at Hudson's head and said to Samantha, "Time for some answers my little vixen, time for lots of answers. And if you don't answer correctly, I will take your life, possibbly the life of your young companion, and who knows, maybe my own. But all that may not be neccessary. Although they haven't released the names, by the reported address and description of events it seems George and his brother are dead, as are Kevin Jackson and Amanda Stone. Leaving Parker - he never knew anything anyway. That only leaves you. Where are your ritual tools? And how did you get into my temple to steal them? And why?"

Samantha thought for a second, but the gun was pointed at Hudson's head, and she figured her uncle may very well be crazy enough to end their three lives in a rage. "I destroyed my ritual tools. You beat the hell out of me, why should I keep playing your games. That whole satanic ritual thing, whatever, that's your deal, not mine. I don't want to play anymore. I threw away my magical weapons in a dumpster, all my regalia. They're long gone in a landfill by now. I'm no threat to you, with the brothers gone and your blackmailers dead and Stewart fucked for life you're safe and in the clear. We've won. You got your revenge, I did, too. I just don't want to do that stuff any more. It's over."

Dying for her sins was one thing. She wasn't about to have Hudson die for her sins, too. It was time to talk, talk like she never had before. Phineas was a living time bomb. She had to defuse him. "If everybody who knows anything is dead, except for me and you, then you have no problems. Did you get rid of your tools?" She had to stall him, keep him talking."Yes. Everything in the temple is gone. I still might burn the house to be sure. How and why did you get in there?"

"How - I watched you, it wasn't complicated. Why - you got drunk and beat me senseless, I thought you were going to kill me. Beating someone so bad you make them think you might kill them does not exactly bring out trust and affection. I came to you to be safe from Stewart, and then *you* beat the crap out of me. I wish you no harm Phineas, Stewart's no threat to me or anybody else any more, we should go our seperate ways. And try to forget everything that's happened."

***

I turned up the hot water and let it pound on me. I needed sleep at least for a few hours, then find how it went between Father Murrell and Samantha. Then, figure out how I could get Samantha and Danny together, and get her to tell the truth, all the truth. I needed to know everything. Danny needed it worse. I still felt real bad about bringing Samatha out without giving Danny the heads up - I was tired, wired, and anxious, despite the long and gruesome night.

***

Hunter was woken up by the noise of the baby's continued crying and everything else that followed. Like children so often do, when one is crying, the other starts. Hunter started crying just as the baby began to nurse. Betty walked in with the baby on her breast and said, "Quit crying, let's go see what's up with Samantha and Hudson. You can eat some Lucky Charms." The twin's favorite cereal.

That was enough, he wasn't really crying. So mother, baby, with Hunter in tow headed into the kitchen. Betty noticed things were wrong immediately. There was a chair near the security box, where she never left one. Betty realized she hadn't warned Sam sbout it. The chair looked like it had been snatched up, not placed with intention. The lights indicated the gates had been opened but not closed. She hit the button to turn on the gate camera, and walked to the window.

She gasped. There was an unfamiliar Mercedes in park, idling between her house and the pond. Samantha and Hudson were leaning against the far side passenger door. There was a man in front of the car, standing on the passenger side about ten to fifteen feet from her child and Samantha. He had a large revolver. Betty studied him with the eye of a trained shooter. He was gesturing with the gun, not aiming it. He was angry, but not to the flash point.

She moved quickly with lightning effeciency. In short seconds, she made the baby a bottle of juice, grabbed two of her favorite stuffed toys and took her back to her bed. She cranked the mechanical musical plastic animal mobil that hung above the bed. That would keep her happy for a few minutes while it played. Betty put the juice filled baby bottle in her baby's mouth, closed the door, and walked rapidly back to the window to watch the man. He was still talking, not in a pre-firing phase.

Grabbing a bowl and the box of Lucky Charms she swept up Hunter and took him back to his bed. She put him down and poured a bowl full. "Hunter, for once, and only once, you can eat all the colored pieces you want, and put the brown ones back in the box. Have fun, this won't happen again." She closed the door and walked rapidly back to the security box and hit the silent alarm, then moved to the gun cabinet in the living room. She took off her necklace, it had a silver Madonna and child, a green jade Budda John had worn in Nam for luck, and a small key. She slid the key in the first lock and turned it. She reached under the cabinet, behind the first leg, where on the head of a nail hung the second key. She grabbed it, and quickly inserted the key in the second lock and opened the cabinet. She didn't think about choices, the distance was not long enough to be a problem. She grabbed the Austrian Steyr 5.56, slid the clip out, checked the ammunition, slid it back in, took off the safety, and jacked a round in the chamber. She had sniper rifles, but they were unneccessary this close.

Surveying the area in front of the house she saw no sign of other intruders than the lone guman. The phrase "lone gunman" bounced around in her head. Is their a phrase in the English language more associated with insane violence than the phrase "lone gunman?" They killed presidents, shot school kids, climbed towers and rained down bullets. She walked to the side door, which faces Spooky's house more than the pond, but which still gave her clear vision of the car, her target – the lone gunman, Samantha, and Hudson. She quietly cracked open the door. The central AC was running, she didn't think the sound of the door opening quietly would be heard near the pond, and it wasn't.

***

Delores looked at the board upon hearing the loud beeping. She couldn't believe her eyes. She slid her chair over to the appropriate area, grabbed a mike, and hit a button. "Betty, are you there?"

The sound on the box was turned down medium low, and she didn't think the gunman could hear them from that distance over the airconditioning, and looking, violence didn't seem imminent. Betty walked back to the security box and hit the switch. "Yes, Delores." She talked quietly at the box. "I'm here and here's the deal. There is a potential hostage situation here on the compound. The potential hostages are Samantha Faulkner and my son, Hudson. I do not recognize the gunman, he's thin, white, tall, bald, appears to walk with a limp. I don't know how he got in, but I found the gates open. I'm leaving them open. 'Mosby's Rangers' are overdue." She looked back at the misplaced chair. "The gate was probably opened by Hudson. Now, Delores, I'm totally sreious here. I do *NOT* want you to contact or send any of our people and do *NOT* want you to contact the county police. What I do want you to do is keep the silent alarm on for a while, let it alert Spooky to what's happening. I was feeding the Baby early this morning, when I heard Spooky's cycle come in. So I know he's home, so keep those lights flashing. I want you to contact APD and tell them you have an urgent, life or death message from Spooky for Danny Fagan. When you get Danny on the phone, tell him that there's a *potential* hostage situation, tell him who, and to come, immediately. Tell him he can bring one or two people, but two max. This is my son involved, I'll make all the calls. I don't want anyone out here I don't know. I'm serious as death here, Delores, you got it?

"Yes, Betty. How about John?"

"You call him down in Savannah and tell him to get here the fastest way possible. Now Delores, listen, maintain the link, but don't talk for a while. I need to check things out."

Gordy was driving, Moose was still awake to keep Gordy awake, Sanchez and Walter were snoozing in their bunks. As soon as Gordy pulled around the last turn and saw the gates wide open, he knew something was wrong. Since the compound was used to showcase security systems, *and* it was a compound rule - it was *always* locked. He looked closely and saw what others might have missed. The two small American flags on wire cables on either side of the gate had been electronically changed, they were upside down. Gordy remembered John mentioning it as part of the silent alarm package. It's a universal distress signal in the US military.

Moose was unaware until he heard and recognized the tone or Gordy's voice. That tone meant trouble. "Get everybody awake. Break out the gear. Upside down flags and an open gate means we have a *situation* here."

Gordy drove the RV through the gates and stopped right past them, blocking the driveway, leaving only enough room for the wheelchairs to get off the lift and into the compound. Moose had already opened two cabinets as well as shaking and talking to the sleeping beauties. Time to go to work. Moose handed Gordy his headphone/mike set, a pair of binoculars, and a Steyr rifle almost exactly like the one in Betty's hands. Gordy quietly almost shut the door and crept forward to do surveillance. He moved like a cat, the latest prosthetic foot was that good. Walter and Sanchez tried to act pissed off at the interruption to their sleep and that there was no hot coffee, but Moose paid them no attention. He handed each one their communication headsets and told them to get it together quickly, the Mosbys might be in danger. The two dressed and hopped into their wheelchairs in short seconds.

Before the first chair came down the lift, Gordy reported in. "We have what appears to be a hostage situation, with one armed hostile out in the open, holding at bay a young woman and one of the twins. We have a definite sniper situation."

Moose went to the gun cabinet, and said, "Gentlemen?" Walter responded, "British." Sanchez, "Russian."

Moose selected and handed to Walter the British L42A1 with the telescopic sight and a clip of ammo. He handed Sanchez a similarly scoped Russian 7.62mm Dragunov, the only semi-automatic military issue sniper rifle in the world, and a clip. Both men checked their weapons, inserted their clips, and then each sunk the barrell inside the top of their boots and leaned the stock of the rifle back between their knees, a hands free way of carrying the weapon.

In seconds they were on the ground, using the lift's unusual ultra high speeed setting. Gordy had already picked out their two sniping positions. They lifted themselves out of the chairs and down on the ground in a standard chair to ground transfer with the fast sure moves of gymnasts. On their stomachs they wriggled the last few feet forward to their firing positions.

Gordy, acting as spotter for both snipers said over his mike, "violence does not seem imminent, hold your fire, unless it looks like he'll shoot. Take turns spotting for each other. I'm going back to the box to find out if Betty and the other kids are okay, see if there are any more hostiles." Gordy was born for situations like this. It's not that he was happy Hudson was in trouble, he wasn't. But he admittedly loved the intensity of the moment in crisis situations. He was a thrill junkie, but he was the good kind because he was on the side of right.

***

I wasn't really paying attention the first time all my lights blinked off and on. I had my eyes closed as the shower pounded on my face. The second time they blinked, I recognized it as the silent alarm. If I didn't respond in three minutes, an alarm clock ringing sound would be heard throughout my house. The first three minutes the flashing purple light on my security box and the repeated flashing of lights was the silent alert, once the alarm sounded, it would stay on. It wasn't a loud alarm that could he heard at a distance outside, but it was annoying and persistent.

There were several possibilites. It was switched on by accident at John's, or it was an unusual electrical malfunction, or else it was somebody coming to get even with John or me, or coming for Samantha. After turning the water off, I kind of dried off and opened the gun box sitting on top of the toilet's water chamber. John and I both had them built into the bathrooms. It's a dry and nearby place to store your weapon while you bathe. I checked my weapon, a fourteen shot 9mm. I hid it in the back of my bluejeans, at the small of my back, just the way Malcom X described in his autobiography.

Moving quickly through my house, I checked to make sure Samantha hadn't come over from John's and set off the alarm accidentally. Looking outside the window, I couldn't believe my eyes; standing there was Phineas standing talking and waving around a large revolver. Surprise turned to rage when I saw him pointing and waving it at my nephew and Samantha.

Betty must have tiggered the alarm. Then I realized with horror, I had brought Samantha here. If Hudson got hurt or killed, it would always be my fault. Always. A possibility I would do anything to avoid.

I went to the alarm box, switched off the alarm, and got on the intercom with Betty.

"Betty!"

"I'm here Spooky. I'm armed and in position. Who is that asshole with the handgun and a deathwish?" She'd turn her head to talk to the machine five feet away, just loud enough to be heard, she stayed in position, rifle ready. Between the air-conditioning noise, the natural insect noise of a morning pond, the Mercedes idling, and Phineas own ranting she considered it safe.

"It's Samantha's fucked up asshole evil uncle. I'm going out there to try to calm things down. If that won't work, I'll create a diversion."

"Fine. I'll be ready. Nobody threatens my babies. Nobody hurts my babies. And lives. Defuse this Spooky, if you can, before somebody dies."

***

Phineas, still wild eyed, was laying it out, very rapidly. "Samantha, there is only one way out of this alive. We walk the child back to the house and put him in. You come with me. I'll go on sabatical, we leave the country, and go to Costa Rica - or some other place without extradition, and stay there until this thing blows over and we know we're safe. It's a simple solution, but it will work."

"No." Samantha replied. "I'm not going with you, anywhere. That's the worst thing we could do, and it would make us both look guilty. Me disappearing is also the worst possible thing that could happen to you. If I go missing, two different law firms will go to two different lockers at two different terminals, insert the keys I gave them, and discover everything, the whole truth. But as long as I'm healthy and visible, our secret is safe, and so are you. I gave them copies of my diary; it's here if you want to see it. You're a main character, but not in a good light." She was winging it for her life.

***

Raul Sanchez and Wallace Hunting Elk were in position, target in sights. Moose, wearing his headset, was making coffee in the RV. These things could go on for hours, sometimes days. Besides that, he wanted some coffee, and the snipers were bitching. Gordy was at the security box at the gate. There had been no sign of other hostiles, Gordy had two snipers in place, one could act as the other's spotter while he was gone. It was time for him to make contact with the house.

"Betty, are you there?" The unmistakably calm voice of Gordy in a crisis situation.

"Yes, Gordy. Thank God, ya'll're here. But Gordy, no heroics. This situation is under my control. This is my house, my land, my child, my guest, and *MY* call."

"Then, I can assumed you're armed, there is only one hostile, you have him in your sights, and my men are to take a back-up role."

"Correctamundo, Gordy." Later she would wonder why the heck she used a phrase "the Fonz" had used twenty-five years earlier in a TV sit-com. "My kid, my call, my shot."

"And we're just back-up."

"Correct again. And now, I need some peace and quiet. But first, Spooky's friend Danny Fagan and probably one or two others will show up, sometime. Let them in, but hold and control them up there. I'm primary, your team is secondary, the cops do nothing. I don't want any trigger happy mistakes to cost me Hudson. Now, Spooky's gonna try to talk things out. If that doesn't work, he'll create a diversion. You guys, only act if we fail. Not otherwise. Absolutely clear?"

"Absolutely."

***

I silently slid out the carport door at the back of my house. Walking barefooted, I quietly made my way along the dirt and grass driveway, up along the porch, past the jacuzzi, towards Phineas' Benz. If I made it soundlessly, unseen, I could possibly rush and tackle Phineas from behind. But with him pointing his weapon at his captives, off and on, as he ranted and raved, someone could get shot.

***

Phineas screamed at Samantha over his gun, pointing at her face. "YOU DID WHAT?"

Samantha was starting to tremble and shake uncontrolably. Oddly, Hudson was not crying, maybe he was too scared to cry. He was watching, obviously afraid, and clutching on to Samantha for dear life. Hudson knew this ugly man brought no presents or candy. All he did was scare them, yell at Sam, and point his gun at them, like the bad guys on TV.

"I kept a diary." She spoke clearly and slowly. There was a trembling, wavering quality in her voice that revealed the depth of her fear, but she kept it together. "I made some copies of my diary, for insurance, whatever. It sure looks like I needed it. Phinnie, you need to go home and chill. What you're doing here will only make things worse. If *you* want to leave the country, then you leave. They've got nothing on you or me, and no reason to suspect us unless we give them some reason. Which is exactly what you're doing, right now. Put that stupid gun away, and go home and take a chill pill before somebody sees you here acting crazy."

In his mind, Phineas knew that if what she said was true, she was correct. But being betrayed, frustrated, and outsmarted by a teenager only infuriated him even more. She was still holding Hudson, next to the car, but no longer leaning on it. Phineas began pacing, storming and limping back and forth a few steps in each direction, out in front of his still running car.

He suddenly faced Samantha, "Maybe I'll just shoot you at close range, wipe off the gun and put it in your hand. I'll say I saw you commit suicide and then I'll wash off the gun powder residue in the pond. Whatever writings show up afterwards are the phantasies and delusions of a deeply disturbed young woman, who suffered abuse at the hands of her brother for years."

Samantha saw me approaching. She looked away quickly, but it was too late. Phineas was watching her, saw the glimmer of recognition, and he followed her eyes back and saw me - approaching with nothing on but bluejeans, walking towards him with my hands empty, palms up.

Phineas barked, "That's close enough Brutus, Judas, Benedict. It's a sad day in America when you can no longer trust your hired guns." Phineas said it with such disdain it pissed me off on top of everything else. But the doctor looked insane, had the wild eyes of the no longer rational.

The distance was still too far away for me to make a move. Phineas had the gun and was still waving and pointing it. The job now was to keep him talking.

"Dr. Faulkner, I get paid to protect your family. Your neice called me scared to death, so I went to her school and took her into protectice custody, at her request. I protected her, which is exactly what your family pays me to do. Now, I don't know what this situation we have here is all about, but what you're doing here, doctor, can't be making anything better. Surely you, as a pyschiartist, can see that. You haven't been arrested, charged, or indicted for anything that I know about. Why throw your career away for no reason. You haven't done anything here, yet, that can't be undone. Let's talk this thing out."

I was taking what was called "baby steps" when we played Simon Says as a kid. When Phineas looked at Samantha I'd move up a little. Although I was trying to calm him down - his anger, confusion, frustration, and uncertainty seemed to be building rapidly to the crisis point. Phineas had his back to John's house and was facing the pond, Samantha to his right, next to the car, and me to his left. Phineas raised his arm and leveled the .357 on Samantha's face, for the first time, assuming something near a real firing position. He was a hair away from the crisis point, and was either about to start blasting, or put the gun away and leave. I was close enough for a clear shot, but I had to get him to take his gun off them before I could make my move. Also, I had to pull mine out of the back of my bluejeans, and move it in front, and aim, all he had to do was aim and squeeze. With his gun on them, he looked back at me and warned, "If you move, I shoot them."

***

The mother red tail hawk was out searching for food, while her mate watched over the nest. Her nestling ate well and would soon fly, he was strong and healthy. As the mother hawk flew in high circles, looking for prey she was irresistably drawn to an area she seldom hunted, near where the crows nested.

***

After Betty and Gordy's conversation, "Mosby's Rangers" all talked on their headsets. They had to respect Betty's request. Moose distributed the coffee, all they could do now was watch and wait, taking turns as sniper/spotter. They all watched Spooky's approach, and his attempt at negotiating. If anything, things looked worse than before. That's when Sanchez spoke out, "Man, that dude's gonna lose it, everybody get ready."

***

"Dr. Faulkner, **please**, let's talk this thing out. You're a doctor, respected in the community, from a prominent family. Think of all the ramifications of your actions here. This isn't going to solve anything. You've got money. If there is a serious problem, hire fucking Johhny Cochran, buy your way out. *This* is certainly not the answer."

***

The mother hawk saw a fledgling crow down below, standing at the edge of its nest, flapping its wings. She saw the sentry crows, and on any other day would have passed, but today, at that moment, she inexplicably could not resist. She dove down at full speed.

One of the sentry crows cawed an alarm just in time. The fledgling crow dived into the nest, an adult dived down to sheild the nest, and the mother hawk missed.

***

John's house faces the south, mine faces the west. The pond is due south of John's house, with Phineas' car in between. Out of the west, right where the woods end and the pasture begins, an ungodly cacophony of noise erupted. It sounded like every crow within a hundred miles had begun cawing, at once, in that one place. It was a loud and urgent noise, growing louder, coming nearer.

***

When the mother red tail went for the fledgling she became the instant taget of the whole murder of crows. As she flew rapidly over the pasture, the mother red tail hawk was not just being persued and harrassed by the crows as is normal and almost daily. These crows were not playing, but trying to do real, lethal damage. Her infringement on the nest area had elicited a response far beyond that of the normal mock combat.

The mother hawk kept going up and down, darting back and forth, but the crows kept attacking her, nipping with their beaks, trying to rake her with their claws. The mother hawk had had enough and was getting desperate. They neared the two legged on the ground below them, but since the two legged here had never harmed crow or hawk, they were not considered a concern by either.

***

The Sacred Pipe had been loaded with all of Creation and the Creator, and Leonard was sending a voice to and with all of Nature. He'd sent a voice to the Great Spirit, the Earth Mother, The Powers of the four directions, and to his healing spirits. As he was praying to protect Spooky his inner vision percieved a bright and surrounding light and his head became a wolf. As his wolf sprit he began runing in the light and came out in a foggy light over the Mosby's pond. He heard something coming at him from the air but as it neared a huge hawk flew down and struck it, taking it in its talons. The bat-monkey beast was dead but the wolf felt something coming behind it. The wolf turned to see a grotesque snake set to strike him. The wolf moved to one side and then lunged forward as the snake struck. The wolf got the viper behind its neck and bit hard, almosy all the way through. As the wolf threw the lifeless snake down, the was a loud explosion. The wolf and the environs dissolved instantaneously and Leonard was himself again. His Pipe had gone out, he finished smoking his Pipe and saying his prayers. As he put the Pipe up the first rays of sunshine lit the top of the mountain.

***

Samantha and Hudson looked up. Phineas looked up. I did, too. The cawing was deafening and coming towards us. I saw something I'd heard about in folklore but never personally seen before. It looked like a dozen or so crows, all cawing loudly, were in hot pursuit of the local female red-tailed hawk. The large red-tail shifted her wing position to increase drag, turned, hovered momentarily and kicked out with her powerful claws, striking the crow hottest on her trail. There was a spurt of blood and black feathers flew as that crow dropped twelve feet, regained equilibrium, and erratically flew back towards its nest. The cawing of the other crows became even more intense. Everyone had been looking up, momentarily spellbound by the noise and aerial combat, but Samantha, still holding Hudson, began edging her way to the back of the car.

*****

The red-tailed hawk, followed by all the crows but the wounded one, dove down towards the tallest two legged. The mother hawk planned to use the two legged as a screen.

*****

Phineas still had the gun pointed at Samantha and the child, but the incredible noise above him had attracted his attention momentarily, but as he turned his head to look back down the barrell of his gun at them, the hawk flew under his levelled arm, then swept behind him, low to the ground, and then up and away. Followed by the dozen crows. They were instantaneously all over Phineas, cawing loudly and he instinctively flailed his arms and protected his face. Some of the crows got caught up in his flailing arms, and were cawing, defending themselves in terror and chaos.

*****

The whole murder of crows was in hot pursuit of the red-tail. Although much louder and more intense than normal, it was not an unusual sight to me. After the short glance, I shifted my eyes back to the doctor, who remained looking up a second longer. I dropped to one knee as my hand flew back to my piece, as I kept my eyes on my target, his mid-chest.

Perception during intense life, or life and death situations - carwrecks, fistfights, shootouts, battle, lethal combat - is different. There are moments your consciousness achieves a temporary state of hyper-awareness. Because you perceive every mili-second, everything seems to be moving in slow motion. Although you know you are moving at full speed, you are so aware of the actions of every mili-second, you seem to be in slow motion along with everything else.

As I dropped in this seeming slow motion my knee hit the ground, taking a shooters position, I saw the hawk dive under Phineas' arm. Simutaneously, I felt my right hand grasp my Colt's handle. As the hawk swept low behind him, I felt the gun come loose from my jeans and my finger found the trigger. I saw the crows engulfing Phineas as I raised my weapon. While flailing away with an open hand and the large revolver in his hand, he hit some of the crows who shrieked loudly. In retrospect, he looked like a character from Hitchcock's *The Birds* as Samantha and Hudson made it behind the car and dropped out of sight. The crows were deafening as my finger began to squeese the trigger. Before my finger finished squeezing, Phineas' head exploded. Red blood, white bones, and grey brain matter erupted sideways, shooting straight out from where the side of his head had been. I put two shots in his body, before it crumpled. I felt myself rising without thinking, running forward to the kids. I put two more in his body as I ran to the back of the car. Samantha and Hudson were croutching on the ground, both whiter than snow. Jamming the Colt back in my jeans, the barrell warm on my butt, I reached down and scooped up Hudson, grabbed Samantha's hand, and ran toward Betty.

Betty came out of the open door, rifle barrell slightly down, scanning the area for other hostiles. We ran past her into the house, then she backed in after us. She had the coldest, hardest, deadliest face I'd ever seen on a good person in my life. With one possible exception.

***

The mother hawk had made the dive at the two legged and escaped from the crows. The two legged had slowed them down. The mother hawk hadn't seen the face explode, but had heard five sharp noises like thunder. All the crows had scattered at the first thunder and headed back to their nests. They didn't understand what happened to the two legged, but they planned to return to feed. The mother hawk made it safely home, but without food. As the nestling loudly kept demanding food upon her return, her mate went hunting.

***

Betty closed and locked the door. She scooped Hudson off me with one hand and handed me the rifle with the other. "Danny's on his way. Lock that up till he needs it." She went to the security box, "Gordy, Gordy, Moose, who's there? Guys? Who's there?

Moose's deep voice answered, "I'm here, Gordy's coming." You could hear Moose panting a little from the run. Same with Gordy when he got on. He can run well with his prosthetic left foot, but not real fastover rough terrain. "Nice shooting, champ. But tell Spooky, next time, not to riddle the corpse with bullets."

You could hear Moose's bellowing laugh. I couldn't help but think, "Great, I'm the comic relief for these guys."

What do you want us to do?" Gordy asked. "Was that the only hostile, or might there be others."

Betty looked at me, impatiently, waiting. I responded, "Shouldn't be. Not that I know of." It felt like such an inadequate answer, but as I far as I could figure, correct. Then Samantha spoke up, "Phineas came alone. From what I could see."

"We don't think so, but why don't you get that noisy dirt bike of yours off the RV and look around on it just in case. Tell your boys to let Danny down when he shows. Remember Father Murrell, he'll probably show up, too. Let him down. Nobody else without my permission. Thanks, Gordy."

"No prob."

504

Betty went to the phone and called Father Murrell. "Father, it's Betty. I've just shot and killed a man who threatened Samantha and Hudson. I need you to come over here immediately. Thanks. Gordy and the boys are here, they'll let you in at the gate."

With all the neccessities taken care of, and with Hudson still in her arms, Betty went to Samantha and hugged her. "I don't know what it's all about and I'm not sure I want to, but I know you took good care of my baby out there." She hugged her again. The she looked over at me, "Spooky, I'm gonna hang out with my kids. Give me a yell when all the authorities show up and they need me." I said sure as I watched her carry Hudson back, gather all her children around her, and close the door.

Samantha walked over and buried herself in me. I put my arms around her and could feel her whole body shaking. She knew how close to death she had been. Scared deeply, she had kept it together. Understandably, now she let go. Maturing in prison and then working as a private detective, I'd been around more than my fair share of violence. I'm lucky in that I've always been cool, maybe cold and ruthless, when things go down. That's my natural reaction. It's afterwards, when all threats are past and the fight or flight adrenalin rush is over, that's when I get shaky. Hands shake, legs shake, but only afterwards. I could feel my own inner vibration inside, that shakiness now that it was over. But mine was nothing compared to Samantha, her whole body was shaking, violently, almost convulsing. I held her tighter and then she began to cry, then sob. I held her, let her cry into my chest, and I stroked her hair and told her everything was going to be all right. That went on for a few minutes. But then there was a transition. She started hugging me in a more aggressive, sensual way.

She looked up at me, needy as could be, stood up on her tip toes, and kissed me lightly on the lips. God help me, I let her kiss me a couple of times. I didn't pull back or push her away, she just seemed too hurt. Now, in my defense there was no tounge or anything crazy like that. But I knew it was inappropriate as hell for a man my age to kiss a girl that age. Thank God, I was saved by the bell.

Moose's voice came in loud and clear through the security box. "Betty, Betty, you there? Danny's here with an ADA Diaz and an Alpert Faulkner. Do I let them down, or what?"

I pulled myself free, thankful for the excuse, and went over to the box. "Let them come on down Moose. There'll be others. Check 'em all through like this."

"Roger."

Samantha came back to me and nestled in. I let her. She started to try for another kiss, but I stopped her with conversation. "Samantha, I've got to go square all this with Danny and Diaz, which is not going to be easy. You can come with me or hang out with Betty and the kids. But if you come with me, please remember I work for APD and your family, and please, please, don't do anything either would consider inappropriate."

We went out in the bright sunlight of what was still the early morning, and watched the car come down. I still had on only bluejeans and a gun at the small of my back. She still had on only Betty's nightshirt. As the car came to a halt, we walked over. Samantha stayed close beside me, but didn't touch or try to physically hang on. Although she wanted to.

Danny got out quickly, somewhere between professional, pissed off, and concerned. Moose had told him everything was resolved, and filled them in a little. Great. Another killing related to this case. The bodies were fucking piling up, and Danny still didn't understand it all. A dead pregnant mother and baby, mutilated animals, four more dead in a related shootout, one Faulkner an almost vegtable, and another - a well known shrink - now dead. Danny wanted some fucking answers, yesterday.

"Spooky, Miss Faulkner. I understand you are both okay, good. Excuse us, Miss Faulkner, I need a few words with Spooky, alone." We left Samantha there with her uncle and the ADA and walked towards the corpse. I saw Alpert walking toward Samantha.

It looked awkward.

"Spooky, buddy, just what the hell is going on here?"

"Well. It just ended, but we haven't called the county cops, yet. You better do that soon, so we don't get in trouble. But I wanted to give you the heads up. Samantha called me Tuesday, seeking protection. I took her into protective custody Wendsday, although she made me give my word of honor I'd tell no one. Which is what I've done (except for Betty and John). I've tried to gain her trust and get the truth out of her, and had succedded somewhat, but then had to work for ya'll last night. Phineas found out she was here, somehow, and came after her. He held a gun on Samantha and Hudson. She tried talking to him, and I tried, but when it looked like he was going to shoot, Betty took him out with a clean head shot. I think we avoided a possible murder/suicide situation with an obviously justifiable head shot."

Hearing another car, we turned and saw Father Murrell's car park next to Danny's. He got out and Samantha ran over to him. They hugged and started talking. At Phineas' car, I reached in and turned off the still running engine. Danny took a look at the corpse. "Head shot, hell, this body is riddled with bullets." I'd forgotten to mention my contribution. I explained it to him. A couple of times. He was cool with my first two shots, he thought the last two were overkill. I kept repeating the mantra "my nephew was in danger" and he finally gave up and accepted it, shaking his head unfavorably.

"Danny, we'd better call the locals. You've been hear five - ten minutes - we've already waited too long. But we need this judged justifiable homicide, immediately, today. We've got to use every connection we've can to make this go away. You keep telling me how the mayor, the

chief, the convention burea, the Chamber of Commerce, and everybody else in Atlanta politics

want this thing solved. *Now it is*. Time to get this case out of the papers and off the news. It's all

over. Danny walked back to his car, and radioed APD to contact the county, to send cops, their

ME, and a meat wagon.

Danny was far from over the anger of me taking protective custody of Samantha and not

telling him. Danny did not appreciate being kept in the dark, ever, at all. "Spooky, giving your

word of honor, this whole sense of honor thing may very well cost you your license and my

friendship."

"I gave my word."

"We still have to find out what she knows, what this whole fucking mess is all about."

Danny got a call on his cell. He mostly listened, and for a long time. I could hear what

sounded like an unhappy black woman speaking loudly, angrily, but I couldn't understand that

many individual words. He didn't look all that happy when he looked over at me as he said,

"Well then, I've got good news for you Ma'am. All the bad guys are in custody or dead." He

paused, looked over at Alpert and the ADA, and began walking toward them very rapidly.

"Ma'am, you do understand this case is not even a week old. Yes, Ma'am, I know it's been on

the national news and the tabloids are going crazy with it, and understand your concern about

tourists and conventions. No Ma'am, we don't want Atlanta known as the new hub of the satanic

South. Ma'am, if you can hang on for just a few seconds, we might be able to resolve the entire

case, this whole situation today…"Danny held his hand over the phone, looked at ADA Diaz and

Alpert. "Mr. Faulkner, if you want to protect your family, and put all this unpleasantness behind

us, I need the name of the nearest state superior court judge you have in your pocket."

Alpert stammered, "I wouldn't use that phrase, but Judge Bert Williams has received large contributions, is a friend of the family, and has jurisdiction over the original crime scene, and I believe this county as well."

Danny raised the phone, "Madam Mayor, you get State Superior Court Judge Bert Williams out here today, with a stenographer who's a notary, and we'll get this resolved and off the news. Wrapped up, done, over, and gone. Thank-you Ma'am, I'll be waiting for his call." Danny looked at Alpert and said thanks.

We all turned as Father Murrell and Samantha walked up. She looked at us, turned, and went into Betty's. Father looked at all of us, "Samantha has asked me to relate some of the details of her life. And about the ritual murder. She's embarrassed and ashamed to talk about this, and wanted me to break the ice and lay the groundwork. She'll answer your specific questions, but let me get this out of the way before this place becomes a circus."

Danny had all the information but the Faulkner family angle. He was all ears. Father Murrell revealed it as he understood it. "What Samantha has told me leads me to believe the ritual murder was about revenge, and the dream of a disturbed man to lead a large satanic cult. Samantha's involvement is best explained by a long history of abuse….

The sirens of the county boys could be heard as Father Murrell concluded the summary. Alpert was white, ashen, with tears streaming down his face. He couldn't understand how he and the rest of his family had missed the depth of his brother's mental illness and depravity, or Stewart's abuse of Samantha. He was shaken to the core.

Things might have gone badly, but the first five county cops to show up had been greeted at the gate by the highly respected warriors who trained them at SWAT school. The county DA had gone to the University of Georgia with Diaz, who had already made a call to him for cooperation. When the sherriff showed up, he spent ten minutes at the gate talking to Gordy and the boys. State Superior Court Judge Bert Williams called Danny, got directions, picked up his stenographer and came straight away. The Sherriff and the ME talked to Gordy and the boys and got their version. Then they had Samantha, Betty, and me tell our stories seperately. Then each person went to the scene and told exactly what happened. The only problem was those last two shots I fired into a corpse. But they decided they didn't want to charge me with unneccessarily shooting a lifeless body. So I thanked them, then suggested to the ME that he drive a stake in Phineas heart, cut his fucking head off, and then creamate him, you know, just to make sure - because that's what I'd do. I was laughing as I walked away, but they didn't know quite what to think.

The judge came and his stenographer took the statements we gave to the county boys, typed them up, and then we read and signed them - Samantha, Betty, the four highly regarded SWAT team trainers, and me. The judge talked to Diaz, Danny, the Sherriff, and the ME. It was ruled on the spot as a justifiable homicide to protect two lives. Unless the autopsy indicated foul play, which they all knew it wouldn't, that was it. End of story, the meat wagon took the body, and the locals went home.

That left the rest of us to resolve the whole Samantha situation. Father Murrell and I developed a plan. We huddled for about twenty minutes, made a few long distance phone calls, and held an impromptu meeting/court session. After a couple of hours it was worked out, signed, sealed, and notarized. Samantha would be charged as a minor with two counts of conspiracy to commit murder - she knew about Phineas' plans and what the ritual entailed. She might have been a hesitant and drugged participant, but if she'd made one phone call, she could have prevented the whole thing. Samantha wanted to get Stewart out of her life, and was willing to go along with Phineas' house of horrors to achieve that goal. She was sentenced to six years court supervised probation during which time her records will be sealed. The terms of her probation require continual psychological treatment for those six years. If her probation is successfully concluded, the sealed recordes will be destroyed on her 21st birthday.

A panel was created to oversee her probation by the judge, consisting of the judge as chairman, Father Murrell, Alpert, and me. The plan was for Samantha to finish the few remaining days of summer school with her family. The same day school was over she would leave for a Jungian psychological and spiritual healing center in Big Sur, California. The friend of mine who runs it specializes in, among other things, victims of child and sexual abuse. She would be in outpatient therapy during the school year, and each summer alternate between Big Sur and participating in Leonard's Personal Quest program in Owens Valley. Leonard would counsel her and cleanse her in the old ways, the Jungians in the new. When all that was figured out and agreed upon, more confirmatory phone calls were made, and then the stenographer prepared it and everybody signed.

The case, with two exceptions, was closed. Parker would be tried and found guilty of impersonating the police. His willingness to do anything for unknown employers earned him the max in time. The charges against Stewart would be deferred until Stewart was competent to stand trial. Which, short of divine intervention, meant never. Danny, as instructed by the chief, called the mayor, and in a brief outline told her how everything had been resolved. Within the limits of protecting the privacy of the minors involved, the mayor and police chief would issue a joint statement, hopefully putting the story to rest.

The mayor told Danny normally they would have had a big press conference for such an occasion to celebrate his success, but with the facts being: they only had one minor court case, they had an embarrassingly high number of corpses, and they had Stewart nearly beat to death while in custody, so any celebration was out. This one was to be put to sleep quietly. The Stewart fiasco and the four fatality shootout/arson guaranteed no flashy news conference with Danny standing next to the mayor and the chief. Although privately, they were all glad it was over and done, and the taxpayers were saved a huge chunk in trial and prison costs.

The judge gave Danny the necessary paper work to take with him. Danny was to take Samantha and book her as a juvenile. Danny, Father, and me took Samantha outside and explained what had been worked out. I doubt she was thrilled to know her life was planned out for the next six years, but she knew it was better than being tried as an adult and doing life for conspiracy to commit murder. John came flying down the driveway and rushed to be with Betty and the kids, said he'd talk to me later.

Danny was ready to take Samantha, when she asked could she talk to me alone. Danny gave me a hard look, but said yes. He gave her ten minutes. We walked to the gazebo. "All these places you're sending me, you know them, trust them?"

"Yes, Samantha. You'll be with Alpert or your folks through exams. Then you'll fly off to be treated by friends of mine who understand the power of symbols and symbolism, of ritual and ritual practice."

She agreed to give Danny her diary and the notebook she'd made with the corrections. It was part of what would be sealed for six years. She stepped forward and hugged me again, and I hugged her back. She tried to kiss me again, and I met her lips for a second, but then I took her face in both hands and made full eye contact. I told her I was her friend and protector, but what she seemed to have in mind was inappropriate and illegal. She mentioned one day she'd be eighteen and I told her I was sure by then she'd have found an interesting young man, and forgotten all about me romantically. I walked her to Danny's car, and told her she now had lots of good people looking out for her interests. Danny, Alpert, and Daiz would be with her at juvy for her booking and immediate release. She was one of the few people in the legal history of Georgia to be adjudicated and placed on probation before being offically arrested and charged. She looked back and waved at me until they were out of sight. I waved back as they went out of sight, and headed back in, thankful it was all over.

Father Murrell left and I went into John's kitchen just in time to hear Gordy's voice on the box asking if they could quit playing watchdog and start having fun. "Sure," was my response, but as we were talking Laura arrived in my pickup. I told them to let her through, close the gates and head on down to the lake cabin and have fun, after thanking them for everything they had done. I hoped they behaved around Laura.

Chapter Seventeen – the Wrap Up

Over the next few days, I caught Laura up on all she'd missed. I talked to Leonard, thanked him, and we congratulated each other on our victory. We had fought one small battle in the spiritual war between good and evil and prevailed, and one lost soul seemed on the path to redemption.

Danny read Samantha's diary and put all the pieces together. He came to understand the motivations, that Phineas was planning to use the regional penal pilot progam to recruit a core of Satanists. He had delusions about being the nexy Anton LaVey, but secretly, with demonically sharp teeth. He really wanted to build a secret satanic underground, the kind Crazy Larry and the anti-Satanists imagined was out there. Phineas, although not fully ordained or defrocked, had trained for the priesthood and did somewhat fit the classical Satanist pattern. He considered himself self-ordained and self-defrocked.

He beileved that with his skills as a shrink he could pick out from a large pool of regional young offenders those who would take to the practice of ritual evil. His selection of George Sanders proved he could pick 'em. George singlehandedly provided Phineas so many skills for this operation. To set up Gary - George, a skilled forger, made the APD ID's, car smart, he helped buy the old cop car at auction and fix it up. That, with an APD uniform from Atlanta Costumes, police belt from a Stromer catalog and a street gun, cash and instructions, and Gary was done.

To set up Kevin - more fake ID's showing George as Kevin. Acting as Kevin, he befriended and seduced their victim. His job at the animal shelter/hospital provided access to the sacrified animals. Between his job and Phineas - they had access to all the drugs they needed for animals and victims. Setting up Stewart was as easy as sending Tonya at Stewart and collecting blood from the ritual to spray on Stewart's clothes and shoes. Kevin being linked to Amanda, all Tonya had to do was get Stewart to remember Amanda's name. The Sanders did the break-ins and planted the blood evidence.

Tarps can be bought anywhere thwey sell camping or painting equipment. Phineas thought he could control the old cottage. He did a public ritual because the pilot penal program was a public program. In his arrogance, he thought the frame would stick. Of course, the Sanders job at the junkyard allowed them to put any and all evidence inside a junk car before it was crushed and sent off to be smelted. All the pieces fit, except fot the human equation. Why would a rich and respected shrink turn to Satan? His father's hardness, pushing him to be a preist, so angered him that when his father died and he rebelled, he rebelled in heart, against it all. Or maybe he was just born evil.

So it ends - Kevin and Amanda, George and Bobby - dead. Phineas - dead. Gary goes down for impersonating an officer of the law and congenital stupidity. Stewart remains in the ABI unit at Shepherd Center, not a total vegtable, but severley brain damaged, with no control of bodily functions. Jasmine is teaching Tonya and Deseree the art of wise investing, and Tonya still thinks about Stewart, and how much richer she could be. Danny and I were satisfied there were no loose ends.

Samantha called me every day through her exams and we talked about her future. I didn't see her again until Danny and I put her on the plane. She did hug me and kiss me lightly on the lips. Danny raised his eyebrows, but let it go.

Laura and I had a couple of wonderful weeks. The first few days we stayed home and put together our notes on the case, and the outline for the book. We heard lots of gunfire and the occassional small explosion from "Mosby's Rangers" but they left after five days. After they left we went on picnics and midnight moonlit horse rides. The second week we went down to Savannah and Tybee Island and had a honeymoon without getting married. We discovered each other and in the process found pasion, friendship, romance, and just plain fun. At times, making love, there were moments in the Eternal Now that were transcendant.

On her last night she told me which job offer she had decided to accept. CNN had offered her a job in the Bay area, but had promised she could work on Native American stories and issues as they came up. She was excited about her new job, but wished she could have stayed a little longer. So did I.